ARANYAK

THE INDIA LIST

ARANYAK

Of the Forest

Bibhutibhushan Bandyopadhyay

Translated and Introduced by
Rimli Bhattacharya

LONDON NEW YORK CALCUTTA

Seagull Books, 2017

Translation © Rimli Bhattacharya, 2002
First published in English translation by Seagull Books in 2002

ISBN 978 0 8574 2 496 9

British Library Cataloguing-in-Publication Data
A catalogue record for this book is available from the British Library

Book design and typesetting by Manasij Dutta, Seagull Books, Calcutta, India
Printed and bound by Maple Press, York, Pennsylvania, USA

CONTENTS

INTRODUCTION

I will write something about the life in the jungle—rigourous and dynamic, radiant with courage—images of an outcast life. About riding in this lonely forest losing one's way in the dark paths, living a solitary life in a little shelter . . . the poverty of the people here, their simplicity, this Virile [sic], active life, these dense forests of jhau dark in the evening—all of it.

(Diary entry of 12 February 1928, cited in Sen 1995: 136)

I came home and made a sketch of the book about the 'jungle'.

(Diary entry of 1 November 1933, cited in Sen 1995: 103)

Do let me know where you find it monotonous. But you must remember that *Aranyak* does not quite belong to the genre of *thrillers*—and there is one more thing: I prefer a novel to be somewhat *reposeful*. And as you know, there are many *dull* pages to be found in many famous novels.

(Unpublished letter to Suprabha Choudhury [neé Dutt], not dated, cited in Sen 1995: 85)

Aranyak tells us of an innocence that is impossible.

It is begotten in acts of destruction when vast stretches of forestland fall under the cultivator's axe. The incessant summons of a distant landlord in Bengal pushes his manager in Bhagalpur district to engage in screening potential tenants, drawing up new legal deeds and settlements, until miles of jungle are leased out, 'cleared' and settled.

Impossible, not only because of the exploitative function demanded of the narrator-manager—the graduate 'Bangali-babu' whose futile search for a job in Calcutta has led him to accept this one. (In Bibhutibhushan's own life, for a mere fifty rupees a month). Or because, the manager-babu himself is seen as a kind of benevolent (brahman) lord by the people who come to clear and settle in the jungleland. Or because, the promise of 'progress' and 'development' brings in streams of landless labourers, impoverished school-masters and starving boys from the neighbouring districts. But finally, because the narrator's celebration of nature is weighted always with his awareness of the death of the forestlands. The death too, of a way of life of the already impoverished tribals who were once kings of the region. The act of writing is a temporary suspension of death.

Bibhutibhushan's *Aranyak* becomes then a chronicle of the dispossessed in visionary prose. Strangely rich with minute documentation of the hard day-to-day life of gangota peasants, men and women, penurious brahmans, migrant landless labourers and adivasis, it resists ethnography for the most part. All who fight for survival against nature and against man—landlords, rich tenants/moneylenders and their henchmen—are equally the object of the narrator's curiosity. Curiosity impelling an episodic narrative that is threaded by the seasonal links of a baramashyo or baramashya, of an intricately bound social system pervaded by the almost 'normative' hierarchy defined by caste.

To this world, the writer brings his own lifelong interest in the natural sciences and astronomy, his study of historical records and surveys and, above all, his lore of travel books. The whole is irradiated by a lost romanticism—Bibhutibhushan sees the world in a grain of sand, and in constellations that appear familiar from light years away—and shot through with ambivalence.

For *Aranyak* cannot be read today simply as a paean to nature in the wild or an elegy for the marginal and dispossessed. The firstperson narrator is not unaware of his implication in the vagaries of the revenue system governing the rich char-soil—the land that arises from the depths of the shifting river, over which the original owners now have no claim. *Aranyak* is composed as both celebration and expiation; to write is to record a death sentence:

> But these memories do not give me pleasure; they are filled with sorrow. By my hands was destroyed an unfettered playground of nature. I know too, that for this act the forest gods will never forgive me. I have heard that to confess a crime in one's own words lightens somewhat the burden of that crime. Therefore, this story.

Yet, storytelling can make 'natural', even inevitable, the processes and agents of change. The narrator of *Aranyak* is historically unable to probe deeper into this text of complicity, his 'reading' of the local and the immediate is mediated by his readings, 'these memories' sifted by 'other' spaces in far-flung places of the globe, bearing the inscriptions of Western trader-traveller-explorers 'discovering' and 'recording' other lands, other continents. Marco Polo, Columbus, Henry Hudson, Shackleton, Harry Johnston, Sven Hedins.

II

Vignettes that become *Aranyak* are scattered through Bibhutibhushan Bandyopadhyay's diaries or field notes. Sometimes they are transplanted in toto to another time and place: a meek person collecting taxes sighted at a fair (5 February 1928, in Bandyopadhyay 1993: 187); the death of Bengali doctor Rakhal-babu; the wonder of seeing the full moon rise in the glow of the setting sun; the quintessential Bengali woman lighting the household lamp at dusk who reminds the narrator of a home left behind—these have migrated from recorded impressions to fiction.

The entry of 9 December 1925 (Bandyopadhyay 1993: 144–5) describes the Shuarmari settlement that becomes the plague-stricken village in Chapter Six of *Aranyak* where Raju Parey hones his healing skills. Something of the vibhatsa rasa is evoked in an otherwise understated account of the narrator's futile attempts at 'rational' intervention, its lingering afterimage is the girl-widow's corpse being pushed to the river with bamboo staves by low caste ahir men. In other instances, a slight substitution is made in the interests of the narrative: Saraswati Puja becomes the festival of Punyaha in Chapter Four; the invitees are also from the lower castes but doshads instead of gangotas and chamars (27 June 1928 in Bandyopadhyay 1993: 183–4).

Bibhutibhushan's diaries are permeated by a willing and conscious surrender to the fluidity of time, the palimpsest of earth's own history. He fantasizes, for example, that some thirty thousand years hence, a little boy savours the wonders of a sea voyage, unaware that the once grand city of Kolkata now lies buried deep beneath the waters over which their ship ploughs (29 July 1925, Calcutta, in Bandyopadhyay 1993: 141–2). Slightly transformed in *Aranyak*, this marks a climax in Chapter Six to the narrator's reverie about the achievements of 'Aryan civilization': 'I sat in the forest and dreamt the dream of that blue ocean from the past.' In a subsequent entry the vibrant rai-green vegetation around a water body provokes him to imagine a primeval earth when there were no people, no birds, or flowers. The forests await the little boy who will become the artist; but when the human beings do come, most of them are busy calculating the current interest rates. Only a few have the 'vision' to experience 'cosmic' beauty and to leave behind their work in science, songs, poems and pictures (21 August 1925, Bhagalpur, in Bandyopadhyay 1993: 141–2).

As his biographers have observed, Bibhutibhushan himself, unlike his narrator Satyacharan, was never completely cut off from his own social milieu during his tenure in Bihar. He receives parcels of books—including Conrad's novels—from the Imperial Library [National Library] in Calcutta (Bandyopadhyay 1993: 193). He is, besides, a regular visitor to a circle of Bengali bhadraloks to whom he could read out parts of what became *Pather Panchali*. He notes in his diary that he has completed the novel on 26 April 1928 and sent off the manuscript by post to Calcutta. (Also a time when he harvested a crop of short stories.) The entries of this period show this constant slippage into and a grappling with his childhood memories of some twenty-five years ago. Their luminosity irradiates his exile. Etches deeper the lines of his immediate home in the rude and immense forests. The montages of terrain and people that compose *Aranyak* are recovered from lived experience. They are freighted too with the burden of intertextuality, of other explorers in other climes. And he realizes towards the end of his stay, that memory makes endearing what once seemed harsh: 'In 1924, this very Ismaelpur seemed like an exile in the Andaman Islands. As for Ajmabad, even in 1925 it seemed like the outer edges of the civilized world—a wilderness of the Belgian Congo. These days I am saddened even to think that I will have to leave Ismaelpur and Ajmabad' (31 January 1928 in Bandyopadhyay 1993: 186). Struck by homesickness, there is yet the consoling reflection, 'will I ever again experience such unlimited stretches of time, such variety?' Much later, when he has actually left Ismaelpur, he longs for the wondrous moonlit nights he has experienced there.

Bibhutibhushan's own childhood, in turn, transfuses the fictive world of Apu's Nischindipur in *Pather Panchali* and, simultaneously, is born his desire to write about life around the river Ichhamati in his native land. The desire comes to fruition much later when the novel *Ichhamati* is serialized in 1947. A certain distance of space and time kindles the memories of the one while he is elsewhere. The green and shadowy paths of Apu's Nishchindipur (Bibhutibhusan's Barrackpur) become all the more vivid during his 'term' in Bihar. And childhood returns to illuminate the creativity of the young graduate in exile from his native Bengal. Numerous trips made by Bibhutibhushan to the jungles of Saranda from 1934 onwards feed into the novel about the jungle that became *Aranyak*. While travelling, Bibhutibhushan often felt that 'the real and ancient Bharatbarsha' lay in the uneven rugged terrain of Bihar, Madhya Pradesh and Orissa (in contrast to the fertile green plains of Bengal). He never ceased to marvel at the immense capacity for hard work that a hostile environment inspired in its inhabitants, and, in the case of tribals, the simple pleasures they garnered from their precarious and perilous existence. And yet, the question: 'Where, in which direction lies Bharatbarsha?' ('Bharatbarsha kon dike?') asked by the princess Bhanmati towards the end of the narrator's stay, remains unanswered in *Aranyak* (Das 1996: 28–36). Actually a response to the narrator's curiosity about the tribal girl's understanding of space and time, of cities and of the country (as in 'desh'), the question remains to interrogate us, the middle-class inheritors of Bhibhutibhushan's fiction with their overlapping chronotopes.

III

Aranyani aranyani asau ya preva nasyasi
Katha gramam na prchasi na tva bhir iva vindatim

Rig Veda, 10.146.1

Spirit of the forest, spirit of the forest, who seem to melt away, how is it that you do not ask about a village? Doesn't a kind of fear grasp you?

Wendy Doniger O'Flaherty (1981)

Where do they come from—the forests of Bibhutibhushan's title, vast tracts that have lapsed into the past tense even as they are recalled in the shadow of Fort William, seat of the Company's knowledge-makers? Who do they belong to—those strips of char, emerging mysteriously from the womb of the river, to be reclaimed, claimed, fought over, settled, farmed and taxed, until one day, just as unbidden, the river turns its course and the rich but despoiled land sinks beneath the weight of water?

Taking its cue from the Aranyakas, the Books of the Forests (aranya) that constitute the Vedas—compendium of magic ritual and chants, the *Aranyak* of the 1930s evokes the mantra of progress and development that has drawn even its chronicler into its throes. The forests of the night turn into land that must be cleared of its original occupants (real people, not spirits or beasts) by a nomadic pastoral tribe who will become colonial and postcolonial India's 'aryan' lore. To the settlers, the forests were mysterious, life giving and life threatening, fearful because unknown. Through conflict and bloodshed there is always an uneasy alliance between the demon/ized rakshasas and the contemplative aspirants of spiritual prowess who demarcate the ashram in the borders of the forests. Motuknath's *tole*—in the spirit of such idealized ancestral *toles*—is the closest Bibhutibhushan approaches to a parody, especially when it is juxtaposed against the 'original' landless status of all those who finally manage to make good—Motuknath, Raju Parey and others. Such indeed is the inheritance of the modern writer exploring the forests of northern Bhagalpur far away from the metropolis of Calcutta, whose replenishment is always from his rural roots.

The destruction of the forest is a necessary prelude in the Adiparva of the Mahabharata: Khandava vana is consumed by fire to provide a clearing for Indraprastha whose urbane magnificence is only the site of further dissension. In Indian literary texts, the period spent in the forest constitutes the locale of numerous aranyak parvas as either exile, voluntary or enforced, a temporary sojourn, or interlude as also the space to which householders finally retire.

The forests of *Aranyak* are recalled, quite literally, in the shadow of Fort William. They are framed by the green in the frenetic city known as the 'Maidan'. Kolkata is invested with civilizational landmarks, abstract and specific, where the absentee landlord's son hones his talents as a singer of light classical pieces and selects a former college friend to be the estate manager of the invisible 'jungle 'state'. This is true not only for the narrator but for those for whom it exists primarily as a name, reading the 'Bangali-babu' as its representative text. Dhaturia and Manchi (both erased by the end of the novel) desire to go to his city to showcase and realize their talents and ambitions; Kolkata is also where the narrator returns and writes his tale, to the whirr of his wife's sewing machine. 'Nostalgia' is as old as our hoary past.

THE THRICE-BORNE TEXT: OUT OF BENGAL
A Note on the Translation

Aranya, vana, vipina, atavi, kanana, jangala, kantara.

Not surprisingly, the two most frequent adjectives used in *Aranyak* are 'janamanabheen' (bereft of human beings) and 'bonyo' (from sanskrit *vanya*) which has been variously rendered in English as rude, rustic, wild, savage and uncivilized. An 'unpeopled' forest is conceived as a lack, the very definition of 'people' excluding tribals, beasts and birds, spirits and all other creatures of the imagination who inhabit it.

Bibhutibhushan Bandyopadhyaya's *Aranyak* is the story of plants and trees, crops and jungle, birds, beasts and peasants and tribals as much as it is the story of the teller.

Written in Bangla but speaking of a land not only outside the Bengal Presidency, but outside of the usual topos of Bengali literature, Bibhutibhushan was already 'translating' the topos and the people for his Bengali readers. The Hindustani spoken by the various people encountered by the narrator is not of any single kind: the 'chhikachiki' is only one of the many versions of Hindi. The tribals of his story, albeit recontextualized in *Aranyak* (probably Gonds, not Santals) would have spoken in yet another language.

The linguistic layering is compounded by the intricacies of land and labour relations inflected by caste, gender and region that form the warp and weft of *Aranyak*. The revenue terms that the Bangali-babu has to master go back to an Arabic or Persian genealogy, while the place names vary according to region and the nature of the terrain. Thus 'baihar' is a Santali word meaning first grade land (Das 1988: 21), but as a suffix it combines to form proper nouns of place names: Narha-baihar, Phulkia-baihar, Lobtulia-baihar, Sungthia-baihar.

In 1911, Bihar was bifurcated from the Bengal Presidency and was made into a state. In the 1920s and 1930s, Bhagalpur district was much larger than it is at present, comprising the area to the south of the Ganga as well as a sizeable area to the north of the river. Similarly, Purnea district was larger in size including what is now Saharsa district. Besides these political divisions, the Ganga keeps changing its course : moving from the south of Bhagalpur to the north in the space of a few years.'Diara' (conflated with'dvira') indicates the elevated strip of land that is formed of the char-soil when the river shifts its course. The social and political economy of Bibhutibhushan's *Aranyak* rests on the fortunes (and certainly the misfortunes) of all those involved with this diara land. As Rusati Sen (1998: 24–6) has elaborated, a specific kind of land settlement known as hal-hasila, determined by the shifting course of the river, was practised on the banks of the Ganga and Kushi rivers, in Purnea and Bhagalpur districts. Revenue collection involved assessing the nature of the crop raised on the hali land, as it was called, measuring the land after the harvest, with intricate rules of falling back on the last year of assessment in case there was no fresh surveying and examination. This elaborate (and unfair) process of fixing taxes and collecting rents required the maintenance of katcheris. The ryot had to contend with the uncertain whims of the river if he wished to cultivate this diara land. According to the Permanent Settlement Act, the rate of taxation increases with fertility and there comes a time when the original ryot becomes a potential threat. (Sen points out that the 1859 Santal Revolt in Birbhum was over the same issue.) Unable to pay the higher revenue, the ryot was evicted from the land he had made fertile, and had to go elsewhere. More prosperous tenants (such as Rashbehari Singh in *Aranyak*) now take over and put their own labourers to work the fields, creating intermediate levels of exploitation.

Fairly detailed and illuminating expositions have been written on the socio-economic and political histories of the terrain, the precise implications of the grains, cereals, and other edible plants or roots that comprise the staple diet of most of Satyacharan's'characters' (Bagchi 1996; Das 1998; Sen 1995, 1998.)

I have tried to suggest some of these specificities of ecological culture in the text; the appendix of plant names and land and labour terms that follow the translation of *Aranyak* may allow the reader to imagine something of the 'original' or inspire him/her to forage further.

This translation is based on the centenary edition of Bibhutibhushan Bandyopadhyay's collected works: Roma Bandyopadhyay, Gajendrakumar Mitra et al. (eds) , *Bibhuti Rachanabali*, Volume 5 (Calcutta: Mitra and Ghosh, 1996). All other translations from Bandyopadhyaya's diaries and notes and secondary sources are mine.

The Bengali/local Hindustani name for months and seasons; and flora and fauna whose English names are not commonly known have been retained.

Occupational identity/rank (e.g. patowari, tehsildar) have been retained, as have been caste names (e.g. gangota, rajput). Unless used as a title, the lower case has been used in both instances.

Indian kinship terms usually appear a trifle apologetic, awkward in English and yet one cannot entirely forgo them. Bhanmati would not have used the Bangla term, Jethamoshai, in any case, but something else in their language. 'Elder Uncle' or something equivalent in English would therefore be more appropriate.

For measures, Bibhutibhushan himself uses both miles and kos/kros (kos is the Bangla variant of Sanksrit kros); I have standardized it to mile.

For weight, I have stayed with the original: maund, seer, chhatak. Other measures such as rashi and kanoa are more obscure and have been changed to handful and so on.

I have retained the units of rupee, anna and paisa: the poverty of most of those who people *Aranyak* makes the use of anna and rupee an exception, and paisa the norm.

In spelling proper names I have tried to romanize according to the local pronunciation: neither anglicized, nor standard Bengali: e.g. Bishnuram Parey (Pandey). Abbreviations or local variants have been retained, e.g. chhatri for kshatriya; bhuiyar for bhumihar. In the case of quotations from Sanskrit slokas and sayings, the verse is presented in the text in romanized form and glossed at the bottom of the page.

Obscure or specialized words have been explained contextually or in the text. A longer gloss appears in the form of endnotes only when it is felt that it will help recreate the atmosphere or bring out the symbolic field, as when the drought-stricken land is evoked through the image of Bhairavi.

References

BAGCHI, Amiya Kumar. 1996. 'Sreni-Bibhakta, Jatonate Gatha Samaj-Pattaner Shokgatha.' *Anushtup* (Annual Issue), pp. 60–70.

BANDYOPADHYAY, Sibaji. 1996. *Bangla Upanyase 'Ora'*. Calcutta: Pratikshan Publications.

BANDYOPADHYAY, Bibhutibhushan. 1993. *Smritir Rekha* in *Diner Pore Din* (An Anthology of Diaries). Calcutta: Mitra and Ghosh Publishers, pp. 135–206.

DAS, Khudiram. 1988. 'Bhumisanglagna Jiboner Aro Ekti Dalil—*Aranyak*' inTarun Mukhopadhyay (ed.), *Bibhutibhushan Bandyopadhyay: 'Aranyak' Nana Chokhe*. Calcutta: Roma Prakashan, pp. 19–27.

DAS, Sisir Kumar. 1996. 'Aranyak: Bharatbarsha Kon Dike', *Visva-Bharati Patrika* (January–March), pp. 28–36.

O'FLAHERTY, Wendy Doniger (ed. and trans.). 1981. *The Rig Veda*. London: Penguin.

SEN, Rusati. 1995. *Bibhutibhushan Bandyopadhyaya*. Calcutta: Paschimbanga Bangla Academy.

———1998. 'Aranyapad O Manabgatha' (1993) in *Bibhutibhushan: Dwander Binnaysh*. Calcutta: Papyrus, pp. 17–44.

ARANYAK

Of the Forest

I was sitting on the Maidan, close by the side of the Fort after a whole day of backbreaking work at the office.

Near me was an almond tree. I sat quietly, letting my gaze travel beyond the tree towards the Fort area when my eyes fell on the undulating land beside the moat: suddenly, it seemed to be evening and I was sitting by the waters of Saraswati kundi on the northern borders of Lobtulia. The next instant, the sound of a car horn on the road to the Palashi gates shattered my delusion.

It seems like it was yesterday, although it is a tale of events long ago.

Submerged without respite in the hubbub and the frenetic activity of the city, when I think now of the forestlands of Lobtulia-baihar or Ajmabad —the brilliant moonlight, or the still dark nights; banks of flowering kash and sparse stretches of jhau trees and the range of grey hills merging into the horizon; the quick-drumming hooves of herds of wild neelgai passing by in the depths of night, and in the intense mid-day heat, thirst-maddened wild buffaloes at the waters of Saraswati kundi; wild flowers in glorious colour in that wonderful stretch of rocky ground and the dense forest, blood-red with the flowering palash—I feel as though it had been a dream of a world filled with beauty, dreamt in the half-awake slumber of a holiday evening. As though there is no such land to be found in all the world.

Not just the forests, what a variety of human beings had I seen.

Kunta . . . I remember Musammat Kunta . . . as if I can see, even now, the poor woman with her trail of children picking wild berries in the jungle of Sungthia-baihar, forever anxious, searching ways to eke out her everyday life.

Or, it is a bitter cold moonlit night: Kunta stands near the well in a cor-ner of the katcheri courtyard in Ajmabad hoping to take for her children some rice left over from my meal.

Dhaturia. I remember the boy Dhaturia ... the dancer, the *natua* lad ...

Southwards in Dharampur district, the crops had failed: Dhaturia had come to the sparsely populated wildish villages around Lobtulia to keep body and soul together with his singing and dancing. I'd seen such a smile of pleasure on his face when he got to eat some molasses with the fried grains of what they called cheena-grass in these parts. Curly hair, big eyes, and somewhat girlish in the way he moved—he was a good-looking boy of thirteen or so. He had no father, no mother, nobody at all anywhere in the world, and so his own efforts to look after himself at that young age ... Where to, I wonder, had the turbulent course of life swept him away once more.

I remember Dhautal Sahu, the simple moneylender. He sits in a corner of my thatched bungalow, slicing slivers off big areca nuts with his nutcracker. In the heart of the forest by his little hut sits the poor brahman Raju Parey singing his refrain Daya hoi ji as he grazes his stock of three buffaloes.

Spring has descended on the huge expanse of forest at the foot of the Mahalikharoop range and a crowd of yellow golgoli flowers swamps all of Lobtulia-baihar. In mid-afternoon a dust storm blurs the copper tinted horizon; at night, a garland of fire hangs around the distant Mahalikharoop: the sal forests have been set on fire to clear the land. I have known the lives of many boys and girls wretchedly poor, the curious lives of so many terrible moneylenders, singers, woodcutters and beggars ... I have sat in the dark courtyard of my thatched house and listened to strange tales told by hunters of the forest: how they had set out in the dark of night to hunt wild buffaloes in the Mohanpura Reserve Forest, and how, on the very edge of the pit criss-crossed with twigs, they had seen the immense frame of the wild buffalo god ...

It is of these people that I shall speak. Our earth has many paths where civilized men seldom tread. Along those paths the strange cross-currents of life trickle their way through obscure pebbly channels. Such currents I had known and the memory of knowing them remains with me.

But these memories do not give me pleasure; they are filled with sorrow. By my hands was destroyed an unfettered playground of nature. I know too, that for this act the forest gods will never forgive me. I have heard that to confess a crime in one's own words lightens somewhat the burden of the crime.

Therefore, this story.

ONE

1

The story begins about fifteen or sixteen years ago. I had graduated with a B.A. degree but then sat idle in Calcutta; despite much running around, there was not a job to be had.

It was Saraswati Puja that day. I'd been living at the lodging house for many years, so they hadn't yet thrown me out, but I was driven to distraction by the summons that came thick and fast from the mess manager. The members of the mess had ordered an image of the goddess and were going to celebrate the puja on their own with quite a bit of fanfare.

Everything is bound to be shut today, I thought, as I woke up that morning. There were a couple of places which had seemed promising but there was no point going anywhere on this day in search of work; far better to wander around admiring the various images of Saraswati that had been put up for the day.

Just then, in came Jagannath, the mess-boy, to hand me a note. Yet another reminder from the manager! They were planning a special treat at the mess on the occasion of Saraswati Puja: as I already owed them two months rent, I was to hand the mess-boy at least ten rupees; otherwise, starting from the next day, I would have to make alternate arrangements for my meals. What the manager had to say was quite fair; however, my resources added to a total of two rupees and a few annas.

There was not much point replying to the note. I walked out into the street which resounded with the music being played all over the neighbourhood; children clustered at the crossroads making a din, and Abhay the

sweetmaker had displayed new trays of sweets in his shop. A temporary platform for musicians had been set up at the gates of the college hostel across
from the main road. Groups of people carrying garlands and assorted purchases needed for the puja were returning from the market.

I wondered where I could go. It was over a year since I had stopped
teaching at the Jorasanko School and had been idle. Well, it wasn't quite right
to say that I'd been sitting idly, for there was not a single merchant office, a
school, a newspaper house, or a rich man's house that I had not visited at
least ten times during this time; but they all had the same thing to say—no
vacancy.

Suddenly, I ran into Satish. I used to live in the same room with him in
the Hindu College hostel. These days he was a lawyer practising at the Alipur
Court (though I doubt that he had much to do there). He tutored someone
in the Ballygunge area: for the present, that was his raft to tide him across
the sea of life. As for myself, let alone a raft, I was quite sparless, barely adrift
and half-drowning. All this was forgotten when I saw Satish.

'Satyacharan! Where are you off to?' called out Satish. 'Let's go to our
old haunt, the Hindu Hostel, and take a look at their Saraswati. Come
along—they're going to hold a musical soirée later in the evening. You
remember Abinash from Ward Six—you know— the one whose father was
a rich zamindar in Mymensingh? Well, he is now a famous singer and he's
going to be peforming tonight. He's given me a card—I do a bit of work for
their estates now and then. Come on, he'll be happy to see you.'

In my college days there was nothing I liked better than having a good
time. Although that was about five or six years ago, I discovered I had not
changed much in this regard. My visit to the Hindu Hostel, made with the
intention of admiring their image of the goddess, drew in turn an invitation
to stay on for the mid-day feast. There were many boys from my home town
who were presently inmates of the hostel and they refused to let go of me.
'Why do you want me to stay on now?' I said, putting up a show of resistance.
'After all, I'll be coming back for the concert later this evening. I'll have something to eat at the mess before I do.' Fortunately, they paid no attention to
my words or I would have had to fast on Saraswati Puja. The sharp note
from the manager rankled; I could never have tucked into a feast, the special

delicacies, not when I'd not even contributed a rupee. The invitation turned out to be a good thing. After a hearty meal I sauntered over to the enclosure and settled down to enjoy the concert. The high spirits of my college days, forgotten in the past few years, took over again. How did it matter whether I had a job or not or whether the mess manager had put on a long face! Drowned in waves of music and immersed in a performance of *thumris* and *kirtans*, I forgot that if I could not repay my debts, I would have to live on a diet of fresh air from the following day. It was eleven at night when the concert got over.

I went up to speak to Abinash. He and I had been the great champs of the debating club in our Hindu Hostel days. We had once invited Sir Gurudas Bandyopadhyay to chair a session; the topic was: 'Compulsory religious instruction should be introduced in schools and colleges.' Abinash led the group for the motion and I, the opposition. After a tumultuous battle of words, the chairman voted our side the winner. Abinash and I had gone on to become good friends, though this was our first meeting since graduation.

'Let me drop you off,' said Abinash, 'I have a car. Where do you live?'

As I was getting off at the mess door, he said, 'Listen, you are to have tea with me at Harrington Street at four o'clock tomorrow. You're not to forget —33/2 is the number. Put it down in your notebook, now.'

The following day, I first located Harrington Street and then hunted out my friend's house. It wasn't a very big house but there was a garden in front and another at the back. The gate was adorned with wistaria, a Nepali gatekeeper and a brass nameplate. A winding path of fine red gravel led to the house: a lush green lawn lay on one side and I could see a huge mango tree and one of muchkund-champas on the other side. A big car was parked in the portico. In short, it was quite impossible to mistake it for anything but a wealthy man's house. I went up the stairs and walked into the drawing room.

Abinash was most cordial in his welcome and almost immediately, we were absorbed in going over old times. Abinash's father was a well-to-do zamindar in Mymensingh, but neither he nor any one of the family members was in their Calcutta home. The entire family had gone to their country home some months ago to celebrate the wedding of one of Abinash's sisters.

'And what are you doing these days, Satya?' Abinash enquired after speaking of this and that.

'I was a schoolmaster at the Jorasanko School,' I said. 'You might say that I've been sitting idle for some time now. I don't think I'm going to do any more school teaching. I'm trying to find other kinds of work—I've been promised something in a couple of places.'

It was not true at all about being promised 'something', but Abinash was a rich man's son—they owned a huge estate; I didn't want it to look as if I was trying to wheedle a job out of him, so I said what I did.

Abinash thought for a while before he said, 'Of course, a deserving person like you should be able to get a job very quickly. I have something to say to you: you've also studied law, haven't you?'

'I've even passed the exams, but I've no desire to practice as a lawyer.'

'Well, we own an estate in the district of Purnea—about twenty or thirty thousand bighas of jungleland. We do have an administrator, a naib of ours there, but it doesn't do to trust him with the responsibility of managing all that land. We are on the lookout for a suitable person. Will you go?'

I know that the ear can play strange tricks. What was Abinash proposing! For over a year now, I'd been scouring the streets of Calcutta for a job, and today, without my having to ask for it, I was being offered a job in the course of an invitation to tea.

Still, there was the question of one's pride. With considerable restraint I suppressed my inner feelings and said indifferently, 'Oh! I see. Well, I'll think about it. Do you think you might be in tomorrow?'

Abinash was an extremely openhearted, generous sort of fellow. 'There's nothing to think about!' he said. 'I shall be writing a letter to Baba this very day. We are looking for a trustworthy person. We don't want one of those hardened products of the zamindari system—that sort is often corrupt. Out there, we need someone as educated and intelligent as you are. We shall be drawing up terms of agreement with our new tenants in the jungleland. Thirty thousand bighas of jungleland—one can't entrust just anybody with such a major responsibility! I've known you for long and I know you inside out. You must agree. I shall have an appointment letter made out by my father right away.'

There is no need to go into details as to how I got the job. The purpose of this story is altogether different. In brief, some two weeks after the tea at Abinash's home, I got off with my belongings at a small station of the B.N.W. (Bengal North-West) Railway.

It was a winter afternoon. Shadows had massed on the open land stretching beyond the track, and in the distance, wisps of mist had gathered on the tops of trees and vegetation. On either side of the railway tracks lay fields of matar crop. The fragrance of the fresh matar carried by the cold evening breeze somehow made me feel that the life I was about to begin was going to be very lonely—as lonely as the winter evening, the melancholy spaces before me and the bluish line of the distant forests.

I travelled all night in a bullock cart a distance of almost sixteen miles. Even inside the covered part of the cart, the blanket and the rug I had brought from Calcutta had turned as wet and cold as the morning frost. Who could have known that it would be so bitterly cold in these parts! The sun came up the next morning and I was still on my way. I noticed that the terrain had changed in the mean time, and nature too, had taken on a different guise: no fields or cultivated land to be seen and very little evidence of human habitation—only forests, big and small, dense in some places and sparse in others. Occasionally, there were stretches of open land, but it was all virgin land.

Around ten in the morning, I reached the office known as the katcheri. An area of about ten-fifteen bighas had been cleared of jungle and a few huts now stood in the clearing. They were made of wood, straw and bamboo—all got from the jungle. The walls of the katcheri were woven of dry grass and slim twigs of the wild jhau, plastered over with a coat of mud.

The huts had been just put together. I entered one and breathed in the smell of fresh-cut straw, bamboos and of grass still not quite dry. I wanted to know something about the place and was told that earlier, the katcheri used to be somewhere else in the jungle. They had made this hut only a short while ago because of a scarcity of water every winter at the older katcheri. A nearby spring ensured sufficient water for this katcheri round the year.

Thus far, I had spent most of my life in Calcutta in the company of friends, and in libraries, theatres, films and music sessions. I could not imagine a life without any of these pleasures. For the sake of a few rupees—a job—to end up in a place so lonely that I could scarcely have imagined it! One day followed another as I saw in the eastern sky the sun rise above the far off hills and the forest tops, and then, in the evening I saw the sun going down, turning the entire jhau forest and the tall stalks of the dry grass into flames of vermilion. Between the two events stretched out an eleven-hour winter day, vast and empty as the wilderness around me. It became a real challenge trying to find ways of getting through these hours. If one was engaged in work, there was certainly much to do, but I was newly arrived: I could not yet understand well the speech of the local people, could not figure out a method of work. I simply sat inside my room and read over and over the few books I had brought with me seeking, somehow, to plough through the time. The people at the katcheri were as good as barbarians; neither did they understand my speech, nor I theirs. Those first ten days were excruciating. Ever so often, I felt that having a job was of no use; it was far better to stay on half-starving in Calcutta than stifle to death here. It had been a horrible mistake to acquiesce to Abinash's request and come to this absolute jungle. This was not the life for me.

One night as I sat in my room preoccupied with these thoughts the old accountant, Mohuree Goshto Chakrabarti, pushed open the door and came in. This was the only person with whom I could speak in my own tongue and feel as though I were breathing freely. Goshto-babu had been living here for at least seventeen years. He came from a village somewhere near Bonpash station in Bardhaman district.

'Do sit down Goshto-babu,' said I.

Goshto-babu sat down on the only other chair in the room. 'I've come to tell you something in confidence,' he began. 'Don't trust any of the locals. This isn't Bengal, you know. They're all very bad . . .'

'Well, Goshto-babu, not everyone from Bengal is good. . .'

'As if I don't know that, Manager-babu. It was because of that and the malaria that I came here in the first place. Oh, it was very hard when I first came here—I used to find the jungle suffocating. But now, it's come to a point, where let alone my home in Bengal, I can't stick it out for more than two days when I have to go to Purnea or Patna for work.'

I regarded Goshto-babu with surprise.

'Why? What is it, does your heart cry out for the jungle?'

Goshto-babu looked at me and gave a little smile. 'That is just it, Manager-babu, you will soon find out . . . You are newly come from Calcutta, your heart longs to fly back to the city, and you're yet young. Spend some more time here. And then, you will see . . .'

'What will I see?'

'The jungle will get inside of you. By and by, you won't be able to bear any kind of disturbance or put up with crowds. That's what has happened to me. Just this last month I had to go to Mungher for a court case, and all I could worry about was when I'd be able to get away.'

May god spare me from such misfortune, I thought. I would have quit my job and returned to Calcutta long before I'd let that happen to me!

'Keep the gun by your side every night whenever you go to sleep,' went on Goshto-babu, 'it's a bad sort of place hereabouts. We had dacoits break into the katcheri one night. However, these days no money is kept here, so that's something.'

'You don't say! How long is it since you had the robbery?' I asked with interest.

'Not that long ago . . . I'd say, about eight or nine years ago. You will come to know everything once you've been here for a while. This is a bad area. Besides, in this frightful jungle, who is to know if the dacoits do get you?'

Once Goshto-babu had left, I went to stand by the window. There was a moon rising above the uneven line of the jungle far away. A branch from a wild jhau struck out against the rising moon. Like a Hokusai print.

What a place to get a job! If I had known earlier of the dangers that came with the place, I would have never given my word to Abinash.

My anxieties notwithstanding, the beauty of the rising moon quite overwhelmed me.

Not far away from the katcheri was a small rocky hillock, and on it stood an immense and ancient banyan tree. The tree was called Grantsaheb's Banyan. I could not find out why it had been so named even after many enquiries. One silent afternoon, after I had been walking for quite some time, I climbed up the hillock to see the glory of the setting sun on the western horizon.

Standing in the dark shadow of the banyan tree as the evening gathered around me, I saw at a glance a huge vista—scenes from my former life in Calcutta: the rooming house at Kolutola, our hang-out at the Kapalitola bridge, and, my favourite bench by the Gol-dighi where I used to go every day around this time and watch the endless stream of people, cars and buses on College Street. What an immense distance seemed to lie between us now. My heart echoed with a terrible loneliness. Where was I! In what god-forsaken forestland was I, a thatched hut for a home, all for the sake of a job! Was it fit for human habitation? Not a soul, not a creature by my side—I was utterly companionless. There was not a single person with whom I could exchange a word. The idiots, the barbarians, natives of this region—were they capable of appreciating a fine thought? Was it in their company that I would have to spend my days? In the endlessly stretching dusk I stood with not a soul in sight and was filled with sadness, even fear. Only a few days remained of the month. I decided then and there that I would somehow stumble through the next month after which I would write Abinash a long letter handing in my resignation. I would return to Calcutta to be welcomed by my civilized friends and acquaintances, eat civilized food, listen to civilized music, be one with the surging crowd of human beings, and, revived by the lively voices of a mass of people, would once again begin to live.

Did I know earlier that I loved so much to live in the midst of men? That I loved human beings so? Perhaps, I had been unable to fulfil my duties towards them at all times, but certainly, I loved them. Were it not so, why should I suffer so much at having left them behind? The old Musalman bookseller who strung his books from the railings of the Presidency College: how often had I stood at his shop and browsed through old books and monthlies. Perhaps I should have bought some, but I hadn't—now, he too, was remembered as the most intimate of friends. How long since I last saw him!

On my return to the katcheri, I went directly to my room. I lit the lamp and had barely sat at my table to read a book when Sipahi Muneshwar Singh, the katcheri guard, came in and gave me a salaam.

'What is it, Muneshwar?'

I had, in the meantime, learnt to speak some patois.

'Huzoor,' replied Muneshwar, 'if you would order Mohuree-babu to get me a *kadha*.'

'What will you do with it?'

Muneshwar's face positively glowed at the possibility of having an iron pot. 'If one had an iron *kadha*, it would be ever so useful, Huzoor,' he said in a humble voice. 'I could take it to all sorts of places with me, I could cook rice in it, store things in it, eat rice from it—it wouldn't break. I don't have a single *kadha*. I've been thinking of a *kadha* for so many days now, but Huzoor, I'm very poor and a *kadha* costs six annas; how can I buy a *kadha* for such a price? That is why I've come to Huzoor, it has been a long cherished desire of mine to have one such *kadha*, if Huzoor permits—Huzoor is the lord.'

I learnt for the first time that a *kadha* could be so worthy of praise, so precious that people could dream of it at night. That there were people on this earth so wretchedly poor that they felt they had entered the kingdom of heaven if they managed to get an iron pot worth six annas. I had heard that the people of this region were poor; I had not known that they were so poor. I began to feel a certain tenderness for them.

The next day Muneshwar Singh deposited on my floor a size five *kadha*, which he had bought from the Naugachhia market on the strength of my signed chit. He salaamed and stood there.

'It is done. Thanks to Huzoor, a *kadhayia* has been got!'

Looking at his smiling face I felt for the first time in the past one month—They're good fellows! What hard lives they lead!

TWO

1

I was unable, however, by any means, to adjust myself to life here. I had only just come from Bengal, all my life so far had been spent in Calcutta; the loneliness of the forestland sat upon my breast like a stone.

On some days, I would set off in the late afternoon and walk far. I might still hear a few voices while in the neighbourhood of the katcheri, but when I had walked on a little further and the katcheri huts were hidden by the wild jhau and the jungle of kash, I felt that I was all alone in the world. As far as the eye could see there were dense forests flanking the expansive fields and it was all jungle and shrub—acacias, wild bamboo, cane saplings and gajari trees. The setting sun splashed the tops of trees and bushes with a fiery orange and the evening breeze carried the fragrance of wild flowers and grass and creepers. Every bush was alive with the cry of birds—among these were also Himalayan parakeets. Before me lay vast open spaces half hidden by grass and the dense splendour of green forestland.

At such times, I felt that I had never before seen such sights as nature had to offer me here. All of this belonged to me; as far as one could see, I was the sole human being, as though there was no one to come and break my quietude beneath the peaceful evening sky. A silent cry would rise within me: let my mind, my imagination, soar to the furthest limits of the distant horizon.

Almost two miles away from the katcheri was to be found a sort of natural hollow. A few tiny springs came down from the hills and trickled through the hollow, and on either side were masses of wild lilies—what they call spider lilies in the gardens of Calcutta homes. Wild lilies I had neither seen before, nor known they make such a magnificent display as these I saw on the banks of the pebbly bed of the mountain stream, their mild fragrance mingling with the wind. Many a time have I found my way there and sat quietly savouring the evening, the sky and the silence.

Sometimes I would go riding. I could not ride well at first but got better at it. And having learnt to ride, I realized that there is nothing in life so pleasurable. How may I share that pleasure with one who has not raced his horse under the silent skies at his will across that vast expanse?

A survey team works about fifteen miles away from the katcheri. Often, after a cup of tea, I get on my horse and give him rein. Sometimes it is evening before I return, and sometimes, the constellations span the sky when I'm homeward bound and Jupiter is all aglow. On moonlit nights the fragrance of wild flowers infuses the moonlight; then, howling foxes sound the hour and the crickets sing in a chorus.

2

Much effort is being put into the work for which I have come: it is not a simple thing to make out terms of agreement and have so many thousand bighas of land settled. There is one more thing I have learnt since my arrival: about thirty years ago, this land was swallowed into the watery womb of the river, surfacing again as *char* land about twenty years later. But those who had gone to settle elsewhere when they found their ancestral land broken up by the Ganga, those original ryots, were now no longer being allowed by the landlord to reclaim the newly risen lands. It was with new ryots that the owner wanted to make terms, desiring a fat deposit and higher revenue. The original cultivators, homeless and shelterless, now desperately poor, had been deprived of their just claims and were not able to lease any of this land, however much they might plead or cry.

Many came to me as well. It was pitiful to see their condition but it was the landlord's orders that no old ryot was to get any land; for, once they settled there, they might very well assert the old rights to which they had a legal claim. For these last twenty years, landless and homeless, the ryots had earned daily wages and worked as wage labourers in far-flung places. Some did a little bit of farming, many others had died: their children were minors or helpless creatures. The landlord wielded the greater power—against his overwhelming force, they would be swept away like chaff.

On the other hand, how was one to get new tenants? All those who came from Mungher, Purnea, Bhagalpur, Chhapra and the other neighbouring districts backed out on hearing the tenancy rates. Only a few had rented some land. At this rate, it would take several decades and more until the ten thousand bighas of jungleland was rented out.

We had a sub-katcheri, also on thickly forested land, about nineteen miles away from where I lived. The place was called Lobtulia and it was just as wild as it was here. The only reason for having a katcheri there was that every year the jungle would be rented out to cowherds for the season as grazing ground for their cattle. In addition, there was almost three hundred bighas of land on which wild berries grew: people leased the forest of berries to raise silkworms. It was to ensure that this money was collected that a patowari was employed at Lobtulia at ten rupees a month. He now lived in the small katcheri.

It was getting on to be the time when the jungleland of wild berries had to be leased out. Between my katcheri and Lobtulia, there lay a ridge of red soil almost eight miles long: it was called Phulkia-baihar, and was thickly forested with a vast variety of trees and vegetation. In some places, the forest was so dense that horse and rider struck repeatedly against branches and twigs. Where the Phulkia-baihar leveled off, Chanan, a mountain river, flowed over the rocks and pebbles. During the rains the waters swelled while in winter there was hardly any water.

I was in Lobtulia now, for the first time. A tiny hut thatched with straw stood on the same level as the ground around it. The walls were made of dried kash strapped together with the leaves of wild jhau. When I got there, a little before evening fell, it was already colder than anything I had experienced; by evening, I was almost frozen.

The guards foraged for dry twigs and lit a fire with the twigs. I sat on a camp chair by the side of the fire and the others sat in a circle around the fire. The patowari had managed to get a rahu weighing about three kilos: the question was who was going to cook the fish. I had not brought a cook along with me. And I did not know how to cook. At Lobtulia, there were at least eight people waiting to see me: Kantu Mishra, a Maithili brahman, was one of them; the patowari appointed him to cook for me.

I asked the patowari, 'Are all these people going to bid for land rights?'

'No, Huzoor,' said the patowari, 'they've come hungering for food. They've been camping at the katcheri for two days now, ever since they heard you were coming. This is common among people from these parts. Many more will probably arrive tomorrow.'

I had never heard of such a strange thing.

'Really!' I said, 'But I haven't invited them.'

'Huzoor, they are very poor . . . they never get to eat rice. Ground gram from kalhai and maize—that's their daily fare, twelve months of the year. When they do get some rice, it's considered a feast. Your coming here meant they would get some rice. The entire lot was enticed by that thought; just wait and see how many more will turn up.'

It seemed to me that people in Bengal had become much too civilized in comparison. I didn't know why it was that on that night I felt such affection for those simple folk, so eager for some food. All around the fire they sat, talking to each other, and I listened to them. At first, they did not wish to sit by my fire, wanting to keep a distance out of respect for me. I called them to me. Kantu Mishra sat nearby. He had lit a fire with wood from an ashan tree and the smoke rising from it was as fragrant as incense. If one ventured beyond the ring of fire, it was as if it was snowing—it was so chilly.

Night fell by the time we—everyone at the katcheri—sat down together for our meal. After the meal, all of us sat in a circle around the fire once more. The cold seemed to freeze the very blood flowing inside one's body. Perhaps it was so cold because of the vast open spaces surrounding us; besides, we were not too far away from the Himalayas.

There were seven or eight of us ringed around the fire and only two small huts of straw. I was to spend the night in one of them and all the others in the second hut. The dark jungle and the open land beyond surrounded us; above us was the endless far-flung dark sky. It all felt very strange to me, as though I had been exiled from our familiar earth and had been drawn into the mysterious life of an unknown planet somewhere in space.

Amongst those in the group, a thirty-year-old man called Ganauri Teowari particularly struck me. He was dark and well built with longish hair, his forehead streaked with two horizontal caste marks. All he had against the piercing cold was a thick cotton wrap. He should have at least been wearing a *merzai*, the thin quilted waistcoat that they wore in these parts, but he did not have one. I had been observing for some time that he regarded the others with some diffidence, without objecting to anyone's comments or anything, although it was not as if he did not speak at all. In response to all my queries, he only said 'Huzoor'. When the local people acknowledge the words of a high ranking person they incline their head to one side and only say, 'Huzoor', very respectfully.

I asked Ganauri, 'Teowariji, where do you live?'

He stared at me in a way which said that he was quite unprepared for the honour: he had not expected me to address him directly. Then he replied, 'I live in Bhimdas-tola, Huzoor.' That evening, he spoke to me of his life, narrating his story not in one go, but in bits and pieces, in response to my many queries.

Ganauri Teowari was twelve years old when his father died. An ancient aunt—his father's sister—had brought him up. When she too, died within five years of his father's death, Ganauri went out into the world to seek his fortune. The familiar centre of his life had been the town of Purnea: the borders of western Bhagalpur district, the lonely forests of Phulkia-baihar in the south, and the Kushi river on the north made up the limits of his experience. Within this area he gathered a living, moving from village to village and sometimes, teaching at the village school, making just enough to subsist on ground kalhai and *rotis* made of cheena-grass, the locally grown coarse species of millets. He had been unemployed for the last two months: the village school at Parbatia had wound up; and, not a soul lived in the ten thousand bighas of forestland of Phulkia-baihar. He had been wandering from one *bathan* to another, where the local cattlemen herded their animals, begging whatever food he could of them. He had come here today with several others having heard of my imminent arrival. Such was the story of his life. Even more remarkable was his version of why they had come.

'Why have so many people come here, Teowariji?'

'Huzoor, they said that the Manager has come to the katcheri at Phulkia, that one would get to eat rice if one came here; so they came, and I came along with them.'

'Don't the people here get to eat rice?'

'Where would they get rice from, Huzoor? The Marwaris of Naugachhia eat rice every day. I myself have not had any rice for three months now—that was last year, at the time of autumn equinox, when Rajput Rashbehari Singh had invited us. He's a rich man and he fed us rice; I've eaten no rice since then.'

Not one among those who had come had a warm garment to cover himself with in this fierce cold. They spend the night warming themselves by the fire. When the temperature plunges in the last hours of the night, they cannot sleep any longer for the cold. Huddling together for warmth, they sit as close as they can to the fire until the day breaks.

I do not know why it was that I suddenly cared for them so much. Was it their poverty, their simplicity and their ability to survive a hard life? The dark jungleland and the harsh outdoors had not allowed them to tread the soft petalled path of luxury but had moulded them into real men. I marvelled at those who had walked nine miles from Bhimdas-tola and Parbatia, without any invitation—only for the pleasure of eating a little rice—and at their intense ability to derive pleasure so easily from so little.

Late that night, I was awakened by sounds that I could not identify. It was so cold that it was torture even to poke my head out of my blanket. I only had with me the blanket I used in Calcutta—I had not brought along adequate warm clothes or bedding for I had not known of the savage winters here. In the hours before dawn, the blanket was icy to the touch. The side I lay on was somehow kept warm by my body heat but when I turned over, I found the other side of the bed to be absolutely freezing. It was like taking a dip in a pond on a chilly winter night in the month of Paush. From the surrounding jungle came the sound of many pounding feet, running breathlessly. Twigs and branches of dry jhau snapped beneath the running, trampling feet. Unable to make any sense of what was happening, I called out to the guard Bishnuram Parey and to schoolmaster Ganauri Teowari. They sat up, their eyes heavy with sleep. In the faint light from the dying fire lit earlier in the evening, their faces wore an expression of deference and sleepiness. Ganauri Teowari had only to listen intently for a few moments before he said, 'It's nothing, Huzoor, just a herd of neelgai running in the jungle'. As soon as he had finished speaking, he was about to turn on his side and drop off to sleep once more.

'But why should the neelgai be running in this manner so late at night?' I asked him.

'Some creature might be after them, Huzoor; what else could it be?' answered Bishnuram Parey in a reassuring tone.

'What sort of creature?'

'What sort of creature Huzoor, but one from the jungle! Could be a tiger, or a bear perhaps ...'

Unconsciously, my gaze moved to the walls of the room in which I was sleeping. The walls, made of kash stems lashed together, were so light that they were sure to give way if even a dog were to push at them from outside. It was hardly reassuring to be informed that somewhere, not too far away, wild neelgai were running for their lives and that a tiger or a bear was giving them chase in the silent jungle night.

A little later, it was dawn.

3

As the days went by, I became increasingly ensnared by my fascination for the forest. I am unable to speak of its particular isolation or describe the jungle of wild jhau which the setting sun splashed with vermilion. I began to feel that I would not be able to return to the hurly burly of Calcutta forsaking the vast tracts of forestland, the fresh fragrance of the sun-scorched earth and the freedom and the liberation they represent.

This was not a sentiment that came upon me all of a sudden. Nature in the wild appeared before my enraptured and inexperienced eyes in myriad forms, her beauty unveiled: evenings came wearing a crown of bloody clouds; the searing afternoon in the guise of a mad Bhairavi;[1] or, draped in moonlight and wearing the cool and pure fragrance of wild flowers in the depths of night came the beautiful muse of music wearing around her neck a garland of stars; and, on moonless nights appeared the immense form of Kali, wielding the flaming blade that was Orion, the radiance extending into space . . .

4

There is one day I shall never forget. I remember it was Dol-purnima, the full moon which marks the spring festival of colour. The katcheri guards had taken leave for the day; all day long, they had celebrated the festival to the beat of their *dholak*. When I found that the singing and dancing showed no signs of abating even after it was evening, I lit a lamp and sat at my table writing letters to the head office till late at night. When I was done I happened to glance at my watch and found it was almost one. Quite frozen with the cold, I lit a cigarette and went to the window for a smoke. What I saw enthralled me so much that I stood rooted to the spot. I was overwhelmed by the indescribable light of a full moon night.

In all the time I had been here, I had never been out so late at night, perhaps because it had been winter. Whatever might have been the reason, this was the first time I experienced the overwhelming beauty of a moonlit night in Phulkia-baihar.

I opened the doors and went outside. There was no one to be seen: the guards had fallen asleep, exhausted after their daylong revelry. The forest was silent as though without a living creature. Never in my life had I seen such unblemished moonlight. There are no big trees in these parts; the wild jhau and the kash are relatively small and do not cast much of a shadow. The moonlight fell on the earth, glinting on the fine white sand and on the forest of kash that had partially dried in the winter sun creating an otherworldly beauty that was frightening even to look at. I felt within myself a sense of liberation, of being supremely detached, untrammeled. As I stood beneath the moonlit skies on that still silent night, I felt that I had chanced upon an unknown fairy kingdom. No mortal would come here to work. Places such as these, bereft of human beings, became the sporting ground for fairies—I had not done well to enter without permission.

That was but the first of the many other moonlit nights at Phulkia-baihar. I have drunk to the full the sweet fragrance of dudhli flowers on moonlit nights when, in mid-Falgun, the dudhli blossoms and carpets the wilderness; and, each time, I have felt that while I was in Bengal I had not known that moonlight could be so exquisite, that it could evoke such fear and detachment—the only word for which would be *udaas*. I will not attempt to describe those moonlit nights in Phulkia; one may not experience them merely by hearing or reading of them. Beauty of this sort comes alive only under the wide-open skies, in silence and loneliness, with the undulating forests stretching as far as the horizon. Such a moonlit night has to be experienced at least once a lifetime; he who has not seen it will never know one of the most exquisite wonders of our earth.

5

I lost my way one evening on the way back from a survey camp at Ajmabad. The forest was not level in all places: there were many hillocks and often, between two such hillocks, a smallish valley. The jungle, however, stretched on uninterruptedly. I climbed to the top of the hillock trying to spot the light near the Mahavir-banner at the katcheri. There was no light to be seen any-where, only the uneven hillocks and forests of jhau and akash trees with a sprinkling of sal and ashan. When, after two hours of searching, I was still unable to make my way out of the jungle, it suddenly struck me: why not try to find my way with the help of the constellations? It was summer and Orion had risen to its position just above my head, but I could not pinpoint where it had come from; nor could I find the Great Bear. Consequently, I aban-doned all hopes of finding out my direction from the stars and allowed my horse to roam as he wished. After we had gone on in this manner for about two miles, I spied a light. When I came to the source of the light, I found myself in a clearing of about twenty square feet, in the midst of which was a low grass hut. A fire had been lit before the hut, even on this summer day. Not too far from the fire sat a man engaged in some task. 'Who is it?' he cried out, startled by the sound made by my horse. Then, recognizing me, he came quickly forward and with great deference, he helped me off my horse.

I was exhausted. I had been on the saddle for almost six hours at a stretch and, while at the survey camp, I had followed the *amin* on his rounds in the jungle. I sat down on a grass mat that the man had spread out for me and asked him his name. 'Ganu Mahato', he said, 'of the gangota caste.' By this time, I knew that in these parts the gangotas carried on their livelihood by farming and animal husbandry. But what was this man doing all by himself in the dense forest?

'Huzoor, I graze my buffaloes here. My home is in Dharampur, at Lachhmania-tola—about ten miles north from where we stand.'

'Are they your own animals? How many buffaloes do you own?'

'I have five buffaloes, Huzoor,' said the man with some pride.

Five buffaloes! The man had chosen to leave behind his village some ten miles away, all for the sake of such a small herd. Here, he had set up his hovel and he paid revenue for the right to graze his animals in this god-forsaken jungle. However did he manage to spend all his time, day after day, month after month, in this little hovel! I who had newly arrived from Calcutta, a youth bred on the metropolitan fare of theatre and the bioscope, found it quite incomprehensible.

But when I had learnt something more of this place, I understood why Ganu Mahato lived thus. There was no other explanation for it but that this was how Ganu Mahato conceived life. They owned five buffaloes, hence it was necessary to graze the animals; and if the animals had to be grazed, then it was necessary to live alone in a little hovel put up in the jungle. This was most natural. Why should it be surprising at all?

Ganu welcomed me by making a long *pika*, a cheroot rolled out of fresh sal leaves, and serving it to me most respectfully. I saw his face by the light of the fire—a broad forehead, high nose, dark skin, gentle eyes and an innocent expression. He must have been over sixty, for not a single hair on his head was black. But he was so handsomely built that even now every muscle on his body rippled with life.

Ganu threw some more logs into the fire and lit a *pika* of sal leaves for himself as well. Inside the hut, the few brass vessels he possessed gleamed in the flames from the fire. Just outside the concentrated circle of fire, lay heavy darkness and beyond that dense forest.

'Ganu,' I asked him, 'you live here all by yourself: aren't you afraid of wild beasts?'

'Huzoor, how would we manage if were to become fearful when this way of life is our very livelihood. The other night there was a tiger just behind my hut. A buffalo had just given birth to two little ones and the tiger was trying to get them. When I hear anything moving about at night I light a flare and bang on the tin, and I yell. That night, Huzoor, I could not go back to sleep. Wolves howl all night long in this jungle, all through the winter.'

'What do you get to eat around here? Where do you get your provisions from . . . rice . . . dal . . . ? There aren't any shops here.'

'Rice and dal, Huzoor! Do we have money enough to buy provisions from the shops? Or do we get to eat rice like the Bangali-babus? I grow about two bighas of kheri in the jungle behind me. I boil the kheri grains and pick the bathua greens that grow wild in the jungle. These I boil with a bit of salt and these I eat. In the month of Fagun, gurmi fruits grow wild in the jungle . . . with a little bit of salt they're quite nice in the raw. It's a creeper, the fruits are small—like those of kakur—and the poor in these parts live off it for a few weeks. The kids come in flocks to have their fill of gurmi.'

'Do you enjoy eating boiled grains of kheri and bathua greens every day?'

'What's to be done, Huzoor. We are poor people. How are we to get rice for our daily meals as the Bangali-babus do? The only people who have rice in these parts are the likes of Rashbehari Singh and Nandalal Parey—they eat rice twice a day. I slave all day after the buffaloes; when I come back home in the evening I'm so hungry I enjoy whatever I get to eat.'

'Ganu,' I continued, 'have you ever been to the city of Calcutta?'

'No Huzoor; I've heard of it though. I went to Bhagalpur once—quite a city, that. I've seen the wind-run cars there: such strange things they are, Huzoor! No horses, nothing, and they move along the road by themselves.'

I was struck by Ganu's excellent health given his age. I had to admit to myself that he was also a very brave man. Ganu's sole means of livelihood were those buffaloes of his. It would be hard to find a buyer for the milk in such a jungle, so he churned butter from the milk and then turned it into ghee which he stored until he had enough in a couple of months to travel to the Dharampur bazar nine miles away. He sold his stocks to the Marwari traders there. For the rest, he had the crop off two bighas of kheri (also known as shyama-grass); the grains of the kheri are boiled and eaten as the staple diet of most poor people here. That evening Ganu escorted me back to the katcheri, but I had taken such a liking to him that I spent many a peaceful afternoon warming myself at his fire and chatting with him. No one else gave me such a melange of information about the place as he did: of flying snakes and live stones, of a child who was up and walking immediately after he was born, and many such like marvels. These stories of Ganu that sounded so mysterious and so delicious in the environs of the lonely forest would certainly, I know, sound absurd and false if one were to listen to them in Calcutta. One may not listen to stories anywhere and everywhere. Nor are stories to be recounted carelessly. A story lover will know how much the pleasure of a story depends on the immediate environment of its telling and the receptivity of its listeners. From all of Ganu's experiences the one that I found most amazing was the story of Tarbaro, the wild buffalo god. As this story has a strange epilogue, I shall speak of this later and not now. I should only mention here that the stories Ganu used to tell me were not fairy tales— they were part of his personal experience. Ganu had experienced life very differently. His words are not to be cursorily dismissed, for having spent all his life in intimate contact with nature, he was an expert on the wilderness. Besides, I do not think that Ganu possessed enough imagination to have made up his stories.

THREE

1

When summer came, a flock of egrets flew from the Pirpainti hill and settled on top of Grantsaheb's Banyan. From a distance, the tree appeared to have sprouted thick clusters of white blossoms.

One day, while I worked at a table I had set up by the side of the half-dried forest of kash, Muneshwar Singh announced, 'Huzoor, Nandalal Ojha Golawala wishes to see you.'

A little later, an elderly man, about fifty-years old, came up to me. He saluted me and seated himself on the stool I had indicated. He immediately took out a small woollen bag from which he brought out a tiny nutcracker and two areca nuts; these, he proceeded to slice. He placed the slices on his hands and held out his joined palms in a gesture of offering in my direction. 'Do take some supari, Huzoor,' he added respectfully.

Although I was not used to having supari in this form, I accepted the one he offered so as not to be rude. 'Where do you come from? What is your business?' I asked.

He replied that his name was Nandalal Ojha, that he was a Maithili brahman. His home was in Sungthia-diara, almost eleven miles northeast of the katcheri. He owned farmland and ran a moneylending business as well. He had come to invite me to his home on the next full moon day. Would I be so agreeable as to please step into his home? Might he dream of such good fortune?

I had no wish to go eleven miles in the blazing sun for a meal; however, Nandalal Ojha begged and pleaded to such an extent that I finally agreed.

Besides, I was most eager to garner information about the domestic life of ordinary people in this part of the country. I could not forbear from wanting to experience as much as was possible.

Late in the afternoon of the appointed day, an elephant with a rider was seen to make its way in our direction through the thick kash forest. When the elephant came up to the katcheri, the mahout informed me that the animal belonged to Nandalal Ojha and that it had been sent to fetch me. It had not been necessary to send an elephant for me; it would have taken me less time to get there on my own horse. However, it was on elephant back that I eventually set off for Nandalal's home.

My feet grazed the tender green shoots of wild grass and the sky seemed to touch my head. Far, far away on the horizon, the chain of blue hills ringed the jungle creating an enchanted world. I felt as though I was an inhabitant of that unreal world, a god from the distant heavens, as though my invisible voyages took place beneath the many cloudy layers piercing the blue atmosphere above the brilliantly green forestland. On the way, we passed the small body of water known as Chamtar Beel. Even now, at winter's end, it was overflowing with flocks of sillis and red ducks. They would fly away as soon as it got a little hotter. Occasionally, we went past some wretched hamlet— fields of tobacco bounded by creepers of phanimansa and poor thatched hovels.

When the elephant entered the village of Sungthia there was a mass of people ranged on either side of the road to welcome me. Nandalal's home lay ahead of us. This was a complex of about ten rooms made of mud, rudely tiled, each one standing separately in an enormous courtyard. As I entered their home, a gun went off twice. I was still in a daze when Nandalal Ojha himself appeared, smiling in welcome. He escorted me indoors and seated me on a chair in the verandah adjoining the biggest room. The chair was wrought of the native shishu tree and bore the craftsmanship of the village carpenter. Then, a little girl, perhaps ten years old, came forward and held out a plate before me. The plate contained a couple of betel leaves, a whole areca nut and a bit of ittar in a little bowl, and a few dried dates. I had no idea of what I was expected to do with the contents. I smiled like an ignoramus and only picked up a little of the fragrant ittar on the tips of my finger saying a few friendly words to the girl as I did so. She set the plate down in front of me and left.

This ritual of welcome was followed by preparations for the meal. I had no idea that Nanadlal had made such elaborate arrangements! An immense asan had been laid out for me. Arranged before this low seat of wood was a metal drinking glass and a brass plate of such enormous dimensions that it matched the one in which we made the fruit and other offerings to the goddess Durga in our part of the world. On the plate there were wheat puris, as big as the elephant's ears, fried greens of bathua, ripe cucumber in curd, a gravy of tamarind sauce, curds made from buffalo milk and peda—sweets made of sugar and condensed milk. Altogether, the strangest assortment of food I have come across! The courtyard was spilling over with people waiting to catch a sight of me; they gazed at me as though I belonged to a rare species. I was told that they were all Nandalal's tenants.

Just before evening fell, as I was leaving, Nandalal placed a small bag in my hands, saying that it was 'Huzoor's nazar'. I was taken aback: the bag contained a lot of money, fifty rupees at least. No one ever gave such a big amount as an obligatory gift, and besides, Nandalal was not my tenant. On the other hand, I believed that not to accept nazar was an insult to the head of the house. I untied the bag therefore, and took out a rupee. 'This is for buying your children some sweets,' I said, as I returned the bag to him. Nandalal was not willing to take no for an answer; I ignored his protests, came out of the house and once more mounted the elephant for the journey home.

The very next day Nandalal Ojha came to the katcheri accompanied by his eldest son. I welcomed both of them but they did not agree to sit down to a meal: I was told that Maithili brahmans do not eat food cooked by any other kind of brahman. After a lot of idle talk Nandalal spoke to me in private: his eldest son was a candidate for the post of tehsildar in Phulkia-baihar; I would have to appoint him to the post.

'But there is already a tehsildar for Phulkia—the post is not open to anyone,' I replied in some surprise.

'Huzoor, you are the master in these matters,' Nandalal responded with a wink. 'If you so desire, there's nothing that cannot be done.'

I was even more astonished. The tehsildar at Phulkia was a good worker; how could I bring myself to end his services all of a sudden? What charges could I bring against him to rid him of his post?

Nandalal answered, 'How many rupees of paan-money[2] would Huzoor be wanting? I shall have the amount sent to him by evening. My son must be appointed as the tehsildar. What is the amount, Huzoor? Five hundred?'

I had realized by now the real reason behind Nandalal's invitation of the day before. Had I known that people here were such crooks, I'd never have accepted the invitation. What a mess I had got into! I sent off Nandalal after telling him some home truths. I sensed though, that Nandalal still clung to his ambition.

Yet another day, I found Nandalal waiting for me on the fringes of a thick forest. It had been an evil moment when I had accepted an invitation to have a meal in his home. Had I known that feeding me a couple of wheat puris would give him ground enough to torment me so, I would have avoided his very shadow.

Nandalal smiled ingratiatingly as soon as he had my attention. 'Namaste, Huzoor,' he said in greeting.

'Hmm. Well, what brings you here?'

'Huzoor knows everything: I'll pay you twelve hundred in cash. Put my son down for the job.'

'Are you mad, Nandalal! I'm not the boss to give him the job. You may petition those who actually own the land, the zamindars. Besides, on what grounds am I to remove the person working there at present, for what offence is he to be fired?'

And without futher ado, I turned my horse around and galloped away.

Gradually, because of my persistently stern attitude towards him, I turned Nandalal into a fierce enemy—both the estate's and mine. I had not yet understood what a terrible person he was, and consequently I was to suffer more.

An event of utmost importance that took place in our katcheri was having the post fetched from the nearest post office, nineteen miles away. It was not possible to send a man so far every day, so he only went twice a week. I do not think that even the explorer Sven Hedin[3] sat waiting in his tent as eagerly for his mail in the lone and arid Takla-Makan Desert, as I did for my mine. I had lost all contact with the outside world living in this lonely forestland: I experienced from one day to another the sun setting, the rising and setting constellations, the rising moon, full moon nights and herds of neelgai running through the jungle. It was only with the few letters I received by post that something of that relationship was renewed—a relationship almost completely lost since my arrival here some eight or nine months ago.

It is one of those precious days today when Jawahirlal Singh has gone to fetch the mail. He is to return this afternoon. The Bengali-babu who is our accountant and I have both been keeping a sharp look out for him, watching the jungle intently. The path lies over a hillock, a mile or so away from the katcheri, and once on this stretch of the path, Jawahirlal Singh is clearly visible. It gets on to be afternoon and there is still no sign of Jawahirlal. I pace in and out of my room at the katcheri. There is always quite a load of official documents that need to be processed in this office: I am required to examine the reports of the various amins, sign the cashbook, reply to the correspondence sent from the head office, check the accounts of revenues collected by the tehsildars and the patowaris, and dismiss legal decrees. Then, there are the cases pending in the courts at Purnea, Bhagalpur and Mungher: I have to peruse and respond to the reports of the lawyers and the accompanying legal papers from these places; these and many other miscellaneous duties which, if not done systematically every day, would pile up to such an extent in a couple of days that it would be exhausting trying to complete the work later. And, a fresh round of papers comes in with every post. Papers from the city, and all sorts of orders—go to this person, meet with that person to settle tenancy agreements and so on.

It was three in the afternoon when Jawahirlal's white turban was sighted glistening in the sun. The Bengali Mohuree-babu called out, 'Do come, Manager-babu, the mailman has come ... here he is!'

I came out of my office. Meanwhile, Jawahirlal had gone down the hill and was once more hidden in the jungle. I looked through my binoculars and found that he was indeed making his way out of the distant forest, between the high grass and the wild jhau. I was no longer able to concentrate on my office work.

What an agonizing wait it was! The human heart tends to value most that which is rare. True, this value is an artificial one, of one's own making; it has no relationship with either the real excellence or the uselessness of the desired object. Yet, it is by infusing such artificial values into most things of this world that we come to define them as great or small, dear or cheap.

Jawahirlal was now visible on the other side of a narrow sandy embankment near the katcheri. I rose from my chair while Mohuree-babu went to meet him. Jawahirlal came over and saluted me; from his pocket he took out a packet of letters which he handed over to Mohuree-babu. There were a couple of letters for me as well, in writing that I knew well. As I read the letters I looked at the jungle all around me and was amazed. Where *was* I! I had never imagined that I would actually spend days on end in such a place abandoning my intense and lively discussion sessions with friends in Calcutta.

I had recently begun subscribing to an English magazine. A copy had come in today's post—By Airmail, it said on the wrapping. I wondered if I would have truly savoured the pleasure of this scientific invention of the twentieth century had I been sitting in the heart of crowded Calcutta. It was only here, in these lonely forests, that one had the opportunity to meditate on and be amazed by every little thing; it was the ambience which drew out such fine sensations. If I were to speak the truth, I would say that it was only since I have come here that I have learnt how to meditate on things. The innumerable thoughts that take shape in one's mind, the countless incidents from times past that are remembered—I had never before enjoyed my own mind in this manner. This was a pleasure I found to be increasingly intoxicating, and it took hold of me despite the thousand and one problems I faced here.

And yet, in truth, I had not been cast away all alone in some remote isle in the Pacific Ocean. The railway station was perhaps only thirty odd miles away. If I boarded a train, I could be in Purnea in an hour, in Mungher in three hours. But, firstly, it was too much trouble to go to the railway station; secondly, that hardship could be endured if only there was anything to be gained by going to Purnea or Mungher. As I did not know anyone in either of those towns, nor did anyone there know me, what was the point in making the trip?

I have missed my books and my friends to such an extent since leaving Calcutta that very often I have thought the kind of life I was leading intolerable. Calcutta was everything to me. After all, who did I have as a friend in Purnea or in Mungher that I should want to visit those places? But I could not go to Calcutta without the consent of the head office, and besides, it was too expensive to travel all the way there for only four or five days.

3

A few months went by as usual, when, at the end of Chaitra, there was the beginning of a phenomenon that I had hitherto not experienced. The month of Paush had seen some rain, but immediately after, a terrible drought fell on the land. There was no rain in Magh and in Falgun, not even in the months of Chaitra and Baisakh. And as the summer heat grew intolerable, we began facing a cruel lack of water.

No simple language would be equal to portraying the face of this fearful natural calamity. From Ajmabad in the north and Kishanpur in the south, further eastwards from Phulkia-baihar and Lobtulia stretching towards the borders of Mungher district in the west, all the water in the jungle ran dry— ponds, ditches, canals or any fair-sized body of water.

There was no water to be had even if you dug a well; if some little water did manage to seep through the sand into the well, it took over an hour for water enough to fill a small bucket to collect inside the well. The agonized cries of the drought-stricken land resounded all around us. In the east, the Kushi was the sole source of hope: the river lay about eight miles away on the easternmost limits of our estate on the other side of the famous Mohanpura Reserve Forest. Between our territory and the Mohanpura Forest, a small mountain stream flowed in from the terai region of Nepal, but now only a dry sandy channel carried the indistinct marks of its pebbly track. Girls carrying their water pots came from far away places lured by the hope of finding a bit of water after hours of digging in the sands. They spent the entire afternoon and more filtering the sand and the water, then walked back home with only half a bucket of muddy water in their pots.

But the river from the mountains—its local name was Michhi—was of no use to us because it was too far away from our estate. Nor did the katcheri possess a deep well; a small sandy well was all we had. It became a real challenge trying to collect water from this shallow well. The clock hand would cross the mark of noon and we had barely managed to get three buckets of water.

It is frightening to go outdoors at noontime and look upon the fiery bronze sky, the half-dried wild jhau and tall forests of grass. Everything appears to be on fire. Tongues of parched wind sometimes sear us. Such terrifying afternoons I had neither seen nor imagined. On some days, there comes a sandstorm from the west—Chaitra and Baisakh are the months when the west wind blows in these parts. Then thick clouds of dust and sand obscure objects that are only a hundred yards away from the katcheri.

Every other day Ramdhania Tahaldar comes to inform me in his Bhagalpuri Hindi, 'Huzoor, there's no water in the well.' On some days, after labouring for an hour at filtering the water, he places before me half a bucket of muddy liquid for my bath. In the fearful heat, even this is invaluable.

One day, on a late afternoon, I was standing in the slight shade of a haritaki tree behind the katcheri. I realized that I had never before seen the noon take on such a fiery guise. Moreover, I would never again see this face of the noon once I left the place. Noontimes in Bengal, I had always seen the dazzling sun in the month of Jaishtha but it was nothing like the fiery incarnation before me. I was overwhelmed by this awe-inspiring ruddy visage of Bhim-Bhairav. I looked at the sun—it was a huge ball of fire: calcium burning, hydrogen burning, iron burning, nickel burning, cobalt burning, hundreds and thousands of gases and metals, known and unknown, burning simultaneously in a live furnace billions of miles in diameter; the waves of fire penetrating layers of ether through unbounded space and touching the vegetation of Phulkia-baihar and Lodhai-tola, soaking up the last drop of sap from the veins and finest capillaries of every blade of green, turning them to shrivelled husks, searing and burning everything else around them for as far as the eye could see—the first steps of Shiva's cosmic dance of destruction, a *tandav lila*. All around me danced the quivering waves of heat and beyond them, I saw the steam rising from the heated ground. Not once in that entire summer did I see a blue sky in the afternoon; it was always bronze, burnt ochre, empty; not an eagle or a vulture in the sky—the birds had all fled the country for less cruel skies.

A terrible beauty was born that afternoon. For long did I stand beneath the haritaki tree indifferent to the heat rising from the ground and the heat engulfing me. I have not seen the Sahara or the Gobi; nor have I seen the Taklamakan desert made famous by Sven Hedin; but here—in the fierce noon that had taken on the fiery incarnation of Shiva as Rudrabhairav— some slight impression of those places came alive before my eyes.

There was still a little water standing in a tiny pond ringed by the forest, about three miles distant from the katcheri. I had heard that in the last few years the rains had ensured an abundance of fish. The pond had not yet completely dried up in the drought because it was deep. But the water had been of no use to anybody: firstly, because it was far away from human habitation, and secondly, because between the water and the bank there was such a treacherous stretch of mud that if you went in you were sure to sink waist deep into it—there was little chance of returning to the bank after filling your pitcher. Yet another reason was that the water itself was not very potable or good for bathing. I do not know what it was that was mixed in the water but it gave off an indefinable unpleasant metallic smell.

One evening, when the heat and fierce west wind had died down some- what, I set off for the pond, riding along a jungle path that lay between wild jhau and the high sandbank. Behind me was the big banyan known as Grantsaheb's Banyan, and behind the tree, the setting sun. I thought of saving some water at the katcheri by watering my horse here in the jungle. However muddy the pond might be, I felt sure that the horse would be able to climb out of it. When I crossed the jungle and went to the edge of the little pond (called a kundi in the local Hindi) an extraordinary sight met my eyes. On one side of the kundi were eight or nine snakes of varying lengths and on the other side three huge buffaloes, drinking water. The snakes were all of the poisonous kind—kraits, and a species of banded kraits, commonly found in these parts. The buffaloes were of a species I had never seen before: they had enormous pairs of horns, long shaggy hair and awesome frames. There was no human habitation or grazing ground in the vicinity; I could not guess where the buffaloes might have come from. I thought, perhaps their owner wished to avoid paying the taxes he was obliged to if he was leasing the sand-bank, and had therefore found a grazing ground for his animals hidden in the interior of the jungle.

I had almost reached the katcheri on my way back when I ran into Muneshwar Singh Chakladar. He started when I told him my story and exclaimed, 'Huzoor, what an escape that was! Hanumanji has saved you this time for sure. Those aren't domestic buffaloes you saw out there—they're aaron—wild buffaloes, Huzoor! They must have come from the Mohanpura jungle in search of water. There's no water in the Mohanpura jungle, you see—they've been driven here by thirst.'

Word of my encounter spread like wildfire in the katcheri. Oh! Huzoor has had a miraculous escape today, ran the unanimous verdict. You stand something of a chance, they said, if a tiger gets you, but there's no getting away from wild buffaloes. If they had charged you this evening in that lonely spot you could never have escaped—not even on your horse!

From this time the pond slowly turned into a watering hole and became a great meeting ground for all creatures of the wild, even as the drought got under way and the heat increasingly became more furious. News came trick-ling in that someone had spotted a tiger drinking at the kundi in the jungle; other people had seen wild buffaloes drinking, and herds of deer, not to men-tion herds of neelgai and wild boars—the last two creatures were to be found in abundance in the jungle.

One moonlit night I, too, set off on my horse for the pond, hoping to shoot some game. Four guards, two of whom carried guns, accompanied me. What I saw that night was unforgettable. To empathize with my experience one would have to conjure up a moonlit night and imagine vast stretches of virgin forest. And, imagine a peculiar silence enveloping the entire forestland. A silence that may not be imagined until you have experienced it.

The warm breeze was permeated with the smell of half-dried kash. We had come far away from human habitation and had lost all sense of direction. At the pond, drinking almost noiselessly, were two neelgais on one side, and on the other, a pair of hyenas. The neelgais looked across at the hyenas who in turn looked back at them, and between the two there was a baby neelgai, about two or three months old. I have never seen such a poignant scene. I did not have any inclination to riddle with bullets the innocent bodies of those thirsty creatures of the wild.

Meanwhile, the month of Baisakh had come and gone. And still, not a drop of water anywhere. There was yet another danger. People would sometimes lose their way in the sprawling forest even before the drought had hit us; now, such wanderers stood every chance of dying of thirst, as there was not a drop of water in the immense stretch between Phulkia-baihar and Grantsaheb's Banyan. Inexperienced travellers would not able to locate the couple of nearly dry ponds that were still left with some water. Let me recount an incident.

4

It was four in the afternoon. The heat had made it impossible to put my mind to my work. I was reading when Rambirij Singh came to tell me that a strange looking fellow—very likely, a mad man—had been sighted on the embankment to the west of the katcheri: he was waving his arms from afar and apparently saying something. I went outside for a look and, true enough, there was someone on the far bank who seemed to be coming our way, lurching drunkenly. The entire katcheri had gathered around and now they stared dumbfounded at the approaching figure. I sent two of the guards to fetch the man.

When the man was brought, I found that he had nothing on but a clean dhoti. He was fair complexioned and had a well-built body. But his face was a terrible sight: he was foaming at the mouth and saliva dribbled down his cheeks; his eyes were hibiscus-red and his gaze wild—indeed, like that of a mad man. There was some water in a bucket in my verandah; as soon as he spotted it, he made for it like a demented creature. Muneshwar Singh

Chakladar took immediate stock of his condition and quickly took the bucket away. When we made the man sit down and opened his mouth, we found that his tongue had swollen to grotesque proportions. With great difficulty we moved his tongue to one side and gently poured in minute quantities of water until he seemed somewhat recovered. We had some lemons in the katcheri; we gave him a glass of warm water with lime juice.

By and by—after an hour or so—he returned to normalcy. He told us that he lived in Patna. He had left Purnea about two days ago with the idea of locating forestland where he might cultivate lac. After he entered our estate, he lost his bearings sometime in the afternoon; it was easy enough, particularly for a stranger, to make a mistake: the forest looked more or less the same everywhere. He had wandered all of yesterday in the fierce heat of the day with the hot westerly wind blowing at him and had not found a single drop to drink, nor had he met a soul in his wanderings. Exhausted, he spent the night under a tree. This morning, he started his wandering again. If he had kept his head, perhaps it might not have been so difficult for him to find his way by the sun—he might at least have returned to Purnea; but frightened out of his wits, he had run hither and thither the entire afternoon. Moreover, he had tried to call out for help. But where was he to find people! The jungleland in Phulkia-baihar where berries grew sprawled on for at least ten square miles until you came to Lobtulia, and the entire stretch was uninhabited. It was hardly surprising that no one had heard his cries. Another reason for his terror-stricken state was that he believed that a spirit, a *jinn-peri* of the jungle, had possessed him and that there was no respite for him but death. He did have a garment on his upper body when he had started out, but extreme thirst had led to such a bad case of itching that at some point in the afternoon he had taken off his shirt and flung it away. If he had not sighted from afar the red Hanuman-banner marking our katcheri, he would certainly have died a dreadful death.

Right in the middle of the severe drought and heat wave, I was informed one afternoon that a terrible fire was raging about a mile away in the southwest and that it was heading straight for the katcheri. We ran out and saw thick coils of smoke and rosy tongues of fire winging their way upwards in the sky. There was a strong west wind that day: the long grass and the jungle of wild jhau, scorched already by the blazing sun, were like kindling—like dynamite ready to ignite. With a single spark, a whole patch would light up. As far as one could see there were only spirals of thick blue smoke with tongues of fire, and all one could hear was the crackling sound of the fire. From west to east came an oblique tongue of fire riding the storm. It came speeding like a mail train towards where we stood by the few thatched huts in our katcheri. Every face froze with fear: if we stayed where we stood, it would mean being burnt to cinders within a ring of fire.

The fire was almost upon us; there was no time to think. The important papers related to the katcheri, the money in the cash box, the official documents and government maps; all this, besides whatever little we owned by way of personal belongings—would all be devoured.

'The fire is upon us, Huzoor', cried the guards in a frightened voice.

'Get everything out,' I said. 'The government cashbox before anything else, then the documents and other papers.'

A few people ran ahead to cut down and slash whatever they could of the jungle that lay between the katcheri and the fire. About a score of people who had rented grazing land came running to protect the katcheri having sighted the fire from their cattle sheds. They had felt the furious power of the west wind and realized the threat it posed to the katcheri.

What an amazing sight it was! Herds of panic-stricken neelagai broke and crashed their way through the jungle on the west and ran eastwards for their lives. Foxes raced past us as did rabbits, their ears upright, and a herd of wild boar simply trampled through the katcheri compound with their young ones, completely oblivious of where they were going. Domestic buffaloes had worked loose their tether—they too, ran for their lives. A flock of wild parrots whistled past just over our heads, behind them came a huge flock of red ducks, and then, yet another flock of wild parrots and some silli.

'Bhai Ramlagan,' Rambirij Singh Chakladar asked wonderingly, 'where *did* the wild ducks come from? There's been no water around this place . . .'

'Curse that man!' exclaimed the Mohuree in vexation. 'Here we are battling for our very lives and the man must know where the red ducks have come from!'

In another twenty minutes, the fire was upon us. The next hour was a veritable battle between the dozen or so men and the fire. There was no water; our only weapons were half-ripened stalks of kash and sand. Scorched by the flames and blackened by soot and ash, every one of the fire fighters looked like a demon. The veins on the hand stood out and many had blisters all over their bodies, whilst the rest of us were still engaged in bringing out the furniture, the bed, cupboards, boxes, dumping them any which way in the katcheri courtyard. Everything got mixed up in the confusion; it was impossible to keep track of one's belongings.

'Keep the cashbox and the box of documents by you,' I instructed Mohuree-babu.

In another moment, however, the fire ran into the space just cleared around the katcheri and then, unable to flow along the northern and southern sides of the katcheri, it made a sharp turn, eastwards. The katcheri had been somehow saved, at least, this one time. The assortment of objects cast pell-mell on the ground were gradually put back in the house, but far away, the destructive tongues of fire burnt all night, their fierce energy reddening the eastern sky. By morning, the fire had touched the borders of Mohanpura Reserve Forest.

A few days later we learnt that ten wild buffaloes, two cheetahs and a couple of neelgai were lying half-buried in the muddy banks of the Karo and the Kushi. The panic-stricken animals had broken out of the Mohanpura Forest and had fled for their lives along the banks of the river until they had fallen into the mud, although the distance between the Reserve Forest and the Kushi and Karo rivers was at least eight miles.

FOUR

1

Baisakh and Jaishtha were over and it was now the month of Asharh. At the very beginning of Asharh was the festival of Punyaha, formally marking a new year of revenue collection from the tenants. Traditionally, a feast is organized by the zamindar for his subjects on this occasion. For my part, I wished to invite many people to the katcheri for a meal; I never got to see many of them at the katcheri otherwise. As none of the villages were located nearby, I sent Ganauri Teowari to all the distant hamlets to invite people to the feast. The day before the festival, the sky became overcast and it was raining little drops; the next day, the heavens broke loose and the rain poured in torrents. Meanwhile, long before noon, and apparently indifferent to the rain, crowds of people had begun arriving at the katcheri in response to the invitation. Soon, it became difficult finding them a place to sit. Many of the invitees were women who had come with their children: I arranged for them to be seated in the katcheri office where they found themselves such space as they could.

It was not much trouble feasting people in these parts. I had not known that there could be a region so poverty-stricken as where I now lived. Compared with the average person here, even the poor in Bengal were better off. My guests had come braving the torrential rains to have a meal consisting of cheena grains, plain yoghurt, coarse jaggery and a sweet laddu each. These items were considered good enough to make up a regular feast.

An unknown boy of about eleven had been working hard since early morning. His name was Bishua, he said. He was a poor boy and must have come from a remote hamlet. Around ten in the morning he asked for some food. The Lobtulia patowari who was in charge of the stores brought him a measure of cheena grains and a bit of salt. I was standing nearby. Dark as ebony, with a beautiful face—the boy was like a living statue of the boy Krishna that had been chiselled out of stone. A delighted smile lit up his face as he anxiously unwound a part of his coarse cotton dhoti and put out the end to receive the trifling meal. I can vouch that even the poorest of Bengali boys would not deign to eat cheena grains, let alone be delighted with them. For I had once tried chewing on cheena grains, and the taste that has stayed with me will prevent me from ever referring to it as a pleasant item of food.

Somehow, despite the rain, we managed to attend to the feast for the brahmans. Late in the afternoon, I noticed three women who sat in the court-yard with their leaf plates before them and their two little ones around them—all of them streaming wet in the rain. There were heaps of cheena-grains on the plates but no one had bothered to serve them with either jag-gery or yoghurt, so there they sat, looking at the katcheri with patient and expectant eyes.

I called the patowari and took him to task: 'Who is serving these people? Why have they been kept waiting? In any case, who has seated them out-doors in the open courtyard?'

'Huzoor,' replied the patowari, 'they are doshads by caste. If we seat them indoors, everything will have to be thrown away—no brahman, gangotri or chhatri will touch the food. Besides, where else can I seat them?'

When I myself went out in the rain to supervise the service for the poor doshad women, the others immediately hurried forward to serve them. Each one of those women ate such vast quantities of cheena grains, jaggery and the sour and watery yogurt, that it seemed miraculous. When I saw how eagerly they ate this humble fare, I made up my mind to invite them to a proper civilized meal. A week later, I had the patowari invite the women and their children from the doshad village. That day they were treated to a typical Bengali feast of meat and fish dishes, fluffy luchis made of flour, chutney, yoghurt, and several kinds of desserts made of creamy milk and rice, surpassing anything they might have even imagined. I will remember for long their wonderstruck and joyous expression, their shining eyes. Bishua, the vagabond gangota lad was also amongst the invitees.

2

I was riding back from the survey camp one day when I came across a man squatting beside a clump of kash making a meal of finely ground kalhai-dal or sattu. For lack of a bowl, he was mixing the sattu on one end of the dirty garment he was wearing. It was such a massive pile that it seemed incredible to me that a single person—albeit a Hindustani with a hearty appetite—could eat so much. The man stood up deferentially as soon as he saw me and salaamed.

'Forgive me, Manager Sahab,' he said, 'it's just a little meal that I'm having, Huzoor.'

I could not see what there was to forgive in a man who sat by himself in the wilderness, quietly having a meal.

'You don't have to get up,' I said, 'do carry on with your meal. What are you called?'

The man continued to stand as he answered respectfully, 'Huzoor, this person is known as Dhautal Sahu.'

He looked as though he was over sixty. His was a tall and thin frame, his complexion dark. His feet were bare and all he wore was an extremely dirty dhoti and a merzai.

This was the first of my encounters with Dhautal Sahu.

'Do you know Dhautal Sahu?' I asked Ramjyot Patowari on my return to the katcheri.

'Certainly, Huzoor,' said Ramjyot. 'Is there anyone in these parts who does not know Dhautal Sahu? He's a well-known rich moneylender, owner of lakhs of rupees—most people in these parts have borrowed from him. He lives in Naugachhia.'

I was taken aback by the patowari's words. It was almost impossible to imagine a Bengali millionaire sitting on his haunches in the middle of the jungle and working his way through a mound of sattu off the dirty end of his garment. I thought the patowari might be exaggerating, but whoever I asked in the katcheri had the same thing to say, 'Oh, Dhautal Sahu! There's no counting his money.'

Since that first meeting there was many an occasion when Dhautal Sahu visited me on his own work. As I got to know him, little by little, I realized that I had come to know a most exceptional character. Unless one saw him in person, it was hard to believe that such a man could exist in the twentieth century.

As I had guessed, Dhautal was about sixty-three. His home was in the village of Naugachhia which lay some twelve or thirteen miles south east of the katcheri. Practically everyone borrowed from him in these parts—tenants and labourers, small and middling farmers, landowners and traders. But the funny thing about Dhautal was that once he had lent the money he could never pressure the debtor to return the loan. In fact, there were many who had cheated *him*. A good-natured innocent creature like him ought never to have taken on the role of a banker and moneylender but he was unable to ward off any appeal. Besides, his own argument was that since they all borrowed money at a heavy rate of interest, he ought to loan the money in the interest of his own business.

Dhautal Sahu came to see me one day with a bundle of old documents tied up in his garment and said, 'Huzoor, would you be kind enough to look through these documents?'

I inspected the contents and found that almost ten thousand rupees worth of deeds had become defunct because of a failure to appeal in the courts in time. Then he opened another fold of the long, flowing urani draped around his chest and took out yet another bundle of equally faded and decrepit looking documents.

'Huzoor, will you have a look at these?' requested Dhautal. 'I thought I should go to the district courts and have the lawyers look through them, but then, I've never filed a case. It doesn't suit me. When I ask them to pay up, the defaulters keep saying they will, but they never do.'

I found they were all defunct deeds. The total value would amount to anything between four to five thousand rupees.

'A good man always gets cheated, Sahuji,' I told him, 'it is not in you to be a mahajan. The only ones who will be successful in moneylending in these parts are professionals like the Rajput Rashbehari Singh—the sort who have eight hired men armed with their sticks to do their bidding. He lets his men loose in the defaulter's fields and extracts both capital and interest by seizing the crops. No one is going to return a loan to a good-natured person such as you. Do not lend out any more money.'

I could not convince Dhautal.

'Not everybody cheats, Huzoor,' he maintained. 'There is still the sun and the moon, and there is still the good Lord above us all—He who looks after the poor and the lowly. Besides, one cannot let money sit idle: Huzoor, money has to be let out at an interest. That is our business, after all.'

I did not understand this bit of logic. What kind of a business was it to lose one's capital in the hope of earning interest? That day, before my eyes, Dhautal Sahu casually tore up fifteen to sixteen thousand rupees worth of defunct deeds. He tore them up as if it was rubbish; of course, they *had* turned into worthless paper. While he was doing this, neither did his hands shake nor his voice tremble.

'I made my money selling raichi and reri seeds,' he said. 'Not a single coin did I inherit from my forefathers: It was I who made the money, and now, the loss is mine. If you want to do business, Huzoor, profit and loss is part of the game.'

All this was true enough, nevertheless, I wondered if there were many who would bear such massive losses with such calm, even indifference. He seemed to suffer from only one weakness: every now and then he would take out a cutter from a little red pouch and nip off bit of an areca nut and pop it into his mouth. He had told me once with a smile, 'Babuji, I have some *supari* every day. This makes for quite a daily expense.'

If it is philosophical to be indifferent to one's property and to regard a huge loss as a trifling matter, then I must say that I have never met a philosopher like Dhautal Sahu.

Whenever I crossed Phulkia I would go past the small hut thatched with leaves of maize that belonged to Jaipal Kumar. In spite of his last name Kumar, he was not a kumbhakar or potter, but a bhumihar brahman.

Jaipal's hut stood beneath a huge and ancient pakur tree. He was quite alone and quite old, with a long and lanky frame and a shock of long white hair on his head. At whatever time I happened to pass his home I would find him sitting quietly at the door of his hut. I never saw him take any tobacco, heard him sing or be otherwise engaged in activity. I could not imagine how a person could sit still for such long stretches without doing anything at all. Jaipal aroused immense wonder and curiosity in me. I could not help but stop my horse before his door every time I passed that way to exchange a few words with him.

'Jaipal, what do you do sitting here?'

'I just sit here, Huzoor.'

'How old are you?'

'I've kept no count of that. But that time, when they built the bridge over the Kushi, I was old enough to be grazing buffaloes.'

'Were you married? Do you have any children?'

'My wife has been dead these twenty years or more. I had two daughters. They died as well. That was about fourteen years ago. Now I'm all alone.'

'Tell me, don't you mind living here all by yourself? You don't go anywhere, you do nothing . . . do you like it? Don't you find it monotonous, dull?'

Jaipal stared at me in some surprise as he replied, 'Why should I mind it, Huzoor? I'm quite well. I don't mind it at all.'

I could never understand this sentiment of Jaipal's. I had been a college student in Calcutta. I did not have a clue as to what a person might do if he was not working or chatting with friends, or if he was not absorbed in books, films, outings and the like. The world had changed immensely in these past twenty years: had Jaipal Kumar kept any track of the many changes that had taken place in the world while he sat silent and unmoving at his post by the door of his hut all this time? Jaipal must have sat in like manner while I had studied in the lower classes at school, and so he had sat even when I had graduated. I compared these unending, lonely and unvaried days that Jaipal must have lived through with the many events of my own life that proved of such interest to me.

Although Jaipal's home was right in the middle of the village, there were fields of maize and some wasteland adjoining his hut, so he had no neighbours. Phulkia was a tiny village of about fifteen households. Almost every person in the village earned his living by grazing buffaloes in the far spreading jungleland. They worked like dogs all day; in the evening, they lit fires from the dry stalks of kalhai, took their pinch of snuff or had a smoke made of twisted sal leaf (very few smoked a hookah in these parts) and the whole lot of them got together for a chat. But I never saw anyone come to chat with Jaipal.

Egrets come to nest on the topmost branch of the ancient pakur tree. From afar, it seems as though the tree has sprouted white blossoms. The place is densely shadowed and lonely; from wherever you look, you can see in the far horizon a ring of blue hills like children holding hands and playing a game. When I stood in the deep shadow cast by the pakur tree and spoke with Jaipal, the quiet peace beneath this huge tree and the unexcitable, calm, detached lifestyle of my host would slowly but surely have a strange effect on me. Of what use was it to run around? What wonderful shade the dark banyan tree gave, where blue-dark Krishna himself might have played his flute, how placid the waters of the Jamuna, how delicious to be adrift in the currents of time, after walking through a thousand centuries!

It was as though something of Jaipal's influence and something of the surrounding nature, which was so free and unfettered, was transforming me into as detached, unruffled and remote a creature as Jaipal Kumar. Besides, the vision I had never known existed inside me was opening up now like a flower, and thoughts I had never imagined now inhabited my world. I had come to love the open spaces and the thick green forests so much that if I went to Mungher or Purnea for work—even for a day—I grew restless with longing to come back to the jungle and plunge once more into its deep silence, the exquisite moonlight, the sunset, the rainbearing dark clouds, and its unsullied starry nights . . .

I come back, leaving all civilized habitation far behind me, past the stakes that Mukundi Chakladar has fashioned of acacia, and immediately upon crossing into the borders of my forest, I am enthralled by the deep green serpentine forests, the rocky masses, flocks of wild parrots, herds of neelgai, the sunshine and the open land.

FIVE

1

All was awash with moonlight and the cold crept into the very bones. It was the end of Paush: I had come over from my headquarters to the sub-katcheri at Lobtulia on supervision work. It got to be about eleven at night before all the cooking and the eating was done with at Lobtulia. One night, after I had finished my meal, I came out of the kitchen to find a young woman standing in the brilliant moonlight. She stood on the fringes of the katcheri compound at that late hour when the sky rained only freezing dew.

'Who is that standing there?' I asked the patowari.

'That is Kunta,' said the patowari. 'She heard you were coming and she asked me, "The Manager-babu will come; my children are in great distress. I shall come to fetch the leftover rice from his plate, may I?" So I told her she could.'

While we were speaking the watchman, Baloa, took away the left-over rice mixed with dal, remnants of the fish and a little bit of the vegetable from my plate and some leftover milk and rice from my bowl; he poured it all into a brass plate with upturned edges that the woman had brought. She left immediately with the food.

I spent about ten days in the Lobtulia katcheri that time. On every one of those nights, I found the young woman standing by the well with only her sari to protect her from the fierce cold, waiting for the leftovers from my plate. After watching her for several days I asked the patowari out of curiosity, 'Kunta—the one who takes away the leftovers from my plate—who is she and where does she live? I never see her at daytime . . .'

'I'll tell you, Huzoor,' said the patowari.

Earlier in the evening, a fire of twigs and roots had been lit in my room. I had been sitting on my chair beside the roaring fire checking the accounts against the instalments due to the estate. After dinner, I felt I had worked enough for the day: I put away my papers and settled down to listen to the patowari's tale.

'Listen, Huzoor,' said the patowari. 'About ten years ago, a rajput named Debi Singh was very powerful in these parts. All the gangotas and the farmers and the tenants of the newly formed *char* land were terrorized by him. Debi Singh's business was to lend money at a very high rate of interest to these people and then to ensure that he got back both interest and principal with the help of his band of stick-wielding men, his lathials. He had at least eight such professional lathials in his employment. Just as Rashbehari Singh is now the chief moneylender in these parts, so too, was Debi Singh in those times. Debi Singh had come from Jaunpur district and had settled down in the district of Purnea. Here, he managed to control the lot of timid gangota tenants by lending them money and using force to settle dues. A few years after the move he went to Kashi where he became very close to the fifteen-year-old daughter of a baiji whose singing had drawn him to their quarters. Debi Singh eloped with the daughter and brought her here. He was then in his late twenties. He married the girl. However, when it was found out that she was a baiji's daughter, his own kind—the rajputs—decided to have nothing to do with him. They stopped eating with him and virtually out-casted him. Because he had a lot of money Debi Singh could afford to dis-regard their contempt. He put on airs, became extravagant and reckless and eventually got involved in a lawsuit with Rashbehari Singh, and so he lost everything he possessed. He has been dead these four years. The Kunta we are now speaking of is the widow of the same Debi Singh Rajput. There was a time when she went to bathe in the sacred confluence where the waters of Kushi and Kalbalia met, riding in a palanquin decked with brocade fringes. She drank water only after sweetening her tongue with Bikaneri michri or sugar crystals; and now—just look at her wretched condition! What makes it worse is that she is believed to have no caste status because everyone knows she is the daughter of a baiji. Neither her husband's rajput relatives, nor the local gangotas accept her. After the wheat has been harvested she goes around the fields picking up bits of broken grains in her basket and that is all she has to feed her half-starved children with for a couple of months in the year. But I've never seen her beg, Huzoor. You have come here as the manager of the zamindar, equal to a king: it is not insulting or humiliating if she has your leftovers.'

'Her mother, the baiji,' I asked, 'has she ever been traced?'

'I've never seen her, Huzoor,' The patowari replied. 'Neither has Kunta ever enquired after her mother. It is she who tries to take care of the children with great difficulty, using her wits and with constant effort. What you see of her now, Huzoor, is nothing compared to her beauty in those times. No one in these parts had seen anything like her. She has grown older, and since she became a widow, nothing of her former looks has stayed with her through her travails. Kunta is a good woman, a quiet creature. But, no one here can abide her: they scorn her and look down on her, probably because she is the daughter of a baiji.'

'That is as it may be,' said I, 'but she walks all by herself at midnight through heavy jungle to get to her home in Lobtulia. It's a distance of at least a mile and half, is it not?'

'Does it pay her to be afraid, Huzoor! She has to cross the jungle all by herself ever so often. Does she have any that she may call her own, who will look after the lot of them?'

This was in the month of Paush. Once I had put pressure on the tenants for the month's dues, I came back to my base. It was around the mid-Magh when I needed once more to go to Lobtulia to rent out a tiny strip of land over a newly risen *char*.

Winter was not yet over and the west wind that blew every evening after sundown doubled the intensity of the cold. One day, I had left the katcheri far behind while wandering in the northern limits of the estate. All I could see was a jungle of wild berries stretching into the far horizon. Cultivators belonging to the kalaor caste from Chhapra and Muzaffarpur had rented these lands; they raised silkworms in the land and made a great deal of money out of it. I had almost lost my way in the forest of berries when suddenly I heard the piercing cry of a woman, young voices crying and screaming and a string of abuses in a harsh male voice. Moving closer to the cries, I came across the servants of the silkworm rentiers dragging a woman by her hair. The woman wore tattered clothes and the little ones around her were sobbing. One of the two rajput servants carried a basket half filled with ripe berries. Enthused by my sudden appearance, the servants informed me that it was just as well that Huzoor had come upon the scene for they were about to take this gangotri woman and her lot to the patowari to be judged: they had all been caught stealing berries. My first task was to threaten them and free the woman from their clutches. By then, the woman, cowering in shame and fear, was trying to screen herself behind a bush of berries. I was struck by her pitiable state. The entire episode saddened me immensely. The servants were most reluctant to let go of their victim so easily. I reasoned with the fellows: 'If a poor woman does pick half a basket of sour berries and tries to feed her children, in what way is it going to affect your lac crop? Let her go home.'

'You don't know the whole story, Huzoor,' said one of them. 'Her name's Kunta and she lives here, in Lobtulia. It's an old habit of her's to steal berries. There was one other time, last year, when I caught her red-handed. If we don't teach her a lesson this time . . .'

I almost jumped in surprise. It *was* Kunta. Why had I not recognized her? One reason was I had never seen her in daylight, I had only seen her at night. I immediately threatened the rentier's men and made them set Kunta free. She was overwhelmed with shame and immediately set off homewards with her children, leaving behind her basket and the hook she used for picking berries. Perhaps she was both afraid and ashamed. When I ordered one of the people gathered there to pick up both items and take them to the katcheri they were very pleased, assuming that the master was certainly going to make her forfeit them.

'Why are your people so cruel?' I asked Patowari Banowarilal on reaching the katcheri.

Banowari was grieved by the incident as well. He was a good soul and, in comparison to the others, he truly had some compassion in his heart. He immediately had someone carry Kunta's basket and hook to her home in Lobtulia.

Kunta has not come to the katcheri for the leftover rice since, perhaps out of shame.

2

Winter was over and now it was spring. Every Phalgun, during the festival of Holi, a famous village fair was held about eight miles beyond the south-eastern borders of our jungle territory, appproximately fifteen miles away from the main katcheri. I was determined to go to the fair this time. I had not seen crowds of people for very long and I was curious, too, to see the local fairs. But the people at the katcheri were bent on dissuading me: they argued that the path was difficult, it ran through hilly terrain and through jungle; besides, there was the threat of tigers and wild buffaloes for almost the entire route. Although a few hamlets were scattered here and there, they were too few and far in between—they would be of no use if I fell into danger. And warnings of a similar nature.

I had never done anything daring in my life. If I ever had to do anything of that sort it had to be undertaken while I was here and now, for once I returned to Bengal and to Calcutta where was I to find jungles and tigers or wild buffaloes! I imagined a scenario in which I saw the sparkling eyes and the enraptured expressions of grandsons and granddaughters listening avidly to my tales; this gave me enough inspiration to dispense with all the advice bestowed upon me by Muneshwar Mahato, the patowari and the accountant, Nabin-babu. On the morning of the fair I set off on my horse. It took me almost two hours to get beyond the limits of our territory because the jungleland within our jurisdiction lay to the south-west.

There was no path to speak of. Only someone on horseback would be able to make his way over the rugged terrain. The trail, such as it was, was strewn with boulders of varying sizes and wound its way through forests of sal and jungleland of kash and wild jhau. It was all uneven going, sometimes having to cross a sandhill that climbed up steep banks of red soil, and some-times over hillocks and dense thorny vegetation atop the hills. I rode at my own pace, quickening and slowing down the horse by turns, for it was not possible to go at a steady trot; the bad road and the boulders along the way kept breaking the horse's rhythm. And so we went, now at a trot, now at a gallop and sometimes walking along the path.

I was beside myself with joy since having left the katcheri. Imperceptibly, from the very first day of my coming here on work, the vast and open fields and the forestland had been growing on me, making me forget my native land and the hundred and one creature comforts and habits of the civilized world—even to the point where I thought I would soon forget my friends. Did it matter whether the horse went slow or fast whilst the red palash flowers, the first harbinger of spring, shone in clusters on the mountain slope and the branches of the thick trees all over and below the hill were weighed down with dhatup flowers? From between the leafless and milkwhite stalks of golgoli flowers burst forth huge yellow flowers like sunflowers which made languid with their scent the midday air—who cared then for the vagaries of the path or kept an account of how far we had travelled?

Nevertheless, it was necessary to keep some track of my whereabouts, otherwise there was every possibility of losing my sense of direction, even of losing the path. This thought had occurred to me me even before I had left the limits of our jungleland, but I had gone on absentmindedly for a while, when suddenly, spreading across the horizon, there came up before me a line of the smoky blue rim of a forest. How did such a huge forest appear all of a sudden? No one at the katcheri had warned me that I would encounter a huge forest on the way to the fairground at Maishandi. I knew then that I *had* lost my way: the line of forest in front of me could be none other than the Mohanpura Reserve Forest which lay straight in a north-easterly direction from our katcheri. There was no clear trail, nor was there a wayfarer to be seen. To add to my confusion, every thing, every feature of the landscape looked exactly same—the bank, the hill, the same clusters of golgoli and dhatup flowers down to the heat waves emanating from the fierce sun. It did not take long for a newcomer to lose his sense of direction.

I turned my horse in another direction. Becoming more cautious, I fixed a landmark in the distance as a point of reference and headed towards it. In the vast unknown expanse of an unpeopled forest, guiding my horse to its destination was something akin to steering a ship in the limitless ocean or piloting an aeroplane in the endless skies.

Again, I passed the leafless gulmraji wilting in the sun, inhaled the sweet mild scent of wild flowers, saw again the ring of barren hills and marvelled yet again at the splendour of the blood-red palash blossoms as I passed them by.

The sun rose high. It would be nice to have a drink of water, I thought, even as I realized that excepting for the river Karo, I would pass no source of water on the way. I was unsure exactly when I would cross the limits of our jungle estate, and Karo was still further away; my thirst grew as I struggled to find my way.

I had told Mukundi Chakladar that he was to plant a stake or fly a banner —Mahavir's banner—to mark the boundaries of our jungleland as I had never before come this way. I now estimated I was somewhere near the limits but evidently Mukundi Chakladar had not followed my orders; he must have thought it most unlikely that the Manager-babu from Calcutta would make his way through the jungle on foot and come to inspect the estate borders. Hardly! It was a fool's errand to go around flying banners . . . let well alone!

After I had crossed the boundary and gone on for a while I sighted smoke, so I made for it. A group of men were charring wood in the forest to make charcoal that they would hawk from village to village in winter. The poor survived the cold months by burning charcoal in earthen bowls. It sold at four seers a paisa, but even at this rate, there were many who could not afford it. I did not quite understand what these people got by selling four seers of the stuff for just a paise, when they put in so much labour in making the charcoal. Clearly, money went a long way in these parts as compared to Bengal.

The men had just boiled maize in an earthen pot, and now, when I had come upon them, they were sitting around the pot with their sal-leaf plates. The maize had no other seasoning than salt. This part of the forest was packed with amlaki trees and kund berries: the men had made themselves a little shelter of dry kash and sabai grass. Branches and twigs burnt inside big holes that had been dug into the earth near the shelter. A young boy stirred the fire with a stick of tender green sal.

'What is there in these holes?' I asked them. 'What is burning?'

They left off eating and huddled together in some confusion. 'Huzoor it's wood-coal,' one of them said, looking at me with fear. The apparition on horseback must have looked alarming: I realized that they had mistaken me for a personnel of the Forest Department. These forests were part of the government's protected areas; it was illegal to fell trees or make charcoal without permission.

I reassured them that I was not an employee of the government—they needn't be afraid of me. They could burn as much coal as they wished to; but where might I get some water? One of them left off eating and disappeared into the forest. When he came back running a little later, he held out to me a shiny metal bowl brimming with clear water. The water came from a nearby spring in the forest, I was told.

'A spring?' I asked, full of curiosity. I was intrigued. 'Where is it? I had not heard that there was one in the area.'

'It's not a spring, Huzoor,' they replied. 'It's what we call an *unui*: the water drips into a stone hollow and within an hour you get about half a seer of water. It's clear water and very cool.'

I went to see it for myself. The forest path, which led to it, was lovely! Birds probably sought out the secluded and cool glade and sported in the water in the dark of night or at daytime in spring. At a point where the forest was at its most dense there was a hollow ringed by twigs of piyal and kend. The bottom was of black stone: it looked like a huge stone bowl crafted by nature, or as though a huge stone seat had eroded with time becoming like the inside of a pestle. The branches of a piyal tree heavy with flowers fell over it creating dark shadows on the water. In the lap of the stone the water grew, drop by drop. They had only just fetched water, there was less than half a cup of water collected yet.

'Most people don't know of this little spring, Huzoor,' they said. 'We do, because we roam the forests.'

I came to the Karo only after I had gone on for another five miles. There was little water in the river at present. There were high sandbanks on both sides; the river could be reached only after a steep drop. The sandy stretches on either side looked deserted; as I made my way down, I felt as though I was climbing down a mountain. I began fording the river on my horse; the water gradually came up to my saddle. I pulled up my feet along with the stirrups and carefully crossed the remaining stretch. On the other side of the river was a forest of blood-red palash: the boulders were red with palash blossoms; everywhere, there was only palash to be seen. And once, I sighted a wild buffalo emerging from a clump of dhatup flowers. He stood on the rock and pawed at the ground with his hooves. I pulled up my horse and came to a halt. There was no one by my side: what if it were to suddenly lower its head and charge? But I was fortunate; soon, it disappeared into the nearby forest.

Beyond the river, the scenery around the forest path became even more beautiful. The afternoon sun was still fierce. There was no cool evening shade, no moonlight: only the long chain of green hills on the left, the uneven ground in the south strewn with iron ore and pyrite, and flowering trees of golgoli and forests of red dhatup in the still blazing afternoon. What a strange place it was—so rude and wild, yet so beautiful. As wild a stretch of jungle as I have ever seen, with the fiery afternoon sun above, the sky intensely blue. There was not a bird flying, the sky was completely empty. And, on the ground, in the heart of wild nature, there was not a man or a living creature —only a frightening loneliness. I was lost in this mysterious and lonely beauty. Until this time, I had not known that there were such places to be found in India. It was like the deserts of Arizona and Navajo in the south of America that one sees in films or like the Gila River Basin described in Hudson's books.[4]

It was one in the afternoon by the time I reached the fairground. It was a huge affair. The fair had been set up in the fields by a small village located in the southernmost tip of the very range that had been accompanying me for the last three miles. It was ringed by hills whose slopes were forested with sal and palash. People had come from places as far away as Mahishardi, Kadari-Tintanga, Lachhmania-tola, Bhimdas-tola and Mahalikharoop. The bulk of the fair-goers were women. Young tribal women had come with blossoms of piyal or dhatup adorning their hair; some had slipped their hair into a lopsided knot held together by a wooden comb. Most of them were slender and healthy looking. They were having a lot of fun buying beads and necklaces, cheap Japanese trinkets and German soapcases, flutes, mirrors and some awful scents or essences. The men bought cigarette bundles of Kali brand—ten for a paisa, while the kids gorged themselves on sweets of tilua, reuri, little laddus made of ramdana and vegetables fried in batter.

Suddenly, I was startled to hear a woman wailing frantically. A group of young men and women could be seen on the top of a high bank, engrossed in laughing and chattering amongst themselves: the wails appeared to come from one of the group. What had happened? Had someone 'shuffled off the mortal coil'? Nothing of the sort, was the answer I got: one of the girls had met up with a woman friend from her parental home. It was the local custom that if a married woman met a girl friend, relative, or kin who lived elsewhere they embraced each other and began wailing. The naive bystander might suppose that they had lost forever someone dear to them, whereas, this was merely an accepted way of being courteous. Not to cry would be to invite censure: if they did not cry before people from their natal home, the implication was that they lived a happy life in their husbands' home—this was considered a shameful situation for a young woman!

Spread out for sale on some jute sacking were books for sale. I spotted a Hindi *Gul-e-bakawali*, *Laila-Majnu*, *Betal Panchisi*, *Premsagar*[5] among the titles. A couple of elderly people were browsing through the display. It struck me that the standing reader of a bookstall whether in the Paris of Anatole France or in the wilderness of the fair of Kadari-Tintanga was pretty much the same. Few would buy a book when there was a possibility of browsing through it and reading it free. In this instance, however, the stallholder was unequivocally business-minded. 'Are you going to buy a book or not?' he demanded of a certain engrossed reader. 'If you aren't, best put that down and look for something else to do.'

At some distance from the fair was a sal forest where groups of people were busy cooking. Little stalls selling vegetables and other kinds of food had been set up for them in this part of the fair. Dried fish, tiny shrimps and ants' eggs were on sale in packets made of sal leaves. The eggs of red ants were a local delicacy. In addition, there were tender green papayas, dried berries, kend fruits, guavas and wild legumes.

I heard someone cry out, 'Manager-babu!'

I spotted Brahma Mahato, brother to the Lobtulia patowari, pushing through the crowd and making his way towards me.

'When did you come, Huzoor? Is there someone accompanying you?' he wanted to know as he caught up with me.

'Brahma! What brings you here? Have you come here to enjoy the fair?'

'No, Huzoor, I'm in charge of collecting the taxes from the fair; but do step into my tent for a moment.'

The tents of these collectors of public revenue, the izeradars, had been set up in a corner of the fairground; Brahma took me to his tent and most respectfully seated me in an old Bentwood chair. I met a man there, the likes of whom I shall probably not see again in the world. I do not know who this person was; quite likely, he was an employee of Brahma Mahato. About sixty years old, bare-chested, dark-skinned, with salt-and-pepper hair; he had a big sack of money in his hand and a notebook under his arm. He appeared to be going around the fair collecting taxes from all the rentiers and then turning in the accounts to Brahma Mahato.

The extraordinary humility and gentle expression on his face caught my attention and moved me; I noted a degree of fear on his countenance. Brahma Mahato was no king, no magistrate, not someone who could strike off heads at his will; he was simply a prosperous tenant of the government estate. Even if he had bid for the rights to the fair—why did this man have such a humble expression before Brahma? Then, with Brahma Mahato himself escorting me inside the tent with much deference, the man hardly dared to look at me, excepting for darting a couple of quick glances which revealed his extreme fear and regard for me. I wondered why he had such an utterly abject look about him. Was he terribly poor? There was something in his face that made me look at him, again and again. 'Blessed are the meek for theirs is the Kingdom of Heaven'; I had never seen such gentle and humble features.

I asked Brahma Mahato about him. He said that the man came from Kadari-Tintanga, the same village as Brahma's; his name was Giridharilal, his caste, gangota. His circumstances were—as I had guessed—wretchedly poor. He had no one of his own but a little boy. Brahma had recently hired him to collect dues from the stalls at the fair; for this, he was to be given meals and a daily wage of four annas.

I was to encounter Giridharilal several times after this, but the circumstances of our last meeting were very distressing; I shall speak of that later. I have seen all kinds of people, but I have not seen one as honest as Giridharilal. I have forgotten many in the course of these long years, but Giridharilal is amongst the handful who will forever be engraved on my mind.

3

It was getting on to be evening. I told Brahma Mahato that I should be on my way and took leave of him. Brahma Mahato looked astonished, as did the other people in the tent: they all stared at me. To travel thirty miles at this late hour—impossible! Huzoor could say such a thing because he was a Calcuttan; he had no knowledge of the roads in this region. The sun would be down before I had gone ten miles; what if it was a moonlit night, the path lay through dense jungle and hills, and not a human being the entire distance. A tiger might be out, then, there were wild buffaloes; it was the season for ripe berries, so bears would certainly be out; why, just the other day, on the other side of the Karo in Mahalikharoop jungle, a tiger had struck and killed a cartman: the poor man had been driving his cart through the jungle and was by himself. Impossible, Huzoor! Do spend the night here and have a meal since you have been kind enough to come to our humble shelter. It would be best to take your time and start tomorrow at a leisurely pace.

Such arguments notwithstanding it became impossible to forswear the temptation of riding on my own through the uninhabited hills and forests on this night of spring when the moon was so resplendent. It would never happen again in my lifetime—perhaps this was my only chance. I recalled the exquisite vision of forest and hill on my way here; if I was not to see it by moonlight, then it made no sense to have endured so much trouble and to have travelled all this distance.

I set off, evading the excessively anxious entreaties of all the people there. Brahma Mahato had been right: a little before I reached the Karo, the huge ball of glowing red dipped into the low chain of hills in the western horizon. I saw it just as I was riding up the sandy bank of the Karo, before I climbed down into the riverbed; and almost simultaneously, on the east, far away above the black line that was the Mohanpura Reserve Forest, I saw too, the newly risen full moon. I reined in my horse and stood absolutely still, looking on at this twin vision. On the unfamiliar riverbank, empty of human life excepting for me, the scene was unreal.

The jungle sprawled all over the slopes and on the bank of the river, sometimes closing in on both sides and sometimes moving away to a distance. I was in the midst of a terrifying isolation. It had been somewhat different during the day; now, when the moon was full it was as though I was travelling though an unknown fairyland, beautiful and mysterious. The next moment, I was afraid at the thought of tigers: I recalled that Brahma Mahato at the fair and almost everybody else at the katcheri had warned me repeatedly against taking this path and travelling on my own at night. I remembered Nandkishore Gosain, one of our cattle-grazing tenants, recounting a month or so ago to a group at the katcheri a tale of someone having been devoured by a tiger in this very jungle. Big trees, their branches drooping with the weight of berries, dotted the path. The ground beneath them was strewn with dried leaves and ripened berries: it was more than likely that bears would be on the prowl. Although wild buffaloes did not live in these forests, it would not take much for a loner to come this way from the Mohanpura forest as had happened this morning. Another fifteen miles of riding through the lonely forests still lay ahead of me.

Fear sharpened the edges of the beauty around me. In some places, the path rose steeply from the south to the north and then turned east, accompanied always on the left by an unbroken range of low hills whose slopes were filled with golgoli and palash flowers; on the hilltops grew sal and tall grass. The shadows of the trees were shrinking as the moon shone brighter, and the scent from an unknown flower embraced all the fields washed by the moonlight; in the faraway hills, Santals had lit fires to clear the land as they do for their jhum cultivation. What a remarkable sight it was—as though someone had entwined garlands of fire over this hill and that one!

Had I been told that there were uninhabited tracts of forest and hills so close to Bengal, and that they were in no way inferior to the rocky deserts of Arizona or the veldts of Rhodesia, I would not have believed it until I had come here myself. It was no less dangerous here: no one ventured to walk in these paths after sundown for fear of tigers and bears.

This was a very different sort of life, I mused, as I rode through the moonlit forest. This was a life for the eccentric wanderer—one who did not care to remain confined within the four walls of his house, did not have housekeeping and domesticity in his blood. When I had left Calcutta and come to this terrible loneliness, to an utterly natural sort of lifestyle, how intolerable the uncivilized life here had seemed; but now, I feel this is the better life of the two. Nature—rude and barbaric here—had initiated me into the mysteries of freedom and liberation; would I ever be able to reconcile myself to a perch in the birdcage of a city? I was racing my horse past rocky boulders and forests of sal and palash with no real path to fix my way and savouring the radiant moonlight under an open sky. I would not wish to exchange this happiness for all the wealth in the world.

The moon shone even more brilliantly, making the constellations almost invisible. I did not seem to be on our familiar planet—but in a land of dreams. In the far-spreading moonlight, unreal creatures descended in the depths of night—they were to be glimpsed through hard austerities; they were creatures of the imagination, of dreams. Those who do not love the flowers of the forest, who do not recognize beauty, who have never been lured by the horizon will never be able to glimpse this other world, the veiled face of our planet.

Within four miles of the Mahalikharoop began our estate. When I reached the katcheri, it was almost nine at night.

4

I heard the sound of drumming and looked out to find that a group of people had come into the katcheri compound, and one of them was playing the dhol. The sound of the dhol drew the guard and the other staff of the katcheri to the group. I was about to summon someone to find out what was happening when Jamadar Muktinath Singh came to the door and said with a salaam, 'Will Huzoor be kind enough to step out for a moment?'

'Why, what is it Jamadar, what's up?'

'The crops have failed in the south, Huzoor: the people can't survive on what they have, so they've put together a troupe of singers and dancers and are now touring the region. They've come to the katcheri because they wish to dance before Huzoor; if Huzoor grants them permission, they will show him their dance.'

The troupe of dancers now entered my little office.

Muktinath Singh asked them what dances they knew.

'Huzoor, we know the Ho-Ho dance and Chhakkarbaji,' answered a sixty-year-old man from the group.

The majority of the members did not look as though they knew much about dancing; clearly, people of all ages had joined the troupe with the sole hope of filling their stomach. For long, they sang and danced. It was late afternoon when they had come to the katcheri; gradually, the moon rose, and still they were dancing—holding hands, whirling, singing song after song. It was a strange sort of dance and they sang to a tune I had never heard. Yet, both song and dance were suited perfectly to these unfettered natural surroundings so far away from civilization, hemmed in by the forest in the shadowless moonlight that stretched over vast distances.

One of the songs had this to say:

My childhood was a happy one:
On the top of the hill behind our village grew a forest of kend:
I picked ripe fruits in the forest, and strung garlands
of piyal blossoms.
The days passed happily:
I did not know then what love was.
I went one day to shoot the karara bird
by Panch-nahari Falls,
A bamboo reed and gummy trap in my hands.
You came to fetch water, in a yellow printed sari;
You looked at me and said, For shame!
Does a man shoot a wild bird with a *sat-nali*!
Ashamed, I threw away my reed of bamboo,
Threw away too, my gummy trap.
The wild bird flew away,
But the bird of my mind was trapped for ever in my love for you.
What is this you've done to me,

Forbidding me to kill the bird with my *sat-nali*?

Was this right of you, my friend?

I understood very little of their language; perhaps that was why I found their songs so strange. They had been strung to the music of the hills and the piyal forests of this land. They sounded well here.

The fee for this lengthy performance was only four annas. The katcheri officials said in one voice, 'Huzoor, even this they do not get in most places; don't make them greedy by giving them more; besides, you will be spoiling the market rates. If you give more, the poorer families won't be able to afford them to have them sing and dance in their homes.'

I was horrified. There were at least eighteen people in the group and they had worked hard for almost three hours at a stretch: four annas would mean even less than a paisa for each dancer. They had crossed the forest and walked through desolate land to come and perform at our katcheri. This would be their only earnings for the entire day; there was no other village nearby where they might perform tonight.

I made arrangements for their meal and for putting them up for the night at the katcheri. The next morning when I gave their leader two rupees he stared at me, his mouth agape. No one had ever given them a meal after a performance, and now here was a fee of two rupees as well.

They had a young boy of eleven years in the group. He looked exactly like those boys who played Krishna in the jatra troupes of Bengal—a head of thick curly hair, beautiful eyes and features set off by his jet-black skin, and a gentle disposition. It was he who stood in front of the group and began the first line of singing. He danced with bells tied around his ankles while a smile lurked in the corners of his mouth. Moving his hands in beautiful gestures, he sang sweetly:

We salute you King; we from another land . . .

The boy was travelling with the troupe for the sake of a square meal. He certainly did not get much by way of money. As for the food they got, it was of the most basic kind: grains of cheena-grass with some salt, and at the most perhaps, some cooked vegetables—not potatoes or a delicacy like patol—but fried gurmi fruit or boiled bathua greens or fried dhundul. This austere fare was enough to keep him smiling all day long. His lithe body glowed with health and sweetness.

'Why don't you leave the boy Dhaturia here, with us?' I asked the group leader. 'He can work in the katcheri and be with us.'

The group leader, a bearded old man, was a strange sort himself—a child-like person, although he was all of sixty-two. 'Huzoor,' he said, 'the boy will not be able to stay here. He travels together with all the others from his village and that is why he is happy. He will fret if he is here without them; he's just a little boy, how can he live by himself? I shall bring him here to you again, Huzoor.'

SIX

1

The survey was on in various parts of the jungle. For some time now, Ramchandra Singh, one of our amins, had been on the job in Bombaiburu jungle, about six miles from the katcheri. One morning, I was told that Ramchandra Singh had gone quite mad some three days ago.

I immediately got together some people and we set off for his place. Bomaiburu was not a particularly thick jungle: it was made up of wide stretches of undulating land; you saw an occasional wild bush in the distance and sometimes, huge trees from which creepers hung like the thin ropes tied to the high masts of a sailing ship. But Bomaiburu was completely desolate.

Far away from the trees in an empty field were two small thatched huts shaded by kash. One was a little bigger than the other—Ramchandra Amin lived in this one; in the smaller hut next to it lived his peada, Ashrafi Tindale. Ramchandra lay on the wooden platform inside his hut with his eyes shut. He started up as soon as he realized we were there.

'What is it Ramchandra?' I asked him. 'How are you?'

Ramchandra greeted me with folded hands and sat there silently.

It was Ashrafi Tindale who answered on his behalf. 'It is a most amazing thing, Babu,' he said, 'you will not believe it if you were to hear of it. I would have gone myself to the katcheri with the news, but I could hardly leave Amin-babu on his own. The matter is as follows: for some time now, Amin-babu has been telling me that a dog has been troubling him every night—I sleep in that little room and Amin-babu sleeps here. Two or three days went by in this manner, and every day he tells me, "Curse that white dog, I don't know where it comes from every night! I make my bed on this wooden plat-form and the dog gets under the platform and starts whimpering, it tries to snuggle up to me and lie down beside me." I hear this story, but don't give it much thought. Then, about four days ago he tells me, "Ashrafi, come out, quick! The dog's come and I've caught it by its tail. Bring along your stick."

'I woke up and dashed inside with the stick and a light, when I saw—you won't believe me, Huzoor, if I were to tell you, but I wouldn't dare to lie before Huzoor—I saw a young woman come out of the room and go into the jungle. At first, I was quite dazed. When I entered Amin-babu's room I found him going through his bedding looking for matches. "Have you seen the dog?" he asked me. I said, "It wasn't a dog, Babu, it was some girl who slipped out." "Idiot! You dare to joke with me? Would a woman come here into the jungle in the dead of night? I had held on to the dog's tail; in fact, its long ears even touched my body. It had been whimpering away beneath the platform—have you taken to drinking then? I shall report you to the head office."

'The next night I was up until very late. The moment I nodded off, Amin-babu called out to me. I tried to run out quickly and had just reached the door of my hut when I saw that a woman was scaling the fence to the north of his hut, and then, she went off towards the jungle. Immediately, Huzoor, I went into the jungle after her. Where was she going to hide in that little time and how far could she go anyway? Particularly, Huzoor, as we are surveyors in the jungle, every one of its twists and turns is known to us. I searched hard and for long, Babu, but there was no sign of her. Finally, I got a bit suspicious and shone the light on the ground and found that there were no footprints, only the marks from my nagra shoes.

'I did not tell Amin-babu anything of what I'd found that day, Huzoor. The two of us live in the heart of this terrible jungle with each other for com-pany. My spine tingled with fear at what had happened. Besides, I had heard some bad things of Bomaiburu jungle too. That banyan tree you see there far away on top of Bomaiburu hill—I'd heard my grandfather say that once, he was returning from Purnea with the money from the sale of his kalhai crop, and as he rode back on a moonlight night, he came to that same banyan tree and found a group of beautiful young girls holding hands and dancing away in the monlight. They are like jinn-peris, they're called 'damanbanu' in these parts, and they live in lonely forests. If they chance upon a human and he is taken unawares, they kill him too.

'Huzoor, the next night I lay down in Amin-babu's tent and stayed up the entire night busying myself with the accounts from the survey. Huzoor, I could swear touching your feet, I saw a woman looking and smiling at me. I saw her clearly—I even saw that she had thick black hair. The lantern was next to me where I had been doing accounts, about five feet away from me. Just as I had put my hand to the lantern to get a better look at her, a creature of some sort came out from under the bed and tried to run out of the room. The light from the lantern fell in a slant on the door, and by that light I saw it was a big dog but it was white from its tip to tail. There was not a spot of black on its body, Huzoor.

'Amin-Sahib woke up and cried out, "What is it?"

'"It's nothing," I said. "A fox or a dog had got into the room."

'"A dog?" said Amin-sahib, "What sort of a dog was it?"

'"A white dog," said I.

'As though despairing, Amin-sahib said, "Are you sure it was white? Or was it black?"

'"Not white, Huzoor," I said, "it was black."

'I cannot say that I was not a little surprised at his question; I could not understand how it would help the amin if it were a white dog instead of a black one. Anyway, he fell asleep but I felt so afraid and uneasy that for the rest of the night I could not shut my eyes to sleep. I got up very early in the morning and on an impulse began to look under the bed. I found a strand of a black hair. Huzoor, I've kept that hair; here it is. Undoubtedly, it's from a woman's head. How did it come here? Such soft black hair! This happened last Sunday, that is, three days ago. Amin-saheb has almost gone mad. I am afraid Huzoor,' said Ashrafi to me, 'I wonder if it is going to be my turn next.'

It was quite a wild tale. I examined the hair but it didn't make sense to me. I had no doubts however that it did belong to a woman. Ashrafi Tindale was a youngish chap. All swore to the fact that he was not addicted either to cannabis or liquor.

The only tent in that huge expanse of uninhabited jungleland was the amin's. The nearest habitation was in Lobtulia, about six miles away. How could a woman travel such a distance down a lonely forest path when none dared to walk in the evening for fear of tigers and wild pigs?

If I were to believe Ashrafi Tindale's account, it was indeed a most mysterious affair. The twentieth century had not yet found a point of entry into this god-forsaken land of vast empty spaces and in the jungle where no human beings lived. Perhaps even the nineteenth century was yet to find its way here. Everything was shadowed in the mysterious darkness of past ages. Here, anything seemed possible.

I had them bring down the tent and brought Ramchandra Amin and Ashrafi Tindale to the main katcheri. Ramchandra's condition grew worse day by day and gradually, he turned completely insane. He shouted and sang, and was delirious all night. I had a doctor come to examine him but nothing worked. Finally, a brother of his came to take him away.

The story has an epilogue, although it took place some seven or eight months after the incident I have just recounted. Let me narrate it here.

Six months later, in the month of Chaitra, two people came to meet me at the katcheri. One was an elderly man not less than sixty-five, and the other, his son, was twenty or twenty-two years old. They had come from Balia district and wanted to rent out the stretch of *char*; that is, they wanted to pay revenue to graze their cattle in our junglelands. The other lots had already been rented out; the only stretch that was left was Bomaiburu jungle. I rented this out to the two of them. The old man even went to inspect the land and came back with his son, very pleased with the long grass he had seen. 'Huzoor, it is very good forestland,' he declared. 'If Huzoor had not been so kind to us, we would never have got such a jungle.'

At the time I was renting out the land, Ramchandra and Ashrafi Tindale's story slipped my mind; even if I had remembered it, I would not perhaps have spoken of it to the old man. For it would go against the interests of our estate if he got scared and ran away. Ever since the incident involving Ramchandra had taken place none of the local people had attempted to rent that particular stretch.

A month later, in early Baisakh, the father came up to me at the katcheri. He seemed very angry; the boy followed him with a sheepish expression.

'What is it?' I asked.

The old man was trembling with rage as he said to me, 'I've brought this wretch before you to seek justice. Give him a beating with your shoe, Huzoor, hit him at least twenty times. That'll set him straight.'

'What has happened?' I asked.

'I am ashamed to even speak of it before Huzoor. Since we have come here, this monkey has been turning into a complete degenerate. I'm ashamed to say it Huzoor, but in the last seven days or so, I've noticed that a woman often slips out of our house. It's just a hut about eight feet wide and thatched with grass where he and I both sleep. It's not so easy to deceive me. After I saw this thing happen on two days, I questioned him. He looked as though he was thunderstruck, as if this was the first time he had heard anything about it! "Why, I don't know anything about it!" he says. Then, when I saw the same thing happen on two more days, I gave him a sound thrashing. I'm not about to let my son come to a bad end before my eyes. But then, when I saw the same thing again—just the night before yesterday—Huzoor, I thought I should bring him to you. Now, if Huzoor will please punish him.'

I suddenly recalled the incident of Ramchandra Amin. 'How late at night was it when you saw the woman?' I asked him

'Almost towards the end of night, Huzoor. I would say a couple of hours before daybreak.'

'And you are sure it was a woman?'

'Huzoor, my sight has not been so dimmed yet. Certainly, it was a woman—and a young one at that—sometimes wearing a white sari, sometimes a red one, sometimes, a black one. One day, as soon as the woman ran out I went after her. I couldn't figure out exactly when she disappeared into the kash forest. I came back and found that my son was lying down pretending to be in deep sleep. He started up when I woke him up. I realized that there was no way to cure this disease unless it was treated at the katcheri, so I've brought him before you, Huzoor.'

I took the boy aside and asked him, 'What is all this that I hear of you?'

He fell at my feet and said, 'Will you listen to me, Huzoor? I don't know anything of any of this. I spend the whole day grazing buffaloes and sleep like the dead every night, then wake up only at daybreak. I wouldn't even know if the house caught fire.'

'You've never seen anything enter the room, have you?'

'No, Huzoor. I become almost unconscious as soon as I fall asleep.'

No more words were exchanged on the subject. The old man was very happy: he thought I had used strong words to rebuke his son in private. About fifteen days later, the boy came back to me.

'I would like to speak with you Huzoor,' he said. 'That time when we came to the katcheri, why did you ask me if I had ever seen anything enter the room?'

'Why do you ask me that?'

'Huzoor, I've become a light sleeper since then, possibly because my father has been so angry. These past few days I find that a white dog turns up from somewhere, it comes in late at night. Some days when I awake, I find that it's somewhere near the bed. It runs away as soon as I awaken and make a sound; some days it runs away as soon as it hears me wake up. It seems to sense somehow that I've woken up. This I've been observing for a while now, but last night Huzoor, something else happened. My father, Bapji, doesn't know, I've come to tell you in confidence: when I woke up very late last night—I hadn't realized when the dog had got in—it was slowly moving out of the room. After the dog got out—it probably took as little time as it takes to blink—I saw through the window, a girl going past the window into the jungle that lies behind our house. I ran outside immediately: there was nothing to be seen anywhere. I didn't let my father know; he is old and he was fast asleep. I just can't make any sense of the matter, Huzoor.'

'Oh, it's nothing,' I said reassuringly, 'it's an optical illusion.' I told him that if they were afraid to stay there, they should come to sleep at the katcheri.

The boy went back; he appeared to be somewhat ashamed at his lack of courage. But my uneasiness persisted; I thought if I heard from them again I would send two guards from the katcheri to sleep there during the night.

I had not yet realized how dangerous the situation was. The mishap took place very suddenly and in the most unexpected way.

A few days went by. I had just got out of bed in the morning when I heard that the night before the old tenant's son had died in Bomaiburu jungle. I went over immediately and found the boy's corpse still lying in the jungle of kash and wild jhau just behind their home. An expression of great fear still showed on his face, as though he had been terrorized by the sight of an unimaginable horror. The old man told me that when he got up in the last hours of the night and could not find his son in the room, he began searching for him with a lantern, but he hadn't spotted the dead body until it was light. It looked like he had suddenly got up in the middle of the night and had gone alone into the jungle to follow something because a stout stick and a lantern were found near the body. It was hard to say what had made him go into the jungle in pursuit. On the soft sandy soil, there was no mark of beast or man other than the footsteps of the youth himself. The body bore no marks of an injury. Nothing was resolved of the mysterious event that took place in Bomaiburu jungle. The police turned back unable to do anything. People were made so afraid by this incident that long before it got dark they stopped venturing into the jungle. On some days, it became so bad that lying by myself in my room in the katcheri and looking out at the dazzling-white shadowless moonlit night, remote and indifferent, an unknown terror would shake my very being. I felt like running off to Calcutta. These were forbidding places. The moonlight was like the demoness of fairy tales who took you unawares, seduced you and killed you. These places were not meant to be inhabited by us mortals, but were home to some other creatures from strange lands. They had been living here for aeons, and they did not care for men who intruded suddenly into their secret kingdom. They would not forgo any chance to avenge themselves.

2

I remember well, even now, the first time I was introduced to Raju Parey. I was working in the katcheri when a handsome and fair-complexioned brahman came up to greet me. He was about fifty-five, but it would be a mistake to call him an old man: many young men in Bengal do not have the strong physique he did. He had a tilak mark on his forehead, a white wrapper over his shoulder and a small bundle in his hand.

When I asked him his business, the man said that he had come from very far and that he wished to rent some land and grow crops. He was extremely poor and did not have the means to pay the customary advance, the salaami; could I make out an arrangement whereby he might rent out a little bit of land and keep half the share for himself, giving the other half to the estate?

There are some who cannot speak on their own behalf, but it is enough to look upon the expression on their faces to know that they have borne much suffering. When I looked at Raju Parey I felt immediately that he had come from distant Dharampur district with the hope of some land; if he did not get any, he would of course turn back without saying anything, but he would return feeling hopeless and dejected.

I worked out a deal for Raju Parey whereby he would have use of two bighas of land in the dense forest that lay north of Lobtulia-baihar. It was given to him for almost nothing. I told him that he was to clear the jungle and start planting; he wouldn't have to pay anything the first two years, but he would have to pay four annas per bigha as revenue from the fourth year onwards. Little did I realize what an odd person I had settled on the land!

Raju had come to meet me around the month of Bhadra or Ashwin and had then gone away to take possession of the land. In the midst of my many duties, I forgot all about him. Around winter the next year, I was on my way back from the katcheri at Lobtulia, when I sighted someone sitting beneath a tree reading a book. As soon as he saw me he quickly shut the book and stood up. I recognized him then: it was Raju Parey. But why had he not visited the katcheri even once since he had taken the land last year? What could it mean?

'How are you, Raju Parey? Are you working in these parts? I thought you had perhaps abandoned the land and gone elsewhere. Haven't you done any farming?'

I saw that his face was frozen with fear. He stammered, 'Yes, Huzoor, some crops . . . this time . . . Huzoor.'

I was angry. Such types spoke sweetly enough; they knew quite well how to wheedle things out of people by tricking them. I said, 'I haven't had a glimpse of you for a year and a half. You've been cheating the 'state of its rightful dues and transporting all the crops directly home! You don't recall, I suppose, that you were to give a share of the crops to the katcheri?'

Raju opened his eyes wide in surprise as he repeated, 'Crops, Huzoor? But I did not even think of giving a share to the katcheri of the cheena grass that I've been raising.'

I could not believe him. 'You've been living off cheena grains for all of these six months, have you? Why, isn't there any other crop? Haven't you planted any maize?'

'No, Huzoor, there are too many gajari trees around. There's only me, I couldn't trust myself to do the work all alone. It's with a great deal of trouble that I've managed to clean about fifteen kathas of land. Why don't you come Huzoor, and grace my place with your presence?'

I followed Raju. The jungle was so dense that from time to time my horse found it difficult to find a path. A little later, we came across a roundish clearing about a bigha in diameter; in the middle, were two low hovels made of wild grass. Raju himself lived in one; he had stored the harvest from his fields in the other. Heaps of cheena grains lay piled up on the earthen floor; there was no bag or sack in the hovel.

'Raju,' I said to him, 'I did not realize that you were so lazy and shiftless. Couldn't you clear a jungle of two bighas in a year and a half's time?'

Raju replied with some trepidation, 'Time, Huzoor—I have very little of it . . .'

'Why, whatever do you do all day?'

Raju looked shy and remained silent. The hovel that was Raju's home had not an extra item of use. I could not see any other vessel excepting for a lota, biggish in size; it was used for cooking rice. Not rice actually, but the grains of the cheena grass. If the boiled cheena grains could be eaten off a sal-leaf, what was the need for a vessel? As for water, there was a pond nearby. Was it necessary to have anything else? But then, in a corner of the hovel, I saw a small stone-black image of Radha-Krishna draped with vermilion and I realized that Raju was a true devotee. The tiny stone seat was adorned with flowers from the forest and a couple of manuscripts and books lay beside it. Therefore, when he said that he didn't have time, he probably meant that he was occupied with worship and devotion throughout the day. If so, when did he work on the land?

I was beginning to understand Raju.

Raju Parey was well versed in reading and writing Hindi, he even knew a little Sanskrit. Not that he read all the time; in his leisure hours he would sometimes sit beneath the tree with a particular Hindi book, but more often than not, he was to be found sitting quietly, gazing at the far away sky and the hills. One day I found him using a quill to write down something in a small notebook. What could he be writing? Did Raju Parey write poetry as well? But he was such a reserved and shy sort that it was impossible to get anything out of him. He was reluctant to say a thing about himself.

'Pareyji,' I asked him one day, 'do you have others in your family?'

'Yes, Huzoor. I have three sons, two daughters, and a widowed sister.'

'How do they get by?'

Raising his hands to the sky Raju said, 'There is the Lord who takes care of them. It is because I wanted to make sure they had something to eat that I have taken the land and have come to depend on the goodness of Huzoor. Once the land is made ready for farming . . .'

'But, is it possible for anyone to support such a large household on only a couple of bighas of land? Besides, you've hardly been working to get it ready for raising crops.'

Raju took some time before he replied, 'Life is so short, Huzoor—as I begin to cut through the jungle, there is so much that comes to my mind, so I sit down and reflect on it. The forest you see here is very beautiful. The flowers have been blooming since a long time and the birds sing, each with their own call; the gods themselves have merged with the wind and have left their mark on the earth. But wherever there is money or transactions of cash, loans and receipts, the air becomes polluted. Then the gods choose not to stay on any longer. So, whenever I pick up the cutter and the axe, the gods come and snatch away my tools. They whisper such thoughts into my ears that all thoughts of land and property are driven away from my mind.'

Raju was a poet, and he was a philosopher as well.

'But Raju,' I said, 'surely the gods do not say that you shall not send any money home or that you should let the children fast. None of that Raju, you should get down to work; I shall take the land away from you otherwise.'

Several months have gone by since that first meeting. I keep going to Raju's for I like him very much. I cannot imagine how he can live for days on end in the jungles of Lobtulia quite alone in that little grass hut of his.

Raju was a man of a truly pure disposition, of satvik qualities. No other crops had flourished on his plot excepting for grains of cheena grass: for the last eight or seven months this had been all that he consumed so happily. He hardly met any one and there was no one that he could talk to, but he didn't seem to mind this at all. Whenever I went past his plot in the afternoon, I found him working the land in the heat of the afternoon sun. In the evenings, he sat quietly beneath the haritaki tree—some days with a book in his hand, and sometimes without it.

'Raju,' I said, 'I will give you some more land, why don't you do some more farming—your family will starve to death at home otherwise.'

Raju was of a very gentle disposition; it was not too difficult to persuade him. He did take up my offer of the land, but even after six months or so, he was unable to clear it for farming.

It took him until ten in the morning to complete his puja and recitation of the *Gita*, after which he set off to work on the land. He worked for two hours and then it was time to have a meal. He worked through the afternoon until five. Then he quietly sat down under a tree and was lost in his own thoughts. Once evening fell it was time for prayers again.

That year Raju grew some maize; he did not eat any of it, but sent the entire crop to his home. When his eldest son came to take the maize away, he stopped by at the katcheri to meet me. 'Aren't you ashamed to be enjoying yourself,' I rebuked him, 'sitting at home while your old father is left to fend for himself in the jungle? Why don't you try and earn something yourself?'

3

News came to me at the katcheri that there was a violent outbreak of cholera in the hamlet of Shuarmari. Shuarmari was not part of our estate; it was about ten miles away, situated on the banks of the Kushi and Kalbalia. Such large numbers of people died every day that there were always corpses floating on the Kushi and there was no means of cremating the dead. I heard one day that Raju Parey had gone to Shuarmari to treat the sick. I had not known that Raju Parey was a medical man. I myself had dabbled in homoeopathy at one time and I thought that perhaps I could be of some use in these parts where there were no doctors or practitioners of traditional medicine. Many others from the katcheri also accompanied me.

I met Raju Parey at the village. He was moving from house to house looking after the sick, carrying a little bag full of medicinal herbs, roots and the like. 'You are very kind to have come, Huzoor,' he said, greeting me. 'Now that you have come these people might survive.' He seemed to suggest that I was the district civil surgeon or another Doctor Goodive Chakraborty, the legendary Calcutta physician. Raju took me along with him to the various homes he visited in the village.

I found that Raju gave them all the medicines on credit. Apparently, the deal was that the amount would be paid back once the patient recovered. In every hut, one saw the fierce face of extreme poverty. The houses were either thatched or had rudely tiled roofs. The rooms were tiny in size and without windows, there was no way fresh air or sunshine could enter these huts. In almost every home, one or two people had fallen sick: they lay on the floor on dirty bedding. There was no doctor, no medicine, and no proper diet. Of course, Raju tried his very best; even when he had not been sent for, he went from house to house treating the sick with his stock of herbs. I was told that he had sat up and nursed a little boy all of the previous night. But all his efforts had no effect on the epidemic; if anything, it was on the rise.

Raju called me to his side and took me to a hut. It was a single room made of straw where the patient lay on a mat woven of palm leaf. The man was at least fifty years old. On the threshold, weeping her eyes out, sat a girl not more than sixteen years old. 'Don't cry any more, my daughter,' Raju said comfortingly, 'there's no more cause for fear, for Babu has come. The sickness will be cured.'

I was exceedingly ashamed contemplating my own helplessness.

'Is she the patient's daughter?' I enquired.

'No, Huzoor,' said Raju, 'she is his wife. She does not have anyone else in this world. She had a widowed mother who died soon after she got the daughter married off. Save him, Huzoor, otherwise this girl will be out on the streets.'

I was about to reply when my eyes fell on a wooden rack on the wall, about three feet above the floor where the patient lay. On the rack sat a stone bowl with day-old rice soaked in water. The bowl was completely uncovered and I saw that at least a dozen flies had settled on the rice. Here, in this very room, was a man afflicted by the deadly Asiatic cholera and within three feet of the patient sat the uncovered bowl of rice! Perhaps, exhausted after a hard day of nursing the sick man, the girl would take down the bowl and eagerly sit down to eat the bit of rice seasoning it with salt and a couple of chillies. It was poisonous food, every mouthful of which held the germs of cruel death. Looking at the innocent tear-filled eyes of the young girl, I trembled at the thought.

'Tell her to throw away this rice,' I told Raju. 'Imagine, keeping food inside this room!'

The girl looked quite shocked when she was told to throw away the rice. Why should she throw away the rice? What would she eat instead? The rice had been given to her last evening by Ojhaji's family.

I was reminded that rice is considered a treat in these parts, in the same manner that we think of puffed flour luchis, or rice pulau. Nevertheless, I ordered her somewhat sternly, 'Get up and first throw away the rice, immediately.'

The girl got up fearfully and threw away the rice.

There was no means of saving her husband. The old man took his last breath later that evening. How the girl wept! With her, Raju too, wept bitterly.

Raju took me to one more hut. It was the home of a person distantly related to him by marriage. When he had first come to the village, it was to this house that he had come and where he had his meals. Now, mother and son were both struck by cholera at the same time; the patients lay in two adjoining rooms, each one crying to see the other. The son was only eight years old.

As it turned out, the boy died. His death was kept from the mother. Gradually, the mother seemed to respond to my homoeopathic treatment and her condition began to improve. She began asking after her son. Why did she not hear him in the next room? How was he?

We would tell her that we had given him sleeping pills, that he was asleep and resting . . .

Meanwhile, the dead boy was secretly removed from the house.

The villagers did not know the first thing about hygiene. There was only one pond in the village. They bathed and washed their clothes in this same pond. I simply could not explain to them that bathing in the water was equal to drinking the water. Many had abandoned their own people and fled the village. In one room lay a sick man; everyone else in his house had left. The patient was a son-in-law of the house; his wife had died the year before. In spite of this, his in-laws had left him to die, perhaps because he was a poor man . . . Raju began to nurse him night and day while I arranged for medicines. I realized that living as he would on the charity of his in-laws, still more sorrows awaited him.

I saw Raju open up his bag and count the amount he had earned through this period of tending the sick.

'How much does it come to, Raju?' I asked.

Raju calculated. 'One rupee and three annas,' he said.

He was quite happy with the amount. People rarely get to glimpse a single paisa in these parts; one rupee and three annas was no mean sum. Raju had slaved away well over a fortnight—he had been doctor, nurse and all in one.

Late at night, the village resounded with the sound of wailing. Yet another one had died. I could not sleep that night. Many in the village did not sleep; they sat up all night before bonfires of wood into which they had poured sulphuric acid. They sat talking to each other as they sat in a ring around the fire. Excepting for tales of sickness and death, they had no other stories to tell. The face of every individual was marked by the same fear, the same terror in the unasked question: whose turn was it going to be next?

In the early hours of the morning, I heard that the newly widowed girl had been struck by cholera. We went to look for her and found her lying in a cowshed near her husband's home. She had been afraid to come back to sleep in her own home, but no one had given her shelter because she had been attending a cholera patient. The girl lay writhing in agony in a corner of the cowshed on a bit of jute sacking tossed over a few sheaves of hay. Raju and I tried our best to treat the hapless girl, but it was impossible to lay our hands on a lantern or even some water. Not a person came in to spare her a glance. The disease had created such terror that by now no one ventured remotely near a person stricken with cholera.

Day broke.

Raju was very good at feeling the pulse of his patients. He held the hand of the young girl and said, 'Huzoor, it does not bode well.'

What could I do, I was not a doctor myself. Some saline might have helped the patient but where was one to get a doctor in these parts?

The girl died at nine in the morning.

I doubt whether anyone would have come to take away her dead body had we not been there. After many entreaties and requests on our part, two farmers of the ahir community used bamboos to push the body along towards the river.

'It's a blessing she died,' Raju exclaimed, 'she would've been a widow otherwise, and that too, such a young lass—what would she have lived on, who would have looked after her!'

'Yours is a cruel land, Raju,' I said.

I have continued to grieve that I had not let her eat that little bit of rice she had cherished so much.

4

In the silent afternoon, the hills of Mahalikharoop and the forest in the distance appeared to be full of an exquisite mystery. I had often thought that I would go and explore the hills but I had never managed to find the time. I was told that Mahalikharoop was filled with impenetrable forests which were a den for the deadly king cobra; there were wildfowl, rare chrysanthemums and vast quantities of the shrub known as bhalluk-jhar. Even the woodcutters never ventured to Mahalikharoop because there was no water on top of the hills and more so, because they were afraid of the deadly snakes.

The dark blue line on the horizon that was the range and forest was the source of many dreams as I saw them in the afternoon, in the evening and at night. As it was, this part of the region had begun to seem like a fairyland—the moonlight, the wild flowers, the vegetation and the forests, the silence, the mystery and the people—all appeared mysterious. They brought me a strange joy as well as a deep sense of peace that I had never found elsewhere. The Mahalikharoop range and the blue line of the Mohanpura Reserve Forest added to the strangeness in greater measure. The hills resonated with an exquisite beauty be it afternoon or evening or on a moonlit night; they filled my heart with *udaas*.

I set forth one day wanting to see the mountain. For nine miles I rode my horse and then took a narrow path between the ranges. The hills on either side were thickly forested, the path wound its way through thick vegetation, sometimes climbing up and sometimes wending down; at times, a rocky spring flowed right through the path. I had not yet seen wild crysanthemums in flower for the autumnal coolness was still with us, but the forest abounded in wild trees full of shefali flowers. The flowers lay scattered like white fluff all over the ground and pebbly path near the spring. The rainy season had come to an end. Besides the arjun and the piyal, and creepers and orchids of various species, an assortment of strange flowers in full bloom gave off a medley of fragrances of such a heady brew as to make people drunk on it like bees.

How long I had lived here, and yet, the beauty of the place was still unknown to me. I had been afraid of Mahalikharoop and the forest from afar—it had tigers, snakes, of bears there was no counting, so I had been told—thus far, I had not sighted a single bear. It was not as fearful as people made it out to be.

Gradually, it seemed as though the forest was pressing down upon me from both sides of the path. Branches from huge trees met above me to weave a canopy. Green ferns sprang from and twirled around the black gnarled roots of trees, and saplings, whose names I did not know, covered the ground. Now the path moved upwards: the forest became even darker and the extraordinarily high peak of the hill appeared before me. From my vantagepoint the trees that grew just a little below its unadorned peak looked like tiny bushes. It was a majestic sight. I climbed still higher following the path; then, coming downhill, I stopped after a while and tethered my horse to a piyal tree. I sat down on a slab of rock, wanting to rest my horse for a bit.

The high peak had suddenly moved to my left. This was something funny I've often noticed in the mountains: you only had to turn a corner and the same view would appear to have become different. In the space of a few steps what had appeared to be directly to the north was now to the west.

I sat there for long. The deep silence of the forest and of its rocky crown on the hill was accentuated by the gurgling of a nearby waterfall. All around me were steep rocky peaks and far above them, the cloudless blue sky of early autumn. The forest and hills had been thus for many centuries. So must this forest have been when the Aryans had crossed the Khyber long ago and had entered the land of the five rivers; when Buddha had silently left his home at night leaving behind his newly-wed wife—on that night, long ago, the mountain peaks must have laughed as they do on this moonlit night ... And so it was, when the poet Valmiki, immersed in composing his epic Ramayana in his hut by the Tamasa river must have started to find that the day was gone—the sun was setting in the peaks, cascades of blood-red clouds cast their shadow on the black waters of the Tamasa and the deer had returned to the ashram; on that day from another age, the peaks of Mahalikharoop must have been reddened by the last red streak of light on the western horizon, just as it was now reddening before my eyes. So it had been when Chandragupta first ascended the throne and the Greek king Heliodorus[6] built the victory pillar with the garuda inscription; when the princess Sanjukta garlanded the statue of Prithviraj as her chosen groom amidst the assembled people; the night when the hapless Dara lost the battle of Samugarh and fled secretly from Agra to Delhi; when Chaitanyadev sang the *sankirtan*[7] in the home of Sribas, when the Battle of Plassey was fought—through all these episodes of history the peak and the forest of Mahalikharoop had stood exactly thus. Who had inhabited these forests in those distant times? Not too far away from the jungle, I had noticed a village consisting of only a few thatched huts and something like an oil press to crush oil out of mahua seeds, and I had seen an old woman who could have been anything between eighty to ninety years old. Her skin was parched and rough, her hair rough and unkempt—perhaps she was picking out lice from her hair—the absolute embodiment of the poet Bharatchandra's rendering of Ma Annapurna[8] as an ancient and decrepit woman. Now, I suddenly remembered the old woman—she was a symbol of the civilization of the forest: for generations, her ancestors have been living in this forest. They had been crushing the mahua seed for oil when Jesus had been put on the cross exactly as they were doing it this very morning. Thousands of years ago, they had been capturing birds with their gummy traps and their *sat-nali* in the same manner as they did now. They had not moved forward an inch in their understanding of the world or of god. I was ready to sacrifice upto a year of my salary to find out what the old woman might have been thinking of.

I do not understand in which races might the seeds of civilization lie hidden, why some improve themselves as time goes by, and there are others who stay fixed in the same place for centuries. The Aryan race who came as barbarians composed the Vedas, Upanishads, the Purans and epics, developed the sciences of astrology, geometry, medicine, conquered the country, established an empire, created the Venus de Milo, the Parthenon, the Taj Mahal, the Cologne Cathedral, composed the raga Darbari Kanada as well as the Fifth Symphony, and invented the aeroplane, ship, railway, wireless, electricity—all within a space of five thousand years, while the natives of Papua New Guinea and the ancient aborigines of Australia, and the Mundas, Kols, Nagas, and Kukis of India have not moved on in these five thousand years.

In some long ago past, there was an ocean here, right where I was now sitting. An ancient ocean whose waves must have fallen upon this sandy shore from the Cambrian Age—what has since then been transformed into a huge mountain. I sat in the forest and dreamt the dream of that blue ocean from the past.

On the sand-strewn mountain peak, the forgotten ocean from the past had left behind a sign—a very distinct sign it was—easily decipherable by geologists. Man did not exist then, nor was there any plant life of the kind I now saw; whatever forms of life had existed in those times had left behind their imprint in rocks, in the fossils that we may now see in museums.

The afternoon sun was turning red above Mahalikharoop. In the forest of shefali-scented trees, there was a hint of the coolness of the coming season, of hemanta.[9] It would not do to linger here for too long. It was going to be a moonless night. A pack of foxes cried out suddenly from the forest: I would rather that a bear or a tiger did not come my way.

On the way back, almost at the edge of the forest, I spotted my first wild peafowl. They were a pair perched on a rock: the peacock flew off as soon as he heard my horse approaching, but his companion did not move. Although I did not tarry for there was the fear of tigers, I stopped abruptly to look at the bird. People had said that the place was full of wild peafowl but I had not believed them. I could not afford to linger, for who knew whether the rumour about tigers in Mahalikharoop might also turn out to be true!

SEVEN

1

Most wonderful it is to long for one's homeland. Those who spend their entire lives in their native village, never venturing beyond the next one, would not know how intriguing is this feeling. Only one who has lived for many years without his kin in alien lands will know how the heart cries out for Bengal, for Bengalis, for one's own village, and for one's dear friends and relatives. The most trivial event takes on a unique flavour, and, as the world becomes intolerable and *udaas*, every little thing belonging to Bengal becomes dearly beloved.

This was exactly my condition after having lived here for many long years. Many a time I have thought to write to the head office asking for leave, but always, there seems to be so much work piled up that I have hesitated to do so. At the same time, how difficult it has been to pass year after year in this no man's land of forests and hills, with tigers, bears, neelgai and other wild creatures for company. There were times when I gasped for breath. I had forgotten what Bengal was like—the changing seasons and the procession of festivals. For many years I had not been part of the Durga Puja in autumn, heard the beat of the dhak played through the month of Chaitra to mark Charak, inhaled the fragrance of incense in places of worship or savoured the birdsong of early spring. The tranquil flow of everyday household life in Bengal—of ritual vessels of copper and bronze heaped on a low wooden platform, the fluid white lines of alpana on the wooden seat, the shell cowries saved up in a little niche in the wall—all seemed like the dream of a forgotten life.

These feelings overwhelmed me most when winter was gone and spring had come. Stirred by these memories I rode off one day in the direction of Saraswati kundi. When we came to a low valley I got off my horse and there I stood in the quietness. Banks of earth, thick with tall kash and dense forests of jhau surrounded me on all sides. Directly above me was a bit of blue sky. Purple flowers that looked like English cornflowers hung in clusters from a thorny bush: a single flower did not have any special appeal, but here, in their profusion, they had woven a sari of purple in the hollow. Beneath the monotony of the drab half-dry forest of kash, the flowers had taken over the hollow to enact their own rites of spring; above them, the ancient and huge spread of wild jhau was a still and rude forest, looking down with indifference at these childish pranks and looking away in some scorn, enduring it all with the patience born of age. Those purple wild flowers heralded for me the coming of spring: not batapi flowers or those of ghetu, nor the buds of mangoes, or kamini, palash, shimul, but the unknown, obscure anonymous flower of a wild and thorny plant. It became for me the very symbol of exuberant spring, of all flowers of forest and glade. I was rooted for long to the spot. It was new to me—a native of Bengal—to discover how a few wild flowers could honour spring. In contrast, wearing the coarse garments of a renunciate, absorbed in contemplation with no thought of luxury, the vast forest above me had such a sombre radiance! The two came together in my mind: the dispassionate spirit of the half-dried blossomless forest above, and the youthful, almost barbaric zest of the wild flowers below. I felt it to be a moment of epiphany. I simply stood still while in that little strip of blue above me, a couple of constellations came alive. The sound of approaching hooves abruptly cut through my reverie. It was Puranchand, the amin, on his way home after having finished with his surveying for the day. He dismounted as soon as he saw me.

'Huzoor?' His greeting held a note of enquiry.

'I've come for a ride.'

'You shouldn't be here alone in the evening, Huzoor, come back to the katcheri. This isn't a safe place, Huzoor: my tindale has seen one with his own eyes—a very big tiger it was—in the kash forest over on that side. Come away, Huzoor.'

Behind us, far away, Puranchand's tindale, Chottulal, had struck up a song—*Daya hoi ji* . . . Be kind my Lord. Since then, whenever I saw the purple flowers, my soul cried out for Bengal. And every evening, as he made his chapatis, Puranchand's tindale would sing just that song—*Daya hoi ji* . . .

I thought, never again in my lifetime would I stand in shadowed woodland fragrant with ripening mangoes and flowering sheuli and listen to the cuckoo cry on the other side of the sandbank. It seemed more likely that I would lose my life in this forest some day to a tiger or a wild buffalo.

But the forest of wild jhau continued to stand still and the distant line of forest in the horizon looked bleak and indifferent.

On such a day of homesickness, I received an invitation to Rashbehari Singh's home, the occasion being Holi, the spring festival of colour. Rashbehari Singh, a rajput, was the most powerful mahajan in these parts. He rented government land that lay on the other side of the Karo. The village he lived in was a little more than twelve miles to the north of the katcheri, adjoining the Mohanpura Reserve Forest.

It did not look good to refuse the invitation; yet, I was very disinclined to go to Rashbehari Singh's. He had become rich feeding on the blood of the poor. He played banker to all the poor gangota tenants. Under his tyrannical rule, not a man could whimper. He had a band of mercenaries—his lathials— who he controlled with land and money. They were always on the prowl with their weapons: if he demanded that a certain person should be brought to him, the order was forthwith executed—the victim was bound and delivered to him. The hapless object of his wrath was quite defenceless if, for whatever reason, Rashbehari Singh happened to feel that so and so was not giving him due respect or that his prestige had somehow been tarnished. There was no respite for him until Rashbehari Singh had found out a way, by cunning or force, to punish his victim.

Rashbehari Singh was a virtual king. Poor ryots and householders trembled on hearing his name, even the relatively well-off did not dare to say anything, for Rashbehari Singh's lathials were violent; they were particularly adept at beating up people and fomenting riots. Even the police was said to eat out of his hands. The circle officer and the manager of the estate visited

Rashbehari Singh's home and accepted his hospitality. Why then should he care for anyone in this jungle?

Rashbehari Singh tried often to establish his control over my tenants. On my part, I resisted these attempts. I let it be known openly that he could do whatever he wished within the limits of his own land but that I would not tolerate it if he dared to even touch a hair on the head of any of the subjects on our estate. In fact, a battle of some sort had taken place last year between his lathials and my guards under Mukundi Chakladar and Ganpath Tehsildar. There had been some problems last Sraban as well; the matter had been taken up by the police and was finally settled by a sub-inspector. After this incident Rashbehari Singh had left alone the people of our estate for a few months. It came as a surprise to me, therefore, that the same Rashbehari should now invite me for Holi. I summoned Ganpat Tehsildar and sit down to discuss the matter with him.

'I don't know, Huzoor,' says Ganpat, 'there's no trusting this man. He's capable of anything—who knows why he wants to invite you to his home? If you ask me, I think it's better you don't go.'

I could not agree with him: not to accept the Holi invitation would be tantamount to insulting Rashbehari Singh, for Holi is celebrated as a major festival by rajputs. He might even think that I had been too scared to go. If indeed he reasoned thus, it would be insulting to me. It looked like I must go whatever might lie in store for me.

Almost everyone in the katcheri sought to convince me against accepting the invitation, using various arguments. Old Muneshwar Singh said, 'Huzoor, you are set on going, but you don't really know the law of the land. They murder at the slightest pretext. They're treacherous people hereabouts —after all, there's not one who is educated. Besides, Rashbehari Singh is an extremely dangerous man—there's no keeping track of the people he's killed. There's nothing that he will stop at—murder, arson, perjury, false lawsuits— he's game for anything and everything.'

I ignored all talk of this kind and found my way to Rashbehari Singh's home in the government estate. His house was made of bricks and tiled in the manner of the houses of well-to-do people here; it also had a front verandah supported by tar-lined wooden poles. A couple of people sat on the two string-cots in the verandah smoking a long-stemmed hookah, called a farsi.

As soon as my horse entered the yard, two shots boomed out from somewhere. I understood that Rashbehari Singh's men had recognized me and in accordance with the local laws of hospitality, the shots had been fired to welcome me. But where was the host? It was not considered proper to dismount until the host himself came forward to receive his guest.

A little later, Rashbehari Singh's elder brother, Rashullas Singh came out of the house, his hands joined in a gesture of welcome.

'Do come in, Janab,'[10] he said to me with great deference and in courteous Urdu, 'please be kind enough to step into this humble home.'

I was reassured: Rajputs do not harm anyone they have acknowledged as a guest. Had no one come to welcome me I would have turned around and headed straight back to the katcheri.

The yard was filled with many people, mostly gangota peasants. Their clothes were dirty and torn but splashed with festive colour. They had come to play Holi at the mahajan's, whether or not they had been invited to his home.

Rashbehari Singh himself turned up about half an hour later. He seemed very surprised to see me, as though he had never in his wildest dreams imagined that I would step into his home to honour the invitation. He too, was quite deferential and attentive in his hospitality. He took me to an adjoining room with a bench and three chairs of Indian rosewood, their thick legs and handles attesting to the talents of the local carpenter. In a niche in the wall was a statue of Ganesh, smeared with sandalwood and vermilion.

A little later, a young boy held before me a big plate which had a small heap of powdered colour, a few fruits, some rupee coins, a strand of flowers, and bits of sugar crystals and sugar-coated cardamom seeds. Rashbehari Singh smeared some of the colour on my forehead; I did the same to him, and picked up the strand of flowers. As I kept staring at the plate not knowing what else I was expected to do, Rashbehari Singh said, 'Your nazar, Huzoor. You have to take it.' I took out some money from my pocket and placed it with the rest of the money.'Use this to treat everyone here to some sweets,' I told him.

Rashbehari Singh then took me on a tour to show off his wealth. There were about sixty to sixty-five heads of cattle in his cowshed. In his stables, there were eight horses: two of them were wonderful dancers, he said; he would show me their dancing some day. He did not yet possess an elephant but was soon going to acquire one. (An elephant was considered essential in order to be treated as a somebody.) They got about nine maunds of wheat from the land; more than eighty people had meals twice a day, and he himself breakfasted on one and a half seer of milk and a seer of michri from Bikaner after his daily bath. This was the only kind of michri he had; the kind that was commonly sold in the market he never ate. Washing down a meal with michri-sweetened water was one of the other distinguishing features of a wealthy personage.

I was then conducted to a room where about two thousand cobs hung from the beams. These were seeds of maize being stored for the following year's planting. I was also shown a huge kadhai made of an iron sheet plated with nails in a roseate pattern. One and a half maund of milk was boiled daily in this kadhai; this was the amount of milk consumed every day in his household. Another small room was stocked with such vast quantities of sticks, spears, shields, axes and halbreds that it was a veritable armoury.

Rashbehari Singh had six sons, the eldest of whom was not less than thirty years old. The first four sons were strapping youths, tall as their father; already, they sported luxuriant sets of moustaches and massive sideburns. After having met the sons and seen the armoury it did not seem surprising that the poor and malnourished gangota peasants should be in perpetual terror of Rashbehari Singh and his clan.

Rashbehari was a proud man, exceedingly conscious of his dignity. He was offended and felt his prestige affected at the slightest deviation from what he felt was due to him; one had, therefore, to be ever vigilant and fearful in dealing with him. The gangota peasants were always on tenterhooks lest their slightest move was detrimental to the master's honour.

That day, I saw in Rashbehari's home the very embodiment of all that could be termed as rude plenty. A plenitude of milk, wheat, and maize, enough michris from Bikaner, enough honour, and certainly, sticks and spears enough. Yet, what was it all for? There was not a single beautiful picture or book to be seen anywhere in the house. Let alone a couch or a chair, there was no clean bedding arranged attractively with cushions and pillows on the floor. The walls of his rooms were stained with lime and streaked with juice from betel nuts while the open drain that ran right behind the house was choked with slimy water and rubbish of all kinds. It was squalid and ugly—both inside and outside. The children did not go to school or receive any education elsewhere; they had on dirty clothes and ungainly looking shoes. Several of the children in the household had died of the small pox the year before. Of what use then was this barbaric plenty? Was it advantageous for anyone to have acquired this wealth by beating up simple gangota peasants? Rashbehari Singh's prestige, of course, was ever on the rise.

I was, however, quite taken aback by the abundance of the feast set out for me. Was it possible for one person to eat so much! There were about fifteen wheat puris, each the size of an elephant's ear, all sorts of vegetable dishes in earthen pots, plus yogurt, laddus, fried malpuas, chutney and papad. Enough food to take care of four of my meals! Rashbehari Singh, apparently, could polish off twice as much food at one go.

When I came outdoors after having finished my meal, the light had gone. The gangotas were all seated in the courtyard happily partaking of a meal of yogurt and cheena grass. Their beaming faces were wreathed in smiles, their clothes dyed with splashes of red colour. Rashbehari's brother was moving around supervising the meal. It was the simplest sort of meal but the gangotas were delighted.

After many days, I saw again the performance of the natua lad, the boy-dancer Dhaturia. Dhaturia had grown up somewhat, and his dancing too, had improved considerably. He had been specially engaged for the Holi festival.

I called him to my side and asked him, 'Do you recognize me, Dhaturia?'

He smiled and gave me a salaam: 'Yes, Huzooor, you are the Manager-babu. Are you well, Huzoor?'

What a lovely smile he had. I was filled with tenderness and compassion whenever I looked at him. He had no one to call his own and had to earn his own keep at such a tender age by singing and dancing and entertaining others, particularly the likes of Rashbehari Singh who was nothing but a philistine glorying in his wealth.

'You still have to dance for a good part of the night, how much will you get for your pains?' I asked.

'Four annas, Huzoor, and food enough to fill my stomach.'

'What will they give you to eat?'

'Madha, yogurt and sugar. They might even give me laddus—at least, they did so last year.'

Dhaturia looked very happy at the thought of the coming meal. 'Is it the same rate at every place you perform?' I wanted to know.

'No, Huzoor,' said Dhaturia. 'Rashbehari Singh is a wealthy man so he will give four annas, and enough to eat besides. If I dance for the gangotas, they only give two annas, and no food, although they do give me half a seer of ground maize.'

'Is this enough to live on?'

'Babu, dancing hardly fetches anything; it used to before. People are in such trouble themselves nowadays: who has the time and money for a performance? When I'm not called to dance, I work in the fields. I had helped with the harvesting the year before last. What was I to do, Huzoor, I had to survive. I had taken so much trouble to learn the Chhakkarbaji dance from Gaya, but no one wants to see it—the fee is higher for performing the Chhakkarbaji, you see.'

I invited Dhaturia to come and dance at the katcheri. Dhaturia was an artist and had in him the aloofness of the true artist.

When the full moon shone brightly, I took leave of Rashbehari Singh. Once more, as soon as my horse crossed their yard, he sounded the two guns in my honour.

It was the full moon of the Dol festival. Between the open fields the road of white sand glistened in the moonlight. Far away, a silli was calling out. In that moonlit night, in the midst of that huge expanse, unpeopled and vast, it sounded like the frantic call of a lost traveller in danger.

'Huzoor, Manager-babu . . .' called out someone behind me.

I looked back to find Dhaturia running to keep up with my horse.

'What is it Dhaturia?' I asked, as I reined in my horse.

Dhaturia was panting. He stood a while regaining his breath, hesitated a bit before he finally said, very shyly, 'There was something Huzoor . . .'

'Well, what is it? Tell me,' I said encouragingly.

'Will Huzoor take me once to his place in Calcutta?'

'What will you do there?'

'I've never been to Calcutta; I've heard that people there greatly value dancing and singing and music. I have learnt so many wonderful dances, but there is no one here before whom I can perform, it makes me sad. I've almost forgotten the Chhakkarbaji dance for lack of practice. Oh! It's such a story as to how I learnt that dance! It's a tale worth listening to.'

We had left the village behind us. The fields shone in the moonlight. It seemed to me that Dhaturia sought to meet with me in secrecy; he was afraid that he would be punished if Rashbehari Singh were to find out about such a meeting. A young simul tree, heavy with flowers stood in the field next to us. I got off my horse and sat on a stone beneath the simul ready to listen to Dhaturia.

'Tell me your story,' I invited him.

'People said that a worthy man called Vitthaldas lived in a village in Gaya district—that he was a master of the Chhakkarbaji dance. I desired to learn the Chhakkarbaji by any means. So, I went to Gaya district, roaming from village to village, always enquiring about Vitthaldas. But no one could tell me anything. Finally, one evening, when I had taken shelter in a cattleshed of the ahirs, I heard them talking about the Chhakkarbaji dance. It was very late at night, and frightfully cold too. I was lying on some hay in the corner of the shed; the moment I overheard them speak of Chhakkarbaji, I leapt up from my place in the corner and came to sit by them. I cannot tell you Babuji how thrilled I was! As though, I'd made a great find. I found out from them where Vitthaldas lived. His home was in a village called Tintanga about seventeen miles away.

I quite enjoyed listening to this tale of a young artist's intense desire to learn his craft.

'And then?' I asked.

'I walked to his home. Vitthaldas, I saw, was an old man—he had a full white beard. "What do you want?" he asked, when he saw me. I said, "I've come to learn the Chhakkarbaji dance." He seemed to be amazed. "Do young boys still like the dance in these times?" he asked, "I thought people have forgotten all about it." I put my hands on his feet and pleaded with him, "You have to teach me, I've come from far away having heard of you." He cried on hearing this. Then he said, "We've been performing this dance for seven generations in my family; but I've no son, and all this time as I have got old no one else has come to me wanting to learn the dance. You are the first one to have come. All right, I shall teach you." So you understand Huzoor, this is how I've learnt the dance, with so much effort and work. Now what use is it to perform before the gangotas? In Calcutta, they care for quality. Will you take me to Calcutta, Huzoor?'

'Come to my katcheri one of these days, Dhaturia. We shall talk further about this.'

Dhaturia went away, reassured.

I felt that there would hardly be anybody in Calcutta who would want to see the rustic dance he had learnt with so much labour and love; besides, once there, how would he fend for himself in the city?

EIGHT

1

What nature gives to her own devotees is invaluable. However, it is a gift not to be received until one has served her for long. Besides, she is an exceedingly jealous mistress: if you want her, you will have to stay only with her; if perchance you glance elsewhere, like a hurt maiden she will not unveil herself again. But if you lie immersed in her, the greatest gifts of nature—beauty and exquisite peace—will be showered on you so abundantly that they will drive you to ecstasy. By day and night the thousand faces of alluring nature will enchant you, extending the furthest reaches of your mind, drawing you closer to immortality.

When I try and write about this store of precious experience, I only write page upon page, without ever being able to express all I wish to. There are very few who truly love nature, fewer still who would want to listen to such things. Nevertheless, I shall share something of these riches.

Now, all over the fields and along the edges of the forest, the dudhli grass begins to flower letting us know that spring is here. The flowers are very beautiful, yellow and shaped like stars; the grass tip extends like a delicate creeper clutching on to the soil, and the yellow flowers appear wherever it touches the ground. The flowers illuminated the fields in the early morning and the adjoining paths shone with their colour, but as soon as the sun rose higher in the sky they folded themselves up into bud-like shapes; next morning, the same buds would have opened up into flowers once again.

Blood-red palash made a riot of colour in the Mohanpura Reserve Forest, in the jungle outside our borders, and along the foothills on the Mahalikharoop range. It took four hours' riding to get to any of these places where the springtime buds of the sal filled the air with fragrance and the simul reddened the forest's horizon. But no birds like the cuckoo, the doel or the bou-katha-kau ever sang there: perhaps, birds did not care to sing in forests that were so out of the way and so wild.

There were some days when my heart would ache with longing for Bengal. In my imagination I would relive the sweet spring of rural Bengal: a young woman returning from the many-stepped ghat, her clothes still wet after a bath; wild clumps of ghetu flowers along the fields; and the shadowy afternoons heavy with the fragrance of batapi-lebu. Only since coming to foreign lands had I come to know my own; I had never felt such anguish for my homeland when I lived there. This was a precious feeling—one who has never tasted this hungering for home remains a stranger to one of life's supreme experiences.

At any rate, what I have been trying so hard to delineate but have not been able to quite express, is the exceptional beauty that lies in vast, fearful, mysterious and endlessly stretching spaces. How am I to speak of it to one who has not seen it!

Alone on my horse on a still afternoon, Lobtulia-baihar—vast and unpeopled—and the tall jungle of wild jhau and kash merging into the horizon entered my consciousness with a sense of mystery. Sometimes, it took on the shape of fear, sometimes, it was a sombre mood that made me detached and distant, and at other times it was like a sweet dream or a song of pain endured by men and women all over the world. It was like an exquisite unvoiced melody composed on unreal moonlit nights to the rhythm of the faint light from the constellations, the strain of the crickets' cry, and in the light of the shooting star's fiery tail.

It is better for those who have to live within the strictures of domesticity never to catch sight of this beauty. In this bewitching guise, nature makes men abandon their homes, fills them with wanderlust as it did Harry Johnston, Marco Polo, Hudson and Shackleton.[9] He who has heard the call of the wild and has once glimpsed the unveiled face of nature will find it impossible to settle down to playing the householder.

I have come outdoors late at night by myself and have drunk in the beauty of open spaces, of darkness, or of shadowless moonlight. Beauty that makes one mad—I'm not exaggerating even one bit; such fierce beauty is not for the faint-hearted. Yet it is a rare vision afforded to a fortunate few. It is not easy to come by such a huge expanse of forests, stretches of wild jhau and a range of hills. To this add the silence of the night in darkness or in radiant moonlight. But if all of these conjunctions were to be easily found, our land would soon be full of poets and mad men!

Let me speak of one such night.

I had a wire from my lawyer at Purnea saying that I would have to be present at the court by ten o'clock the next day, failing which we were sure to lose a major case.

Purnea was about fifty-five miles from our estate. Only a single train that ran at night connected the two. By the time the wire came to my hand, it was not possible to catch this train from the nearest station at Kataria, another seventeen miles away. It was decided that I would immediately set off on horseback for Purnea. The path was long and dangerous, especially at night: it was also decided that tehsildar Sujan Singh would accompany me.

We set off in the evening. Soon after we left behind the katcheri and entered the jungle, the moon—now in its third week—rose in the sky. In the indistinct light the forest looked even more mysterious than usual. We rode abreast—Sujan Singh and I.

The path lay through undulating land. The light from the moon shone on the white sand. Excepting for a few bushes it was only forests of kash and wild jhau. Gradually, the moon shone brighter—the forests, the sandbank took on sharper outlines. For very long there was a only a single continuous line of the top of the forest visible below us—as far as the eyes could see there was open ground on one side and the jungle on the other. To our left came a low range of hills. All was silent and, other than us, there was not a soul. There was no other movement or sound—as though there were just the two of us living creatures on a lonely path in the forest of an unknown planet.

Sujan Singh reined in his horse at one point. What was the matter? From the jungle on our side, a fair-sized wild pig was crossing over to the other side with her numerous piglets. 'Well, that's not so bad,' said Sujan Singh, 'I had thought they might be wild buffaloes. We're close to the

Mohanpura jungle and that's full of wild buffaloes. They killed a man just the other day.'

After we had gone on for a while we did sight a dark shape in the moonlight.

Sujan said, 'Stop, Huzoor, the horse will take fright.'

But whatever the thing was did not move at all. When we cautiously approached it, we found it was only a little hut made of kash. Again, we let our horses race. Fields, forests and riverbeds—an empty world throbbing with the moonlight. Ti-ti-ti-ti-ti . . . the cry of a companionless bird came from deep inside the forest; the hooves threw up quantities of sand, there was not a moment to rest the horses—it was only a continuous flying forward.

My back was hurting from riding in the same position for too long, my saddle felt heated, and the horse had ceased to gallop and was now going at a steady trot. My animal was a nervous sort, so I had to ride very carefully, scanning the path far ahead of me; if I had to rein in abruptly, I would undoubtedly go flying.

Knots tied onto the tips of kash stalks at regular intervals marked the path; there was no other path in the jungle. One could decipher the way only by sighting these knots. Once Sujan Singh said, 'Huzoor, this does not seem to be the way, we've made a mistake.'

I used the Great Bear to find the Pole Star: Purnea lay directly to the north of our estate. In that case, we were going in the right direction, I explained to Sujan.

'No, Huzoor,' Sujan reminded me, 'first there's the crossing at the Kushi, only then do we go directly northwards. Now, we have to go north-easterly for a while.'

Finally, the path was found.

The moon grew even more radiant—such marvellous light! Such a wonderous night! Moonlight, special to the lonely sandy banks by the deep forests, not to be savoured by those who have not seen it. Beneath the open skies, a moonlit night without shadows, the light falling on the bank, over the hills and the forests and the fields. What a ride it was! Both the horses had begun panting and despite the cold, we too, were sweating.

We paused for about ten minutes to rest our horses beneath a simul tree. A small river ran past us flowing into the Kushi not too far away. The simul tree was full of flowers; the forest seemed to surround us from all sides so that not a trace of the path remained. Yet, it was a forest of small trees and bushes; the simul stood out tall amongst them. But by now, we are both dying of thirst.

The moonlight begins to dim. The path is dark; the moon now dips behind the western horizon in the last phase of the night. The shadows lengthen. No sound of birds anywhere, only shadow upon shadow, dark fields and forests. The wind grows sharper as the night ends. It is four by my watch. We fear that a herd of wild elephants might appear suddenly in these waning hours of the night. There is a herd of wild elephants in Madhubani jungle.

Now, small hills appear beside us, the path winds through them: a gologoli tree, bare of leaves, stands on the hilltop, forests of the blood-red palash in other places. Everything—the forest and the hills—looks eerie by the light of the sinking moon. Then the eastern sky lightens, gradually a cool breeze begins to blow and one hears the birds begin to chirp. The horses are dripping with sweat. They are good creatures; that is why they have run so hard on this difficult path. It was evening when we had left the katcheri—now it is dawn. The path seems unending: still the same forest and the hills.

A ball of vermilion red is rising behind the hill that lies directly in front of us. We stop for a bit to drink some milk that we buy at a wayside village. A few more hours and we are in Purnea.

I completed the work I had to do for the estate in Purnea; it was done almost in a half-hearted manner, for my heart still lay with the path through the jungle. My companion wished to set off as soon as the work was done, I asked him to wait: I could not give up the delight of enjoying a moonlight ride once more.

And so we rode again that night. The moon rose late but the moonlight stayed with us longer. Marvellous moonlight—calm, restrained and mysteriously beautiful—choreographing an unknown dreamlike world. And the stunted forest of kash, yellow golgoli all along the sides of the hill, the same path going up and down. We flew like spirits after death on an unknown heavenly body, flying towards Buddha's nirvana where the moon does not rise, but where there is no darkness.

One afternoon, many years later: I have left behind my life of freedom and have become a householder. I sit in my room in a narrow little lane in Calcutta and listen to my wife at her sewing machine. I think so often of this night, of its exquisite delights, the beauty of the forest in the moonlight, the golgoli tree on the top of the hill in the last hours of the dark night when the moon has set, the fresh fragrance of the forest of new kash. How many times I have imagined that I was once more riding to Purnea . . .

2

It was the middle of Chaitra when news came to me that a certain Rakhal-babu, a Bengali doctor, had suddenly died the night before in the village of Sitapur.

I had not heard his name until his death. In fact, I was not even aware that such a person had been living in Sitapur village. I was told that he had been settled there for the last twenty years or more. He had quite a practice in the area and had even built a house in the village where he lived with his wife and children.

I grew very anxious, wondering how the sudden death of a Bengali bhadralok in an alien land of non-Bengalis had affected his family: what was the condition of his wife and children, who was looking after them, had it been possible to perform the last rites for the dead man? I thought that my first duty was to go to their home and find out personally how the bereaved family was faring.

I was told that the village was about twenty miles away, near the border of the Kadari estate. I reached there in the afternoon and after asking around, located Rakhal-babu's house. The house had two big rooms with tiled roof, and three smaller ones. Outside, there was a sitting room in the local style— open on all three sides. There was no way of identifying it as a Bengali's house: everything was typical of the region—from the string-cot in the sitting room to the Hanuman-banner flying in the yard.

A twelve-year-old boy came out in response to my call and asked me in the Hindi peculiar to the region, 'Who are you looking for?'

There was absolutely nothing about his appearance to suggest that he was a Bengali boy. His hair had been shaven off with a long strand left on the top of his head, and he had wound around his neck the usual white cloth of mourning. All this I understood; but how was it possible that the very expression on his face was that of a Hindustani boy?

I introduced myself and asked if he would call whoever was the most senior person in the family at present.

The boy said he was the eldest son. He had two younger brothers. There was no other guardian.

'Tell your mother that I should like to speak with her,' I said to him.

A little later the boy came back and led me into the house. Rakhal-babu's wife looked very young, less than thirty years old. She wore the stark white sari of the newly widowed and her eyes were swollen with crying. The furniture was that of a poor household. A small stack of paddy stood in one corner, a couple of string cots, some torn quilts, a brass vessel of the local kind, a gurguri for smoking and a tin trunk was all that there was in the room. 'I am a Bengali and a neighbour of yours,' I said by way of introduction. 'I came to know of Rakhal-babu's death and so I have come—I feel that I have a certain obligation in this regard. If I can help in any way please let me know without any hesitation.'

Rakhal-babu's wife began weeping silently as she stood half hidden behind the door. I tried to reassure her and said that I would come again. At this, Rakhal-babu's wife came out and spoke to me. 'You are like an elder brother,' she said, 'God has sent you to us in these terrible times.'

In the course of our conversation, I learnt that this Bengali family living in an alien land was now quite destitute and helpless. Rakhal-babu had been laid up with illness for the past year. All their savings had been spent on his treatment and household expenses. At present, they had no means of even performing the shraddha, the after-death rites.

'But Rakhal-babu has been living in this area for quite a while; could he not earn enough during this time?' I enquired.

Rakhal-babu's widow had, in the meantime, got over much of her initial shyness and embarrassment. Her expression suggested that she was infinitely relieved at having met a fellow Bengali, so far away from her native land and in such difficult times.

She said, 'I don't know what he used to earn earlier. I had been married to him for the last fifteen years—he married me after his first wife died. Ever since I came, we seemed to have barely enough to run the house. Very few people give cash for 'visits' made by the doctor; they pay in kind—wheat, maize and the like. He fell ill last year, in the month of Magh; we've not got a paisa since then. But they're not bad people in these parts: whatever was owed to us, was paid back. They came to our house carrying wheat, kalhai, maize . . . that is how we have survived, otherwise we'd have starved to death.'

'Where is your home? Have you informed your people?'

Rakhal-babu's wife was silent for a while. Then she said, 'There's nobody to inform. I've never seen my natal home. I have been told it's somewhere in Murshidabad District. I have always lived in Sahebganj, at my brother-in-law's. My parents died long ago. My own sister—the one in Sahebganj—died after my marriage. My brother-in-law has married again. I have no connection with him.'

'Are there no relatives of Rakhal-babu—anywhere?'

'I had heard that he had distant cousin brothers in Bengal, but neither they did they enquire after us nor did he ever go on a visit to Bengal. We were not on good terms with them; it's all the same whether we let them know or not. I had heard that I have an uncle-in-law in Kashi, but I don't know his address.'

No one to call her own, with three little boys, she—a widow—without any means or resources in a land where she was without friends: my heart sank as I thought of her helpless situation. I returned to the katcheri after I had done what I could for the time being. I wrote to the head office and sanctioned a hundred rupees from the estate accounts to have the rites performed for the dead man.

I went a couple of more times to Rakhal-babu's home. I had got the family a monthly stipend of ten rupees sanctioned from the estate; I went personally to hand over the first instalment. Rakhal-babu's wife, whom I called 'Didi', always took great care of me, treating me most affectionately. Living as I did so far away from my native land, I cherished her care and concern. I so longed for this affection; I went to their home whenever I had the time.

3

The northern part of Lobtulia was a huge lake. Such a body of water was called a kundi in these parts. This one was named Saraswati kundi.

Thick forest enfolded all three sides of Saraswati kundi. Neither our estate nor Lobtulia had a forest quite like this. The foliage here was dense: perhaps it was because of the proximity of the kundi or for whatever reason, the forest had a thick undergrowth of creepers and wild flowers. It encircled the vast blue waters of Saraswati kundi like a half moon; only from the unenclosed side could you see a vista of the far reaching blue skies and the distant mountain range. If you sat therefore on a particular part of the of the shore and looked southwards and to your left, the exceptional beauty of Saraswati kundi struck you. If you looked to the left, your gaze would go right into the forest and lose itself in the greenery. If you looked southwards across the clear blue water, you saw the blue strips of the sky and the indistinct outlines of hills—a sight that filled your mind, letting it fly and soar far above the earth like a balloon.

I would often go to this kundi and find myself a rock to sit on. Sometimes in the afternoon, I would wander in the forest. I'd sit beneath the shade of some huge tree and listen to the birds. Sometimes I would gather plants or the flowers of wild creepers. We do not have as many birds as did the forest in Saraswati kundi—I identified them by their calls. The number of birds around the kundi was extraordinarily high, possibly because they had such a choice of wild fruits and the tall trees made nesting easier. The forest had a variety of flowers as well.

The forest ran all along the shores of the lake that was about three miles long and a mile and a half wide. All along the lake a narrow path wound its way through the forest for the entire length of three miles. I followed this path. You glimpsed the blue waters of the lake from between the leaves and the plants; above it, the blue sky seemed turned upside down, the hills becoming invisible on the horizon. A mild and cool breeze blew and the birds sang, as you inhaled the fragrance of flowers.

One day I climbed up a tree and made myself comfortable on a branch: an indescribable joy filled me. Above me was a vast spreading mantle woven only of green leaves with sudden patchwork pieces of the blue sky, and swaying in front of me were clusters of flowers hanging from a huge creeper. Far below me in the moist soil, mushrooms had sprung up. One can only wish to think leisurely in such surroundings. One becomes aware of new sensations, insights, and an infinite consciousness extending beyond mortality emerges from the core of one's being. It finds shape in the mind, bringing in its wake a profound happiness. It is almost as if one can match the heartbeat of every plant and tree with one's own.

We do not have such a variety of birds in our estate where nature seems to follow a set of different rules. Spring may descend upon the whole world but you will neither hear the cuckoo in Lobtulia, nor see a single familiar flower in bloom. Spring in Lobtulia has a rude, rough and stern visage like the goddess as Bhairavi, undoubtedly beautiful, but lacking in sweetness. It captivated the mind with its immensity and fierceness: like music without the softness of a komal note, a sombre composition like a dhrupad played in the Raga Malkaus in the twelve-beat chautal measure, leading the mind to its graver and higher reaches.

In contrast, Saraswati kundi was composed like a thumri, its sweet and gentle notes transporting the mind to a mellower and dreamier world. Listening to the cries of birds on a still afternoon of a Phalgun or Chaitra month as I sat in leafy shadow, my thoughts would travel far away: the wind carried the fragrance of the wild neem blossoms and in the water the red lilies bloomed. Only when evening fell did I leave the place.

Narha-baihar was being surveyed so that the land might be allotted to the tenants; I would often have to go there to supervise the amins in their work. On my way home, I would make a detour of two or three miles to the southeast with the sole thought of enjoying the verdurous forest around Saraswati kundi.

I was coming back home around three in the afternoon one day. When I entered the forest, I was drenched with sweat, having crossed the vast stretch of fields in the fierce heat of the sun. I moved deeper into the shade until I had reached the edge of the water. The water was at least a mile and a half from the forest, or even further away in some places. I tethered my horse to a tree and immediately fell asleep on an oilcloth that I laid out in the shade of a tree. On all sides, I was so surrounded by trees and thick foliage, that no one could have seen me from outside. Just a couple of feet above me were branches—a canopy had been made by the thick twisting stems of a climbing vine—and almost immediately above my breast, swaying gently in the breeze, were the green pod-like flowers of a wild plant I did not know. There was another tree nearby; its branches covered almost half of a bush that had tiny little flowers sprouting from it. The flowers were so tiny that you only saw them when you went up close but their perfume was strong and intense. The weight of the flowers had almost pulled to the ground the lower part of the bush.

I have already said the Saraswati kundi was where all the birds of the wild would flock. An amazing variety it was—magpies, pheasant crows, wild parrots, sparrows, chathares, ghughus, harials, shyamas and harteets. On the top of the bigger trees, bajbauris, kullos, and kites; and, in the blue waters of the lake, many-coloured ducks, sillis, maniks, and other water birds. The upper part of the bushes resounded with the cries of an assortment of birds; their incessant chatter almost deafened the ear. Often, they seemed not to care at all about human beings. They sat unconcernedly on the swaying branches and boughs around me, barely a foot or two away from where they could see me lying on the ground.

I greatly enjoyed their free movements. Even when I got up they were not afraid; they might fly off, but it would only be to settle down a little distance away and not a real exit. A little later, chattering and squawking, they would make their way back very close to where I sat.

It was by the *kundi* that I saw my first wild deer. I knew that there were wild deer in our jungle estate but I had never spotted any thus far. One day as I lay down I suddenly heard footsteps and looked up to find a fawn standing in the midst of the creepers and plants in the most secluded part of the bushes. He had spotted me and was gazing at me with wide uncomprehending eyes, wondering what strange creature I was!

The moments passed: the two of us in our places, speechless, motionless.

About half a minute later the fawn came forward a little, as though to look more closely at me. In his eyes was the curious and eager excitement of a human child. He might have come even closer, but at that moment my horse suddenly stamped his foot and shook himself; the startled fawn broke through the bushes and sped away to tell his mother of our meeting.

I sat quietly by the bushes for a long time. Between the trees one glimpsed vignettes of the blue waters of Saraswati kundi, extending in a half moon towards the foothills. The sky was a cloudless blue: the water birds who inhabited the *kundi* were engaged in incessant and noisy warfare, a grave and old manik bird perched high atop a plant on the edge of the water expressed his displeasure every now and then with sudden cries. On the big trees that bordered the water sat innumerable white egrets looking from afar like masses of white blossoms.

Gradually, the sky reddened.

The hilltop across the water took on a copper tint. The egrets began spreading their wings and flying away. Light fell on the upper branches.

The chattering and singing of the birds sounded louder, and the fragrance of the unknown wild flower became more pervasive. It seemed sweeter and stronger. A mongoose looked unblinkingly at me from a distance.

Peace of an unbroken quiet. And wondrous solitude. I have been here for at least three and half hours, and I have heard nothing but birdsong, and the rustling and snapping of twigs in the undergrowth as the birds moved around, the sound of a dry leaf or a broken twig falling. No sign of a human being.

The last of the day's red falls on the strange forms of many an unknown plant or tree and casts on them an unusual glow. Creepers have found their way up clinging to the topmost branches of these trees; one such creeper was known in the local language as the bhionra. I called it the honeybee creeper. It would cling on to all the sides of whichever tree it made its home. Now, the honeybee creeper was in flower—many of the big trees had a radiant crown of the little white flowers. The fragrance was wonderful, something like the mustard flower, though not as strong.

Wild sheuli trees abounded in the forests of Saraswati kundi sometimes giving the impression that it was only a sheuli forest. A species of tall coarse grass grew next to them around which were entangled thorny bushes. Thousands of sheuli flowers lay scattered over the grass, the stones and the thorny bushes. The place was warm and shady so the flowers had not dried although they had fallen in the morning.

I saw Saraswati kundi in all its many forms. People say that there are tigers in these forests. In my desire to see the waters in the light of the full moon, I have deceived Banowarilal and pretended to have gone to the main katcheri at Ajmabad, but instead, have come here directly on horseback from the sub-katcheri at Lobtulia.

True, I did not see a tiger, but on that occasion, I felt that most certainly enchanted creatures did come to the lake to delight and sport in the water. In the forest on the eastern shore all was quiet save the sound of a fox calling; far away, you could see the faint outlines of the hills; the cool breeze carried the mild smell of the trees and night flowers like the honeybee creeper into the moonlit night. Before me, the still waters of the lake brimmed over with moonlight. A heavenly moonlight, shadowless and full, refracted into a thousand little drops on the surface of the water while the huge tops of trees were illuminated by the white blossoms of the honeybee creeper, like the white fluttering garments of sprites and fairies . . .

An insect chirped monotonously, the sound was like a cricket's. Only the soft rustle of an occasional falling leaf or the crackling of dry leaves as a wild creature prowled the jungle at night broke the silence.

The forest goddesses do not come whilst we stay. Who knows how late in the night they come! I cannot bear the late night dew; I leave after an hour or so.

I have heard a legend concerning the sprites of Saraswati kundi.

In the month of Sraban, I had to spend one night in our northern borders on survey work. Amin Raghubir Prasad accompanied me. He had formerly been a government employee; for almost three decades he had been intimately acquainted with the Mohanpura Reserve Forest and the other forests in the area.

When I spoke to him of Saraswati kundi he immediately said, 'That is a magical *kundi*, Huzoor: fairies and sprites come there at night; on moonlit nights they take off their clothes and drape them over the stones, then they go to play in the water. If a mortal happens to glimpse them they lure him to the water and kill him. In the moonlight, their faces are sometimes to be seen in the water like lotuses. I have never seen them, but Head Surveyor Fatehsingh did one day. Then, once he had to travel through the forest past the lake late at night to get to the survey tent. The next morning they found his corpse floating in the waters of the lake—one of his ears had been eaten up by the big fishes. Huzoor, do not go there by yourself.'

It was by the waters of the Saraswati kundi that I chanced upon a strange person one afternoon.

I was on my way back from the survey camp and had taken the path that went around the lake when I saw a man digging away in the thick of the forest. At first, I thought that the man had come to dig up bhui-kumro, a species of pumpkin: the fruit is huge and lies so well hidden in the leaves of the creeper sprawling on the ground that it can hardly be seen from above. The pumpkin is used for medicinal purposes and sells for a good sum. I got off my horse and out of curiosity went up to the man: but it wasn't pumpkins that he was picking, he was busy planting seeds.

He seemed taken aback by my sudden appearance and looked at me in some confusion. He was getting on in years; his hair was a mix of salt and pepper. He had with him a little jute sack from which peeped out the edge of a spade, beside him on the ground lay a pick and few bits of scattered paper.

'Who are you?' I asked, 'What are you doing here?'

'Huzoor, are you the Manager-babu?' he asked in turn.

'Yes, I am. Who are you?'

'Namaskar. My name is Jugalprasad. I am a cousin of Banowarilal, the patowari at Lobtulia.'

I recalled then that Banowari Patowari had once in the course of a conversation mentioned this same cousin. The reason being that there was a vacant post—a mohuree's—at Ajmabad katcheri, that is, the one where I lived. I had asked him to find me a good man for the job. His own cousin would have been just the right man, Banowari had said sorrowfully, but he was of a strange temperament, whimsical and completely indifferent to worldly matters. Excepting for that failing, there were few people to be found in these parts to match his cousin either in their learning or the wonderful hand he wrote in Kayethi Hindi.[10]

I had asked him, 'Why, what does he do?'

Banowari had replied, 'Huzoor, he has many quirks—one of them is to simply wander around. He doesn't do anything; he is married, but he doesn't look after his family, just wanders around in the forest. Yet, he's not a sadhu or somebody who has renounced the world. That's the sort of fellow he is.'

So, this was Banowarilal's cousin!

The man had probably been working in secrecy; he spoke in embarrassed tones, as though he had been caught doing something wrong: 'Nothing, just ... this seed ...'

I was very surprised. The seed ... of what tree? This was not his own land, but dense forestland, what sort of a tree was he planting here? Of what use was it? I asked him.

'Huzoor, I have all kinds of seeds,' he said. 'I had seen a wonderful English creeper in a saheb's garden in Purnea: it had lovely red flowers. This seed is of that creeper, and then, I have the seeds of many other kinds of wild flowers. I've collected them from far off places, the forests here don't have these species of flowers and creepers. I'm planting them now; in another two years they will come up and start flowering. How nice it will look.'

I felt a great deal of respect for the man when I had understood his purpose. The man was spending his own time and money in order to beautify huge areas of forestland where he had no claim over any piece of land. All this work, with no selfish motive. A strange fellow!

I called Jugalprasad over and we both sat down beneath a tree for a chat.

'I've done this work before, Huzoor,' he said. 'All the wild flowers and flowering creepers that you see in Lobtulia—all of those—I planted some ten years ago. Some I'd brought from the forests in Purnea, some from the hilly forests of Lachhmipur 'state in South Bhagalpur. Now there's such a jungle of those flowers.'

'Do you enjoy this work very much?'

'The jungle in Lobtulia-baihar is beautiful—I have long wished to make the hills there and the forests here bloom with new flowers.'

'What sort of flowers did you plant?'

'Let me tell you Huzoor, how I first got drawn into this work. My home is in Dharampur district. We had no wild bhandi flowers in our part of the world. I would graze buffaloes on the banks of the Kushi, about fifteen miles away from our village. And there I saw the beauty of the wild bhandi flowering in the jungle and forests. So I took some seeds and planted them in our land, and now there is such a jungle of bhandi flowers wherever you look—by the wayside, in abandoned yards, in backyards. That's when the idea got into my head. I wished only to introduce those flowers and creepers and trees which were unknown to any one place. I've been doing this all my life. I have now grown old in the task.'

Jugalprasad knew many of the wild flowers and beautiful looking trees and plants which were native to the area. Most certainly, he was a specialist in the field.

'Do you know of the aristlochia creeper?' I asked him.

I described what the flowers looked like and he immediately said, 'Do you mean the hansalata? The flowers look like ducks, don't they? I've seen them in Patna, in the gardens of the babus.'

His knowledge was remarkable. Such selfless lovers of beauty are rare. He had nothing to gain from scattering and planting seeds all over the forest-land. He was so very poor himself and he did not earn a paisa from this work. Yet, such an intense desire and such unceasing toil to add to the splendour of the forests.

'Babuji', he told me, 'there's not such a wonderful forest as the one in Saraswati kundi in these parts. So many kinds of trees, and then, just look at the water—tell me, do you think we could have lotus growing here? There are lots of lotuses in the ponds at Dharampur. I thought I'd get some tubers and plant them here.'

I decided that I would help him. From that day onwards, I was seized almost by an passionate desire to adorn this forest with flowers, creepers, plants and trees of all kinds—the two of us working together. I knew that Jugalprasad often went hungry and that theirs was a needy household. I wrote to the head office and had him appointed to the mohuree's post at Ajmabad katcheri at a salary of ten rupees.

That year, I had English wildflowers ordered from the Sutton Seeds Company in Calcutta and the wild jui creeper brought from the Duars range and had them planted in great numbers in the forest around Sarawati kundi. Jugalprasad's joy and excitement know no bounds! I advised him that he should not reveal his emotions before the people in the katcheri; not only would he be considered quite mad, but I too, would be seen in a similar light. The next year, thanks to heavy rains, the creepers and the trees we had planted began growing at an astonishing speed. The soil around the lake was very fertile and the trees that we had planted grew well in this environment. Only the seeds in the Sutton packets created a problem: every packet carried the name of the particular flower, and in some cases, even a one-line description of the flowers. From these I picked out the colourful and attractive ones. Amongst these, the white beam, red campion and the stichwort showed exceptional progress; the foxgloves and the wood anemones did not do too badly either; but despite our best efforts, the dog-roses and the honeysuckle could not be saved.

I had also planted something that had yellow dhatura-like flowers all along the lake. These blossomed very soon. Jugalprasad had brought seeds of the wild baira creeper from Purnea; in seven months, the bushes were covered with the creeper. The flowers had a mild scent and were beautiful to look at.

At the beginning of autumn, I noticed that the baira creeper had given out innumerable buds.

As soon as I sent the news to Jugalprasad, he dropped his pen and came racing to Saraswati kundi all the way from Ajmabad katcheri, seven miles away.

'People had told me', he said, 'that even if you did manage to transplant the baira creeper, and even if it grew well, it would never blossom. All creepers do not flower, I believe. But just look at these buds!'

A tuber of the flower called the watercroft had been planted in the waters of the lake. It had multiplied so fast that Jugalprasad grew afraid that it would take over the lotuses in the lake.

I had also wanted to plant bougainvillaea but it was so much a part of urban parks and gardens that I had misgivings of it taking away the special character of the forest around Saraswati kundi. Jugalprasad shared my sentiments on these matters. He too forbade me from getting bougainvillea.

A lot of money went into the project. One day I heard of an unknown flower from Ganauri Teowari—he said it grew on the other side of the Karo, in the Jayanti Hills. In those parts, they called it the dudhia. The leaves were like those of the turmeric, the tree was as big, very tall with a stalk that stuck out for three or four feet. Not only was it nice to look it, it also gave off a very beautiful scent; at night particularly, the fragrance spread far and wide. A single plant multiplied so fast that in a couple of years there would be a forest of trees.

I could think of nothing but this flower from the time I heard of it from Ganauri. I was determined to have the flower brought. Ganauri said that one could bring it only in the rainy season: the tubers had to be planted and they needed enough water to survive. I sent off Jugalprasad with enough money on this mission. He searched for long in the impenetrable forests of Jayanti Hills and finally came back with several dozen tubers of the plant.

NINE

1

Almost three years have gone by.

I have gone through many changes in these three years. Nature—in and around Lobtulia and Ajmabad—has so captivated me that I have almost forgotten the city. I am so drawn to the attractions of solitude, of the constellated open sky, that once, when I had gone to Patna only for a few days, I suffered greatly from the narrow tarred roads and longed to return to Lobtulia-baihar. To see once more the inverted dome of a blue sky above fields of unending green, forest after forest unscarred by a highway; where foxes howling in the dark forests sound the hour to those immersed in deep slumber and the clattering hooves of herds of neelgai or the sonorous lowing of the wild buffaloes alone break the silence.

My employers were forever sending me memos to hurry up with the leasing out of the land. I knew that this task was indeed one of my duties, but I was loth to settle people and destroy the peace of the forests. Those who would rent the land would certainly not be doing so to keep the forests pristine. As soon as the sale was complete they would clear the land, prepare it for farming and plant crops, they would raise settlements to live on the land. The quiet forests, the *kundi*, the range of hills and everything else would be transformed into human settlements. And, with the surge of people, Bonolakshmi—the forest goddess, would fly breathlessly elsewhere. With the influx of people, the enchantment of the forest would disappear, all beauty lost to the claims of habitation.

As for the settlements, I could visualize them clearly. The way to Patna, Purnea or Mungher was full of such settlements: ugly lean-tos, one piling up on the other, clumsy one or two-storeyed thatched huts, phanimansa scrub, cows and buffaloes staked around mounds of dung, water drawn up from the well, crowds of men and women in dirty clothes, the banner fluttering over a temple dedicated to Hanuman, naked little children dust-covered, with silver chains around their necks playing by the roadside . . .

A strange sort of exchange it would be!

Such vast tracts of forestland, uninterrupted and open, so exquisitely beautiful, comprised a rich national resource. Had it been any other country, they would have made this into a national park. Exhausted city dwellers would have come now and then to refresh their weary minds, here in the midst of nature. There was no such hope now; why should the owner let his land lie fallow when he could rent it out to cultivators?

I had come here to settle new tenants in these forests. Having come to destroy the forestland, I have instead fallen in love with the beautiful forest maid. Now, I only tried to stall the day that would fulfil my objectives. Whenever I went riding in the shadowy afternoons or found myself alone beneath the open sky of a moonlit night, I wondered, was the forest going to be destroyed by my hands? She had won my heart like a cunning seductress!

However, I had come with an assigned task and I had to fulfil my task. At the end of Magh, a rajput named Chhotu Singh came to the katcheri: I fell into a great dilemma as soon as he submitted his application to lease a thousand bighas of land. Letting him have the thousand bighas was to sound the death knell over a huge area—all the trees, creepers and all kinds of plant life would be ruthlessly cleared. Chhotu Singh began pestering me: I forwarded his application to the head office and tried to stall, for a while at least, the imminent dance of death.

2

One afternoon as I was on my way back from the jungle of Narha-baihar that lay to the north of Lobtulia, I came upon a person seated atop a big rock by the side of the road.

I drew in my horse as I came up to him. The man was at least sixty years old. He had on a dirty dhoti and a torn *chaddar* covered his upper body. What on earth was he doing in this lonely place?

'Babu, who are you?' asked the man.

'I work in the katcheri here,' said I.

'Are you the Manager-babu?'

'Why do you ask? Is there something that you want? Yes, I am the Manager.'

The man got up and put out his hand in a gesture of benediction. 'Huzoor,' he said, 'my name is Motuknath Parey, a brahman. I was on my way to see you.'

'Why?'

'Huzoor, I'm a very poor man. I've come on foot from a long way off, having heard of Huzoor. I've been walking for the last three days. If you would find me a means of livelihood . . .'

'What have you been eating in the jungle for the past few days?' I asked curiously.

Motuknath showed me a bit of ground kalhai dal that he carried in a corner of the dirty *chaddar* he wore on his shoulders. 'I had a seer of it when I left home,' he explained. 'I've been living off this for the past three days. It's work I'm looking for Huzoor; my ration of ground kalhai has run out today . . . God will find me something or the other to eat.'

I could not conceive what sort of work he expected to find in the desolate stretch between Ajmabad and Narha-baihar carrying that bit of ground kalhai in his *chaddar* for a meal.

I said to him, 'Why did you not go to the big towns—Purnea, Bhagalpur, Patna, Mungher—and why have you chosen to come to this forestland, Pareyji? What will you do here? There are hardly any people in these parts. Who will give you work?'

Motuknath looked at me despairingly: 'Is there no means of earning anything here, Babu? In that case, where am I to go? Those are big towns, I don't know a soul there, nor the streets, they scare me. So I thought if I came here . . .'

The man seemed a sad and innocent sort of creature and very helpless. I brought him back with me to the katcheri.

A few days went by. I could not find any work that I could give Motuknath for he did not know any work. He had a little Sanskrit and could serve as a brahman priest. He had earlier taught students in a traditional school for teaching Sanskrit, a *tole*. He would turn up at odd hours to recite strange sounding Sanskrit verses to me; perhaps he thought this would be a diversion for me.

'Huzoor,' he said one day, 'please give me some land near the katcheri so that I can set up a *tole* here.'

'Who is going to study at your *tole*, Panditji?' I asked him. 'Are the wild buffaloes and herds of neelgai going to savour Kalidas' *Raghuvamsa* and the subtleties of Bhatti's grammar?'[11]

Motuknath was a complete innocent; possibly, he had proposed setting up a *tole* without thinking very deeply about the matter. I thought he would desist from making such a proposition in the future, but a few days later he brought up the matter again.

'Kindly set up a *tole* for me,' he entreated. 'Let me try it out at least and see what happens. Where else can I go otherwise?'

What a mess! Was the man mad? On the other hand, one felt sorry looking at him: he did not understand the affairs of the world and was only a simple and uncomprehending sort of man; yet, he had come here with tremendous hope and a certain faith—on whom, I did not know.

I tried in vain to explain to him that I was willing to give him land that he could farm in the manner of Raju Parey.

Their family had been brahman priests for generations, living off the sacred texts, the shastras, said Motuknath in a tone of entreaty. He knew nothing of farming; what would he do with the land?

I could have retorted, Why then had a brahman priest living off the shastras chosen to come and die in this god-forsaken place? But I did not have the heart to tell him a harsh word. I had come to like the man very much. Finally, yielding to his incessant entreaties I had a room put up for him and said, 'Well, here's your *tole*; now it's up to you to find the students.'

Motuknath inaugurated his school with a ritual puja and a feast for a couple of brahmans. There was nothing much that he could find in the jungle; he himself cooked thick rotis of maize and a vegetable dish made of wild dhundhul. He had set also some yoghurt with the buffalo milk he got from the cattlesheds. Naturally, I was one of the invitees.

For a few days after the inauguration, Mokutnath was in great spirits.

What odd creatures are to be found on this earth!

Every morning after he had bathed and completed his rituals he went to his schoolroom and sat on a palm-leaf mat. A copy of the traditional Sanskrit grammar, *Mughdabodh*, lay open before him and from this he would recite, exactly as though he was indeed teaching someone. He shouted out the verses so loudly that I could hear him from my office as I worked.

'The Panditji is a complete lunatic,' Tehsildar Sajjan Singh would say, 'Just look at what he is up to, Huzoor!'

A couple of months went by in this manner. Motuknath continued his instructions to an empty room, once in the morning and again in the late afternoon, with unvarying enthusiasm. Meanwhile, the day of Saraswati Puja came around. Every year, instead of an icon of the goddess, Saraswati was honoured at the katcheri with an inkstand—a symbolic representation of learning—for how was one to mould a clay image of the deity in the jungle? I was told Motuknath had determined to observe the puja independently in his *tole*; he was going to make the image with his own hands.

I marvelled at the faith and enthusiasm in this old man of sixty ...

Motuknath did make a small image of the deity with his own hands. A separate puja was performed in the *tole*.

'Babuji, this is our ancestral worship,' the old man informed me with a smile. 'Ever since I was a child, I've seen my father making the image and per-forming the puja in his *tole*. Now, again in my *tole* ...'

But was there a *tole*!

Of course, I did not actually say this to Motuknath.

About twelve days after the celebration of Saraswati Puja, Motuknath Pandit came to inform me that a student had come to admit himself in his *tole*. He had simply turned up that very morning.

Motuknath presented the student before me. He was a thin boy of about fifteen years, a Maithili brahman, and wretchedly poor: excepting for what he wore he did not possess another garment.

Motuknath's enthusiasm however, was unbelievable. He had hardly enough to feed himself, yet, in a moment he had taken on the responsibility of supporting his young pupil. This was the custom of their *tole*, he explained: in the past, the various needs of the pupils had been taken care of by their *tole*; he could not do otherwise and send home this fellow who had come in the hope of learning.

Within a couple of months, there were two other pupils at the *tole*. They ate only one meal a day and fasted for the other meals. The guards pooled together their resources and got him wheat, maize, cheena grains; I too, contributed something from the katcheri. The pupils picked bathua greens from the jungle; on some days they simply boiled the greens and managed a single meal. Motuknath himself fared much the same way.

From my office I could hear Motuknath instructing his pupils as late as eleven at night and even upto midnight, as he sat under a haritaki tree in front of his *tole* surrounded by his pupils. The instruction went on sometimes in the moonlight and sometimes in the dark, for he had no money to feed his lamp.

I have been astonished by something I observed. Apart from his initial request to give him the land and to set up the schoolroom, Motuknath has never asked me for any financial help. Not for once did he say, 'I cannot manage, please help me out a bit.' He never asked anyone; the guards had contributed of their own free will.

Between Baisakh and Bhadra—in these five months—the number of pupils in the *tole* rose quite substantially. About a dozen young lads who had been neglected, abandoned, and even chased away by their parents, turned up at Motuknath's; they were evidently attracted by the idea of a place where they would get free meals and lodging for little labour. News of this sort spreads fast; in these parts even the crow was a messenger. His pupils looked like they had hitherto been cowherds; not one showed a glimmer of intelligence. Were these boys to study Sanskrit syntax and poetry? They found Motuknath an easy victim and had come to eat off him while they pretended to study at his *tole*. Motuknath, however, was quite oblivious of all this; the mere fact of having pupils delighted him.

One day I was told that the students had not got any food and were perforce fasting. And so was Motuknath.

I called Motuknath and asked him what was up.

It was actually so. The ration of wheat and maize the guards had pooled together and contributed to the *tole* had run out. For a few days, master and students had lived on a meal of boiled bathua greens at night, but even that had not been possible today. Besides, many of the boys had fallen ill after these *ad hoc* meals; they were unwilling to eat the greens any more.

'Well, Panditji, what are you going to do now?'

'I can't think of anything, Huzoor. These little boys, going without food ...'

I arranged to have cereal rations measured out for all of them: rice, dal, wheat and some ghee, enough to see them through a couple of days.

I turned to Mokutnath: 'How will the *tole* run, Panditji? You had better wind it up. What will you eat, and what will you feed them with?'

He was hurt by my words. 'Is that possible, Huzoor!' he said. 'Can one simply wind up a running *tole*? Ours is an ancestral affair.'

Motuknath was an ever-optimistic creature; it was no use expostulating with him. He continued in good spirits with his handful of students.

Thanks to Motuknath, this part of my forestland was transformed into an ashram run by the sages of yore. The pupils pursued their studies with a great deal of noise, recited sutras from *Mugdhabodh*, and amongst other activities, stole pumpkins and gourds from the thatched frames of the katcheri, plucked flowers, destroying twigs and foliage as they did so. Soon enough, things started missing from the katcheri: the guards held that the culprits were the *tole*-pupils.

The naib had left open his cash-box in his room one day: someone made off with a few rupees and an old gilt ring of his. The incident created a great stir. Within a few days, the ring was recovered from one of Motuknath's pupils. He had tied it up in the slender little pouch he hung around his waist. Someone had spotted it and had reported him. The pupil was caught with the booty.

I sent for Motuknath. He was genuinely a hapless sort; the rampaging students were taking advantage of his good nature and doing whatever they wanted to. There was no need to shut down the *tole*, I said, but he would have to send away at least a few of his pupils. As for the ones who remained, they would have to do some farm work and earn their keep. I would give the land, and they would have to raise maize, cheena grains and some vegetables. They would survive on what they got from the land.

Motuknath took this proposal to his pupils. Eight of the twelve boys promptly fled. Four stayed back, but I doubt whether it was because they were desirous of learning. They simply had no other option. In former times they had grazed cattle, they were reconciled to a bit of farming now. Since then, Motuknath's *tole* has been running reasonably.

4

Chhotu Singh and other tenants had a great deal of land allotted to them — a total area of almost a thousand and a half bighas. We had to give them the thousand and a half from the land in Narha-baihar because the soil was extremely fertile there. The forest on the edges of the land was very beautiful: so often, when I had gone riding in the afternoon I had thought this forest in Narha-baihar to be one of the world's most beautiful places. Goodbye now to the beauty spot.

I would see from afar that they had set fire to the forest. It was impossible to clear a dense forest like this until at least some of it was first burnt down. Not all of it had been jungle though; creepers, wild flowers, plants and bushes of all kinds had once filled the stretches of open land . . .

From far, I heard the forest crackling as it burnt; I sat quietly and imagined the destruction of so much wonderful plant life. I experienced a curious sense of pain; I could not bear to go in the direction of the fire. A national resource that might forever have given so much peace and joy to people was being destroyed for a mere fistful of grain.

It was only in the early part of Kartik that I went to see the place. They had sown mustard in all the fields, here and there houses had been built. Already, people had brought their wives and children and their cattle and had settled villages.

In mid-winter, when the fields were golden with mustard flowers I saw before me an incomparable sight. A carpeted expanse of a thousand and a half bighas of gold, unending and uninterrupted lay before my eyes. The sky above—blue as sapphire, and golden yellow beneath, as far as eyes could see. This was not bad either, I thought.

I set off one day to inspect the newly settled villages. With the exception of Chhotu Singh, the other tenants were all poor: I would set up a night school for them. This was what I thought of before everything else when I saw innumerable little children playing in the mustard fields.

But soon, the new tenants created a major problem. I came to realize they were not peaceloving. News came to me at the katcheri one day that serious fighting had broken out amongst the tenants of Narha-baihar. The fighting had erupted because there was no clear demarcation of the plots; those who had five bighas of land were now trying to harvest ten bighas and so on. I was also informed that Chhotu Singh had secretly brought over many rajput mercenaries armed with big sticks and spears from his native village several days prior to the actual harvesting; it was now quite clear why he had done so. In addition to harvesting his own three to four hundred bighas, he was now set upon taking over the harvest from the entire thousand and a half bighas (or the maximum he could) of Narha-baihar.

'This is how it is in these parts, Huzoor,' the amlas at the katcheri said to me, 'whosoever has the might of the stick has the right to the harvest.'

And those who did not have the might of the stick came to me at the katcheri and wept. They were helpless and poor gangotas who had cleared little plots of ten to twenty bighas of jungleland and had planted crops. They lived with their families in little huts by the edge of the fields. It looked like they were about to lose the whole year's labour at the hands of a tyrant.

I sent two guards from the katcheri to the trouble spot to find out exactly what was happening. They came back running breathlessly and announced that fierce fighting had broken out in the northern boundary of Bhimdas-tola.

I set off immediately with Tehsildar Sajjan Singh and all the katcheri guards. We could hear confused shouts and cries, the buzz of a disturbance long before we arrived at the trouble spot. A small river flowed down from the hills and cut through Narha-baihar: most of the noise seemed to come from that source.

When we came to the river bank we found people amassed on both sides—about seventy on this side and on the other, about forty of Chhotu Singh's rajputs. The latter were attempting to cross over; the people on this side had formed a wall to thwart the crossing. A couple of people on this side had, in the meantime, been wounded. Chhotu Singh's men had tried to behead one of the wounded who had fallen into the river: he had been saved by the prompt intervention of his comrades on this side. There was not much water in the river: it was the end of winter and besides it was a mountain stream.

When the contingent from the katcheri made its appearance both sides stopped warring and came up to me. Both sides proceeded to tar the opposite camp and whitewash their own behaviour: each side tried to set itself up as Yudhishtir the Wise and the Just, branding the other as Duryodhan the Evil. In the ensuing din and confusion it became impossible to weigh the justice of the case. I asked both parties to come to the katcheri. The injured were not badly hurt: they had been hit on the head with sticks. I had them brought over to the katcheri as well.

Chhotu Singh's men said that they would come to see me at the katcheri in the late afternoon. I thought everything had been taken care of. But I was yet to learn about the locals. A little after noon, news came to me that the warring groups at Narha-baihar were at it again. Once more, I rushed there with my men. I also sent a man on a horse to the police post at Naugachhia about nine miles away. I found the situation much the same as in the morning, but this time, Chhotu Singh had massed a larger contingent on his side. I was told that Rashbehari Singh Rajput and Nandalal Ojha Golawala were all helping Chhotu Singh. Chhotu Singh himself was not present at the site. His brother, Gajadhar Singh sat on his horse some distance away; he moved away as soon as he saw me coming. I saw that this time two of the men in the group of rajputs had guns on them.

From the other side, the rajputs called out to me, 'Huzoor, move aside, we want to teach those gangota sons of slaves a lesson.'

Acting upon my instructions, my men went forward and stood between the two groups. I told the rajputs that I had already sent word to the Naugachhia police post; the police must be half way through by now. Those guns they carried, in whose name had they been registered? It was definitely a jail sentence for him if he but fired a shot. The law was very strict about such matters.

The two men with the guns backed away a bit.

I called over the gangotas on this side of the river and told them that they had no need to indulge in a battle. They should turn back. I would stand guard here. All the amlas and the katcheri guards would be with me. If the harvest were to be looted, I would be personally responsible.

The gangota leader trusted me and took his men some distance away where they stood around the bakain trees. 'No, not there,' said I, 'you must go home directly. The police are on their way.'

The rajputs, however, were not to be cowed down so easily. They stood their ground and began conferring amongst themselves.

'What is up, Sajjan Singh?' I asked the tehsildar. 'Are they going to descend upon us?'

'Huzoor,' said the tehsildar, 'it's that Nandalal Ojha Golawala I'm afraid of—he's a real villain.'

'Then be ready. I am not letting any one of them cross over. Just keep them at bay for a couple of hours. The police should be here in the meanwhile.'

I don't know what the rajputs decided amongst themselves, but some of the group came forward and said, 'Huzoor, we want to cross over to the other side.'

'Why?'

'Don't we have land on the other side?'

'Tell that to the police. The police are almost here. I can't let you come over.'

'Have we paid the katcheri such a huge amount of money as salaami for nothing? This is an unfair demand on your part.'

'You can tell that to the police as well.'

'You will not let us cross over?'

'No, not before the police are here. I will have no warring on my territory.'

Meanwhile, other people from the katcheri had also joined us. They came crying that the police was on their way. One by one, Chhotu Singh's men gradually slipped away. The fighting had been stopped for the time being, it was true, but it was also the beginning of an ever-rising tide of incidents including bloody confrontation between the two groups, and the police. I realized that the root of the problem was in my having let out such a huge area of land to a man as ruthless as Chhotu Singh. I called him over to the katcheri one day. He said he had no clue of whatever I was telling him. As for himself, he spent most of his time in Chhapra town: how was he to be held responsible for what his people might or might not do in his absence?

I realized that the man was an old hand at the game. There was no way that a straightforward settlement would work in such a case. I would have to look for other ways to teach him a lesson.

From that time onwards, I completely stopped leasing land to anyone but gangotas. But there was no way to redeem the mistake that had already been made. Narha-baihar had forever lost its peace.

5

We had settled tenants in almost six hundred acres of land in the northern part of our twelve-mile long estate. When I was required to go there around the end of Paush, I found it completely transformed.

I came out of the jungle at Phulkia and my eyes met a golden carpet of flowering mustard stretching to the horizon, unwinding without a gap or a pause all the way upto the foot of the blue range of hills. It was winter and the sky was a cloudless blue. This dazzling field of gold was dotted with sheds of kash belonging to the tenants. I could not imagine how they and their wives and children withstood the bitter cold, living as they did in these slight huts made of kash stalks.

It was not too long before the crops would ripen. Already, the reapers who would help in the harvesting had begun arriving from far away places. Their's was a strange life: they came with wife and children from Purnea, the Terai and the hills of Jayanti and northern Bhagalpur, built these little huts and did the harvesting. They got a part of the harvest as their wages. Once the harvesting was over they left behind their little huts and went away with their families. They belonged to many different castes: most were gangotas, but some were chhatris, bhumihar brahmans, even maithili brahmans.

It was the rule of the land that the revenue had to be recovered on the field, while the harvesting was on. Otherwise, the tenants were so miserably poor they were unable to pay taxes once the harvest had been taken away from the fields. It became necessary for me to spend some time in the mustard fields of Phulkia-baihar to supervise the collection of taxes.

'Shall I have the small tent pitched there?' the tehsildar asked me.

'Wouldn't it be possible to put together a small hut of kash in a day?'

'Will you be able to live in a hut in this weather, Huzoor?'

'Certainly, I will. Do get a hut built.'

That is what they did. There were about four of these kash huts built side by side. One was for me to sleep in, the other was a kitchen, and the others were for the two guards and the patowari. The huts were called *khupri* in the local language. Instead of windows, a little bit of the kash wall was cut out; there was no way you could shut it and the icy wind blew in through the walls every night. The entrance to the hut was so low that you had to crawl inside. Dried heaps of kash and the pods of wild jhau were laid out on the floor, a rug was spread on top of the heap, and above that, a mattress and sheet, to make up my bedding. My *khupri* was seven feet long and three feet wide. It was impossible to stand up straight inside, as the height was only four and a half feet.

But the *khupri* was most enjoyable. I had never lived in such comfort and joy even in a four-storeyed mansion in Calcutta. Perhaps, I was getting to be quite wild myself, having spent so many years here. Who knew whether the open forestland and nature had some small but definite impact on my tastes, on my attitude and my likes and dislikes?

What I liked most about the *khupri* as I entered it was the fresh fragrance of the newly-cut kash stalks of which the walls were made. What I liked next best, was the view I had of the blossoming mustard flowers from the square-foot opening in my hut. It was a most unusual perspective, as though I was lying down on a yellow carpet that covered the entire earth. The keen wind brought with it the sharp tang of the mustard in flower.

It was as cold as it could be for the time of the year. There was no respite from the west wind even for a day; it was fierce enough to melt the strong sunshine. On my ride back through the jungle of berries, I would see the winter sun set behind the low range of bluish hills of the Tirashi-chauka. The sky reddened from the south-western corner to the south-east and became a sea of liquid light as the sun like a huge fire ball dipped behind the hills. I thought I could feel the planet rotate, a huge mound of earth turning eastwards from the west; if one looked long enough, the eyes played tricks and it seemed as though the western horizon was in fact moving towards the spot where I stood.

The cold became intense as soon as the last of the sun disappeared. After a long day of hard labour and hours of riding we lit a fire before my *khupri* and sat down around it. In the sky the mass of stars burnt as though they were electric lights—I had never seen such a resplendent Great Bear or such a set of the Pleiadas. I saw them so intensely that they became like intimate friends. The silent and mysterious night, the dark forests beneath and above me the uncountable stars, my nightly companions. On some days, a slice of an unreal moon would appear like the beam of a distant lighthouse in a sea of darkness. And the black darkness would be criss-crossed by the sharp arrows of shooting stars. They were to be seen on all sides of the compass— south, north, south-western, south-eastern, east and west. There goes one, and another, there go two at one time, and yet again, one more—every minute, every second.

Ganauri Teowari and many others turn up at my camp from time to time. All sorts of tales are swapped, and marvels related. It was here that I heard a fantastic story. We happened to be talking of hunting when someone mentioned the wild buffaloes of Mohanpura jungle. A rajput called Dashrath Singh Jhandawala who had come to the Lobtulia katcheri to bid for land on the sandbank happened to be with us. He was known to be a top-notch hunter and there was a time when he had roamed the length and breadth of the jungles here. 'Huzoor,' said Dashrath Jhandawala, 'I once saw Tarbaro when I went hunting wild buffaloes in the Mohanpura jungle.'

I remembered then that Ganu Mahato had also spoken to me of the same Tarbaro.

'What is it all about?' I asked.

'Huzoor, it all happened a long time ago. The bridge over the Kushi had not yet been built. There was a pair of boats at Kataria and people coming on the passenger-train had to take the boat across the river with their belongings. We were quite taken up with dancing horses in those days— Chhotu Singh of Chhapra and I. Chhotu Singh brought horses from the fair at Hariharchhetra, and the two of us would teach those horses to dance and then sell them at a higher price. There are two kinds of dances that you teach horses: *jamaiti* and *fanaiti*. Horses that had a long training in *jamaiti* sold for better prices. Chhotu Singh was a master at teaching the *jamaiti*. We made a lot of money, the two of us in those two or three years.

'Chhotu Singh suggested that we should get a license and do business with the wild buffaloes we could capture from the Dholbajya jungle. Every-thing was fixed up. Dholbajya was a reserve forest belonging to the Maharaja of Darbhanga. We greased a few palms and got ourselves a permit from the officials. Then we spent our time tracking the whereabouts of the wild buf-faloes in the jungle. Such a huge forest it was, Huzoor, spotting a buffalo was quite a job! Finally, we put an old tribal, a Santal, on the job. He showed us the hollow in a bamboo forest and said that the *jera*, a herd, of wild buffaloes would go that way late at night for a drink of water. We dug a deep pit across the path and covered it well with bamboo and mud. The buffaloes would fall into the trap when they passed that way at night.

'The old Santal watched us while we were doing all this and then he said, "Whatever you may do, there's one thing that you should know: You will never be able to kill a wild buffalo of the Dholbajya jungle. Tarbaro lives here."

'We were astonished. "Who is Tarbaro?" we asked him.

'The old man said, "Tarbaro is the god of wild buffalo herds. He will not let a single buffalo come to harm."

'"Lies!" said Chhotu Singh, "We don't believe such things. We are rajputs, not Santals."

'Huzoor, you will be amazed at what happened next. I get shivers down my spine to think on it even now. In the dead of night we stood, silently, hidden behind a bamboo thicket next to the path, when we heard the sound of hooves. A jera of buffaloes was coming our way. Then they were almost there, only seventy feet away from the pit. Suddenly, we saw by the side of the pit, about ten feet away from its edge, a man, tall and dark, standing there with his hand upraised. The figure was so tall that it seemed as though he touched the very tips of the bamboos growing around him. The herd of wild buffalos came to a sudden stop as they saw him, and then the herd broke and fled here and there. Not one came anywhere near the trap we had laid for them. Believe it or not, this I saw with my own eyes.

'I have since asked a few other hunters about the matter, and they have all told us, Abandon all thoughts of capturing a wild buffalo in this jungle. Tarbaro will not let a single animal be killed or even be captured. We simply wasted our money to get a permit, not a single wild buffalo fell into our trap that time.'

When Dashrath Jhandawala had finished his tale, the Lobtulia patowari said, 'We have also heard stories of Tarbaro ever since we were children. Tarbaro is the god of wild buffaloes, he is always on the alert lest his herds lose their lives in any unnatural way.'

I did not care to find out whether the story was a true or a false one—I would look up at the sword-bearing Orion now visible in the sky while I listened to the story. Over the dense forests, the sky was turned upside down. A wild cockerel was heard somewhere far away. The dark and silent sky had come together to whisper conspiratorially with the earth, also dark and silent;

I would shiver involuntarily looking on at the black line of the Mohanpura Forest on the far horizon remembering the story of a forest god I had not heard of before. It was wonderful to listen to such stories before a fire on a dark winter's night in the heart of a lonely forest.

TEN

1

I spent fifteen days in my *khupri* living an open-air life as did the gangotas and poor bhumihar brahmans. It wasn't entirely out of choice that I lived in this manner. What could one have brought to the jungle anyway? I ate rice and the wild-dhundhul cooked in a curry; the guards picked kankrole from the forests or gathered sweet potatoes; these we fried or boiled. There was no fish, milk or ghee to be had.

Of course, there was no dearth of wild sillis or peafowl, but somehow, I couldn't bring myself to kill birds although I had a gun. I stayed vegetarian.

There were tigers in Phulkia-baihar. And this is what happened.

It was cold enough to chill one's bones. I had gone early to bed as soon as I finished my work, around ten, and had promptly fallen asleep. Suddenly—I don't know how late at night it was—I was awakened by shouts and screams. Some people had gathered by the edge of the forest and they were screaming at the top of their voices. I got up and quickly lit a lamp. My guards came out quickly from the adjoining *khupri*. While we were all speculating as to what it could mean, a man came running to me: 'Manager-babu, come quickly with your gun, a tiger has taken a little boy from a *khupri*.'

A gangota tenant called Domon lived in a *khupri* only three hundred feet away from the edge of the jungle. His wife had been sleeping with their six-month-old son inside the *khupri*; they had lit a fire inside to fight the terrible cold and had kept the opening a little ajar to let the smoke escape. A tiger had got in through the opening and had made off with the infant.

How did they know it was a tiger? It might well have been a fox. Once I reached the spot, however, my doubts were dispelled: the pug marks of a tiger were clearly visible on the soft soil of the field.

Anxious that nothing adverse be said against the estate, my patowari and guards began proclaiming in a loud voice, 'Huzoor, this tiger is not one of ours, it has come from the Mohanpura Reserve Forest. Just look at how big the pug marks are!'

Did it matter where the tiger had come from or where it belonged? I ordered them to gather as many people as possible and light some torches. I said, 'Let us go into the jungle and search. The mere sight of the huge pug marks in the dead of night had frightened everyone to death; not one person was willing to go into the jungle. After a lot of scolding and cursing, I managed to round up about ten people. Carrying torches and beating on tins we searched through various parts of the jungle all through the night, but in vain.'

The next day, around ten in the morning, the bloody remains of the child were found beneath an ashan tree about two miles away in the south-eastern part of the jungle.

Immediately after this incident, the fearfully dark moonless nights of the month came upon us. I had Bankey Singh Jamadar brought over from the main katcheri. Bankey Singh was a hunter and familiar with the habits and habitats of tigers. He said, 'Huzoor, these man-eating tigers are a cunning lot. Some more are going to be killed. Warn all the people to take especial care.'

Exactly three days later, around evening, the tiger got a shepherd boy. People stopped sleeping after the incident. A remarkable scene took place every night. All over the huge *baihar*, people beat on canisters in their little *khupris*, sometimes they lit fires with kash stalks, while Bankey Singh and I let off our guns every hour. And, as though it wasn't enough having to deal with the tiger, a herd of buffaloes came charging from Mohanpura Forest and destroyed quite a bit of the crops ready for harvest.

The guards had lit a big fire right in front of my kash *khupri*. I would sometimes throw a log or two into the fire. I could hear the guards talking in the adjoining *khupri* as I lay inside mine. From the peephole near my head, I could see the immense spread of fields, the blurred outline of the forest in the dim light of the stars. Looking up at the dark sky it seemed as though waves of icy cold wind from dead constellations were speeding their way towards the earth; my mattress and quilt had turned into sheets of ice. The fire was burning out and the cold was monstrous. All through the night, the icy wind howled across the open fields.

How did the people here brave this punishing cold? How did they spend their nights on the cold floor of these primitive kash *khupris* that lay beneath the open skies? Add to that the hardships of guarding the crops against the depredations of wild buffaloes, wild pigs, and even tigers. Could our peasants in Bengal endure so much? They farmed a fertile land and lived in a rural environment free of these hazards, yet, there was never plenty and they could not free their lives of suffering.

About five hundred feet away from my *khupri* lived a family of reapers, wage labourers who had come with their families from southern Bhagalpur to help with the harvesting. One evening as I passed by their *khupri* I found the entire family sitting outside, warming themselves by a fire they had lit at the mouth of their home.

I still knew very little about them. I thought I'd find out something of their lives.

'Babaji, what are you doing?' I asked this of an old man in the group. He got up to greet me with a salaam and then he invited me to warm myself at their fire. This was a local custom: in the winter, it was a mark of courtesy to invite a guest to warm himself by the fire.

I sat down. Peering into the *khupri* I saw that there was nothing inside that looked like bedding or furniture of any sort, only some sheaves of dry grass laid out on the floor. As for vessels, all they had were a biggish sized bowl of bell metal and a small *lota*. There was not a scrap of clothing inside. However that might be, where was the quilt or covering to protect them against the fierce weather? How did they sleep at night?

I asked them this question.

The old man was called Nakchhedi Bhakt, a gangota by caste. 'Why,' he said, 'don't you see the sheaves of kalhai that are piled up in a corner of the *khupri*?'

I did not quite comprehend: Did they make a fire of the sheaves of kalhai every night?

Nakchhedi laughed at my ignorance. 'No, Babuji, the children snuggle inside the sheaves and go to sleep, and we grown-ups cover ourselves with the kalhai. Don't you see, there are at least five maunds of kalhai piled up inside. This stuff is warm as anything, its full of *om*, of goodness; even two blankets will not give you this sort of *om*. Besides, tell me, where would we ever get any blankets?'

While this conversation was going on, the little boy's mother was getting him ready for the night: she fitted him inside the sheaf and covered him from top to toe so that only his head poked out. How little we humans know of our fellow creatures, I thought to myself. Had I ever known anything of this? I was only now coming to terms with the real face of my country.

On the other side of the fire sat a young woman, busy cooking.

'What are you cooking?' I asked her.

Nakchhedi replied, 'It's *ghato*.'

'What is *ghato*?'

Where has this Bangali-babu turned up from! The girl engrossed in cooking must have wondered at this point. He's quite an idiot, I can see. Does he keep no track of the world? Her laughter rang out as she asked me, "Don't you know what *ghato* is Babuji? It's boiled maize. Like you call boiled paddy, rice, so you call boiled maize, *ghato!*'

The girl picked up a bit of the above-mentioned item from the pot on the tip of her flat cooking spoon and showed it to me in a benevolent attempt at dispelling my ignorance.

'What do you eat it with?'

From this point, it was the girl who spoke. 'With salt, or with spinach; what else can you eat it with?' she said laughingly.

'And have you also cooked spinach?'

'Once the *ghato* is done, I'll put on the spinach. I've picked some greens of the matar crop.'

The girl was very self-assured. 'Do you live in Calcutta, Babuji?' she wanted to know.

'Yes.'

'What sort of a place is it? They tell me that there are no trees in Calcutta: have they cut down all the trees there?'

'Who has told you that?'

'Someone from our village who works in Calcutta told me once. What does it look like, Babuji?'

As far as was possible, I attempted to explain to this innocent country girl what a big city of our modern times might look like. I don't know how much of it she understood, but she said, 'I wish very much to see Calcutta—who will show it to me?'

I continued chatting with her for long. It was getting on to be night and the darkness thickened. They finished cooking, brought out the big vessel from the *khupri* and poured into it a mess that looked like rice starch. They sprinkled salt over it and all the little ones sat in a circle around it and began eating from it.

'Will you be going back to your village once you are done here?' I asked.

'It will be a long time before we get back home,' said Nakchhedi. 'We go on to Dharampur to cut the paddy; rice doesn't grow in these parts, but it grows there. After that is over, we go to Mungher to harvest the wheat. By the time the wheat harvesting is done, the month of Jaishtha will be upon us. And then, it will be time to harvest the kheri in your estate. Then we take a rest for a few days! In Sraban-Bhadra the maize will have ripened and will need harvesting. When we are done with that, there's the winter crop of paddy in Purnea-Dharampur district. This is how we roam the land all the year through.

'Don't you have homes?'

Now the young woman spoke. She was in her mid-twenties, very healthy, dark as varnished wood, with a beautiful figure. She spoke well and the strain of the southern Behari dialect in her speech gave it an exceptional quality.

'Of course, we have homes,' she said. 'We have a home and everything, but if we stay put there, we wouldn't survive. We shall go home at the end of summer and shall stay there until mid-Sraban. And then once again we will have to go wandering in foreign lands.'

Quietness surrounded us. Through the darkness, came the distant sound of someone beating on a tin. They were brave people, I thought, to spend night after night with their children in flimsy huts made of kash stalks on the very edge of the forest. Only a few days ago a child had been taken away by a tiger from his mother's embrace, from one of these very *khupris*. These people too, did not have any security. Yet, I noticed that they acted as if the incident had not even taken place. Nor did they seem frightened. Why, it was quite late even now and they had been sitting beneath the open sky chatting away and cooking their meal!

'You must be careful,' I said, 'You know that a man-eating tiger is out, don't you? A man-eater is a terrible creature, and very crafty too. Keep the fire going in front of the *khupri* and get inside your *khupri*. The forest is just a stone's throw away, and it's getting late . . .'

'Oh, we are quite used to it, Babuji,' said the girl. 'In Purnea district, where we go every year to harvest wheat, wild elephants come down the hills. That is a jungle even more terrible than this one. Specially, at the time of harvesting, herds of wild elephant are on the rampage.'

The girl threw in some more dried twigs of the wild jhau into the fire and then she came over and sat down on one side. She went on: 'That time, when we had gone to the foot of the Akhilkucha Hill, I was cooking one evening in front of our *khupri* and I looked up to find about five wild elephants standing within seventy feet of where I was. In the darkness, they looked like black mountains—as though they were heading straight for our *khupri*. I dropped my pot and put my little son to my breast and caught the girl by her hand and shoved them inside the khupri. There was no one else . . .when I came out I saw that the elephants had paused for a bit. My throat was tight with fear. We were saved because elephants don't see very well, although they can smell human beings from very far away. Perhaps the wind was blowing in the other direction that time; whatever it was, they went off somewhere else. In Purnea too, we kept the fire going and beat on tins all night long for fear of the elephants. It's wild buffaloes here; it's wild elephants there, that's all. We're quite used to it.'

I came back to my own dwelling for it was quite late.

In another fortnight, Phulkia-baihar was completely transformed. Just as soon as the mustard plants were dried and the seeds threshed, all sorts of people found their way here. Marwari businessmen came with scales and sacks from Purnea, Mungher, Chhapra and like places to buy up the crops. With them came bands of men who were going to work as coolies and cart-men. Sweet-makers turned up and set up temporary stalls of kash: they did brisk business in salty *puris* and *kachauris*, and sweets like *laddus* and *kalakand*. Peddlers appeared with an assortment of cheap and attractive wares: glass bowls and dishes, dolls, cigarettes, soap, printed bolts of cloth and such like things. Besides the traders and vendors, came the entertainers who put on all kinds of shows, wanting to make some money: some danced, others dressed up as Ram and Sita for devotees; and the priest came with a vermilion-smeared icon of Hanuman to pick up what he could earn by way of offerings. This was the season for everyone to make a little bit of money.

I was startled to see how the deserted jungle and fields of Phulkia-baihar that I had been scared of crossing in the evenings even on horseback just last year were now transformed into a joyous festive ground. Young girls and boys laughing, chattering, the sound of cheap tin whistles, rattles, the tinkle of the dancers' anklets—as though all of Phulkia-baihar had turned into an immense fairground.

The population too had shot up. New *khupris* and thatched huts made of kash cropped up overnight. It did not cost much to build a home—the forest supplied the kash, the wild jhau, the trunks and branches of the kend tree, and strong rope was made in these parts from twisting the dried-up kash stems. Add to this, the reapers' capacity for hard work.

The tehsildar at Phulkia came to let me know that these were all outsiders who had come to earn money; I would have to extract taxes from them on behalf of the landlord.

'You must hold a real court, Huzoor,' he urged me, 'I shall bring them to you one by one; settle a sum of money per head as taxes.'

What a variety of people I got to see in this connection!

I sat at this makeshift katcheri from early morning upto ten, and then through another shift from three in the afternoon until evening.

'They won't stay here for very long,' said the tehsildar, 'They'll all run off as soon as they are done with the cutting and winnowing and their trading. We must make them pay up before that happens.'

One day, I spotted some Marwari moneylenders weighing grain in a grain shed. It looked to me they were cheating with weights and short-changing the simple tenants. I asked my patowari and the tehsildar to check each and every one of the scales and other instruments of measurement. The two began presenting a couple of moneylenders before me from time to time—those who had been caught cheating with the weights or manipulating the hand balance. I had such men thrown out of the estate. At least in my estate, I would not let anyone deprive the tenants of what they had grown and harvested with so much labour.

It wasn't just the moneylenders; I noticed that many others too, lay in wait to trick the tenants and get a share of their money. There wasn't much of an opportunity to make cash in these parts so people bartered away their mustard crop to buy things from the peddlers. Invariably, they were cheated. This was more so the case with the young women. They were so guileless and simple that it was very easy to deceive them with some ridiculous argument and get four times the real value of the item that was sold. Not that the men were particularly worldly wise: they bought English cigarettes, shoes and clothes for equally high prices. Both men and women became quite giddy with the money they could command once the harvesting was done. The girls listed out purchases of colourful cottons, household utensils of glass and enamel; little bags full of sweets and savouries were bought from the sweetmaker; they even blew away their money listening to songs. And of course, there were pujas and offerings galore for Ramji, Hanumanji. Finally, heading the list, there were the guards and the henchmen of the landlords and the moneylenders who had to be dealt with. The peasants had stayed up nights in the dead of winter, safeguarding their crops against the ravages of wild pigs and wild buffaloes, not hesitating to throw their lives at the mercy of tigers and snakes. But whatever they had earned labouring for the whole year, they happily blew away in a little over a fortnight. There was one thing in their favour, though, and that was, not one among them drank liquor or toddy. Such addictions were not usual amongst the gangotas and bhumi-har brahmans; many made a drink of *bhang*, and that, they didn't have to buy, for wild cannabis grew in abundance along the edges of Lobtulia and Phulkia. All you had to do was tear off the leaves and make the drink and no one was any wiser.

One day Muneswhar Singh informed me that a man was seen 'in flight' with a view to cheat the landlord of his tax; I had only to give the order, he would immediately nab the offender.

'What do you mean, in flight?' I asked in surprise, 'You mean he is running away?'

'Huzoor, he is running as swiftly as a horse; he must have crossed the big *kundi* by now and gained the edge of the jungle.'

I gave the order for the culprit to be captured and brought to me.

In an hour, four or five of the guards had caught the accused and had delivered him to me.

When I saw the man they had brought I was speechless. I was sure that he was at least sixty years old—the hair on his head was white, the skin on his face wrinkled. He looked like someone who had been hungry for aeons, and had only now been able to have a full meal, after having come to the cattle sheds at Phulkia-baihar. I was told that in the last few days, costumed as the the boy Krishna as *Nanichor Natua* or the divine butter-thief, he had amassed a huge amount of money, that he had been camping in a *khupri* beneath Grantsaheb's Banyan, and that, for the last few days the guards had been badgering him for taxes as the harvesting season was almost over. He was supposed to have paid his dues today. Suddenly, in the middle of the afternoon, the guards got wind of the fact the man had packed his belongings and had set off. When Muneshwar Singh went to investigate, he found that the 'accused' had already crossed the *baihar* and was on his way to Purnea; upon Muneshwar Singh's calling out, the man had started running. And then this.

I was suspicious of this account given by the guards. Firstly, if *Nanichor Natua* indicated the butter-thief, Krishna's child incarnation, it was most unlikely that the man before me could impersonate the little stealer of curds and cream. Secondly, I was told that the man had been running at top speed; this too, seemed quite improbable!

But all present swore that both of these were factually correct statements.

'What made you act in this wicked manner?' I asked the man sternly. 'Don't you know that taxes have to be paid to the landlord? What is your name?'

The man was trembling like a palm frond battered by the wind. My guards always went for overkill in their duties: if they simply had to fetch someone, they delivered him bound. It did not take me long to understand that they had not been very gentle or compassionate in their treatment of this ancient performer.

The man trembled as he pronounced his name: 'Dasharath.'

'Of what caste? Where is your home?'

'Huzoor, we are bhuinhar brahmans. My home is in Mungher district, in Sahebpur Kamal.'

'Why were you running away?'

'Why no, why should I be running away, Huzoor!'

'Well then, pay up the tax.'

'Where am I to pay the tax from? I've not earned anything. Whatever grains I got for my dancing, I sold—to eat something in these few days. I swear by Hanumanji.'

'He's lying, Huzoor,' cried out the guards in a chorus, 'don't listen to him, Huzoor. He's earned a lot of money. He has it on him. If you give us leave, we shall search his clothes.'

The man joined his hands and implored, 'Huzoor, I will tell you myself how much I have.'

He took out a slim pouch that was tied to his waist and turned it out completely. 'Huzoor look, here's the total—thirteen annas. I have no one of my own; and anyway, who will give me anything in my old age? This is when I earn, in the harvesting season, when I go wandering from one harvesting ground to another and show people my dances. This is all I will have to live on until the wheat is harvested—another three months to go before that happens. All I can do with this money is get a bit of food. The guards say that I should pay eight annas as tax; that means all I will have left is five annas. How will I eat for the next three months with these five annas?'

'What do you have in that bundle in your hands?' I asked. 'Open it.'

The man opened his bundle and showed me the contents: a little mirror with a tin frame, a crown made of silver foil complete with peacock feathers, some paint for his face, a necklace of beads and so on—his accessories to make up as god Krishna.

'And look, Huzoor, I still don't have a flute,' said the man. 'A big-sized tin whistle would cost at least eight annas. I've managed here with a reed flute; its easy to deceive these folks—they're gangotas after all, but the people in our Mungher district are great connoisseurs. They'd laugh if I danced without a flute. No one would pay for the performance.'

'All right,' I said, 'if you can't pay taxes, show us a dance instead.'

The man looked as though he had been granted a seat in paradise. When he had painted his face and put on his crested crown, I did not know whether to laugh or cry: the old man presented a truly bizarre sight as he swayed and danced in the manner of a twelve-year- old.

The guards stifled their laughter and tried their best to hide their sar- castic smiles. In their eyes, the dance of *Nanichor Natua* was a monstrous affair. The poor fellows could not laugh heartily in front of their Manager- babu and yet, they were hard put to curb the waves of unquenchable laughter that shook their very being.

I have never seen such a strange dance. The sixty-year-old sometimes pouted like a spoilt child and moved away, as in a game, from his imaginary mother Yashoda; sometimes, he doled out the stolen butter and cream to his young cowherd friends; and at times, he would plead with folded hands with his mother who had tied up his wrists, and then, he would wipe away his tears, sniffling for all the world like a hurt little boy. The whole thing was utterly ridiculous, enough to make one burst with laughter.

The dance got over. I applauded and praised the performance.

'I have never seen a dance like yours, Dasharath,' said I. 'You dance very well indeed. All right, I exempt you from paying the tax, and here—I would like to give you from my side two rupees in appreciation. Excellent dancing!'

In another twelve days or so, when all the buying and selling related to the harvesting was over, all the migrant folks returned to their own homes. Only those who farmed the land stayed on. The stalls were pulled down, the dancers and the vendors left for other places to ply their trade. The wageworkers had stayed on simply to enjoy something of the celebration that was taking place after the harvest; now, they too, were ready to uproot themselves.

2

Returning to camp one day, I stopped by at Nakchhedi Bhakt's *khupri* to meet him and his family.

It was nearing evening. In the west, a huge red sun was slowly sinking into the deep green line of the forest. The sunsets here were so unreal, so beautiful, particularly in winter, that from time to time I would climb up Mahalikharoop and quietly wait for that astonishing event to take place.

Nakchhedi quickly got up when he saw me and saluted me. 'Manchi!' he called out to someone, 'Give Babuji here a place to sit.'

An elderly woman was to be seen inside the *khupri*; it was not hard to determine that she was Nakchhedi's wife. She was usually occupied with a host of outdoor chores—chopping and splintering wood, fetching water from the well in distant Bhimdas-tola and the like. Manchi was the girl-woman who had told me the story of her encounter with the wild elephants. She came now and laid out a mat woven of dried kash stalks for me.

'Babuji,' she said, laughing and moving her head in rhythm to that beautiful 'chhikachhiki' dialect peculiar to southern Bihar, 'What do you think of the fair you saw in our *baihar*? Didn't I tell you that there would be so much dancing and fun, and so many things would be sold? Wasn't it so? How long it has been since you have visited us, do sit down. We shall soon be on our way.'

I seated myself on the mat, spreading it over the still wet grass right in front of their doorway so that I might have a direct view of the setting sun. A washed-out red tinted the world around us. An indescribable peace and quietness had settled over the huge *baihar*.

I was perhaps a little late in responding to Manchi's many queries. She had come up with yet another question for me in the meantime, but I did not understand too well her 'chhikachhiki' dialect. In order to hide that I had not quite understood what she had just been telling me, I asked her, 'Will you be leaving tomorrow?'

'Yes, Babuji.'

'Where will you go?'

'We will go towards Purnea-Kishanganj.'

Then she asked me, 'Babu, how did you like the dancing and the other amusements? The singers who had come this time were quite good. There was a man who played the *dholak* with his mouth in Jhollu-tola one day, beneath the bakain tree; did you hear him? So wonderful it was, Babuji!'

Manchi was delighted with these shows exactly like a little girl. Now she sat down and began most enthusiastically to describe in detail all that she had seen and heard in the fair.

'Come, come,' said Nakchhedi, 'Babuji is a Calcuttan: he has seen and heard much more than you have. She loves this sort of thing, Babuji; we've stayed on for so long only for her sake. She said, "Let's spend some more time and enjoy all the sights and shows that will take place in the harvest ground." She's such a child, still!'

All these days I had not asked as to how Manchi was related to Nakchhedi, although I assumed she must be the old man's daughter. His words today left me in no doubt at all.

I asked him, 'Where have you married your daughter?'

'My daughter!' said Nakchhedi in astonishment, 'Where do I have a daughter, Huzoor?'

'Why, isn't Manchi your daughter?'

At my words, Manchi burst into laughter before anyone else. Nakchhedi's elderly wife too disappeared into the *khupri* covering her face with her sari-end.

Nakchhedi said in an offended tone, 'What do you mean, daughter, Huzoor! She is my second wife.'

'Oh!' I said.

For a while there was silence. I was so embarrassed that I couldn't find anything to say.

'Let me make a fire,' said Manchi, 'It's so cold.'

It was indeed very cold. As soon as the sun set, it felt as though the Himalayas had descended into our midst. The lower half of the western sky was still red, the upper half blue-black.

The twelve feet high dry kash a little away from the *khupri* flared up instantly as Manchi lit it. We went to sit by the blazing copse of kash.

'Babuji, she's still such a child,' said Nakchhedi, 'she's so fond of buying things. Just think of it, this time we must have got anything between eight to ten maunds of the mustard crop as wages, and she has already spent three maunds of that on fancy things. I told her, why do you buy such trifles with wages of sweat and blood? But she's such a child she won't listen. She starts crying. Well then, go ahead and buy the stuff, I say.'

An old man with a young wife, I mused, hardly has much of a choice.

Manchi said, 'Why, I've told you I'm not going to buy anything when they have a fair at the time of wheat harvest. Such wonderful things got so cheap—'

'Cheap!' said Nakchhedi angrily. 'Those shopkeepers and peddlers have all cheated her, like they cheat all the women—Huh, cheap! She's bought a comb for five seers of mustard, Babuji. And the year before, in the wheat granary at Tirashi Ratanganj—'

'Babuji,' broke in Manchi, 'let me fetch the things, I leave it for you to judge and tell me if they're cheap or not.'

Manchi had run off into the *khupri* even as she was speaking and came back with a woven kash basket with a lid. She opened the lid and one by one took out her purchases and exhibited them before me.

'Now, look at this *kankoi*, isn't it big? Can you ever get such a big comb for less than five seers? Isn't the colour just wonderful! Isn't it a precious piece? And now, just look at this bit of soap! Just smell it—they took five seers of mustard for this as well. Tell me, Babuji, isn't it cheap?'

How could I consider it cheap! The same bar of soap wouldn't cost more than an anna in the bazaars of Calcutta; five seers of mustard would at the very least be worth seven and a half annas. Simple countrywomen like her had no idea of prices, it was easy enough to trick them.

Manchi showed me many more items. In her delight she would show me first one thing and then quickly show me another. A ring with a false precious stone, a porcelain doll, a small enamelled dish, a bit of broad red ribbon and such like things. I discovered that all girls, from whatever country or culture, were fond of the same sort of things. There was not much difference between rustic Manchi's taste and that of her sophisticated sisters. The desire to collect and acquire, and to possess things was natural to both. Even if it did make old Nakchhedi angry!

I did not know then that Manchi had kept hid for the very last what she thought was the best buy of the lot.

She took it out now with a mixture of pride and joy and anxiously held it out to me for inspection.

It was a necklace of blue and yellow hinglaj.

The smile on her face was one of such intense pride and delight! Unlike her urban sisters, she had not learnt to hide her emotions; an innocent and unalloyed feminine spirit shone through beneath her sense of possession of these assorted things. There is little chance in our civilized society of being witness to such a frank expression of a woman's feelings.

'Now tell me, what do you think of it?'

'It's wonderful!'

'How much would it cost, do you think Babuji? They must be wearing such things in Calcutta as well?'

I do not wear a necklace of hinglaj in Calcutta. No one in Calcutta would wear one. However, I did not think that it would cost more than six annas, at the very most. 'You tell me,' I said to her, 'how much did it cost?'

'Seventeen seers of mustard he took. Isn't it a bargain?'

Was it any use telling her that she had been swindled? This was bound to happen in such remote places. Why should I destroy her exquisite pleasure in her purchases by telling her the truth and have Nakchhedi scold her for her foolishness?

Such trickery had been possible because of my own inexperience. I should have kept a stern eye on the prices being quoted by the vendors. Yet, I was new to the place, how was I to have known the way things ran here? As it was, I hadn't even known that a fair was held at the time the grain is threshed. I would have to ensure that it didn't happen the coming year.

The next day Nakchhedi left with his two wives and his children. Before he left, he came to my *khupri* to pay the revenue, and with him came Manchi. I saw that she had the necklace of hinglaj around her neck. 'We shall come again in the month of Bhadra to harvest the maize', she said. 'You will be here, won't you, Babuji? We pickle wild hartaki berries in Sravan—I shall bring some for you.'

I had liked Manchi very much and was saddened when she left.

ELEVEN

1

I had a very strange experience around this time.

News came to us that a huge forest of sal and of tendu which lay about twenty miles south of the Mohanpura Reserve Forest was going on the block at the Collectorate Auction. I quickly sent word to the head office and a telegram came back instructing me to bid for the forest of tendu from which bidis are made.

I was, however, unwilling to bid for the jungle without knowing exactly what we were going to buy and wished to see it for myself. As the day of the auction was imminent, I set off for the jungle the very next day after I had got the wire.

Some of my men had already started at the crack of dawn with boxes, bedding and various other bundles loaded on their head. We met up with them as they waited to cross the Karo on the border of the Mohanpura Forest. With us was Banowarilal, our patowari.

The Karo was a narrow mountain stream of knee-deep water that wound its way through stones and boulders. The two of us got off our horses—they could have stumbled with riders on them over the riverbed strewn with gravel and rocks. The sandbanks on both sides were of a bleached yellow colour. It was not possible to ride our horses over the sand, for we sank knee-deep into the sand as well. By the time we gained the lease-hold land on the other side, it was eleven in the afternoon. Banowari Patowari suggested, 'Let us cook here, Huzoor. We may not get any water after this stretch.'

On both sides of the river were virgin forests of kend, palash and sal, no huge trees, but dense and expansive forestland nevertheless. No sign of a human, anywhere.

Although we were done with our meal in the quickest possible time, by the time we set off once more it was already one o'clock.

The day was almost gone and we were still inside the forest. I thought it better not to go on ahead but to try and find a tree where we might pitch camp. Of course, we had passed a couple of rude settlements on the way— one was called Kulpal and the other Burudi— but that was around three in the afternoon. Had we known then that we would not be able to get out of the jungle by evening, we might have spent the night in either of those places. As it was, just before it got dark we moved into even thicker jungle! Where the jungle had been sparse, huge trees and bushes now crowded into the narrow track we were following. Where we presently stood there were only massive tall trees surrounding us, not a bit of sky was to be seen and the night was almost upon us.

It was beautiful wherever the jungle had thinned out a little. An unknown white flower grew in clusters illumining the top of the forest beneath the dark blue sky. For whose pleasure had such delicate beauty been laid out, so secluded from human eyes, so far away from the civilized world? 'These are flowers of the wild teuri, Huzoor,' Banowari informed me, 'they flower around this time of the year—wild creepers.'

Wherever one looked one saw only the tops of trees and thickets illuminated by the faintly bluish flowers of the wild teuri—exactly as if layers of freshly carded bluish cotton had been scattered randomly on the tree tops. I'd rein in the horse and stand still for long spells. Some parts of the forest looked so strange that it was unsettling. One was seized by feelings of vast distance and alienness, as though one was far from the civilized world, in a remote, unknown, mysterious and exquisitely beautiful part of the world with which no human had any contact, into which no human had the right of entry either. It was only a world of creepers, plants and trees and other living creatures.

Perhaps, we had been delayed because of my stopping every now and then to stare at these sights. Banowari Patowari, poor fellow, worked under my orders, so he couldn't very well protest outright. He must have been thinking though, A mad chap, this Bangali-babu! For how long will he be able manage the business of the estate?

The ten of us in the group took shelter beneath a big ashan tree. Banowari said, 'Let's make a big fire and huddle around it for warmth. Do not go tramping all over the place, this forest is dangerous at night.'

I sat on the camp chair beneath the tree. Before me was a wide stretch of the sky. It was not yet dark. All around us, high in the jungle, white flowers of the wild teuri blossomed in hundreds. Long grass, parched golden, grew right next to my camp chair. The fragrance of an unknown wild flower came wafting to me, enclosing me like the silver foil that dressed the icon of Durga at festival time. The freedom of these wild regions had brought a sensation of joy, of liberation, to my mind—not to be found anywhere but in such vast spaces, unpeopled and unspoilt. Only those who have experienced it may understand the exuberance of such an untrammelled life.

Just then, a coolie appeared to tell the patowari that he had gone to forage for dry branches in the jungle and had sighted something odd a little distance away from where we were. This wasn't the best spot to have struck camp— it was the haunt of ghosts and *peris*—it would have been better if we had gone elsewhere.

'Come, Huzoor,' said the patowari, 'let us find out what is this thing he has seen.'

After we had gone on for a while in the jungle, the coolie stopped and indicated a spot. 'It's over there; I shan't go any nearer,' he said.

Emerging from the dense vegetation of creepers and thorny bushes was a tall pole on which was carved a hideous face. It was scary enough in the twilight.

Undoubtedly, human hands had made it, but I could not understand how such a pole might come to be in a jungle where there was no human habitation. Nor could I make out how ancient it was.

The night passed. The next morning we reached our destination by nine. We were met by an employee of the present owner. He escorted me around the forest I had come to inspect. Suddenly, the tip of a stone pillar peeped out from the thick jungle on the other side of the dry nullah. It was exactly like the one I had seen last evening. It had the same hideous face carved on it.

Banowari Patowari was accompanying me; I showed him the pole. 'There are three or four more of those scattered in the jungle hereabouts,' said my escort who was a local man. 'They are pillars to mark the boundary.'

'How do you know they are pillars?'

'I've always been told so,' said the man. 'Besides, the descendant of those rulers is still around.'

I was exceedingly curious: 'Where is he?'

The man pointed with his finger, 'There, on the northern edge of the jungle is a small hamlet—that's where he lives. He's very highly regarded in these parts. I've heard that his forefathers were kings of the entire forest and mountain region—up to the Himalayas in the north, and Chhotanagpur in the south, the Kushi river on the east and Mungher in the west.'

I remembered then, Ganauri Teowari the schoolmaster had once told me that there was still a descendant of the tribal rulers of this region. All the tribes still looked upon him as their king. The local man, who was called Buddhu Singh, was an intelligent fellow. He had been in service for many years and I found him knowledgeable about the local history.

Buddhu Singh continued, 'These people fought the Mughal army when the Mughals were ruling the country. They disrupted their passage with their bows and arrows whenever the army passed through these forests en route to Bengal. Eventually, they lost their kingdom when the Mughal commanders, the *subedars*, started residing in Rajmahal. They come from a line of very courageous people; now there is nothing left. Whatever was left was all gone in the Santal Revolt of 1862.[12] The leader of the Santal Revolt is still alive— he is the present Raja. His name is Dobru Panna Birbardi. He is very old and very poor, but all the indigenous people of the land give him the respect due to a king. He's still regarded as a king, although he doesn't have a king- dom any more.'

I wished very much to meet the Raja.

If one went to meet the Raja, it was necessary to take a gift, a *nazar*. Not to give him the respect due to him would show a lack of sense of duty on my part.

By one in the afternoon I had bought some fruits and a couple of big chickens from the nearby hamlet. Around two, once I finished the work for which I had come, I said to Buddhu Singh, 'Come let's go to meet the Raja.'

Buddhu Singh did not appear to be equally keen on the meeting. 'What, will you go there?' he said surprised. 'He's not worthy enough for people such as you. It is true he's king of the uncivilized hill people, but he's not worthy enough to speak on equal terms with the likes of you—he's not that great, Babuji.'

I did not listen to him. Banowarilal and I set off for the capital, but we took Buddhu Singh along with us too.

The royal capital was a small place comprising not more than a score of households—little mud huts, roofed with rough tiles, the walls neatly plastered with mud: snakes, lotuses, creepers and other images had been etched on the walls. Little boys were busy playing and the women were engaged in domestic chores. The little girls as well as the slightly older ones were well built and healthy—every one of them beautiful and sweet looking. They all stared at me in surprise.

'Is the Raja here?' Buddhu Singh asked one of them in the local language.

The woman said that she hadn't seen him, but where else could he be but at home?

2

We went a little further into the village. I gathered from the expression on Buddhu Singh's face that we were now standing before the palace. The only difference between the royal dwelling and the other huts was that a stone wall encircled the former. The stone had been brought from the low hills just behind the hamlet. Many children were to be seen in the royal household, some very still very young: they wore bead necklaces, some strung from the beads of the neel fruit. Some of the children were very pretty looking. Buddhu Singh called out and a girl of sixteen or seventeen years came running out of the house. She was taken aback at seeing us, somewhat afraid too, it seemed from the expression in her eyes.

'Where is the Raja?' asked Buddhu Singh.

'Who is this girl?' I wanted to know from Buddhu Singh.

'The daughter of the Raja's grandson,' said he.

The Raja's longevity must have deprived many a young and old man from their claim to the royal seat.

'Come with me,' said the girl. 'Elder Uncle is sitting by the stones at the foot of the mountain.'

I thought to myself as we followed her, that whether one accepted it or not, this girl who was now showing us the way was indeed a princess—her ancestors had for long ruled over this forestland. She was their descendant.

'Ask the girl her name,' I said to Buddhu Singh.

'Her name is Bhanmati,' said he.

Bhanmati! What a lovely name! The Princess Bhanmati!

Bhanmati was a slim and healthy young girl. Her face was endearing and full of warmth. However, the garments she wore would not have been considered modest in civilized society. Also, her hair was dry and unruly, and she wore a garland of shells and beads around her neck. From far she pointed out a big bakain tree: 'Go ahead, Elder Uncle is sitting beneath the tree grazing the cattle.'

Grazing cattle! I almost jumped out of my skin. The king of this vast forestland, the leader of the Santal Revolt, Raja Dobru Panna Birbardi, grazing cattle!

But the girl had turned away before I could question her further. We soon gained the bakain tree and came across an old man engrossed in his smoke—a home-made cheroot of tobacco in a twist of tender sal leaves.

'Salaam, Rajasaheb,' said Buddhu Singh.

It appeared that Raja Dobru Pannu suffered from poor vision although he was not hard of hearing.

'Who is it, Buddhu Singh? Who is with you?' he asked.

'A Bangali-babu has come to meet you. He has brought you *nazar*, you have to accept it.'

I went forward and laid the chickens and the other things before him.

I said, 'You are the king of the land, I've come from very far to meet with you.'

Looking at his tall frame, I was sure that Raja Dobru Panna must have been very handsome in his youth. His face was marked by intelligence. The old man was delighted.

'Where is your home?' he asked, regarding me attentively.

'Calcutta.'

'Ah, that is very far away. It's a grand place, I'm told—Calcutta.'

'Have you never been there?'

'No. Is it possible for us to go to the cities? We are better off here in the jungle. Sit down. Where has Bhanmati gone? Bhanmati—'

The girl came running: 'What is it, Elder Uncle?'

'This Bangali-babu and the people with him will stay with us today, they will eat here.'

'No, no,' I protested, 'that's not right! We shall be off in a little while. Just to meet you ... about our staying on...'

'That is not possible, said Dobru Panna. Bhanmati, take these things away.'

At a sign from me, Banowarilal Patowari carried the things to the king's home, Bhanmati following him. I could not disregard the old man; I was filled with respect for him at first sight. The leader of the Santal Revolt, the brave descendant of an ancient royal race (albeit a primitive tribe), Dobru Panna, was requesting me to stay. The request was tantamount to an order.

It was obvious that Raja Dobru Panna was very poor. True, I had initially been shocked to find that he was grazing cattle, but later, I pondered that in the history of India many another king, mightier and more powerful than Raja Dobru Panna, had been forced to take up an occupation lowlier than grazing cattle.

The Raja himself made a cheroot of sal leaves and handed it to me. There were no matches: he lit a leaf from a little fire that burned near the tree and held the cheroot before me.

I said, 'You are part of an ancient royal race belonging to this land. It is a worthy thing to be able to meet with you, to have your *darshan*.'

Raja Dobru said, 'There's hardly anything left. We are of the solar dynasty, descendants of the Surya clan. These forests and the hills, all the earth, was once our kingdom. I have fought against the Company[13] when I was young. Now I am many years old. We lost our battle. Now there is nothing left.'

It looked like Raja Dobru did not keep himself informed of the affairs of the world beyond the limits of the forestland. I was about to reply when a young man came up to us.

'My youngest grandson, Jagru Panna,' said Raja Dobru. 'His father is away at present: he has gone to visit the Rani-saheb of Lachhmipur. Jagru, make arrangements for Babuji's meal.'

The young man had a body like a young sal tree, muscular and supple.

'Does Babuji eat porcupine-meat?' he asked.

Turning to his grandfather he said, 'I had laid a trap on the other side of the hills, two porcupines were caught last night.'

I was told that the Raja had three sons, and between them, the sons had ten children. All the members of this extended family lived together in the same village. Their livelihood was hunting and cattle grazing. Besides this, when other tribes living in the forests and hills in the area came to the Raja for settling quarrels and other disputes they brought with them a little tribute—milk, chickens, a goat, birds, fruits and the like.

'Do you have any farmland?' I asked Raja Dobru.

'That sort of thing is forbidden to our race,' Dobru Panna replied with some pride. 'The greatest honour lies in hunting, and of that, there was a time when hunting with spears was considered the most prestigious. Hunting with bows and arrows does not appease the gods, it is not something a brave does. Of course, nowadays anything goes. My eldest son has bought a gun from Mungher; I never touch it. Real hunting is done only with spears.'

Bhanmati came once more and placed a stone bowl before us.

'Rub yourselves with the oil,' said the Raja. 'After you are done, you can bathe—there's an excellent spring nearby.'

Once we had bathed, the Raja ordered that we should be taken to one of the rooms in the royal house.

Bhanmati brought rice and potatoes in a flat woven basket. Jagru skinned the porcupines and brought us the meat on tender sal leaves. Then Bhanmati came again with some milk and honey.

We had no brahman who could cook for us; Banowari sat down to peel the potatoes and I tried to get the fire going. It was quite difficult trying to light the fire only with big logs. After a few unsuccessful attempts on my part, Bhanmati quickly went and got an old dried up bird's nest. She shoved this into the fire and immediately, it kindled. Once she had done this, Bhanmati promptly moved back; she stood watching us from a distance. Bhanmati was a princess, but she was a very easy-going and unselfconscious one. Yet, she had a certain natural poise and an inherent sense of dignity.

Raja Dobru Panna sat continously at the door of the kitchen to ensure there was not the least lapse in hospitality. After the meal he told us, 'I do not have many rooms—your stay has been uncomfortable. There are still signs of the huge house that my royal forefathers had on the hilltop in the forest. I've heard from my father and grandfather that in ancient times our ancestors lived up there. But those are bygone days! Our ancestral god is still there.'

I was filled with curiosity: 'Would you have any objection, Rajasaheb, if we go up there once, just to see the place?'

'Why should one object! However, there is nothing much to be seen now. But come, I too shall come along. Jagru, come with us.'

I protested. I did not like the idea of dragging a ninety-two-year-old man up the hill. But my protests did not have any effect. Rajasaheb laughed, 'I often have to climb up the hill: the burial ground of our ancestors lies on the slopes of the hill. I have to go there on every full-moon night. Come, I shall show you the place.'

A low range of hills, known locally as the Dhannjhari, rose from the north-eastern corner, and as though making a sudden turn eastwards, had created a cleft beneath which was a valley. The forests on the hillside appeared to flow into the entire valley like a vast wave of green, like a waterfall cascading down the side of a mountain. The forest was sparse in these parts and was to be found only in patches: on the top of the trees was the line of blue hills on the horizon, probably in the direction of Ramgarh or Gaya. As far as the eyes could see, it was only the green tops of the forest, sometimes high with the foliage of big trees, sometimes low, only saplings of the sal and palash. We climbed up the hill following a narrow track.

Then we came to a place where there was a heap of huge stones planted crosswise, shaped exactly like cowries or grindstones. Beneath them lay a huge hole, such as potters have in their kiln to fire their pots or like a hole that a vixen makes in a field. A clump of sal saplings guarded the entrance to the hole.

'You will have to enter this hole,' said Raja Dobru. 'Come follow me. There is nothing to fear. Jagru, lead the way.'

I entered the hole, my heart in my mouth. For all I knew, there might be tigers or bears inside; if nothing, at least snakes.

After one had crawled along for a while it was possible to straighten up a bit. The darkness seemed impenetrable at first, but once the eyes got used to the lack of light, it wasn't so bad. We were standing inside a huge cave— a little more than twenty feet long and fifteen feet broad. In the northern wall was yet another fox-hole like opening which, I was told, led to another cave just like this one, but I wasn't keen to enter that one. The roof of the cave was not too high: if you stood straight, you could touch it with the tip of your outstretched hand. The cave had a musty smell, it was obviously the haunt of bats; foxes also frequented the cave, we were informed, besides wild creatures like civets and polecats.

'Huzoor,' whispered Banowari Patowari to me at this point, 'let's get out of here quickly. Don't linger too long inside.'

This was Dobru Panna's ancestral palace-fort.

In fact, it was a big-sized natural cave. In ancient times, it must have been possible to seek shelter inside the cave and withstand the onslaught of the enemy.

The Raja said, 'The cave has yet another secret entrance, but I am not allowed to reveal it to anyone. It is handed down only to members of our family. Of course, no one lives in the cave any more, but the tradition has continued in our family.'

Only after we came out of the cave did I breathe freely.

Then, when we had climbed a considerable height we came across an immense banyan tree whose innumerable branches had dropped down like pillars, some slender, others thick and heavy. The tree was spread over an area covering a bigha of land.

'Please be kind enough to take off your shoes,' said Raja Dobru Panna.

In the shadow of the banyan there were huge upright slabs of stone, shaped like grinding stones.

This was their royal ancestral burial ground the Raja told us: beneath each of those stones was the grave of a member of the royal family. The stones were spread all over the land beneath the canopy of the immense banyan tree. Some stones, held in the pincer-like grip of roots descending from the banyan tree, seemed ancient; in other places, the stones had quite disappeared into the tangle of branches. You could tell how ancient the ground was from these signs.

Raja Dobru told us that earlier, there had been no banyan tree in the area, but all sorts of other trees. A small banyan sapling had grown to these immense proportions killing off all the other trees in the process. Now, the banyan had itself become so old that the original tree was long since gone. The trunk we now saw had come down from the original tree at some time. 'If you were to cut through the trunk,' said Raja Dobru, 'you would find many other burial stones that have now been pushed underground. That's how old this place is.'

As I stood there beneath the spreading banyan, I was filled with a sensation that was quite new, one that I had not experienced when I met either the Raja (the Raja had seemed to me like any old Santal coolie), or the princess (I had not noticed any difference between her and any healthy young Ho or Munda tribal woman); and, certainly not when I saw the palace (that had seemed ghost-ridden and likely to be haunted by snakes); but once on top of the hills, the burial ground of olden times shadowed in the arms of the huge and ancient banyan aroused in me a strange and wondrous feeling.

The place had an indescribable mystery and solemnity. The day was almost gone: golden sunshine shone on the leaves, the branches and on the other peaks of the Dhannjhari range. The lengthening shadows of the afternoon lent an added element of mystery and grandeur to the burial ground.

'The Valley of the Kings' in Thebes, the ancient burial ground of the Egyptians, has now become the sporting ground of tourists from all over the world. Publicity and massive advertising ensure that the big hotels in the area are filled to capacity with seasonal tourists. Time had once shrouded and kept obscure the Valley of the Kings; now, smoke from expensive cigarettes and cigars darken it. But no less mysterious and innately dignified was this burial ground of kings belonging to the indigenous, non-Aryan people, that has always hidden itself in the shadows of the dense forests and would continue to do so. Their burial ground lacked the pretension, the polish and the wealth and splendour of the works of the wealthy Egyptian Pharaohs, for they had been poor people. Their civilization and culture, like that of ancient man's, was rude and simple; a child-like mentality had created that palace of caves, the royal burial grounds, and planted those poles to mark the boundary. As I stood on the hilltop beneath that immense tree, it was as though in the shadows of the afternoon I could glimpse quite another world, in comparison to which the Puranic and Vedic age seemed like time present . . .

I saw the nomadic Aryans cross over the north-west mountain ranges and come down like a torrent into an ancient India ruled by primitive non-Aryan tribes. Whatever history that India had, became subsequently the history of this Aryan civilization—the history of the vanquished non-Aryan races was not written down anywhere, or perhaps, it was written only in such secret mountain caves, in the darkness of forests, in the lines of calcified skeletal remains. The victorious Aryan had never been anxious to decipher that script. To this day, the vanquished wretched tribes continue to be ignored, shunned and disdained. Aryans, proud of their civilization, had never spared them a glance, never sought to understand their way of life and they do not try to do so even now. Banowari and I were representatives of that victorious race; old Dobru Panna, the youthful Jagru and the maiden Bhanmati those of the suppressed race. Both races now stood together, one facing the other, in the dark evening. I, with the pride of the Aryans, was looking upon Dobru Panna of royal lineage as an old Santal, Princess Bhanmati as a Munda coolie woman, the royal palace that they cherished and were so proud of, as an ill-ventilated, ill-lit cave, a den of spirits and snakes. Before my eyes that evening was enacted the great tragedy of history. The actors of that drama comprised the defeated, poor, disdained king of non-Aryan origins—Dobru Panna, the young princess Bhanmati, the young prince Jagru Panna on one side, and on the other, myself, my patowari, Banowarilal and my guide, Buddhu Singh.

We came down from the hill before the evening shadows covered the royal cemetery and the spreading banyan.

On the way, we passed by an upright stone, daubed with vermilion. Around it were marigold and sandhyamani flowers, obviously planted by human hand. Yet another big stone stood before us, and that too, was daubed with vermilion. It was a sacred space, dedicated long long ago, I was told, to the ancestral god of the royal family. Formerly, humans were sacrificed—right here—on the big stone; pigeons and chickens were offered these days.

'What is the name of the god?' I asked.

'Tarbaro,' replied Raja Dobru, 'the god of wild buffaloes.'

I recalled the story told by Ganu Mahato last winter.

'Tarbaro is a powerful god,' said Raja Dobru. 'Were it not for him, the hunters in their greed for hide and horns would have surely decimated the wild buffaloes. It is he who preserves the herds. Just before they are about to plunge into a trap, he stands before the herd, his arms spread out—so many have seen him.'

No one in the civilized world reveres this god of an ancient forest people, no one knows of him. Yet, as I sat in the shadow of the hills, in the exquisite beauty and mystery of the forest abounding with wild animals, I felt it all to be true.

Much later, when I had come back to Calcutta, I saw once in Burrabazar in the frightful heat of Jaishtha, a cartman from the western regions whip his two bullocks mercilessly with a leather thong. Alas Tarbaro! I thought that day, this is not the forestland of Chhotanagpur or Madhya Pradesh; how will your kindly hands save these tortured beasts? This is twentieth-century Calcutta, of Aryan lineage. Here, you are as helpless as the defeated Raja Dobru.

I set off immediately after the day was over in order to take the bus from Nauada to Gaya. Banowari returned to camp with our horses. I met Princess Bhanmati once more. She stood waiting for us at the door of the royal house with a bowl of buffalo milk.

TWELVE

1

Raju Parey informed the katcheri that a herd of wild pigs was attacking his crop of cheena grass every night. He was afraid of a couple of old tuskers in the lot and was unable to do much more than beat on a tin cannister; unless the katcheri did something to stop this assault, nothing would be left of his crops.

That evening, arming myself with my gun I set off for his fields. Raju's hut and his bit of farmland lay deep in the dense forests of Narha-baihar. It was still an unpeopled area and very little of the land had yet been made cultivable; there was much to fear from the depredations of wild animals.

I found Raju working on his land. He came running up as soon as he spotted me. He took the reins of my horse and led it to a nearby haritiki tree where he tethered the animal.

'I don't see much of you these days, Raju,' said I. 'Why don't you come to the katcheri sometime?'

All around Raju's hovel was a forest of kash, with an occasional kend or haritaki tree. How did he manage to live in this inhospitable forestland with not a soul to talk to at the end of his day? Here was a strange sort of fellow!

'Huzoor, do I have the time to go anywhere?' said Raju. 'I'm worn out trying to guard the crops. And then, I have the buffaloes to look after.'

I was about to ask him how he could be so busy looking after only three buffaloes and farming a plot of a bigha and a half that he didn't have the time to go anywhere. But, if one were to go by the list of daily activities that Raju volunteered to narrate, it really did seem that he wouldn't have a moment to spare. Work in the fields, grazing his cattle, milking them, making butter, his rituals and worship, reciting the Ramayana, cooking and running the household—the list left me breathless. What a hard-working man! On top of everything, he had to stay up nights to beat on the canisters and fend off the pigs.

'Exactly when do the pigs come?' I asked.

'There's no saying when, Huzoor,' said he, 'but they do come every night. Just wait for a while, and you will see how many of them will turn up.'

What intrigued me most however, was how did Raju manage to live in such a lonely spot? I was obliged to put the question to him.

'Babuji, it has become a habit,' was Raju's reply. 'I've been living in the same manner for many years, it doesn't seem a hard life to me; on the contrary, I quite enjoy my days. I work all day long, sing my devotional songs every evening, praise the lord, and so the days pass.'

I discovered new worlds in people like Raju or Ganu Mahato or Jaipal (and there are many such others who live in these forests), worlds that I had not been aware of.

I knew there was a particular worldly item that Raju was terribly addicted to—he was exceedingly fond of drinking tea; yet, I had no idea where he would manage to get the wherewithal to make tea in the jungle. So, coming to call on him, I had brought along some sugar and milk. Now I said to him, 'Raju, make us some tea. I've brought everything we need.'

Raju filled a huge lota capable of holding several seers of water and put it on the fire. He seemed delighted. Soon the tea was ready, but excepting for a small bowl of bell metal, there was no other vessel to be had. Raju poured out my tea in the bowl while he drank from the huge lota.

Raju had studied some Hindi, but he had no idea of the world outside the jungle. He had heard of a place called Calcutta, but had no idea where it was. To him, Bombay or Delhi was as vague and unreal a place as the moon. He could count Purnea as the only city he had seen, and that too, on a short visit.

'Have you seen a motor-car, Raju?'

'No, Huzoor. I've heard it moves without being pulled by a horse or a cow and lets off smoke. I'm told that these days many of them are to be seen in Purnea. I haven't been to Purnea for many years though; we are poor folks and it costs money to live in the city.'

I asked Raju if he was interested in going to Calcutta. If he was, I would take him there on a visit. He wouldn't need to spend any money.

Raju replied, 'A city is an evil place; I'm told that it's the haunt of thieves, gamblers and thugs. They tell me that you lose caste if you go there. They are all wicked out there. One of my countrymen had gone to a hospital in a city, to get his leg treated. The doctor begins cutting his leg with a knife and asks him, "Well, how much are you going to pay me?" He says, "Ten rupees." Then the doctor starts to cut some more into his leg. "Now tell me," he asks again, "how many rupees are you going to give?" "I'll give you five more rupees, Doctor saheb, please don't cut any more," says he. "That won't do," says the doctor, and begins to cut again. He was a poor man, but the more he cried and begged, the more the doctor cut with his knife, and so it went on, until the whole leg was just cut off. Oh! What a horrible business it was, Huzoor, imagine!'

It was a hard job controlling my laughter as I listened to this story. I remembered that this was the same Raju who on seeing a rainbow come up in the sky had once told me, 'This rainbow that you see Babuji—it always rises from a termite heap. I've seen it with my own eyes.'

We were drinking our tea sitting beneath a big ashan tree that was next to Raju's *khupri*. Wherever you looked, you could only see the dense jungle and kend, amloki, clumps of bahera creepers in flower; the flowers filled the evening wind with their sweet mild scent. It was a rare experience in one's life, I felt, to drink tea in such surroundings. Where would I find such a forest, such a kash-hut enfolded in the forest, and a fellow being such as Raju? The experience was as strange as it was rare.

I said to him, 'Raju, why do you not bring your wife here? You wouldn't have to worry about cooking every day.'

'She is dead,' said Raju. 'It has been almost eighteen years since she died and I have not been able to settle down at home since then.'

It was difficult to imagine that there had been a romance in Raju's life, but the story that Raju told me following this exchange made me feel that the word was appropriate enough.

Raju's wife was named Sarju (the local variant of Sarayu). When Raju was eighteen years old, and Sarju fourteen, Raju had gone to study grammar in the *tole* run by Sarju's father in Shyamlal-tola, in northern Dharampur.

'For how long did you study there?' I asked him.

'Not very long,' said Raju, 'for just about a year, but I never sat for the exam. That is where we first met and then, little by little . . .'

Out of deference to me Raju just coughed a little and stopped at this point.

'And then, carry on . . .' I said in an encouraging tone.

'But Huzoor, her father being my teacher, it became difficult to speak to him of this matter. One day—it was the festival of Chhat—Sarju had gone to the Kushi to bathe with her girlfriends; she was wearing a sari dyed yellow, and I . . .'

Raju coughed and fell silent again.

'Carry on, not to worry,' I encouraged him yet again.

'I hid myself behind a tree to watch her. The reason being that in the last few days I had not seen much of her, there was matchmaking going on already with some one else. The group of girls went singing—you know Babuji that during the Chhat Festival the girls go singing in a group to the river and set afloat the *chhat* in the water! Then, as they went singing towards the river, they passed me by and she saw me standing behind the tree. She smiled at me and so did I. I gestured to her and asked her to stay behind and she shook her hand and said not now, on our return.'

As he was saying this Raju's fifty-two-year-old visage took on the shy expression of a twenty-year-old lover and a far off dreamy look came over his face—as though his companionless ancient heart was seeking out the sweet fourteen-year-old of his first love.

He was weary living all by himself in the dense forest. The one whom he now liked to think of, whose company his soul thirsted for, was that little maiden Sarju who was not any more on this earth.

I was rather enjoying his story. 'And then?' I asked eagerly.

'Then, we met on the way back. She fell behind her group a bit. "Sarju," I told her, "I am suffering deeply: I'm unable to see you or meet you, I know

I shan't be able to continue with my studies; and why should I suffer without any reason; I'm thinking of leaving the *tole* by the end of the month." Sarju started weeping. "Why don't you ask my father?" she said. Sarju's tears made me desperate. What I otherwise would never have dared to tell my teacher, I blurted out one day to him. There was no obstacle to our marriage—we were of the same caste and everything. And so, we were married.'

Perhaps it was a rather simple and and innocent sort of romance, something I might have laughed off as a rustic idyll, a pre-marital courtship of a feeble tenor, had I heard it amidst the din of city life. But in these surroundings, I was captivated by its singular charm. I realized that day the great mystery that lay in the story of how a man and a woman had come together in this life.

By the time I had finished drinking tea, the evening was gone and a pale moonlight enveloped us. The moon was in the sixth or seventh day.

I picked up my gun. 'Come Raju,' I said, 'let's find out how many pigs have come to raid your crops today.'

There was a big tunth tree on on end of the field. 'Huzoor, you will have to climb this tree,' said Raju. 'I put up a *machan* this morning on one of its forked branches.'

I found this quite a problem. I had given up climbing trees for some time now. Besides, it was already dark. Raju tried to encourage me: 'It won't be a problem, Huzoor. I've driven in bamboo stakes into the trunk and there are lots of branches along the way—it's a really easy climb.'

I handed over the gun to Raju and using the branches as footholds climbed up to the *machan* and settled myself there. Raju followed me with effortless ease. The two of us sat side by side keeping our eyes on the ground.

The moonlight grew stronger. Through the fork of the tunth tree I could see the tops of the forest, some of it distinct and the rest hazy. This was yet another new experience for me.

A little later, a pack of foxes began howling from the forest around us. Just then a blackish sort of animal ran out of the southern part of the thick forest and entered Raju's field.

'Look, Huzoor!' cried out Raju.

I aimed my gun and held it tightly ready to shoot, but when the animal came closer, the moonlight revealed that it was a neelgai and not a boar.

I did not feel inclined to shoot a neelgai and Raju shouted, 'Go away! Begone!' As the animal ran back into the forest I fired a blank shot.

Two hours passed. From the same southern part of the jungle a wild cockerel crowed. I had thought I would get the big-tusked old boar, but not even a pipsqueak of a pig showed up. It had been stupid of me to have fired the blank after the neelgai.

'Climb down, Huzoor', said Raju, 'I will get your meal ready.'

'What meal do you mean? I am off to the katcheri—it is not even ten yet. I can't stay on here: I shall have to set off tomorrow morning to check on the work going on at the survey camp.'

'Do stay behind for a meal, Huzoor.'

'It won't be safe to go through the Narha-baihar jungle if I delay any longer. Let me set off right away. You mustn't mind, Raju.'

While mounting my horse I asked him, 'You won't mind will you, if I come now and then to drink tea with you?'

'How can you say such a thing!' cried Raju. 'I live all by myself in such a jungle, and I'm a poor man. You love me, so you bring tea and sugar and we make tea and drink it together. You must not say such things and shame me, Babuji.'

Raju was rather good-looking even at this age: he must have been a handsome fellow in his youth. Sarju, his teacher's daughter, had shown her discrimination when she was attracted to her father's young and handsome pupil.

It was late at night. I was swept along the plain. The moon was gone. No light anywhere. Instead, an eerie silence as though I had been exiled to a deserted and unknown planet. Scorpio shimmered as it rose on the horizon and in the blackness above my head, the sky held innumerable stars in its clasp. The silent forests of Lobtulia-baihar lay below me, the crest of wild jhau barely visible in the faint light of constellations, in the hesitant darkness. Somewhere, far away, the foxes howled the hour, and even further, the border of the Reserve Forest looked like a long dark black range of hills. There was no other sound but the monotonous kir-r-r-r-r made by an insect. If you listened very attentively, you might have caught the cries of a couple of other insects along with this one. I was struck by the exquisite romance of this open life, the joy of such an intimate relationship with nature. Above all, a certain ambiguous, indefinite, unpronounced mystery—I do not quite know what sort of a mystery—but this I know, that since leaving the forestlands, I have never again experienced it. On a silent and lonely night such as this, one could imagine the gods whose home lies in the constellations, rapt in creation. Their imagining would bring forth in the far future, millions of new universes, new beauty, the seeds of lives yet unborn. They are mysterious apparitions, perceived only by one who spends his time immersed in an unquenchable thirst for knowledge, whose being rejoices and glories in the vastness and the minuteness of the universe, and one in whom the petty grievances of the present have disappeared in the hope of a longer journey through many lifetimes . . .

nayamatma balaheenen labhya[14]

Those who had given up their lives in snowstorms and blizzards in making the Everest ascent had experienced the immensity of the lord of the universe. When Columbus stood, day after day, on the shore of the Azores, seeking to read the news of the unknown continent across the vast ocean from bits of sea borne driftwood—he had understood something of the playful strength of the universe. Those who sit at home nursing their hookahs, discussing the wedding of their neighbour's daughter, busy trying to outcaste their fellow being for offences by denying him community services of the washerman or the barber are themselves denied insight into the mysteries of the universe.

2

The survey was on along the forests and the hills on the northern banks of the Michhi. I have been camping here for the last ten days or so. I probably have to stay on for another ten or twelve days.

This was a spot quite far away from our estate, but close to the kingdom of Raja Dobru Panna. I've called it his kingdom, but of course, Raja Dobru was a king without a kingdom; it would perhaps be more correct to say that I was close to where he lived.

It was a splendid place: a valley with a wide mouth narrowing like a funnel at the end, and range of hills encircling it on the west and east. The undulating valley, shaped like a horseshoe, was right in the middle. It was partly forested with thorny bamboos and numerous other trees and in some parts strewn with pebbles and boulders. Numerous waterfalls and springs came down from the north and flowed out from its mouth. The forest was particularly thick on both sides of the water; in the last few years, I had come to know that it was just the sort of place where a tiger might have his lair. There were deer of course, I had heard wild fowl crowing around two at night and I had also heard foxes howling, but so far, I had neither seen nor heard a tiger.

To the east, in the very heart of the hill, was an immense cave. At the mouth of the cave stood a far-spreading ancient banyan tree, rustling and quivering in the wind at all hours of the day and night. On an afternoon when the sky above was blue, this cave and the deserted wooded valley led one to recall ancient times when, perhaps, this very cave might have been a palace of an ancient tribe, like the dwelling place of the forefathers of Raja Dobru Panna. Something had been carved on the walls of the cave, some pictures—now extremely faint, almost impossible to decipher. The earthern floor, the stone walls, the very air of the cave had absorbed the laughter of many forest dwellers, men and women, their joys and sorrows, the unwritten history of many tears shed in the life of a barbaric society—it was rather nice to imagine all of this.

A little further away from the mouth of the cave, by the side of a spring, was an open space where a Gond family had made their home. There were two small huts, one slightly bigger than the other, thatched with leaves, with a fencing of twigs culled from the forest. They had built a stove of stones in front of the huts. The hut they lived in was under the shade of a big wild badam tree. The yard was almost entirely covered with the dry leaves that had fallen off the tree.

They had two young girls, one about sixteen and the other fourteen years old. They were dark as ebony, but their faces expressed a simple beauty and shone with good health. Every morning the girls went up the hill to graze the few buffaloes they owned and were down before evening fell. I would see them coming back home with the animals when I would return to my camp for my tea.

One day, the elder girl stood waiting by the road and sent her younger sister to my camp. She came up to me and greeted me, 'Salaam Babuji. Do you have a bidi?' she asked, 'My sister would like one.'

'Do you smoke bidis?'

'I don't, but my sister does. Do give us one, Babuji, do you have one?'

'I don't have a bidi. I have a cheroot, but I shan't give that to you. It's too strong, you won't be able to smoke it.'

The girl went back. After a little while I went over to their home.

The head of the house was somewhat amazed to see me come to his home, but he courteously made a seat for me. The girls had just sat down to a meal of ghato; they were eating it off sal leaf plates. It was simply plain, unseasoned boiled maize. Their mother was cooking something on the fire. A couple of children played nearby.

The father was over fifty. He was a healthy and able-bodied man. I asked him where he was from. 'Siuni district,' said he. They had been here for the past year because there was enough drinking water here as well as pasture for his animals in the hills. Besides, it was very easy to use the bamboo that grew here to make all sorts of containers and baskets—*dhamas, chupris*, as well as hats. They made a little bit of money selling these things at the Akhilkucha fair at the time of Shivratri.

'How long do you plan to stay here?' I asked him.

'As long as one may wish to Babuji. But I must say we really like this place a lot, otherwise we hardly ever stay in any one place for as long as a year. There's one other good thing about the place—plenty of custard apple trees on the hills. In the month of Ashwin, my girls would bring down at least a couple of baskets of the fruit they'd picked while they were grazing cattle, and we lived for two months just on those custard apples. You could say we live here because we're so greedy for those apples. You can ask them yourself.'

The elder girl said, while she continued to eat, with a glow on her face, 'Oooh, there's a special spot in the corner of the hill on the east—so many wild custard apples! The fruits ripen and simply fall to the ground and there's no one to eat any. We pick up baskets full of the stuff.'

Just then someone came walking out from the thick forest saying as he came to a stop before the hut, 'Sita-Ram, Jai Sita-Ram—can you give me some fire?'

'Please come in, Babaji, sit down,' said the head of the family welcomingly.

It was an old sadhu with matted hair and all. He had in the meantime spotted me, and now stood to one side, somewhat surprised and perhaps made somewhat afraid too, at my presence.

'Pranam, Sadhu-babaji,' I said greeting him in the customary way.

He blessed me in turn; nevertheless, he still looked apprehensive.

'And where does Babaji live?' I asked him, to put him at his ease.

The father answered on his behalf, 'He lives in the very thick of the jungle where those two hills meet—in that corner. He's been living there for many years now.'

The old sadhu had sat down. 'How long have you been here?' I asked him.

'About fifteen years, Babu-saheb.' He was speaking freely now.

'Alone, I suppose? I'm told there are tigers in these parts; aren't you afraid?'

'Who else will stay with me Babu-saheb? I meditate on the Eternal Spirit—how is one to get on if one is afraid. Tell me Babu-saheb, how old do you think I am?'

I looked at him carefully and said, 'About seventy.'

'No, Babu-saheb,' he replied with a laugh, 'more than ninety. Ten years I lived in a jungle near Gaya. Then the rent collectors began cutting down the jungle and little by little settlements came up. I ran away. I can't stay where there are too many people.'

'Sadhu-babaji,' said I, 'there's a cave nearby. Why don't you live in the cave?'

'Why one, there are any number of caves in this hill. Where I live on the other side, it's not quite a cave but almost like one. I mean it has a ceiling and walls on two sides—only the front is open.

'What do you eat? Do you beg?'

'I don't go out anywhere, Babu-saheb. The Eternal Spirit gets me something or the other. I eat the boiled core of bamboos, and there's a fruit in the forest that's very sweet, like red potatoes—I eat that. The jungle is full of ripe gooseberries and custard apples. The gooseberrries I have a lot of: if you have them everyday you don't age all of a sudden, but stay young for long. When the people from the village come to visit me, they leave behind some milk, sattu and bhura. And so one gets by.'

'Have you ever had to face a tiger or a bear?'

'No, never. However, I once saw a monster of a python in this jungle. It was lying completely immobilized—as thick as a palm tree, black as thunder, green and red markings all over its body. The eyes were burning like live charcoal. That one still lives in this jungle. That time it was lying near the edge of the water perhaps hoping to catch a deer. Now it lies hidden in some cave or the other. Well Babu-saheb, I must be off now, it's getting on to be night.'

The sadhu went off with his fire. I was told that every now and then he would come here for some light and have a chat with them.

It had fallen dark; a hazy moonlight shrouded us. The valley was filled with a strange silence; there was no other sound but that of water gurgling from a neighbouring spring and the sudden cry of a couple of wild fowls.

I came back to my tent. Clusters of fireflies glowed around a huge simul tree which lay in my path, encircling it in slow spirals from top to bottom and then climbing up yet again, tracing a variety of geometric paths in the light and dark air.

3

To this place came the poet Venkateshwar one day. He must have been over forty. A tall thin man, wearing a coat of black serge and a none-too-clean dhoti, his rough hair flying any which way.

I thought he was looking for a job. 'What do you want?' I asked.

'I have come with the desire to see Babuji (he did not say Huzoor). My name is Venkateshwar Prasad. I come from Bihar province, Patna district. I live in Chakmaki-tola, three miles away.'

'I see. Well, what brings you here?'

'I should like to tell you . . . with Babuji's kind permission. I hope I am not wasting your time?'

I still believed that the man had come for a job. He had gained my respect however, by not addressing me as 'Huzoor'. 'Why don't you sit down, you've walked a long way in the heat,' I said to him.

I noted another thing about him: his Hindi was refined, not the sort of Hindi that I could speak. My work had to do with the guards and peons and my rustic subjects; such Hindi as I possessed, had been put together from their mix of local speeches along with the odd Bangla idiom. I'd not even heard such refined and cultivated Hindi as this person spoke; there was no question of my speaking it. I spoke therefore, with some caution: 'Please tell me the reason for your coming here.'

'I've come to recite my poems to you,' said he.

I was taken aback. Well might he be a poet, but what could have possibly urged him to seek me out in the jungle and recite poetry?

'Ah, you are a poet? I'm delighted! I shall listen with pleasure to your poetry. But how did you come to know of me?'

'I live about three miles away—just over that hill. The people in our village were talking about a Bangali-babu who has come from Calcutta. People like you respect learning, because you are learned yourselves. The poet has said:

vidvatsu satkavivacha labhate prakashang
chhatreshu kutumalsamang trinavjadeshu[17]

Venkateshwar Prasad recited his poem to me. It was an elaborate poem and had something to do with a ticket checker, a booking clerk, a station master, and a guard and assorted railway personnel. The poem did not appear to be of a high order. However, I do not wish to be unfair to Venkateshwar Prasad. I could not follow his language very well—in fact, to be absolutely honest, there was very little that I followed. Nevertheless, from time to time I made encouraging sounds or indicated agreement with a particular line.

Time flowed on. Venkateshwar Prasad did not stop reciting his poetry. He gave no indication of departing.

He stopped only after a couple of hours. He turned a smiling face to me and demanded, 'How did Babuji like it?'

'Excellent,' I said. 'I've very rarely heard such poetry. Why don't you send your work to a periodical?'

Venkateshwar replied with some sorrow, 'Babuji, everyone here calls me mad. Do you think there are people here who understand poetry? It has been very satisfying to me that I could recite some to you today. One has to read one's poetry only to the connoisseur. As soon as I came to know of you, I felt I must catch you for a reading.'

Finally, he left. But the very next evening he was back and pleading with me to visit his home in the neighbouring village, at least once. I could not put off his entreaties and found myself accompanying him to Chakmaki-tola.

It was late afternoon. The long shadows of hills lay across the fields of wheat and barley ahead of me. A sort of peace had fallen all around; flocks of sillis were alighting on the clumps of thorny bamboos and the village children bustled around a spring trying to catch fish.

Inside the village the houses lay cheek by jowl, the roofs almost piling one over the other. Many houses did not even have a courtyard. Venkateshwar Prasad took me to a fair-sized thatched house. The front room opened out into the street; I was made to sit in this room on a wooden cot. A little later, I had a glimpse of the poet's wife when she came to serve me food—some *dahi-vadas* and fried maize. She sat herself down in a corner of that same wooden cot but did not speak, although she had not veiled herself. She would have been about twenty-four with a nice complexion and a peaceful expression on her face. The poet's wife might not have been a beauty, but certainly, she was not ugly. There was a certain innocence and grace in her movements.

I noticed something else about the poet's wife—her health. I wondered why it was that wherever I had gone to in these parts, the women invariably seemed to be much healthier than their Bengali sisters are. I've never come across as many women in Bengal of the kind I met here—not fat, rather, quite tall, slim and lithe. The poet's wife was one such.

A little later, she placed a bowl of yogurt made of buffalo milk on one side of the cot and then withdrew behind the door. Venkateshwar Prasad went to her side as soon as he heard the iron chain being rattled, and then he came back to inform me smilingly, 'My wife says that you have become our friend, and one has to cool down a friend—the yogurt has a lot of chili and dry ginger powder!'

'If that be the case,' said I with a laugh, 'I propose that the three of us share the yogurt, then all of us will end up crying.' From behind the door came the laughter of the poet's wife. I wasn't about to yield and made sure that all of us had some of the yogurt.

A little later she went indoors and came back with another plate and this she placed once more on one side of the cot. This time she spoke in a low and playful tone, clearly addressing her words to me: 'Tell Babuji, that now he must soothe his throat with these home-made sweets.'

What beautiful chaste Hindi she spoke.

I really loved listening to the particular strain of Hindi that women spoke in these parts. Because I myself did not speak the language well, I was especially drawn to all forms of spoken Hindi. It was not bookish literary Hindi; but here—in the hills, forests and villages, amidst the unfolding fields of wheat and barley irrigated by the mobile leather *rahat* towed in circles by bullocks, where the flocks of balihans, silli and egrets flying towards the bluish hills traced snaky patterns in the sky suggesting endless spaces, in the late afternoon as the shadows lengthened with the setting sun—here, the abruptly ending, half broken off forms of speech, the unfamiliar verb endings that one heard spoken specially by women, was the language I was most drawn to.

I suddenly addressed the poet: 'Will you please read out to me a couple of your poems?'

Venkateshwar Prasad's face glowed with excitement. He had written a poem about a rural love story and he now recited this. A young man on one side of a small canal kept guard over a field of maize; every day, on the other side, a girl came to fetch water, cradling a pot in the crook of her arm. The boy thought she was very beautiful. While she was there he would turn the other way and whistle a song, chase his goats and cattle, darting an occasional look at the girl. Very often, their glances met. The girl would immediately look away, overcome with shyness. Every day, the boy thought that he would certainly call out to the girl the next day and speak to her. He thought of her constantly when he was home. But time went by, the days came and went—and he never did say what he wished to say. Then, one day, the girl did not come; days, weeks and months went by, but the girl he had come to know by sight everyday, never came back. Every evening, the boy went back home from the fields in despair, too timid to ask anyone about her. Finally, he had to leave behind his village and go elsewhere in search of a job. Many years have gone by. But the boy has not been able to forget the beautiful young girl by the banks of the stream.

I listened to the poem in the twilight hour when the evening had almost turned to night and kept my eyes on the distant range of blue hills and the immense fields of crops. I wondered if it was not Venkateshwar Prasad's own experience. The poet's wife was called Rukma—there had been another poem by that name which he had recited to me earlier—I now wondered if, despite having such a good looking and talented Rukma by his side, a youthful grief did not still live on in his heart?

While he was escorting me back to my tent Venkateshwar pointed out to a big banyan tree on the way, 'You see this tree, Babuji? We had an assembly beneath this very tree; many poets had come to read out their works. Such a gathering is called a 'mushaira' in these parts. I too, had been invited. Ishariprasad Dubey from Patna—you recognize Ishawariprasad? A very talented man, edits the magazine *Doot*—and is himself a good poet too—he treated me most courteously.'

I realized that this had been the one and only time in Venkateshwar's life that he had been invited to stand before an assembly and recite his poems. It was the greatest honour he had ever known; it had become a memorable day for him.

THIRTEEN

1

I was on my way back to my own estate after a gap of almost three months. The survey was finally completed.

Eleven miles of road. This was the road I had taken that time to get to the fair held at the Autumn equinox—the forest of sal and palash, the open fields strewn with rocks, the uneven hills. After I had gone on for a couple of hours a dark line appeared on the horizon—Mohanpura Reserve Forest.

It was a familiar scene, but one I had not seen for the last three months. I have somehow become bound to Narha-baihar and Lobtulia and it is almost painful to stay away from them for too long, as though I had been in foreign lands. Although the limits of Lobtulia was still some seven or eight miles away, like the return of a native I could feel happiness welling up inside me.

They had cleared quite a bit of the jungle at the foot of a small hill to raise kusum flowers and now they were ripening; wage labourers were reaping in the fields. I was riding past the crops when someone called out, 'Babuji, O Babuji—Babuji!'

I looked around to find Manchi. Surprised and pleased, I reined in my horse and Manchi ran up to my horse, all smiles, sickle in hand. 'I knew it was you from far away because of the horse,' she exclaimed. 'Where had you gone, Babuji?'

Manchi was just the same, if anything—healthier. The kusum flowers had reddened her hands and the front of her sari.

'I had some work at the foot of the Bahraburu hills—I've been there for these three months. I'm on my way back. What are you doing here?'

'Harvesting kusum flowers, Babuji! It's quite late, stay the afternoon with us. Our *khupri* is right there.'

My objections went unheeded. Manchi stopped her work and took me to their home. Her husband Nakchhedi Bhakt came home from the fields when he got news of my arrival. Nakchhedi's elder wife was cooking inside their *khupri*. She too, was pleased to see me, but Manchi was ahead of everyone in everything. She laid out straw in layers to make a seat for me. Then she brought me a small bowl of mahua oil and sent me off to have a bath.

'Come, I'll take you there myself,' she said. 'To the south of our *tola* is a small pond. It has lots of water.'

'I won't bathe in the pond, Manchi,' I had to tell her. 'All the people of the *tola* wash their clothes and their vessels, gargle and bathe—in the same water. It's bound to be dirty. Do you drink that water? In that case, I'd better be off. I won't drink that water.'

Manchi looked perturbed. It was clear there was simply no other source of water that they could have drunk from. Did they have an option?

Her hopeless expression made me sad. They had been happily drinking the polluted water all that time, never imagining what might or might not be lurking in it; now, if I refused to accept their hospitality using the water as a pretext, simple as she was, the girl would be deeply hurt.

I told her then, 'Manchi, if you boil the water well, I shall drink it. Don't bother about my bath.'

'Why Babuji, I'll boil you a tin full of the water and then you may use it for your bath. It is not too late yet. Why don't you sit, I'll fetch the water for you.'

Manchi brought me the water and then got busy preparing my meal.

'You won't eat if I cook,' she said, 'so why don't you cook the meal yourself?'

'Why wouldn't I eat if you cooked? Cook me whatever you can.'

'That won't do Babuji, you had better cook. Why should I destroy your caste purity for just this one meal? I'd be committing a sin.'

'Nothing will happen if you do make the food. I'm telling you, there's no harm in it.'

So, Manchi sat down to cook. It was simple fare—she made a few coarse and thick rotis and a dish of the wild dhundhul. Nakchhedi managed to get me a pot of buffalo milk.

While she cooked Manchi began telling me stories of their travels: how she had raised a little kid when they had gone to the hills to cut kalhai, and how the little animal got lost—I had to sit through a host of such details.

'Babuji,' she said, 'did you know that there are hot springs by the Kankoara estate? You had gone quite close to the estate, did you not go to the springs?'

'I have heard of the springs, but it wasn't possible to get there.'

'Do you know, Babuji,' said Manchi, 'I got beaten up when I went to bathe there. They wouldn't let me bathe.'

'It turned out bad: a nasty lot of priests they are at Suraj-kund,' said her husband.

'Why, what happened?' I asked.

Manchi turned to her husband: 'Why don't you tell Babuji? Babuji lives in Calcuta, he will write it up. That will teach those wicked scoundrels.'

Nakchhedi said, 'Babuji, of all those springs, Suraj-kund is the best. Pilgrims go to bathe in the waters there. We were harvesting kalhai at the foot of the Amlatali hills, and then we had the full moon, you see. Manchi stopped her work in the fields and went to take a dip. I had fever so I wouldn't bathe. Tulsi, our elder wife, didn't go either—she's not all that keen on religion. Manchi was about to take a dip in Suraj-kund and then the priests start asking her: "Why are you going down that way?" "I'm going to bathe in the water," she says. "What is your caste?" they want to know. "Gangota," she says. Then they say, "We don't let gangotas bathe in these waters. Begone." You know how spirited she is—she says, "But this is a mountain spring, any one can bathe in these waters. Why, just look around, how many are bathing right now! Are they all brahmans and chhatris?" And then, just as she was going to bathe, two of them came running down and dragged and pulled her away beating her all the while. She came back sobbing.'

'What happened then?'

'What could happen after that? We're poor gangotas, daily wagers. Who will listen to our appeal? I said to her, "Don't cry, I'm going to take you to Sita-kund in Mungher for a dip."'

'Babuji,' said Manchi to me, 'just put it all down in writing. You'll write this up won't you—you Bangali-babus have a powerful pen. The rascals will be punished for sure.'

'Certainly I will,' I said with conviction.

Manchi then served me my meal with great care. I was very moved by her attentive concern.

Before I left them, I made Manchi promise again and again that when they came the following Baisakh to harvest wheat and barley they must certainly visit us at Lobtulia-baihar.'

We will, Babuji,' said Manchi. 'You needn't tell us.'

On my way back, basking in the warmth of Manchi's hospitality, I thought of her as the very embodiment of joyousness, health and of innocence. She was like the goddess of plenty in these forests—brimming with youthful vitality, spirited and vibrant, yet, inexperienced, innocent and unspoilt like a little girl.

I have fulfilled today the promise I had made to this daughter of the woods who had such utter faith in the might of a Bengali's pen. I do not know if it will be of any use to her after all these years. Where has she been all these years, how has she been living—who knows if she is even alive?

2

It is the month of Sravan. For many days now, newly formed clouds had been massing in tiers, like the slope on a hill. If you stood in Narha or Lobtulia-baihar or even beneath Grantsaheb's Banyan and looked around you would see the tender forest of kash swelling like a sea of vivid green.

I received an invitation from Raja Dobru to celebrate the Jhulan festival at the time of the full moon in Sravan. Raju and Motuknath insisted on coming with me as well. They went on ahead of me, for they were going to walk to our destination.

We crossed the Michhi on a small and narrow country boat known as a 'dongah'. That was around one-thirty in the afternoon; it took another hour for all of us to cross over. I left behind the group and sped ahead on my horse.

The clouds piled up thickly in the west. And, soon, came torrents of rain.

I experienced the rains in a wondrous fashion in the forest. The range of hills on the horizon had turned blue with clouds, the sky was overcast with thunderous black clouds carrying lightning in their belly. Suddenly, on the branches of a kend or on a wayside rock, a peacock would flaunt his flaming tail, engrossed in his dance; village boys and girls in high excitement laid traps made of wild bamboo and sal called 'ghunis' to catch the small fry of fish; the grey rocks glistened black in the rain; and the cowherd perched on the rocks, pulled at his smoke of sal leaves. A still and peaceful land, forests unfurling one after another, open spaces, springs, hillside villages, red soil strewn with pebbles with a sudden glimpse of a flowering kadamba or piyal tree.

I reached Raja Dobru Panna's royal seat before it was evening.

The thatched room that we had been taken to on former occasions had been completely refurbished and the walls plastered with fresh lime and smoothened. They were now the colour of the red mountain soil with drawings of lotus, trees and peacocks, while creepers and flowers had been wound around the pillars made of sal. My bedding had not yet arrived since it was coming with the others, but that was of no consequence. A freshly woven mat was laid out on the floor with two fresh pillows on it.

A little later, Bhanmati came in carrying a brass plate full of cut fruits and a bowl of condensed milk; behind her came another girl of the same age bearing a whole pan leaf, a betel nut and various other ingredients, all arranged on a tender sal leaf.

Bhanmati had on a short plum coloured sari that she wore above her knees, a green and red necklace of hinglaj, and she had a spider lily tucked into her hair. She looked more healthy and comely than when we had last met—her slender body brimmed over with a sweet youthfulness, though the expression in her eyes spoke of the same innocent girl I knew.

'Well Bhanmati,' I said, 'how are you? Are you well?'

Bhanmati did not know usual forms of greeting; she simply smiled at my words and said, 'And you, Babuji?'

'I am well.'

'Do eat something. You've been riding all day; you must be very hungry.'

Without waiting for my reply she sat down on her knees on the floor in front of me and taking two pieces of papaya from the brass plate she put them into my hand.

I liked it—this frank offer of friendship. For a native of Bengal this was alien, unexpected, but novel, tender and beautiful. Would any Bengali maiden in her mid-teens behave in this manner with a male who was not related to her? With regard to women, we seem to be always in some kind of a dither, shy and secretive. We are neither capable of thinking of them in an honest open way nor are we able to mix freely with them.

I have noted that like the open and generous countryside—the forests, the clouds, the range of hills, free and untrammelled—Bhanmati was unencumbered, innocent and free in how she conducted herself. So were Manchi and the poet Venkateshwar Prasad's wife, Rukma. The forests and the hills had liberated their minds, expanded their vision with generosity; in like manner, their love was deep, generous and liberating. They could love greatly because of the greatness of their hearts. But nothing could be compared with the experience of Bhanmati sitting near me and putting the pieces of fruit into my hands. For the first time in my life, I experienced a great pleasure— the sweetness of a woman's frank behaviour. When she is affectionate and loving, it is as if the gates of heaven are opened on our earth. The dictates of refinement and the pressures of the civilized world had erased in her sisters the eternal woman that resided in Bhanmati.

She treated me with even greater warmth than she had in the course of the last visit. She had realized that the Bangali-babu was a friend of the family, a well-wisher, and was one of them; she treated me as though she were my very own loving sister.

It has been many years now, but Bhanmati's loving concern, her friendly words are bright in my memory. Many a thing of value that is a mark of our civilized world pales before the gift I had received from the civilization of the forest world.

Raja Dobru had been busy with the preparations for the festival, he came into the room now to keep me company.

'Have you always celebrated Jhulan?' I wanted to know.

'It is an old tradition of our dynasty,' said Raja Dobru. 'Many of our relatives come from far away to dance the Jhulan. We shall be cooking two and half maunds of rice tomorrow.'

Motuknath had come, expecting the traditional offerings made to a pandit; he must have imagined a huge palace and immense preparations. Looking thoroughly disappointed, he walked about the grounds. His own schoolroom must have appeared to him a much better affair than the royal quarters we were in.

Raju Parey, unable to hide his dismay, said frankly, 'Huzoor, this is no king—he's only a tribal leader, a Santal sardar. I'm told, Huzoor, the king does not have as many buffaloes as even I do!'

He had already managed to take stock of the material possessions owned by the Raja. Cattle was the chief measure of wealth in these parts, the number of heads determining the status of the owner.

When, in the deep night, the moon climbed up from behind the screen of huge trees in the forest and cast a magic net of light and shadow over the courtyards of the houses in the village, there came to my ears a strange tune sung by a chorus of women. The full moon marking Jhulan would rise tomorrow; tonight, the princess and her companions and the assembled kinsfolk were rehearsing songs for the festivities and the dancing that was going to take place. All night long they sang and played on their *madal* drums.

I must have fallen asleep listening to them, but the song played on in my ears even in sleep.

3

The next day, Motuknath, Raju, and even Sipahi Muneshwar Singh were charmed by the festivities of Jhulan.

When I awoke that morning I found that about thirty odd unmarried girls, of Bhanmati's age, had come from all the neighbouring settlements and the hills to celebrate the festival. I observed that they followed a sound practice: in the midst of all that singing and dancing none of the women imbibed any mahua, the liquor they traditionally brewed from the mahua flower. When I mentioned it to Raja Dobru he said with a proud smile, 'It is not part of our dynastic tradition that the women drink. Besides, until I give the order, no one would dare drink before my sons and daughters.'

'The king is even poorer than I am,' Motuknath whispered to me in the course of the afternoon. 'He's getting coarse red rice cooked, and ripe white-pumpkins and wild dhundhul for the vegetable dishes. Now tell me, how am I supposed to cook this stuff for so many people?'

I had not seen Bhanmati all morning. Just as I sat down to eat she came with a bowl of milk and sat down before me.

'I enjoyed your songs last night,' I said to her.

Bhanmati smiled, 'Do you understand our songs?'

'Why not? I've been with you for so long, why wouldn't I understand your songs?'

'Will you be coming to see the Jhulan later in the day?'

'That is why I'm here. How far would I have to go?'

Bhanmati pointed to a part of the Dhannjhari range, 'You've gone up that hill, haven't you? You must have seen our sacred site.'

At this point a gaggle of young girls appeared and clustered around the door. They looked on with extreme curiosity at the Bangali-babu having his meal and chattered animatedly amongst themselves.

'Be off with you now!' said Bhanmati to them in mock seriousness. 'What do you want here?'

One girl, more daring than the others, came forward and said, 'Hope you haven't given Babuji salty karamcha berries on Jhulan day?'

The others broke into peals of laughter at her words and fell over each other in their merriment.

'Why are they laughing?' I asked Bhanmati.

'Ask them,' said Bhanmati, somewhat embarrassed. 'What would I know!'

Meanwhile, one of the girls had come back with a big red chilli. She put it on my plate and said, 'Have a pickled chilli, Babuji. Bhanmati's only been giving you sweets; that won't do! Let's make you eat some chillies.'

They all fell to laughing again. Their laughter lit up the room, as the radiance of the full moon.

A little before evening the young people started walking to the hills—we followed them. It was a huge procession. To our east, on the borders of Nauada-Lachhmipur rose the hills of the Dhannjhari range, from its foot the Micchi flowed northwards. A full moon was rising above the forests on the hill: on one side lay the low valley glowing with emerald-green forests and on the other, the Dhannjharis. After we had walked on for a mile, we reached the hills. After some climbing, we came to a level ground atop the hill. Right in the middle was an ancient piyal whose trunk had been entwined with garlands of flowers and creepers.

'It is a very old tree,' said Raja Dobru, 'I've been seeing girls dance around this tree during Jhulan from the time I was a child.'

We put down our palm-leaf mats on one side and there, in the clearing awash in the moonlight, thirty young girls began dancing, encircling the tree in their dance. They were accompanied by a group of young men who played on the *madal*. I saw that Bhanmati was at the forefront of the group. The girls had garlands entwined around their hair and flower ornaments adorned their bodies.

The dancing and the music went on late into the night, the groups only breaking off for short rests before they were at it again. The beat of the *madal*, the moonlight, the rain-washed forestland, the dark and lithe band of dancers made it as beautiful a scene as a painting by a master artist, its haunting appeal like soft music. I remembered from our history the Solanki princess and her companions who sang and danced to celebrate Jhulan, how she had garlanded the cowherd Bappaditya while they were playing . . .

What bliss today, today, as Shyam swings,

On the jhulan, today . . .

I could see, as if before my eyes, scenes enacted from the very earliest times of India's mysterious past; the culture of those primitive times took on life in the dance of the simple mountain girl Bhanmati and her companions. Thousands of years ago, in many such forests and hills, on such a moonlit night, so many young dancers like Bhanmati and her companions had sung and danced. The sound of their dancing feet rising to a crescendo and their smiles lingered still in these girls; in these secret forests and hills hidden from other eyes they continued to send their message of joy and excitement flowing in the veins of their descendants.

It was past midnight. The moon had almost toppled over behind the distant forests in the west. We came down the hill, all of us. Happily, the sky today was free of clouds, but the moist breeze had turned very cold in the last hours of the night. Even so, late at night when I'd sat down to eat, Bhanmati brought me some milk and sweets.

'That was excellent dancing I saw,' I said to her.

She smiled shyly, 'Would people like you enjoy it, Babuji? Would people in Calcutta ever watch such things?'

Bhanmati and her great-grandfather Raja Dobru simply would not let me leave the following day. Yet, there was a lot of work pending at the katcheri. Finally, I had to drag myself away. As I was leaving, Bhanmati asked me, 'Babuji, will you get me a mirror from Calcutta? I used to own one—it broke ever so long ago.'

A pretty young girl of sixteen years, and without a mirror! Why on earth had a mirror been created if not for one such? Within a week, I had a fine mirror bought from Purnea and had it sent to her.

FOURTEEN

1

A few months later and it was the first of Phalgun. I was on my way back to
the katcheri from Lobtulia when the sound of laughter interspersed with conversation in Bangla made me pull in my horse near the *kundi*. My astonishment grew the closer I drew to the sounds—I could even hear women's
voices. What could it mean? I rode my horse deeper into the jungle and came
to the banks of the *kundi*: I found that a party of eight or ten Bengali gentle-
men had spread out cotton rugs by the wild jhau and were chatting away
in a relaxed fashion. Half a dozen young women were cooking nearby
and another half a dozen children were running around, playing. I was still
standing, quite amazed, unable to fathom where so many men and women
with their children had appeared from to picnic so deep inside the jungle,
when all at once their eyes fell on me. One of them remarked in Bangla, 'Here
comes a specimen of a *chhatu*-eater: wonder where he sprung up from!'

I dismounted and going up to them said in Bangla, 'You are Bengalis, I
see. Where have you come from?'

They looked dumbfounded at my words, even somewhat embarrassed.

'Oh, you're a Bengali! Please don't mind—we thought, heh, heh . . .' said
one finally.

'Not at all,' said I. 'But where have you come from—I see you have
womenfolk with you.'

We soon got into a conversation. The elderly man with them was a retired
deputy magistrate, with the title of a Rai Bahadur. The group was made
up of his sons, nephews, nieces, daughters, granddaughters, sons-in-law,

friends of sons-in-law, and so forth. While in Calcutta, the Rai Bahadur had read somewhere that Purnea district was famed for good hunting grounds, and so he had come to find out for himself if this was true, as he had a brother who was a *munsef* and who lived in Purnea. Everyone had maintained that if it was a question of a real jungle, you simply had to see Lobtulia, Bomaiburu and Phulkia-baihar. So they had taken the train to Kataria from Purnea, reaching there around ten this morning; then, they had come along the Kushi on boat to find out this place for their picnic. As soon as the picnic was over, they would walk for another four miles and catch a boat at the Kushi, at the bottom of the Mohanpura jungle; they would reach the Kataria railway station by night.

I was most astonished. They had ventured into this fearful jungle with children, with only one double-barreled shotgun for protection. Admittedly, they showed some courage in doing so; nevertheless, veteran as he was, one would have expected the Rai Bahadur to be a little more circumspect. Even the locals stopped venturing into Mohanpura well before it got dark because they feared the herds of wild buffalo, not to speak of wild boars and snakes. It was not exactly the sort of place to come picnicking with children.

The Rai Bahadur insisted that I sit down and have a cup of tea with them. He wanted to know what was I doing in this jungle and all the rest of it. Did I do business in wood and so on? After I had given them an account of myself, I invited the whole party to spend the night at the katcheri but they would not agree to this. They had to catch the ten o'clock train at Kataria and get back to Purnea by midnight. If they didn't, the people at home would worry, so it was out of the question.

I still could not figure out though why they had come so deep into the jungle for a picnic. I noticed they cared very little for what was beautiful about the place: the far spreading forests and valleys of Lobtulia-baihar, the grandeur of the distant hills, the colours of the sunset, the bird calls, the fantastic wild blossoms that had come out with spring and dotted the forest not ten feet away from us—nothing held any attraction for them. They simply let out little shrieks from time to time, sang, scurried around, and busied themselves with cooking. Two of the young women were studying in a college in Calcutta; the girls were still in school. Of the men and the boys, one was enrolled in the Medical College and the rest were either at school or in college. By a stroke of rare fortune, they had landed in this extraordinary kingdom of nature, but they lacked vision to appreciate what they saw. In fact, they had come with the sole purpose of hunting, as though birds, rabbits, and deer were all awaiting them by the roadside, waiting patiently to be shot.

The women were a motley collection, completely devoid of imagination. They ran about gathering twigs for their fire on the edges of the forest and chattered endlessly, but not one of them were around to see where they were, either at the spot where they were going to cook or at the natural beauty of the forest around them.

'Pass me the tin-cutter!' cried out one of the girls. 'Look at all the rocks lying around: it'll be easy to find something to pound the tin with!'

'What a wretched place!' said another, 'No chance of getting any fine quality rice—I went through all the town yesterday—only look at this horrid coarse rice; and you were saying that we should make fried rice—'

Did they know that only a dozen yards from where they sat, the forest sprites danced in the moonlight?

They began discussing films. They had seen a film last night in Purnea and it was pronounced a horrible one. Immediately, they began comparing it with the films that were to be seen in Calcutta. And so it went on. It was just as the adage said, The mill grinds wheat even in heaven!

They left around five in the afternoon.

They left behind a clutter of empty tins of condensed milk and jam. To my eyes, they had seemed completely out of place in the jungles of Lobtulia.

2

This time the wheat in Lobtulia-baihar ripened just as spring ended. Last year we had an abundant crop of mustard in our estate. Now that wheat had been cultivated in large areas, early Baisakh would see many harvest fairs.

It was as if the reapers had antennas: they had not come at winter's end as they usually do; it was only now that they started coming in gangs, setting up their *khupris* all across the fields and along the edges of the jungle. Almost three thousand bighas of land was going to be harvested and there must have been an equal number of harvest hands who had turned up. I was told that more were on their way.

I would start off early in the morning on my horse and would get off only when evening fell. All sorts of strangers had begun to trickle in; at least some among them were bound to be rascals, thieves, hoodlums or diseased people—I had to keep an eye on them for these were places unsupervised by the police, and anything might happen during the fair.

Let me recount a couple of incidents.

On one of my rounds, I came across two little boys and a little girl crying by the wayside. I got off my horse to speak to them.

'Why are you crying? What is up?' I asked.

Their story was as follows: they lived somewhere—not part of our estate—in the village where Nandalal Ojha Golawala lived. They were siblings and had come here to enjoy the harvest fair. When they got here this morning, they had come upon a gathering of people gambling with sticks and knots. The eldest, a boy, began to try his luck at the game which he said went something like this: you had to take a stick which had one end planted in the ground and the other end had to be wound up with a piece of rope; if you could make a knot while the rope was being untied, the man would give the player four paisa to the original one that had been staked.

The elder boy had ten annas with him, but despite spending it all, he couldn't manage to get the noose on the stick even once. After he had lost his own money, he spent the eight annas of the younger brother and finally, the four annas of his little sister. Now they had no money to eat, let alone try out the other games in the fair.

I told them to stop crying and made them take me to the gambling spot. They could not immediately decide on the location, but after a while they pointed out to a haritaki tree and said that it was beneath the tree that the game was being played. Of course, there was not a living creature to be seen now. With us was the brother of Roopsingh Jamadar from the katcheri. 'Huzoor,' he remarked, 'do gamblers ever stick to one place for any length of time? They must have set up their game somewhere else.'

It was late afternoon by the time the man was caught. He had been carrying on with the gambling in a settlement some three miles away. My guards happened to spot him and brought him before me. The children recognized him at once.

At first, the man was most reluctant to return the money. He hadn't forcibly taken away the money, he insisted. The children had chosen to play and had lost the money, how was he to be blamed? By and by, not only did he have to return all the money to the children, but I also ordered the guards to turn him over to the police.

He then began begging me to release him.

'Where is your home?' I asked.

'Balia District, Babuji.'

'Why do you cheat people in this way? How much money have you cheated others of?'

'I'm a poor man, Huzoor. Please let me go this time. I've only earned two rupees in three days.'

'Compared to the labourers, you've earned quite a bit in three days.'

'Huzoor, I'm hardly able to earn a sum like this through the year. At the most, I make forty rupees in the whole year.'

I let him go, on the condition that he had to leave my estate that very day. He was never been spotted since on our estate.

I was unable to find Manchi among the pickers this time; I was surprised and anxious. She had told me repeatedly that they would be coming to our estate at the time of the wheat harvest. The harvest fair had come and was now on its way out—and still, she had not come; I did not understand it at all.

There was no information to be had from the other workers I kept asking. I reasoned that there was no other estate near at hand which offered such extensive fields, excepting for the diara in Isamaelpur, south of the Kushi; but why would she have gone so far away when the wages were the same in both places?

Eventually, when the fair was at an end, a gangota labourer gave us some news. He knew both Manchi and her husband, Nakchhedi Bhakt. Apparently, they had all worked together in several places at one time. I heard from him that last Phalgun they had gone for harvesting in the government land at Akbarpur. After that, he had lost track of the family.

Around the middle of Jyeshtha when the harvest fair had wound up, I was startled one day to find Nakchhedi Bhakt in the katcheri courtyard. Nakchhedi held on to my feet and began sobbing loudly. 'What is the matter?' I asked him wonderingly, as I unwound his hands from my feet, 'Why did all of you not come this time for the harvesting. How is Manchi? Where is she?'

He replied that he did not know where Manchi was. Even while they were working on the government land, Manchi had left them and run away—where to—he did not know. He had searched hard and in vain, she was simply not to be traced.

I was stunned. I found that I seemed to have no sympathy for old Nakchhedi; whatever anxious thoughts I had were all for that mad girl. Where had she gone? Had someone wiled her away, how was she living now? She was so attracted to cheap ornaments and other trifles that it would not have been very difficult to lure her away using these as bait. That's what must have happened.

'And the little boy?' I asked Nakchhedi.

'He's gone too. He died last Magh of small pox.'

I was deeply affected by this news. Perhaps, maddened by the death of her son, she had gone any which way. I was quiet for a while, then I asked, 'Where is Tulsi?'

'She has come here with me. Huzoor, do give me a bit of land, otherwise how are this old man and woman to live by harvesting crops alone? While Manchi was with us, she was our strength, and so we could venture out; she's left me crippled.'

When I visited Nakchhedi in his *khupri* that evening, I found Tulsi peeling the grains of cheena with her children around her. Tulsi began crying as soon as she saw me. I saw that she, too, was quite heartbroken at Manchi's departure.

'Huzoor,' she said, 'this old man is to be blamed for everything. Someone from the "govirment" came to give us vaccination, but he sent him off with a four-anna bribe. Wouldn't let any one of us get vaccinated. Said that if we did, we would have small pox. It wasn't three days but Manchi's little boy had the pox, and then died of it too. She had gone quite mad with grief, didn't eat or drink, just kept weeping.'

'And then?'

'And then, Huzoor, they chased us off from the govirment land. Your people have died of the pox, they said, we shan't let you stay here. There was a young rajput fellow who used to eye Manchi. Manchi disappeared the night we were to leave. I'd seen that fellow hang around our *khupri* that morning. I'm sure he's done it. Lately, Manchi was always going on about wanting to see Calcutta: I knew then, something would happen.'

I recalled that even last year Manchi had been very keen on visiting Calcutta. It was not impossible that the clever rajput fellow would deceive the innocent country girl, playing on her desire to see Calcutta.

I know that in such situations the last stage for the woman was that of a tea-picking coolie in Assam. Was Manchi fated to end her days in slavery and exile in the friendless hills of Assam?

I became very angry with the elderly Nakchhedi. This man was at the root of all their trouble. In the first place, who had asked him to marry Manchi when he was already such an old man? And secondly, why had he warded off the man that the government had sent with a bribe? If I were to give him land, it would certainly not be for his sake, but for his elderly wife Tulsi, and for his children.

That is what happened. I had orders from the head office to rent out Narha-baihar. Nakchhedi became our first tenant.

Narha-baihar was all dense forest: couple of families had barely begun to clear away the jungle and put together their little *khupris*. Nakchhedi was somewhat overwhelmed by the jungle and wanted to back out: 'Huzoor, it is such a place, a tiger is sure to eat us up in broad daylight—and to set up house with my little ones . . .'

I was short with him: if he didn't like the place he could go elsewhere.

Having no other option, Nakchhedi accepted a piece of land in Narha-baihar.

I had not been to visit Nakchhedi since the time he had come to Narha-baihar. One evening on my way back through the jungle of Narha-baihar I came across two *khupris* of kash in a clearing. There was light in one of the *khupris*. I knew then that it was Nakchhedi's. At the sound of hooves an elderly woman came out of the *khupri*—it was Tulsi.

'Is this where you've settled? Where is Nakchhedi?'

Tulsi was taken unawares by my appearance. She fussed around with a jute mattress stuffed with straw and spread it out for me. 'Do get down Babuji, sit for a while,' she said. 'He's gone to buy salt and oil at the shops in Lobtulia. He's taken our eldest with him.'

'And you are all by yourself in this jungle?'

'I've become used to all that, Babuji. How are we poor folks to live if we are afraid? I never had to be alone all this time—but it's my misfortune! For as long Manchi was with us neither water nor jungle held any threat. What courage, what energy she had, Babuji!'

Tulsi had loved her young co-wife. Tulsi also knew that the Bangali-babu would be glad to hear of Manchi.

Tulsi's young daughter, Suratiya said, 'Babuji, I've kept a baby neelgai as a pet; will you see it? I heard it rustling behind our *khupri* one evening, Chhania and I managed to run and catch it.'

'What does it eat?'

'Only tender leaves and the husk of the cheena grains. I pick tender kend leaves for it.'

'Why don't you show it to Babuji?' said Tulsi to her daughter.

Suratiya sped off like a deer and disappeared behind the *khupri*. A little later, her girlish voice rose in a scream, 'Ayeeee, the neelgai is running away, O Chhania, come here, no there—quick, catch it—'

The two of them dashed around wildly and finally captured the baby neelgai and then, smiling and panting, they brought it up for my inspection.

Suratiya held up a flare for me to see the animal in the dark. 'Well, isn't it nice?' she demanded. 'You know, a bear had come last night to get him. The bear had climbed up that mahua tree over there to drink mahua . . . it was very late at night—my parents were fast asleep, but I know everything about bears and things—then he climbed down the tree and came and stood by our *khupri*. I hug this little creature and sleep with him next to me; when I heard the bear's footsteps I just held on to him, very tight, and put my hand over his mouth and just lay there . . .'

'Weren't you a little scared, Suratiya?'

'Huh! Scared! I'm not one to be scared. I see so many bears in the jungle when I go to gather firewood—even that doesn't scare me in the least. Will it do to be scared, Babuji?'

And Suratiya put on a wise and knowing expression.

All around the *khupri* kend trees as tall as big black chimneys, like a forest of Californian Redwoods, thrust their trunks skywards. The branches were alive with the sound of bats fluttering their wings and the stirring of other night birds—it was hard to imagine how the mother of these children lived with her flock on the edge of the forest. Forest, wise and mysterious, truly you are kind to those who seek your refuge.

'Has Manchi taken all her things away with her?' I asked in passing.

Suratiya replied, 'Chhoti-ma did not take anything with her. That box of her's that you saw that time—she's left it behind as well. Would you like to see it? I'll fetch it.'

She brought the box and took off the lid. A comb, a small mirror, a bead necklace, a green handkerchief of poor quality—it was as though she was showing me a doll's box, belonging to a little child! But that strand of hinglaj beads, the one she had bought at the Lobtulia fair—that was missing.

Who was to say where she had gone away leaving her home and family? After all these years, these people had finally settled down somewhere; only she, the wanderer, remained forever so.

'Babuji, do come again,' urged Suratiya as I got ready to leave. 'We trap birds. I've just woven some new traps. I've snared a dahuk and a bulbuli—they're my pets now. The wild birds hear them call and they fly into the traps and get caught. There's no time today, otherwise I'd have shown you how we catch them.'

It was scary to take the path that cut through Narha-baihar so late at night. A spring gurgled along to my left; wild flowers bloomed somewhere around me—the darkness was heavy with their scent and in some places so complete that I could not even see my horse's mane; elsewhere, it was diffused by light from the constellations.

Narha-baihar was home to a variety of creepers, birds and animals. Nature had bestowed her wealth generously on this stretch of land in whose northern boundary lay Saraswati kundi. Records from the old surveys showed that the Kushi once had its bed there; all that remained of the waters was the *kundi*; in other parts, the ancient river bed had been swallowed up by the thick forests—

pura yatra srotah pulinamadhuna tatra saritaam[18]

The silent and dark night revealed itself to me in its indescribable majesty. Yet, I grieved, knowing that the forests of Narha-baihar would not stand for long. I loved the place so greatly, but my own hands had destroyed it. In two years the entire estate would be settled and would be taken over by ugly *tolas* and dirty hutments. It had taken hundreds of years of fervent meditation, of *sadhana*, to create Narha-baihar; nature had fashioned it lovingly with her own hands. The exquisite forests and the distant winding open spaces would be completely erased. And in their place, what would one be gaining? Thatched houses, unbelievably ugly, fields of maize, gowal and janar, rope-cots, banners flying above temples to Hanuman, an abundance of phanimansa scrub, snuff and tobacco, epidemics of cholera and small-pox.

Forests, primeval and ancient, forgive me.

I went another day to watch Suratiya and her sister trap birds.

Carrying their two cages, the two of them, Suratiya and Chhaniya, led me to the open land beyond the jungle of Narha-baihar.

It was late afternoon; the sun had set behind the hills, spreading long shadows across the fields of Narha-baihar.

The cages were put down on the grass beneath a simul sapling. One cage had a big sized dahuk, the other, a gurguri. Both had been trained: the dahuk immediately began calling to attract other wild birds; the gurguri was quiet at first.

Suratiya began whistling and snapping her fingers; 'Come little sister, how do you sing . . .' she chanted.

And the gurguri called out, 'Gurr-r-r-r-r-r . . .'

In the silent afternoon and in the open fields that strange tune only brings to mind a picture of endless horizons, dreams of open spaces, and of moonlight without shadows. Chhaniya hid her trap in the grass where millions of yellow dudhli flowers had bloomed. The trap, made of bamboo, was like the fencing of a birdcage. She hid the gurguri in its cage with the light fencing.

'Come Babuji,' said Suratiya, 'let's go and hide behind the bushes. The birds will be frightened away if they see people.'

Behind the sal saplings, all three of us waited quietly.

The dahuk would pause occasionally, but the gurguri went on unceasingly —gurr-r-r-r-r—

A melodious and magical call it was.

'Suratiya, will you sell your gurguri; how much will it cost?'

'Ssh ... Babuji, be quiet ... look, there's a wild bird alighting—'

A few minutes of silence. Then, from the forest to the northern side of the field came wafting—gurr-r-r-r-r—

I trembled. The wild bird had called out in response to the caged one!

Gradually the call sounded nearer. For some time you heard the two, distinct and separate, but by and by they merged indistinguishably; and suddenly, only one could be heard—it was the caged bird.

Chhaniya and Suratiya ran to the spot: the bird had been snared. I too ran up. The bird was struggling to set itself free, one of its feet had been trapped. It had stopped calling the moment it was snared. Amazing! Almost hard to believe one's eyes.

Suratiya raised the bird to my level and said, 'See, Babuji, how its foot has been caught. Do you see it?'

'What do you do with the birds?' I asked Suratiya.

'Father sells them at the weekly market at Tirashi-Ratanganj. Gurguris at two paisas each, and the dahuks go for seven.'

'Why don't you sell them to me? I shall pay you for them.'

Suratiya gifted me the gurguri. I couldn't make her accept any money for it.

The month was Ashwin. One morning I received a letter saying that Raja Dobru Panna was dead: the royal family was in great distress, would I please go as soon as I had the time. The letter was written by Jagru Panna, Bhanmati's young uncle.

I started immediately and reached Chakmaki-tola a little before evening. From then on, I was escorted by the Raja's eldest son and his grandson. I was told that Raja Dobru had suddenly fallen down while grazing his cattle and had injured his knee. He died of the wound in his knee.

As soon as their mahajan had heard of the Raja's death he had come and confiscated all the cattle. Until he recovered his money, he was not going to release them. Meanwhile problems came thick and fast: there was to be a coronation ceremony the next evening—and that too, would cost some money; but where were they to get the money from? Besides, if the cattle was taken away by the mahajan, the royal family would become destitute— half their monthly income used to come from the sale of ghee made from the milk. They would simply starve to death.

I listened to everything and sent for the mahajan. He was called Birbal Singh. I found him completely unwilling to listen to anything I had to say. He was adamant about not releasing the cattle until the money was paid up. Clearly, he was not a good sort.

Bhanmati came crying to me. She had dearly loved the great-grandfather she used to address as 'Elder Uncle'. While he was alive, he had been like a mountain, sheltering them with his solidity. In a moment, everything had changed and all was chaos. Bhanmati's tears would not stop falling while she was speaking with me. 'Come with me Babuji,' she urged, 'let me show you Elder Uncle's grave by the hillside. I can't enjoy anything Babuji, I wish only to sit beside his grave.'

'Wait a bit,' I said to her. 'Let's see what I can do with the mahajan, and then we can go.' However, it was not possible to settle the matter with the man right away. He was a formidable rajput, not the type to listen to anybody's pleas. Finally, he relented somewhat and allowed the animals to stay where they were for the time being, on condition that not a drop of the milk was to be used by the family. A way was found of settling the debt only a couple of months later, but I will come to that elsewhere.

I found Bhanmati standing all by herself in front of their house. 'It is getting late,' she said, 'we shan't be able to go later, do come and see the grave.' She set off alone with me and I realized that the innocent girl regarded me as a close relative, as a beloved friend of the family. I was overwhelmed by the simplicity of her manner and the friendship she offered me.

The vast valley was criss-crossed with shadows of the late afternoon.

Bhanmati was walking rather fast, like an anxious doe. 'Bhanmati,' I said to her, 'you must slow down: tell me, where can I find sheuli flowers?'

In their part of the country, they called sheuli flowers by a quite different name. I simply could not explain to her which flower I meant. You could see quite far as you climbed higher up the hill. The blue range of the Dhannjhari encircled Bhanmati's land—Raja Dobru Panna's realm that was not a kingdom—like a girdle. From far came the wind blowing freely past us.

Bhanmati paused in her climbing and turned to ask me, 'Babuji, are you finding it hard going up?'

'Not really. Slow down a bit, that's all. Why should it be hard?'

Then, after we had walked a little further, she said, 'Elder Uncle has left us, Babuji, now I have no one left in the world.'

She said these words tearfully.

I wanted to laugh at her words. Was it not her ancient great-grandfather who had died? Her father, brother, grandmother, grandfather—all of them—were still living; it was a full household! Bhanmati was a female, and a young girl at that, it was natural that she would have a certain feminine way of wanting love and getting the attention of a male.

'You must come every now and then, Babuji, and look after us. Tell me that you will not forget us . . .'

'Why would I? Certainly, I will come now and then . . .'

Bhanmati pouted and said in a hurt tone, 'When you go back to Bengal, and to the city of Calcutta, you're sure not to remember this wild hilly place of ours . . .' She paused for a bit before she went on, 'About us, about me . . .'

'Why, did I not remember, Bhanmati and did you not get the mirror?' I reminded her affectionately. 'Think of it, did I or did I not remember?'

Bhanmati turned a radiant face to me, 'Ooh Babuji, it was an excellent mirror—it's true, I quite forgot to let you know about it.'

When we came to stand under the ancient banyan tree at the burial ground, there was little or no light left. The red sun had almost set in the distant hills. The burial ground was still, as though in expectation of being illuminated once more by the pale moonlight that would dispel the darkness.

I asked Bhanmati to pick some flowers that I could place on her great-grandfather's grave. They did not follow the practice of strewing the grave with flowers. At my urging, she picked up some of the sheuli blossoms that were lying on the ground nearby. Then she and I arranged them over the grave of Raja Dobru Panna.

Just then, a flock of sillis took off with a fluttering of wings from the topmost branch of the banyan tree and flew above us with their haunting cry. It was as though well pleased with my gesture, all the ancestors of Raja Dobru, ignored and unsung, abused and forgotten, were applauding us in chorus. For, perhaps, this was the first time that a descendant of the Aryans had honoured the royal burial ground of a non-Aryan race.

FIFTEEN

1

There was an occasion when I had to become a supplicant of Dhautal Sahu Mahajan. This happened once when we did not get enough money from the estate, but I was nevertheless required to deposit ten thousand rupees as revenue. I was advised by Banowarilal to borrow the remaining sum from Dhautal Sahu. He will certainly not mind lending you the amount, he added. Dhautal Sahu was not a tenant of my estate; he lived on the government estate. He had no obligations towards me; given these circumstances, I doubted very much whether he would be willing to give me a personal loan of three thousand rupees.

But I was made desperate by need. I took Banowarilal with me and secretly set off one day for Dhautal Sahu's; I did not wish anyone in the katcheri to know that I had to borrow money to pay revenue dues.

Dhautal Sahu's house was in the middle of a squalid settlement called Pausadia- tola. A few string cots were laid out in front of a big tiled shed. Dhautal was busy weeding the tobacco field next to his yard with a hoe. He came running as soon as he saw us. For a while he was at a loss, not knowing quite where he would seat us and what he would do with us.

'What is this! Huzoor has come to this poor man's home. Please come. Do sit down Huzoor. Come, Tehsildar saheb.'

I did not see any servants in Dhautal Sahu's home. He had a robust looking grandson called Ramlakhia who was running around, trying to put everything right for us. Neither the house nor the furniture in it looked like a millionaire mahajan's home.

Ramlakhia took off the saddle and the stirrups from my horse and tethered it in the shade. He brought us water to wash our feet with. Dhautal
Sahu himself took up a palm leaf-fan and began fanning us. Another grand-
daughter of Sahuji's ran off to prepare a smoke for us. Their hospitality
embarrassed me. 'There's no need to rush around so, Sahuji,' I said. 'You don't
need to get tobacco, I've got my cheroot with me.'

Despite the sincere hospitality and concern, I was somewhat hestitant
to broach the real reason for our coming; how would I bring it up?

'Has the Manager-babu come this way to shoot birds?' enquired Dhautal
Sahu.

'No, I've come to you, Sahuji.'

'To me, Huzoor? Tell me what is it that you need, Huzoor?'

'Our katcheri is short of the revenue money that we owe the government.
Three and half thousand rupees are urgently required—that's why I've come
to you.'

The words spilled out from me in some desperation, as there was no
other option but to say them.

Without a moment's hesitation Dhautal Sahu said, 'But why should you
have to worry so much about this? The matter will be taken care of, of course,
but why did you take the trouble to come all the way only for this? Your order
would have been carried out if you had simply written a note and sent it with
the tehsildar.'

I would now have to tell him the fact of the matter, I thought to myself:
That I would be taking the money as a personal loan, for I did not have the
power of attorney to take a loan on behalf of the zamindar. Would Dhautal
lend me the money even after he knew of this? I was not native to the place;
nor did I have any property or goods here that he might take as surety for
the money. I said to him with some deference, 'Sahuji, the deed will have to
be made out in my name. Not in the zamindar's.'

Dhautal Sahu said in some astonishment, 'What deed? You have come
all the way to my home to take a bit of money that you're short of. In the
first place, there was no need to have come at all—it would have been enough
to have sent a note, and I would have sent the money. And now that you have

come, where is the need to write out a deed? Take the money right away. Once the katcheri recovers the amount, it can be returned to me.'

'I shall give you a handnote,' I said. 'I've brought along the 'tickets' with me. Or, take out your account book, let me sign there.'

'Forgive me, Huzoor,' said Dhautal Sahu with folded hands. 'You are not to bring up this matter again. It will hurt me greatly. There's no need for a written document; take the money.'

All my entreaties fell on deaf ears.

'Huzoor, I have one request,' said Dhautal emerging with a bundle of notes that he had counted out indoors.

'What is it?'

'You cannot leave now. Let me take out the cereals and provisions; you can go only after you have had a meal at my home.'

Again, I tried to protest, but this time too, it was of no use. I asked Banowarilal, 'Will you be able to do the cooking? I'm not much good at it.'

'That won't do, Huzoor,' said Banowari. 'You will have to cook yourself. They will speak ill of you in the village if I cooked the food. I shall tell you what to do.'

Dhautal Sahu's grandson took out an enormous quantity of provisions. While the meal was being cooked, both grandfather and grandson offered innumerable suggestions about how it was to be prepared.

When Dhautal was away, his grandson said to me, 'We stand to lose everything for that grandfather of mine, Babuji. He's lent money to so many people without any interest or security or document that now it's impossible to recover the money from them. He trusts everyone, although so many have cheated him. He's even gone all the way to their homes to lend them money.'

Another villager who happened to be sitting there added, 'I've yet to see a person who has fallen into trouble and has come to take money from him being turned away by Sahuji. Sahuji's an old-timer—such a wealthy banker he is, but I've never seen him go to court. He's a simple and innocent man and mortally afraid of the court.'

It took me almost six months to return the money that I had got from Dhautal Sahu. Throughout these six months, Dhautal never stepped anywhere near our Isamaelpur estate in case I thought that he had come to remind me of the debt. A true gentleman!

2

I had not been to Rakhal-babu's home for almost a year. When I finally went after the harvest fair, his wife was very happy to see me. 'Why do you not come any more, Dada? You haven't enquired after us. It is such a treat to see another Bengali in the midst of our exile, and then, given our condition . . .'

She began weeping silently.

I looked around me: the house looked as poverty-stricken as it did earlier, but things did not seem to be as chaotic as before. The elder son worked from the house as a tinsmith. It was little he earned, but, however precariously, the household was running.

I said to Rakhal-babu's wife, 'At least the youngest should be sent to Kashi to his uncle for his studies.'

'He has no uncle of his own, Dada. We had sent them several letters telling them of our calamity—they sent us ten rupees—and since then, for the last year and a half, all we have had from them is silence. It is better that my sons cut maize, and graze cattle or something, than go begging to such an uncle.'

I was all set to ride back home, but Didi would not let me. I would have to spend some more time there until she had cooked me something and served it to me.

I had to wait. She made me *laddus* from ground maize mixed with ghee and sugar, and cooked some *halwa* as well. She did as much as anyone could in a poor household.

'Dada, I had put aside the maize in the month of Bhadra for you. Because you enjoy roasted cobs.'

'Where did you get the maize from?' I asked. 'Did you buy it?'

'No. I picked it up from the fields. All the broken and left over bits of maize that the farmers leave behind in the fields after harvesting—I'd go with the village girls and pick a basket-full everyday.'

I was most astonished. 'You went to the fields to pick up maize?'

'Yes, I'd go at night. No one knew. All the village women do it, don't they? I used to go with them; I managed to get at least ten baskets this last Bhadra.'

I felt very sad. This was something poor gangota women did; chhatri and rajput women of these parts, however poor, would never go to the fields to pick up gleanings from the harvest. It hurt me very much that a Bengali woman should have to do this work. Didi had picked up such lowly practices because she lived in a village of uneducated gangotas; of course, her poverty was undoubtedly the chief cause. I could not openly tell her any of this in case I hurt her. This destitute Bengali family would never have any access to culture or education: in a few years, they would become gangota peasants in their language, gestures and everyday life. Already, they were well initiated into that path.

I have met a few such Bengali families in out of the way villages that are far from railway stations. It was such a difficult affair marrying off the daughters of such families! I used to know such another brahman family who lived in an outlandish village of southern Bihar. Their financial situation was quite bad and there were three daughters in the family: the eldest was about twenty-two, the middle one twenty, and the youngest, seventeen. All three were unmarried and there was no means of their marrying in the future either. In these parts, it was very hard getting a Bengali groom belonging to the right caste.

The twenty-two-year-old daughter, the eldest one, was quite nice to look at. Not only did she not know a word of Bangla but in every other way, she was totally a Behari countrywoman: she carried huge bundles of kalhai on her head and sheaves of wheat husks.

This woman was called Dhruba. An unmistakably Behari name. Her father had first come to this village as a homoeopathic doctor, then began farming after acquiring some land here. He died shortly and his eldest son— a Hindustani inside out—looked after the farm work. Despite all his efforts, he could not arrange a match for any of his elder sisters. I knew that they had no means of paying any dowry.

Dhruba was another Kapalkundala.[17] She addressed me as 'Bhayyia' or elder brother. She was extremely strong: she ground wheat, pounded sattu, carried heavy loads, was an expert in grazing cattle and adept in working in the fields. Her brother had even proposed that if he could find a siuitable match he would give all three sisters to the same person. Apparently, the three women were not averse to this proposal.

'Do you wish to see Bengal?' I had once asked the middle one, Joba.

She had replied in the local language, 'No, Bhayyia. The water won't suit me.'

I had heard that Dhruba too was very keen to marry. She had told some-one that whoever married her would never have to hire anyone to milk the cows or pound grain; she was herself capable of grinding five seers of wheat into sattu.

Alas, poor and wretched unmarried Bengali woman! After all these years she must still be preparing the feed for the cattle and carrying back loads of kalhai from the field. Who would ever marry a poor and aging rustic woman without a dowry and carry her home in style in a palanquin? Who would welcome her with the sound of the conch and the ululation of the women that marked the auspicious entry of a bride to her new home?

When evening falls in the quiet open spaces, like a parting in the hair, the narrow path that cuts through the thick forests on the distant hill comes into view. And, Dhruba—poor and with her wasted youth—probably still comes down the path with a bundle of firewood on her head: I see this often enough in my imagination. As I have seen, too, my Didi, Rakhal-babu's widow: perhaps, even now, she slips like a thief into the fields at night to pick up the discarded cobs of maize, like any other old gangota peasant woman.

3

That time, while I was returning from Bhanmati's in the middle of Sravan, the rains came down heavily. It rained unceasingly from morning to night and the sky was overcast with thick clouds, black as kohl. From Narha and Phulkia-baihar the horizon was a blur, misted completely in the rain; Mahalikharoop was invisible, and the top of Mohanpura Reserve Forest seen only in glimpses. I was told that both rivers were in flood, Kushi in the east and Karo in the south.

The forests of kash and jhau that stretched on for miles were now being drenched in the rain. I would take a chair to sit outside in the office verandah, and watch a companionless ghughu getting completely soaked as he sat on the branch of a wild jhau in the midst of the kash forest. For hours together he sat in the same way, occasionally ruffling his feathers in an effort to ward off the water, but sitting still for the most part.

Then, it would become impossible to spend the day sitting in my office room. I would tighten the girth of my saddle, fling a raincoat over my shoulders and set off on my horse. The freedom was a gift of life. Everywhere it was a sea of green. The kash forest had renewed itself in the rainwater and now sprouted eager green shoots. As far as the eye could see—from Narhabaihar on one side up to the blurred blue skyline of the Mohanpura Forest on the other—it was a green ocean and the moist monsoon wind beneath the sky of dark clouds rippled over this greenery. I was a sailor on immense seas, voyaging to a mysterious dream port.

I would gallop through this vast green ocean for miles altogether. Sometimes, I entered the forest of Saraswati kundi and saw how nature's treasures had been embellished by the many plants and creepers that Jugalprasad had planted with so much care. I am sure there are very few places in all our Bharat that can compare in beauty with Saraswati kundi and the forest around it. The rains had brought out a crowd of red campion by the lakeside; bluish white watercroft filled the *kundi*. I know that only the other day Jugalprasad had planted an unusual wild creeper by the lake. It is true that he worked as a mohuree at the Ajmabad katcheri, but his heart lay in the groves and nooks in the forests of Saraswati kundi.

On coming out of the forest I saw again the vast open spaces, lush grassland. Dark blue clouds were massing up again, above the forest line; before they could release their load of water, yet another mass would come in to take their place. A part of the sky had taken on an unusual shade of blue, and a heap of clouds catching the red of the setting sun looked like an unknown mountain peak.

It is almost evening: in the endless Phulkia-baihar I hear the foxes begin to howl. There is the darkness of the overcast sky, and the fast approaching darkness of evening—I turn my horse towards the katcheri.

How often, in the short lull between downpours, as the evening thus crept into the vast open fields, I have dreamt of a god. The clouds, the evening, the forest, the chorus of the foxes, the water flowers in Saraswati kundi, Manchi, Raju Parey, Bhanmati, Mahalikharoop, the poor Gond family, the sky—all of this—had once been germinating like seeds in his imagination. Like the monsoon rains and the garland of blue water-bearing clouds his benediction now seeped into all life in the universe: the rain-soaked evening was his gesture, his voice was in freedom, the voice which awakens the innermost core of man. A god who need not be feared, who was vaster than this vast Phulkia-baihar and even more unending than the boundless sky—his love and his blessings equally inexhaustible. For the lowliest and the most unimportant was reserved the greatest share of the invisible blessings and compassion of such a generous god.

The god of whom I dreamt was not an ancient judge, a lawgiver, wise and far seeing or one couched merely in the obscure philosophical jargon of omniscience and immortality. Many a dusk in the open fields of Narha-baihar or Ajmabad, many a mass of blood-red clouds, many moonlit fields have made me feel that he was love and romance, poetry and beauty, art and intellect. He loves with all his might, creates with the power of his art and exhausts himself in a constant giving for the love of his creatures. And the same god with the power and vision of a mighty scientist creates too, the stars, the planets and the galaxies.

4

On one such rainy day of Sravan, Dhaturia arrived at the Ismaelpur katcheri.

I was very happy to see him after a long gap.

'What news Dhaturia? Are you well?'

He put into my hands the little bundle in which he carried all his worldly belongings and greeted me with folded hands, 'I've come to show you my dance, Babuji. I'm going through a bad time, no one has asked me to perform this last month. I thought, let me go to Babuji at the katcheri—they'll be sure to watch me dance. I've learnt some more dances, nice ones.'

Dhaturia looked thinner. It made me sad to look at him.

'Will you have something to eat, Dhaturia?'

Dhaturia shyly nodded an assent.

I summoned my cook and asked him to give the boy something. There was no rice to be had at that time of the day; the cook brought him some milk and pressed rice. Watching Dhaturia eat, I realized that he must not have eaten for at least a couple of days.

A little before twilight Dhaturia danced for us. Dhaturia had greatly improved since the last time I saw him dance. He had in him the sensitivity and dedication of the true artist. I gave him some money and the others at the katcheri made up a collection for him as well. But how long would it sustain him?

Dhaturia came to me the next morning to take leave of me.

'Babuji, when will you be going to Calcutta?

'Why do you ask?'

'Will you take me to Calcutta, Babuji? I had asked you that time, remember.'

'Where will you be going now Dhaturia? You must eat before you leave.'

'No Babuji, I can't—there is a bhuiyar brahman in Jhallu-tola whose daughter is to be married, they might want to see a dance or two. I'll go and see if I can get any work. It's about eight miles from here: if I set off now, I shall get there by evening.'

I was loath to let go of Dhaturia. I said to him, 'If I give you some land in the katcheri, will you stay here? You can do some farming and stay on here, can't you?'

I noticed that Motuknath Pandit had also taken a great liking to Dhaturia. He was keen on having Dhaturia as a pupil in his *tole*. 'Babuji, do tell him to stay,' Motuknath pressed me, 'I shall get him to complete the *Mugdhabodh* text in two years time. Let him stay here.'

Dhaturia responded to my offer of land with, 'It's most kind of you Babuji; you are like an elder brother to me—but, would I be able to do any farm work? I'm not interested in farming! I am happy as long as I can perform for people. I don't really care for anything else.'

'That's all right, you will continue to perform every now and then. If you do some farming, it doesn't mean that you will be chained to the land, does it?'

Dhaturia was delighted. 'I'll do whatever you tell me. I like you very much Babuji. Let me come back from Jhallu-tola and then I shall settle down here.'

Motuknath Pandit added, 'And I shall enrol you as a student in my *tole* when you come back. You could come at night to learn from me. There's nothing to be gained in being an ignoramus—you must learn some grammar and some poetry.'

Dhaturia sat down and spoke at length on various aspects of the art of dancing, much of which I did not understand very well: the differences between the Ho-Ho dance as it was danced in Purnea and in Dharampur; how he himself had initiated a change in a certain gesture of the hand, and other such details.

'Babuji, have you seen the women dance during the Chhat festival in Balia district? There's one part of the dance that is very similar to the Chhakkarbaji. And how do they dance in your part of the world?'

I told him about the 'Nanichor natua' piece I had seen during the last harvest. 'Babuji, that's nothing but a rustic dance from Mungher,' said Dhaturia with a laugh. 'A dance to entertain the gangotas. There's nothing authentic about it; it's too simple.'

'Do you know it? Why don't you show it to me?'

I found Dhaturia to be well-versed in his art. He gave an excellent rendering of 'nanichor natua'—the same sort of sing-song crying like a little child, the same way of doling out the stolen curds and cream, all of it. Except, it suited him much more, for he was truly a lad.

As he was bidding us goodbye he said to me, 'Since Huzoor has been so generous, can you not once take me to Calcutta? It is a city where they would know how to value dance.'

This was the last time I saw Dhaturia.

A couple of months later, we heard that a little distance from Kataria station, a young boy's body had been discovered on the tracks of the BNW Rail line; it had been identified as the body of the *natua* lad, Dhaturia. I cannot say whether it was an accident or a case of suicide. If it was suicide, what grief could have prompted him to the act?

I came across many men and women in the two years I spent in the region, but Dhaturia was unique. In him, I had found an artist's sensibility, ever active, ever joyous, and unworldly. His was a sensibility rarely found, not only in that wild and godforsaken place, but in any part of the so-called civilized world.

5

Three more years went by.

All the jungleland in Narha-baihar and Lobtulia had been leased out. There were no forests like those of former times left anywhere. All the shady groves that nature had composed in these many years, the creeper-entwined trees and secluded paths were lopped off by the ruthless hands of the labourers. What had taken fifty years to come up was destroyed in a matter of days. Now, there remained no mysterious green where enchanting fairies might descend on moonlit nights or thick jungle where benign Tarbaro, god of the wild buffaloes, put up his hand to save his herd of wild creatures.

Narha-baihar had lost its name and Lobtulia had become just another settlement. Wherever one looked one saw only straggling lines of tiled huts, jostling for space, and the occasional hut of kash—a dense and crowded settlement, split into *tolas*. The vast stretches of open land had been planted over with crops, and wild phanimansa bushes bordered the little plots. They had cut up the unfettered earth into little pieces and had destroyed it.

Only one spot remained—the forestland around Saraswati kundi.

It was true that I had leased out the land to peasants in the interests of my employer, in order to keep my job, but I could not willingly give up for rent that exquisite bit of forest by the side of Saraswati kundi where Jugal-prasad had toiled so hard. How often had people come to me wanting to lease the land around the lake, even offering higher advances and revenues! For not only was the land particularly fertile, the presence of all that water would certainly make the soil yield a better harvest. But I had never agreed to let it out.

Yet, was it possible to hold on to it indefinitely? I got frequent letters from the head office enquiring why I was delaying in letting out the land around Saraswati kundi. I had kept the process at bay by citing sundry problems, but this could not continue for long. Human beings are only too greedy; I know that nothing would stand in the way of destroying such an exquisite grove—all for a handful of cheena-grains and a couple of maize cobs. The settlers did not care much for the majesty of trees, they did not have the eyes to see the grandeur of the land; their only concern was to fill their stomachs and to survive. If it were any other country, they would have had laws to keep the forests intact and preserve them for nature lovers, as they have done with the Yosemite Park in California, the Kruger National Park in South Africa or the National Albert in the Belgian Congo. My distant employers do not care for the landscape: all they understand are taxes and revenue money— the salaami, the *irshal* and the *hustabood*.

How did a Jugalprasad come to be born in this land of people blind from birth to nature's bounty, I wonder . . . I have sought to preserve the forest around Saraswati kundi thinking only of him. But for how long?

Anyway, the task for which I was appointed appeared to be almost completed.

I had not been to Bengal for almost three years. I grew very homesick sometimes. All of Bengal became my home, illumined by the glow of the auspicious lamp with which a young housewife ushers in the evening. Here, it was all vast open stretches and jungles without the soothing touch of a woman's hand.

A sudden and unknown tide of joy leapt up and flooded my being. I set off immediately for Saraswati kundi on my horse, for by then, the forestland of Narha-baihar and Lobtulia was fast vanishing. Whatever remained of the forest's beauty was still to be found on the banks of the Saraswati: the only place where I could give expression to this inner joy.

The waters of Saraswati kundi glistened in the moonlight. Not merely glistened, the moonlight broke in waves upon the lake. The silent and lonely forest encircled three sides of the lake; the cry of red ducks and the scent of the wild shefali filled the air. It was Jaishtha, but here, the shefali blossomed all the year round.

I let my horse wander for a while by the lakeside. In the waters of the lake lotuses bloomed and, on the banks, the watercroft and the spider lilies that Jugalprasad had planted grew in thick clumps. I was headed for home after many years. I was soon to be free from my lonely exile in this forestland. I would live again enjoying the food cooked by Bengali women. I would go to the theatre and the bioscope now and then in Calcutta and, after all these years, I would again meet up with my friends!

Gradually, the pleasure of these anticipated joys broke through the banks and flooded with me with its full force. It must have been by some wonderful coincidence that it was time for me to return home now, when the waters of Saraswati kundi were awash in moonlight, when the wildflowers and the scent of the shefali and and wind whistling past my galloping horse made everything like a dream. It was a deep and joyous intoxication! As though I were a god drunk on youth, unfettered, moving through and beyond time, as though this movement was the victorious sign of my fate, my good fortune, blessings showered on me by some benign deity.

Perhaps I would never return: I might die once I had gone back home. Goodbye, Saraswati kundi, goodbye you line of trees along the bank, goodbye forestland washed in moonlight. I shall remember you in the middle of the crowded bustling avenues of Calcutta like the faint plucking of a *vina*, sounding notes of days gone by; I shall remember these trees brought from far-off places by Jugalprasad and planted here along the lake; the forest of spider lilies and lotuses; the ghughu crying out in the still afternoon hidden amidst the branches; the gnarled stumps of moinakata turning red in the late afternoon sun half hidden by clouds; flocks of red geese and silli making a trail in the blue sky over your blue waters; the soft imprint of a fawn's hooves in the muddy banks; and above all, the quietness, the all-enveloping loneliness. Goodbye, Saraswati kundi.

On my way back, I came across signs of trees having been felled, and about a mile after I had left the lake, of human habitation. The place was called Naya-Lobtulia, the New Lobtulia, like New South Wales and New York. The new settlers had struck off branches and made three low-roofed hovels, thatched with wild grass. There were no big forests nearby, so the branches must have come from the forest around Saraswati kundi. On the wet open verandah in front of the hovel lay a bottle with a broken neck—probably filled with coconut or mustard oil; a thin little naked baby was crawling on all fours around baskets woven of the thin twigs of the sihora tree, while a stocky young housewife, dark as an *yakshi*,[17] with a bracelet around her bare upper arm stood amidst a couple of brass plates and bowls, some flat-bladed machetes, a pick and a spade. These items made up the basic stock of goods in practically every household. It was the same not only in Lobtulia but in Ismaelpur and Narha-baihar as well. I wondered always about where these people had come from—they had no love for their native place or their ancestral land, no love for neighbours. Settled now in the forests of Ismaelpur, on the sandbanks of Mungher a few days later, and then again, at the foot of the Jayanti Hills—they went everywhere. They made their homes anywhere.

I heard a familiar voice and found Raju Parey ensconced amongst one such family of new arrivals, holding forth on theology. I dismounted and went towards him. All got up and made a seat for me. Raju told me that he had come here to practice his herbal medicine. He had been given a fee of eight measures of barley and eight paisas in cash. He was thrilled with the amount and was now engaged in expounding on philosophical matters to his new audience.

'Do sit down, Babuji, and give us your comment on this point: Tell us, is there an end to this world? Babuji, I've been telling them that just as there is no end to the sky, so there is no end to the earth. Isn't that so, Babuji?'

I had not imagined when I had set out on my excursion that I would have to confront such a profound scientific query.

I knew that Raju Parey's philosophical inclinations always led him to spin out complex theories, and I also knew that he always sought to resolve his speculations with very original solutions: rainbows emerged from termite hills, the constellations were the spies of Yama, the god of death—they were sent by Yama to keep track of the population expansion on earth, and so on.

I was trying to throw light on this question, as best as I could, from my understanding of the earth's rotation, when Raju interrupted me with, 'As to why the sun rose from the east and set in the west—has anyone ever been able to distinguish the sea from which the sun rose from the sea into which it set?' Raju had studied some Sanskrit, on his using the word *nirakaran* for 'distinguish', the gangota folk and their families gazed at him with wonder and admiration; simultaneously, they must have felt that their doctor had thrown the English educated Bangali-babu in deep waters with his penetrating questions. It was enough for the Bangali-babu to keep himself afloat in such circumstances!

'Raju,' I said, 'your eyes deceive you; the sun goes nowhere—it stays still in one place.'

Raju stared at me disbelievingly. The gangotas burst forth in derisive laughter. Alas Galileo! You had once been imprisoned in this disbelieving irrational world of ours.

After the first effect of the general amazement had died down, Raju demanded of me, 'Does not the sun god rise in the Uday mountain in the east and sink into the western sea?'

'It does not,' said I.

'They have written this in the English books, have they?'

'Yes, they have.'

Truly, knowledge makes a man courageous. Raju, peace-loving and quiet Raju, who I had never heard raising his voice, the very same Raju now said with fierce pride and energy, 'It's all lies, Babuji! A sadhu from Mungher had once seen the cave in Mount Uday from which the sun comes out. You have to go very far on foot, the mountain is on the very edge of the east, there's a huge stone door blocking the cave, and that's where the sun god's chariot of mica is stored. It's not just any old person who gets to see it; only the holiest of sadhus and temple-heads are privileged to do so. He brought back with him a bit—a huge chunk of shiny mica it was—my *guru-bhai*[18] Kamtaprasad has seen it with his own eyes.'

When he had finished speaking, Raju proudly cast his eyes on his gangota audience.

I was completely silenced that day by such irrefutable proof of the sun rising from the cave in Mount Uday.

SIXTEEN

1

'Let's go to the Mahalikha-roop to look for new plants,' I said to Jugalprasad one day.

Jugalprasad responded most enthusiastically, 'There's a creeper-like tree in the forests on that hill; it is only to be found up there. We call it chihor. Let us look for it.'

The path lay through the new settlements of Narha-baihar. Already, each one of these *tolas* had been named after the local head: Jhallu-tola, Rupdas-tola, Begum-tola, among others. From the tiled houses of mud the smoke rose in coils and thin naked children played in the dust by the wayside.

The northern limits of Narha-baihar still had magnificent forest cover. But in Lobtulia-baihar there was no forest or even many trees left: about three quarters of the beautiful forest of Narha-baihar was gone, only about two thousand bighas of land in the north had not yet been leased out. I could see that Jugalprasad was very distressed.

'The gangotas have come and ruined everything, Huzoor,' he said. 'They don't really make homes. A group of wanderers they are, moving from one spot to another. How could they have destroyed such a forest!'

'They are not to blame, Jugalprasad,' said I. 'Why should the zamindars let their lands lie unused; after all, they pay revenue to the government. How long can they keep on paying the revenue from their own pockets? It is the zamindar who has brought them here; what are the gangotas to do?'

'Don't let out Saraswati kundi, Huzoor. Whatever I've planted there was got with a great deal of effort—'

'It does not depend on me, Jugal. It is enough that I've managed to keep it untouched for all these years. How long can this go on? The tenants are keen on renting that part of the estate—it's good land, you see.'

There were several guards accompanying us. Not quite understanding the drift of our conversation, they sought to encourage me, 'Don't you worry Huzoor, not one bit of land will be left untenanted around Saraswati kundi once the spring harvesting is done.'

Mahalikharoop was almost nine miles away. Its hazy shape could be made out from the office window. It was ten in the morning by the time we got to the foot of the hills.

The sunlight and the blue sky were very special that day. I had never quite seen such a shade of blue sky—I don't know what made the sky take on such a deep blue on some days. The sunlight took over one's being like an intoxicating wine. It fell on tender green leaves and turned them transparent. The birds had no place left for nesting in Narha-baihar and Lobtulia: they had sought refuge in the nearby forests—some near Saraswati lake, some here in the foot of Mahalikharoop and some in the Mohanpura Reserve Forest. They made their presence felt with unceasing chirps and calls.

The quiet dense forest filled one with a sense of peace and freedom. Trees everywhere, and wild flowers, huge rocks scattered all over—sit wherever you like, stretch yourself on the ground if you wish to, or while away the moments of your life in the dark shadow of the blossoming piyal—the vast forestland will always soothe your exhausted nerves.

We have begun the climb up. The sunlight barely filters through huge trees, mountain springs and waterfalls gurgle and sound their way down the slopes, while the big leaves of the haritaki and the kelikadamba rustle and stir in the wind. The piercing cries of wild peafowl also reach us.

'We must start looking for the chihor fruit tree, Jugalprasad,' I remind him.

We come across the tree on much higher ground. The leaves are like those of the sthalpadma; the creeper thick and woody, it has climbed up twisting and turning, using other trees for support. The flowers are pod-like, but the two halves of the pods are as big as the kotki-cloth slippers that are specially crafted in Cuttack, and just as wide and hard; inside, there are round seeds. We have roasted these seeds over dry twigs—they taste exactly like little round potatoes.

We have climbed up quite high. There, far away is Mohanpur Reserve Forest, to the south lies our estate, and there—to be seen only indistinctly— the forest around the fringes of Saraswati kundi. And there, the last little quarter of what remains of Narha-baihar, and over there, the Kushi flowing around the eastern limits of Mohanpura Reserve Forest . . . The land lying beneath us looked like a painting.

'A peacock! Huzoor, look there, a peacock!'

Just above us sat a huge peacock on a tree. A guard who had brought his gun along was about to shoot down the bird. I stopped him.

'Babuji,' said Jugalprasad, 'I'm looking for a cave here somewhere in the jungle; it's got all kinds of pictures drawn on its walls, no one knows how ancient it is.'

Perhaps there were paintings or carvings in the unyielding rocky walls of the cave done by people in prehistoric times! Millions of years of the earth's history would suddenly, in a moment, be uncovered before us—we who would suddenly enter the cave and be sucked into the vortex of time.

We began pushing our way through the jungle impelled by an intense desire to see the cave paintings from prehistoric times, but when we finally managed to find the cave, it was so dark inside that I did not dare to go in. In any case, I would hardly be able to see! We might easily lose our lives to a poisonous snake, perhaps a king cobra or a banded krait, in the darkness. They were to be found aplenty in these places. Let it be. We would have to come prepared another time.

'You must plant some newer species of plants and trees in this forest,' I told Jugalprasad. 'No one will ever cut down the forests on these hills. Lobtulia is gone, and you might as well forget about Saraswati kundi . . .'

'What you say is right, Huzoor,' said Jugalprasad. 'It has struck a chord in me. But you will not be coming here any more; I shall have to do it all on my own.'

'I shall come every now and then to look around. You can begin planting.'

Mahalikharoop was not really a mountain but a range of hills about a thousand and a half feet at its highest point. It made up the lowest rung of the Himalyan foothills, although the Terai jungle and the real Himalayas began only a hundred miles later. From the top of the Mahalikharoop, the plains below looked as though in ancient times the ocean waves had once dashed against the sandy slopes of the mountan. Cavemen were still to come: they lay cocooned in the womb of the future. Mahalikharoop was the sandy expanse of that ancient ocean.

Jugalprasad showed me at least ten new different kinds of plants that were not to be found in the plains. The vegetation in the upper part of the hill range was quite unique.

The day began to wane. We had been inhaling the scent of unknown wild flowers. Their scent grew stronger with the passing of the day. On every branch were flocks of raucous birds, chattering and singing—harteets, cuckoos, wild parrots and many others whose names I did not know.

My companions grew anxious to begin the descent for they were afraid of tigers. I found it hard to tear myself away from the pleasures of this lonely forest on a hill, in the lengthening shadows of dusk.

'Huzoor,' said Muneshwar Singh, 'tigers are a greater menace here than they are in the Mohanpur Reserve Forest. All those who come looking for firewood go down before it is evening. Anyways, they always come in a group. There are tigers and king cobras too . . .'

And so, we had to descend. Through the big leaves of the kelikadamba tree in that forest on the hill you could see Saturn and Jupiter glowing in the twilight.

2

I came across schoolmaster Ganauri Teowari one day sitting in the outer portion of a newly settled tenant's house and tucking into a meal of sattu on a sal leaf.

'It's Huzoor! How are you?'

'Quite well. When did you come? Where have you been? Are these people your kinsfolk?'

'No, they're not. I was passing by and it got late. They're brahmans, so I've accepted their hospitality and I'm having a meal. I did not know them, but of course, now we know each other.'

The host came out and greeted me, 'Do come up Huzoor, and sit with us.'

'No, I won't sit now; I'm fine here. When did you take over this land?'

'It's been two months, Huzoor. I've not been able to plant anything yet.'

A little girl came to give Ganauri Teowari a couple of green chillies. The meal consisted of kalhai sattu, salt and chillies. It was hard to figure out how that huge pile of sattu would fit inside Ganauri Teowari's thin frame. Ganauri was a regular wanderer. In a corner of the verandah, where he sat eating, I could see a bundle of dirty clothes and a thin quilt-like bedding which I knew to be his: these made up his worldly belongings.

'I'm busy now,' I told Ganauri, 'Come and see me at the katcheri this evening.'

Ganauri came to the katcheri in the evening.

'Where have you been, Ganauri?'

'Babuji, I've been travelling in the villages of Mungher district. I've done quite a bit of wandering around in those parts.'

'And what were you doing there?'

'I'd teach little boys. Set up little schools.'

'Not one of those schools succeeded . . .?'

'They didn't run for more than a few months. The boys wouldn't pay their fees.'

'Are you married? How old are you now?'

'How could I marry when I'm barely able to feed myself. I am about thirty-four or perhaps thirty-five years old.'

It was hard to find a person as poor as Ganauri even in these poverty stricken parts. I remembered that Ganauri had once come to my katcheri, without any invitation, to have some rice. This was when I had first come here. It must have been a long time since he last had rice. Accepting the hospitality of gangota households meant all he had for a meal was kalhai sattu.

'Ganauri,' I said, 'tonight you will have a meal here. Kantu Mishir cooks for us; you wouldn't have any objections to food cooked by him?'

Ganauri was delighted. 'Kantu is a brahman like us,' he said with a big smile, 'I've had food cooked by him in earlier times, why should I object? Huzoor,' he added, 'since you've brought up the question of marriage I might as well tell you . . . The year before, in the month of Sravan, I started a school in a village. There was a brahman family same as ours in the village. I lived in his home. My marriage to his daughter was all fixed up, so much so, that I even bought a nice merzai from Mungher. But in the meantime, the neighbours started working against the match: he's a poor schoolmaster, doesn't have a roof over his head, no food, no money, they said, don't give the girl to him. So, the marriage never took place. And I left the village.'

'Had you seen the girl? Was she good looking?'

'Haven't I seen her though! A wonderful girl, Huzoor! Why should she have me? It's true, I've nothing to call my own.'

Ganauri appeared to be very distressed that his marriage had not taken place; he was evidently quite taken with the girl.

He chatted and told me a lot of stories that evening. Listening to him, I felt that life had given him nothing. He had wandered from village to village looking for a handful of food and that too, was often denied to him. He had spent half his life moving from one gangota home to another.

'That's why I've come to Lobtulia after all this time,' he said. 'I had heard that many new settlements have come up recently. I thought I might start a school here, it will run well. What do you think Huzoor?'

Right away, I thought to myself that I would start a school here and keep Ganauri here. Large numbers of little children had come to live in the estate; it was my duty to provide some kind of education for them. Let's see what could be done.

3

On an exquisite moonlit night Jugalprasad and Raju Parey had come over to chat with me. We also had a visitor from a settlement that had newly sprung up not far from the katcheri. It was only four days since he and his neighbours had come all the way from Chhapra district to settle down in our estate.

The man told us his life's story. He had travelled to many places with his wife and children and made his home on *char* land and in forests that they had cleared. Three years in one place, five in another; and ten years when they lived on the banks of the Kushi. But nowhere had they been able to improve their circumstances. He hoped that it would soon happen, now that they had come to Lobtulia-baihar.

These nomadic householders led very strange lives. I have spoken with them and found them completely free of all bonds. They lead the lives of outcasts, they have no social ties and are not drawn to a homestead; they compose their homes beneath the blue skies and live in forests, in valleys and on lonely river banks. They're here today, gone tomorrow.

I found everything about them intriguing and novel: their love, separation, life and death. I was most intrigued above all, by the hope of progress that his man held on to.

It was difficult to imagine the kind of progress he aspired to, cultivating wheat in five or at the most ten bighas of land in the jungles of Lobtulia.

The man was over fifty years old. His name was Balbhadra Sengai. He was a farmer of the kaloar caste, also called the kolu. He still hoped to improve his circumstances, even at this ripe age

'Balbhadra, where did you live before you came here?' I asked him.

'Huzoor, we lived on the sandbank in Mungher district. We were there for two years. Then there came the blight and the maize crops got destroyed. I realized then that there was no hope of making any progress in that place. Huzoor, everyone who lives desires to better his lot and progress. Now that Huzoor has granted me a place ...'

'I had six buffaloes when I first came here, now I have ten. Lobtulia is the place to progress,' observed Raju Parey.

'Buy me a pair of buffaloes, Pareyji,' said Balbhadra. 'After I've harvested the crops this time, I must buy a pair with the money. There's no other way of progressing.'

Ganauri had been listening to their conversation. 'That's right,' he chimed in, 'I too, would like to buy a couple of buffaloes. Just as soon as I can settle down somewhere . . .'

In the moonlight, the trees on Mahalikharoop and beyond them, the Dhannjhari range could now be seen as though through a haze. It was getting to be cold and a little fire had been lit—on one side of it sat Raju Parey and Jugalprasad and on the other, Balbhadra and few other new tenants.

How strange it was to hear their talk of material improvement. Their idea of progress was not an overly ambitious one—it meant owning ten or perhaps a dozen buffaloes in the place of six. As I listened to them and chanced to find out the kind of hope and aspirations a human being might cherish even in these distant and impenetrable forests encircled by hills, the very moonlit night became one of exquisite mystery to me. The mystery enveloped Mahalikharoop, the distant Dhannjhari and the thick vegetation on the mountain.

Jugalprasad alone did not take part in this talk of material advancement. He is a misfit on our earth. He does not like talking about land, crops and cattle, nor does he care to listen to such talk.

'Have you noticed, Babuji,' he said turning to me, 'the hansalata I'd planted in the eastern borders of the jungle by Saraswati kundi, how well it has done? This time the spider lilies around the pond also look wonderful. Will you come there for a walk on a moonlight night?'

I felt sad wondering how long I would be able to keep untouched the forest around Saraswati kundi—the forest Jugalprasad was so deeply attached to. The hansalata, the wild shefali, would they all disappear? In their stead, innumerable stalks of maize would rear their heads; rows of tiled huts would stand cheek by jowl, string cots before them, and muddy yards where the cattle chewed on their fodder.

Just then, Motuknath Pandit came in. Presently, there were about fifteen boys studying traditional Sanskrit grammars like the *Kalap* and *Mugdhabodh* in his *tole*. His situation had improved considerably. At the time of the last harvest, he had received so much wheat and maize from the guardians of his students that he had to make a small stack out of them.

Motuknath was living proof that success was inevitable in the case of those who kept on trying to improve their lot.

Improvement! Progress! —There it was again.

Yet, there was no way of avoiding the issue. It was clear that because Motuknath had bettered his lot, he was getting a great deal of respect these days. I noticed that the very guards and clerks in my katcheri who had once regarded him scornfully, as a mad man, held him in respect and were deferential towards him since Motuknath had his own stack of grain. Increasingly, the number of students in the *tole* appeared to be on the rise. On the other hand, no one cared a whit for Jugalprasad and Ganauri Teowari. Raju Parey had also gained the esteem of the tenants who had newly arrived—you could often spot him making the rounds of the houses with his bundle of medicinal roots and herbs, taking the pulse of this child and that one. However, Raju Parey did not quite understand money matters; he was quite contented with the attention he received and the conversations he had with his many patients.

4

In another four months, tenants had been settled in the entire area between Mahalikharoop and the northern limits of Lobtulia and Narha-baihar. Although the land had been let out much earlier and crops sown, never had so many people been actually settled in the area. This year the people came in droves and set up villages, almost overnight.

Such a variety of people! One family was seen to arrive with their household belongings—bedding, vessels, kindling, a stove, the household deity—all piled up on the back of a thin horse. Another man had loaded his little boys and girls, along with a broken lantern, cooking vessels, and even a string-cot, on a buffalo. Some families had come walking, the parents carrying a litter on their shoulders: their children and goods were squeezed into the litter.

The newcomers included the poor Maithili brahman as well as gangotas and doshads—people from all strata of society. I asked Jugalprasad Mohuree, 'Have these people been homeless all this time? Where are they all coming from?'

Jugalprasad was upset at the influx. 'These people are all of a kind,' he said. 'They've heard that there's land going at cheap rates here and so they come in droves. If they can work out something they will stay on, otherwise, they will pack up and run off elsewhere.'

'Don't they have any love for their ancestral soil?'

'None whatsoever, Babuji. It has become part of their livelihood to grow crops on newly-emerged char or to take over forestland and clear it. Settling down is secondary. They'll stay on for as long as the harvest is good and the revenues low.'

'And then?'

'Then they'll find out where land is going cheap or where the river has thrown up a new bank, and off they'll go. It's their business to keep moving.'

5

The other day I had gone to Grantsaheb's Banyan to have the land measured out. Ashrafi Tindale was doing the measuring; as I supervised him from my seat on the horse, I saw Kunta go by in the path around the *tola*.

I had not seen Kunta for a long time. I asked Ashrafi, 'Where does Kunta live these days? I don't see her . . .'

'Haven't you heard about it Babuji?' asked Ashrafi. 'She wasn't here for quite some time in between . . .'

'How is that?'

'Rashbehari Singh took her over to his home. You are the wife of our kin, he said, come and live at my place . . .'

'Well?'

'She did stay at his place for some time—you've seen her looks, Babuji, even now, after all the sorrows and difficulties she's gone through, she . . . Then Rashbehari said something or the other to her, and even tried to assault her; it's been a month now that she's run away from his place. I'm told Rashbehari threatened her with a dagger. And she said, "Kill me Babuji, I'll give up my life, but I won't give my honour."'

'Where does she live now?'

'She has taken shelter with a gangota family in Jhallu-tola. She lives in a shack near their cowshed.'

'How does she manage? She has several children . . .'

'She begs, or picks up the leftovers from the harvested field; she harvests wheat and other crops. She's a good woman, Kunta. She may have been a *baiji's* daughter but her bearing is like that of a woman from any respectable family. She's not the one to do anything dirty.'

The surveying was done. A tenant from Balia district had taken this lot of land; tomorrow, he would start building his home. The grandeur of Grantsaheb's Banayan was about to end.

The sun grew red above the tree line on top of Mahalikharoop. Flocks of silli flew towards Saraswati kundi. Evening would soon be here.

I thought of something.

Not one bit of land would remain in all of vast Lobtulia and Narha-baihar. Unknown people had come in droves and had taken over the land, but those who had lived forever in these forestlands and who were wretched and utterly poor, would they be forever kept out of its bounds only because they lacked the means to rent out the land? I had to do at least this bit of favour to those I loved.

I turned to Ashrafi and asked him, 'Can you get Kunta here tomorrow morning, Ashrafi? I have some work with her.'

'I can, Huzoor, whenever you say.'

The next day Ashrafi brought Kunta to my office at nine in the morning.

'How are you Kunta?'

Kunta joined her hands in a namaste. 'Huzoor, I am well.'

'And your children?'

'They are well too, by the grace of Huzoor.'

'How old is your eldest son?'

'He is just running eight, Huzoor.'

'Can he not graze buffaloes?'

'Who would let such a little boy graze cattle, Huzoor?'

It was true that Kunta was still good-looking. Sorrow and hardship had left their mark on her face, but courage and purity had endowed it with a rare radiance.

This was the same Kunta, lost to love, the daughter of a *baiji* in Kashi. She still carried in her hand that burning brand of love, and so she was poor and insulted. Kunta had truly honoured her love.

'Kunta, will you take some land?' I wanted to know.

She did not appear to have registered what I just said. She stared at me in surprise and repeated, 'Land, Huzoor?'

'Yes, the land that is now being allotted.'

Kunta seemed to think for a while. Then she said, 'We had so much land in the old days. When I first came, I saw all the land. Then, it was all gone, little by little. How am I to take this land now, Huzoor?'

'Why, can't you give some money as an advance?'

'Where would I get the money? I pick up leftovers of the harvest from the fields at night lest anyone insult me if I do it at daytime. I get anything from half a basket to a basket of kalhai, this I ground and make sattu to feed the children with. There's not enough for me on all days . . .' Kunta stopped speaking and lowered her gaze. Big drops fell from her eyes and rolled down her cheek.

Ashrafi moved a little distance away. The youth had a tender heart; he had not yet hardened his heart to the sorrows of others.

I said, 'Suppose Kunta, you did not have to pay the advance, the salaami?'

Kunta raised her tear filled eyes and looked at me with astonishment.

Ashrafi immediately came up to her and said with a vigorous movement of his hands, 'He's giving you the land for free, for free—don't you understand, Daiji?'

I said to Ashrafi, 'If I give her the land, how will she farm it?'

'That's not so difficult Huzoor. Every one would willingly lend her a hand, help her out with a couple of ploughs. If every one of the gangota familes was kind enough to give her a hand, the land could easily be farmed. I will take on that responsibility, Huzoor.'

'All right, Ashrafi. How many bighas will she need?'

'Since you are kind enough to give her land, give her ten bighas, Huzoor.'

I asked Kunta, 'If ten bighas of land were to be given to you without any salaami, you would be able to farm it properly and then pay off the katcheri with the sale of your crops, wouldn't you? Of course, you won't have to pay any revenue for the first two years. Only from the third year.'

Kunta looked dumbstruck. As though she was still trying to figure out whether we were simply joking at her expense or were indeed serious about what we said.

She exclaimed somewhat helplessly, 'Land! Ten bighas of land.'

Ashrafi spoke on my behalf, 'Yes, Huzoor is giving you the land! You don't have to pay revenue for the first two years. Pay it from the third year onwards. Come now, are you agreeable?'

Kunta looked at me with painful shyness, 'Yes, Huzoor, it is your kindness.' Then suddenly, she broke down into violent sobs.

At a sign from me, Ashrafi led her away.

SEVENTEEN

1

In the hours after twilight, the new hamlets that have come up in Lobtulia look pleasing to the eye. The mist dims the moonlight somewhat, the farm-lands spread into the far horizon and, flung here and there, are the lights blinking from some four or five settlements. So many people, so many families have come to our estate in the hope of making a livelihood, of growing enough to fill their stomachs: they are busy cutting down the forests and clearing the land for farming. I do not even know the names of all the villages, nor do I know all the settlers. Shrouded in the misty moonlight the scattered villages look mysterious. To me, the lives of all those who inhabit the villages appeared as mysterious as the mist enshrouded moonlit night. I had made an acquaintance with only a few, but, from whatever little I gathered from them, their views of life, even their daily routine, seemed very strange.

Consider first, their daily diet: There are three cycles of crop in our estate—maize in the month of Bhadra, kalhai in Paush and wheat in Baisakh. Not too much maize is grown, for there is not enough suitable land, but there is a lot of kalhai and wheat—almost twice as much wheat as kalhai; the staple diet was therefore flour ground from kalhai.

Almost no rice is grown, whether in the leasehold land or in the government estate, as the low-lying land necessary for rice cultivation is not found in these parts. So people rarely have a chance to eat rice; eating rice is actually considered a matter of luxury or excess. A few people with fancy tastes do sell their kalhai and wheat and buy rice with the money, but their number may be counted on one's finger.

Then, as regards their living conditions: The innumerable settlements that have sprung up on the ten thousand bighas of our estate have homes thatched with the kash from the jungle, fencing made of stalks of kash; some have plastered the walls with mud, while others have simply left them bare. There are no bamboos growing in the area; they have used twigs of the trees native to the place—parts of the kend and the piyal—which now form their homes.

It is no use speaking of their religion. They are Hindus, but I have no idea how they have managed to single out Hanumanji from a pantheon of thirty-three crore gods and goddesses. In every village there is the ubiquitious Hanumanji's banner flying high. Ritual vermilion is even smeared on the banner. Ram and Sita are rarely celebrated in song; their servitor Hanuman has usurped the attention due to them and has obscured their importance. Vishnu, Durga, Shiva, Kali and other such deities are hardly worshipped or celebrated. In fact, it is doubtful if they are at all worshipped or celebrated, at least on our estate.

Ah, I had almost forgotten! There was one, who was a devotee of Shiva. He was called Dron Mahato, of the gangota caste. Some ten years ago, some-one had placed a chunk of stone at the foot of the Hanuman banner at the katcheri; every now and then, the guards would daub it with vermilion, or some one might even place a vessel of water as an offering before the stone. Most of the time however, it lay unattended.

In the last couple of months, a new settlement had come up at a little distance from the katcheri. Dron was no less than seventy years of age. He had a name like Dron precisely because he was an ancient man;[18] I believe that the boys and young men of these times would have names like Domon, Lodhai and Maharaj. In earlier times, the parents would be embarrassed to give their children fancy names.

However that may be, the elderly Dron once came to the katcheri and noticed the stone. Since that time, the old man bathed every morning in the Kalbolia river and brought back a vessel-full of water to pour over the stone; then, he circumbulated most devoutly around the stone and bowed before it lying prone on the ground on his stomach. Only after these devotions would he return home.

I told Dron, 'Kalbolia is miles away: you have to walk there and back every day; why don't you take the water from the nearby kundi?'

'Babuji,' replied Dron, 'Mahadeoji enjoys running water. It is my good fortune that I can pour water over him every day and bathe him.'

God is also fashioned by the devotee. As the story of Dron Mahato's worship of Shiva spread from hamlet to hamlet, I saw a few men and women come from time to time to offer their worship as well. A species of sweet-smelling grass grows in the area; the burnt offering of this grass or its stalks gives off a wonderful fragrance. The fragrance becomes more intense as the grass dries. Someone brought seedlings of the grass and planted them around the deity.

Then, one day, Motuknath Pandit posed a question: 'Is it proper for a gangota to come everyday and pour water over Shivji's head?'

'Panditji,' I replied, 'as far as I can see, it was the same gangota who had familiarized the locals with the deity. Why, you've also been around for quite some time now, but I've never seen you make an offering of even a single measure of water.'

Motuknath was so angry that he lost all capacity to argue rationally. 'Babuji, this stone here is not Shiva,' he retorted. 'Unless the god is duly consecrated, he doesn't warrant being worshipped. What's here is just a bit of stone!'

'In that case, why bother? Why should you object if a chunk of stone is watered?'

And, so Dron Mahato became the chartered priest for the shivalinga at the katcheri.

In the month of Kartik, Chhat was the major festival in these parts. From the many *tolas* came groups of women and girls dressed in saris dyed yellow. They sang their way to the Kalbolia, where they immersed the little leaf floats called 'chhats' which gives the festival its name. The whole day was reserved for festivities. When you went past the villages in the evening, you could smell the special sweet savouries called *pitha* being fried to mark the day. The sound of children laughing and chattering and of girls singing continued late into the night in places where once herds of neelgai used to run in the depths of the night, and hyenas laughed and tigers coughed (tigers make a sound that is exactly like a man clearing his throat, as the knowledge-able reader may know). Now, the same place was transformed into a populous settlement resounding with laughter and songs.

On the evening of the Chhat festival, I went to Jhallu-tola to honour an invitation to a meal. It was not just the invitation from this one *tola*, but from all fifteen *tolas* had come invitations for all the katcheri staff. First, I went to visit Jhallu Mahato, the headman of Jhallu-tola.

Jhallu Mahato's home was still surrounded by jungle on some sides. He welcomed us most affectionately and made us sit beneath the torn canopy he had hung up in his yard. All the others who had come from the *tola* wearing fresh dhotis and *merzais* sat on grass-mats. I said to Jhallu, 'I'm afraid I shan't be able to honour your request to have a meal, for I have to visit many another *tola*.'

'You must have some sweets,' he said. 'The girls will be most upset, otherwise. They were very excited that you were going to step in here and they've made special *pithas* for you.'

I could do nothing. Mohuree Goshto-babu, Raju Parey and I settled down to eat. A few *pithas* made of wheat and jaggery arrived on sal leaves. Each one of these savouries was as thick as a one-inch brick: if you hurled one at somebody, he was certain to be injured, if not killed outright. Yet, every one of those *pithas* was decorated with patterns of creepers and leaves as though it had been cast in a special mould. The *pithas* had first been cast in the patterned mould and then fried in ghee.

I could not do justice to the pithas prepared with so much labour and love by the girls. I managed to eat half of one, and that, with a great deal of trouble. It was not sweet in the least, nor was it tasty. I realized that gangota women had little by way of cooking skills. Raju Parey, however, finished about five of those huge *pithas*. Perhaps, out of deference to our presence, he could not ask for more.

From Jhallu-tola, we went to Lodhai-tola; then, on to Parbat-tola, Bhimdas-tola, Ashraf-tola, Lachmania-tola. In every *tola* was heard the sound of revelry, singing, dancing and music. They would not sleep the entire night; they were going to be dancing all night, the people moving from house to house.

There was something though which gave me a great deal of pleasure: I was told that in every *tola* the girls had prepared food for us. When they heard that the Manager-babu himself was to pay a visit, they had spent their entire repertoire of culinary expertise in trying to get the *pitha* right. Although I was most grateful for this generosity on the part of the girls, I was very sad that I could not really praise their culinary attempts. In subsequent stopovers I was introduced to even more inferior specimens of *pithas* than the ones I had had in Jhallu-tola.

In every *tola* I found girls in bright coloured saris staring with curious eyes from their partially covered vantage points at these Bangali-babus sitting down to their repast. On his part, Raju Parey did not disappoint or hurt any one. Ultimately, I despaired of keeping count of the number of *pithas* he consumed, for he soon overtook the limits of the possible. I cannot tell you therefore exactly how many *pithas* he ate.

It wasn't only Raju though, each one of the gangota invitees ate a score and more of those rock-hard *pithas*; I wouldn't have believed that a human being could eat so much if I had not seen it with my own eyes.

We also went to visit Chhaniya and Suratiya who lived in Narha-baihar.

Suratiya came out running as soon as she saw me.

'How late you are Babuji! Mother and I have made special *pithas* for you. We kept waiting and wondering why you were so late. Please come and sit down.'

Nakcchedi greeted everybody most hospitably and invited all of us to sit. I laughed to myself when I saw that Tulsi was arranging Raju's plate with care. Were Raju and his friends in any condition to eat any more?

'Ask your mother to take away some of the *pithas*,' I told Suratiya. 'Who can eat so many?'

Suratiya looked at me wonderingly, 'Why Babuji, aren't you going to eat these few *pithas*? Why, Chhaniya and I had about sixteen each. Ma has put raisins and milk in the *pithas* and Baba went and got fine quality wheat from Bhimdas-tola because you are going to be eating them.'

I had not done right by saying that I was not going to eat the sweets. These girls and boys were starved of such delicacies the entire year. Such longing and such sorrow had gone into the making of the *pithas*. I wished to make the children happy; somehow, I managed to eat two of the *pithas*.

'They're excellent,' I said to Suratiya wanting to make her happy, 'but I've had to eat something or the other in every one of the places we've stopped at, so I cannot eat any more. I'll come and have a go at them again.'

Raju Parey carried a small bundle in his hands. He had carried away something from every household. Given the weight of each *pitha*, his bundle must have weighed at least six kilograms.

Raju was thrilled. 'This kind of *pitha* doesn't spoil easily, Huzoor,' he explained. I shan't have to cook for the next few days. They'll do for my meals.'

The next morning Kunta appeared at the katcheri with a brass plate that she shyly placed before me. The plate was covered with a bit of clean rag.

'What do you have there, Kunta?' I asked.

'*Pithas* from the Chhat festival, Babuji', she said shyly. 'I came with it twice last night and took it back not finding you.'

I uncovered the plate and found a few *pithas*, sugar, a couple of bananas, a slice of coconut and an orange.

'They're lovely *pithas*, I can see!'

Kunta said in her embarrassed low voice, 'Please be kind enough to have all of them. I've made them specially for you. I am sad that I wasn't able to serve them hot.'

'That's all right Kunta, I'll have them all. They look very good'.

Kunta made me a *pranam* and left.

2

One day, Muneshwar Singh came to tell me, 'Huzoor, there is someone in the forest lying on some rags beneath a tree. The villagers pelt him with stones whenever he tries to enter the village. If you will allow me, I'd like to bring him to the katcheri.'

I was shocked by what he said. It was already late afternoon and it would not be long before it got dark. Although it wasn't excessively cold, it was still the month of Kartik: the dew fell heavily in the early hours and the tem-perature went down. I couldn't understand what made a man seek refuge in the forest in such conditions, or indeed, why the villagers would want to stone him.

On the other side of Grantsaheb's Banyan, beneath an arjun tree, a man was lying on bedding he had devised from rags and other dirty scraps. (It was almost thirty years from the day when the Englishman, Grant 'Saheb' came to survey the forestlands of Lobtulia and pitched his tent beneath the tree; the name had stuck since.) I couldn't see the man well for the thick bush that partially covered him. 'Who is it? Where do you come from?' I called out to him. 'Come out.'

The man came out very very slowly, walking on all fours at first. He was over fifty and thin and raggedy looking, his dhoti and *merzai* were dirty and torn. As long as it took him to crawl out of the bush, he kept looking at me with the frightened eyes of a hunted creature.

As he came out from the thick undergrowth into the light, I saw that his left arm and his left leg festered with sores. Perhaps this was why he could not immediately straighten up once he lay down.

Muneshwar Singh said, 'Huzoor, it's because of the sores that they don't let him enter the villages. They don't even give him a drink of water if he asks for it. They stone him and chase him away.'

It was clear now, why the man had sought shelter in the wild bushes braving the cool dew-drenched night of autumn.

'What is your name? Where is your home?' I asked him.

The man had shrunk in fear on seeing me: he looked ill, and in his eyes was an expression of fear and helplessness. Behind me stood Sipahi Muneshwar Singh with his stick; perhaps he thought that we were objecting even to the fact that he had sought shelter in the forest, that I had come only to chase him off.

He said, 'My name? My name . . . Huzoor, it is Girdharilal . . . I live in Tintanga.' The very next moment, he said in the tone of a delirious patient, entreating and cajoling, 'I want some water, a little water . . .'

I had recognized the man by then. He was the same Girdharilal that I had seen in the Brahma Mahato's tent at the fair that time in the month of Paush. The same frightened expression in his eyes, the same gentle features . . .

Does god single out for punishment the poor, the frightened and the meek? I turned to Muneshwar Singh: 'Go back to the katcheri and round up another four or five people and bring a string cot.'

He left.

'What is it, Girdharilal?' I asked him gently. 'I know you. Have you not recognized me? We met that time, at the fair, in Brahma Mahato's tent, don't you remember? Don't be afraid; what has happened to you?'

The tears fell from Girdharilal's eyes. He turned his arm and his leg to show me the sores and said, 'Huzoor, they got infected after I'd hurt myself. There was no way the wounds would heal. I tried every remedy that everyone suggested—it just got worse. Then they told me: You have leprosy. That is why I've been suffering like this for the last four months or so . . . they don't let me set foot in the villages. I beg and somehow, I get by. They don't give me a place to sleep at night so I come back into the forest . . .'

'Where were you heading for? And how did you get here?'

Girdharilal was already panting with exhaustion: 'I was going to the hospital at Purnea, Huzoor. Otherwise, the wounds will not heal.'

I could not but be surprised. How intense is the desire in man to survive. Purnea was at least forty miles from where Girdharilal lived. Before him was the dangerous Mohanpura Reserve Forest; yet, he was on his way to the hospital at Purnea, dragging his afflicted arm and leg all the way!

The string cot came. I put him in a room near the guards' quarters. At first, the guards raised objections because they too believed he was a leper, but when I explained the matter, they understood.

Girdharilal appeared to be starving, as though he hadn't eaten well for long. He picked up somewhat once he was given some hot milk. When I went to his room towards evening, he had fallen into a sound sleep.

The next day I sent for the local specialist, Raju Parey. Raju solemnly felt the patient's pulse for a long while and then examined his sores.

'Do you think you can do something or should I send him to Purnea?' I asked him.

Raju replied in somewhat hurt tone, 'By the grace of your ancestors, I have been doing this kind of work for quite some time now. The wounds will heal within a fortnight.'

I would have done well to have sent Girdhari to the hospital, I realized later. It wasn't because of the wounds—Raju Parey's medicinal roots and herbs changed the complexion of the sores in less than a week's time—the problem arose over nursing the sick man. No one wanted to touch him or apply the medicinal ointments; they even objected to washing the vessel from which he drank water.

On top of everything, the poor man came down with a high fever.

Left without any option I sent for Kunta. I told her, 'Get a gangota woman from the village; I shall pay her. She will need to look after him.'

'I will do it, Babuji,' Kunta replied without a moment's hesitation. 'You don't have to give me any money.'

Kunta had been the wife of a rajput; how could she nurse a sick man who was a gangota? I thought she had not quite understood me.

I said, 'You will have to wash his dishes, feed him—he can't get up. How can you do all of this?'

Kunta replied, 'I will do whatever you order me to do. I'm hardly a rajput, Babuji! Have my kinsmen ever looked after me all these years! I shall do whatever you tell me to do. What use have I with caste?'

Within a month, Girdharilal grew hale and hearty thanks to Raju Parey's herbs and Kunta's nursing. Kunta would not accept anything for her services. I noticed that she had in the meantime begun to address Girdharilal as 'Baba'. 'How can I take money for looking after Baba, he is such an unfortunate man. Is there no just god, no Dharmraj above us?'

Of the few good acts in my life, one of the most important ones was to settle the gentle and hapless Girdharilal in a small plot of land in Lobtulia, free.

I went one day to his hovel.

He had cleared his plot of five bighas all by himself and had planted wheat. Around the hut was a species of lemons known locally as gora-lebu.

'What will you do with so many trees of gora-lebu, Girdharilal?'

'Huzoor, you can make a drink from these lemons. I love the taste. We cannot afford sugar and michri, but with a bit of coarse jaggery it makes a wonderful drink.'

Girdharilal's gentle eyes sparkled in anticipation.

'They're from a good quality graft. Each one will weigh about half a kilo. I have always thought that if I could ever get a bit of land, I would grow a tree of these gora-lebus, and I'd have lemons to make any amount of sweet drink. So often Huzoor, when I've asked others for a few lemons I've been insulted; I shan't have to endure such grief again.'

EIGHTEEN

1

It is time for me to take leave. I had an intense desire to see Bhanmati once more. The Dhannjhari possessed my mind like a dream . . . her forests . . . her moonlit nights . . .

I took Jugalprasad with me.

Jugalprasad was riding Tehsildar Sajjan Singh's horse. Almost immediately after we had crossed the borders of our estate, Jugalprasad said, 'Huzoor, this horse won't do. As soon as I change the pace when we get on to the jungle path, he is sure to stumble and fall, and then I'll be blamed. Let me go and get another horse instead.'

I assured him that Sajjan Singh rode his mount well; consider how often he went to Purnea to keep an eye on his court cases: surely, Jugalprasad was aware of the terrain over which one had to ride to reach Purnea.

Soon after, we crossed the Karo.

After that it was only forests, forests—of beauty and wonder, thick, hushed forests. As I have said earlier, in these forests the trees did not send out their branches so far that they interlocked one with the other to keep out the sky. One saw saplings of kend, sal, palash, mahua and bushes filled with berries and undulating banks of red soil spreading far; occasionally, the footprints of wild elephants, and not a human being.

I began to breathe freely at having left behind the ugly and cluttered settlement newly come up at Lobtulia and the monotonous sight of bleak farmland. There was not such forestland anywhere else in these parts.

By noon, we had crossed two isolated villages, Burudi and Kulpal. The sparse forest soon lay behind us, ahead of us the plant life grew more luxuriantly. It was the end of Kartik and the wind blowing around us was cool. Far, far, away the Dhannjhari range grew more visible.

I reached the katcheri after evening had fallen. This katcheri now belonged to the person who had leased the jungle we had bought at the auction. They grew tobacco here.

The owner was a Musalman called Abdul Wahed: his home was in Shahabad district. He made me stay the night and treated me with great courtesy. 'It's good, Babuji, that you've come here before it got too dark,' he remarked. 'Tigers are a big menace here.'

It was a quiet night.

Through the big trees the wind blew.

We were chatting inside the room with the window open when suddenly a creature called out from the forest.

'What is it?' I asked Jugal.

'It's nothing,' he replied. 'It's a hural.' Meaning a wolf.

Late into the night a hyena was heard laughing—the sound froze the blood in my bones: it was exactly like the spasms of a tubercular patient, sometimes almost choking, and then the exuberance of laughter.

The next morning we set off early and reached Dobru Panna's capital at Chakmaki-tola at nine. How very pleased Bhanmati was at my unexpected arrival! She looked as though her happiness would burst forth from her eyes and her face; it threatened to spill over.

'I thought of you even yesterday, Babuji! Why did you not come earlier?'

Bhanmati looked taller this time, and somewhat thinner as well. Other than that, her features were just as warm and attractive, her figure just as lithe.

'You will bathe in the spring, won't you? Shall I get you mahua or mustard oil? Come and see how the rains have fed the spring this time.'

Something else that I've always noted: Bhanmati is always very clean and well groomed; in this respect, you couldn't compare her with an ordinary

Santal woman. Her dress and her appearance showed a refinement and delicacy that indicated her aristocratic background.

In the yard adjoining the verandah of the mud house where we sat were big ashan and arjun trees. A flock of green wild parrots squawked madly in the branches of the ashan. It was the beginning of *hemanta*; the breeze was still cool even late into the day. In front of me, less than half a mile away, was the Dhannjhari range. A path came down the hill, like a parting riven deep. On one side, very far away, the range of hills in Gaya district was like a bank of blue clouds.

To lease out the forest of tendu-leaves, to live forever in this quiet forest-land, my little cottage on the fringe of a mountain spring! Lobtulia was ruined, but no one would destroy this forest in Bhanmati's homeland. The soil was made up of pebbles and pyrite and crops did not flourish here; otherwise, this forest, too, would have disappeared long ago. It would be quite another story of course, if they suddenly were to begin mining the place for copper ore.

Chimneys of the copper factories, trolley lines, rows of bustees for the coolies, drains overflowing with dirty water, discarded heaps of ash spewed from engines, clusters of shops, tea-joints, cheap films—*Jawani Hawa, Sher Shamser, Pranoyer Jer* (only three annas for the matinee, come and book your seat in advance). Country liquor shacks, tailors' shops. Little pharmacies selling homoeopathic drugs (free treatment for the poor en bloc). The original and absolutely authentic Adarsho Hindu Hotel.[19]

The three-o clock whistle sounds from the factory.

Bhanmati has gone out, a basket on her head, to peddle coaldust in the bazar. C-o-a-l for sale, C-o-a-l, four paise a basket—

Bhanmati stood before me with the oil. All the family members came to greet me and encircled me. Bhanmati's younger uncle, the young Jagru, came up whittling a branch and smiled at me. I really liked this young fellow. He was built like a rajput, with a dark beauty! Of the people in their house, this young man and Bhanmati stood out; it was impossible not to sense that they were the true aristrocrats amongst the wild tribes.

'Well, Jagru?' I asked, 'How is the hunting these days?'

'Not to worry Babuji,' he said with a laugh, 'I'll get something for your meal this very day. Tell me what you would like to eat—porcupine, wild fowl or a harial?'

I came back after a bath. Bhanmati brought me a mirror (the one that I had brought for her from Purnea) and a wooden *kankoi* to comb my hair with.

I was resting after the meal, the day was on its way out, when Bhanmati proposed, 'Come Babuji, aren't you going to climb the mountain? You enjoy it so much.'

Jugalprasad was sleeping. We set off for a walk as soon as he woke up. With us came Bhanmati, and her cousin, Jagru Panna's brother's daughter, a girl of twelve years.

We came to the foot of the mountain after walking for about half a mile.

The forest was so astonishingly beautiful in this part of the hills that you wanted to stop and savour it at every step. Wherever you looked, you saw big trees, creepers, pebbled hollows into which springs trickled, and stone formations of odd shapes and sizes. The sky between the forest and the Dhannjhari had become a narrow strip. A red dusty path went up the forest and climbed up the hill going down on the other side. It was dry soil, not a drop of moisture anywhere. Not even a drop in the hollow of the spring.

As we pushed our way through the thick forest and began the climb up, all of us were equally enchanted by a sweet scent. A most familiar scent it was: I was not able to place it at first, then I looked around me and noticed for the first time the many chhatim trees that grew on the Dhannjhari hills. Now in early *hemanta*, the chhatim had blossomed and it gave off its unique fragrance.

And, it wasn't a just a couple of chhatim trees; there was a forest of them! There were kelikadambas too; not flowers of the kadamba, the kelikadamba belonged to another species altogether: the leaves were as big as those of the segun, the twisted branches giving it the appearance of thick vegetation.

In that late hour of a *hemanta* afternooon, standing in the midst of the thick forest of wild chhatim flowers with the cool breeze blowing around us, I saw the youthful Bhanmati glowing with vitality. I felt as though I had been blessed with a vision of the presiding deity of the forest herself, a goddess as dark as Krishna! She was indeed a princess. This forest, the hills, Michhi river over there, the banks of the Karo, and Dhannjhari on this side, the Nowadar range on the other—all these lands had once comprised the dominion of the now vanquished royal family, and the daughter of this family. The royal family was now threatened with extinction, made poor and lacklustre by its confrontation with the advent of a new ethos, a different civilization, so that in my eyes, Bhanmati appeared today like any other Santal girl. Whenever I saw her, this tragic chapter from the unwritten annals of Indian history flashed before my eyes.

The late afternoon that I was now experiencing merged with many other such beautiful afternoons and shone luminously in a crowd of sweet memories—sweet as in dream, and as unreal.

'Come,' said Bhanmati to me, 'aren't you going to keep climbing?'

'How wonderful is the scent of the flowers, is it not? Shall we not sit here awhile? Let us watch the sun set . . .'

'As you wish, Babuji,' replied Bhanmati with a smile. 'If you ask us to sit, we shall. But aren't you going to put flowers over Elder Uncle's tomb? You had taught us to do that: I go up the hill every day with flowers for him. Now the forests are full of flowers.'

Far away, the Michhi turned northwards, making a loop at the bottom of the hill. The sun set behind the indistinct range beyond Nowadar. The scent from the chhatim flowers grew stronger and the shadows darkened over the forest on the hills, and then spilled into the valley and the barren mountains by Michhi.

Bhanmati plucked a cluster of chhatim flowers and tucked it into her hair. 'Shall we sit here,' she asked, 'or shall we go on, Babuji?'

Again, we started on our way up. Each one carried a branch of chhatim flowers in his or her hand. We made our way to the very top of that ancient banyan tree in the ancient burial ground. Stones, shaped like those we use for grinding, were scattered all over the place. Over the grave of Raja Dobru Panna, Bhanmati and her sister Nichhni scattered their flowers; so did Jugalprasad and I.

Bhanmati was young and she expressed her delight in all innocence. 'Let's stop here for a while, Babuji,' she exclaimed in an endearing manner, 'It's really nice here, isn't it?'

I was overwhelmed by my thoughts. This was the last time: I would not be coming here any more. I would never see again the burial ground on the hilltop, the forest. This was my final farewell to the blossoming chhatim and to Bhanmati. I would carry back with me to the city of Calcutta six long years of a forest life; but why, as the day of departure drew closer, was I clinging even more to all of them?

I wanted to speak of this to Bhanmati; I wanted to know what she would say when I told her that I would never be coming here again; but of what use was it to tell this innocent forest maid of futile love, of affection?

As the evening fell, I became aware of yet another fragrance. There were many sheuli trees in the forest. The evening breeze was heavy with the strong scent of sheuli. The forest of chhatim now lay below us. Already the fireflies could be glimpsed through the trees. How vibrant and sweet was the breeze, how lifegiving. Who would not live longer if they breathed such freshness every morning and evening? I did not feel like going down the hill, but there was the fear of wild animals; besides, Bhanmati was with us. Jugalprasad was perhaps wondering about some new plant he might take away from here and transplant elsewhere. I noticed that his concentration was fixed entirely on a new variety of creeper and a particular leafy tree. Undoubtedly, Jugalprasad was quite mad, although it was madness of a special kind.

It is believed that Empress Nurjahan had the chinar brought from Persia and had it planted in Kashmir. Nurjahan was no more, but the beautiful chinar was now to be found in all of Kashmir. Jugalprasad would die, but in the waters of Saraswati kundi—even a hundred years later—spider lilies, blooming in early winter, would spread their aroma in the wind and the wild hansalata would bring forth its duck-like blue flowers in some bush. Did it really matter if no one mentioned that it was Jugalprasad who had brought such beauty into Narha-baihar?

'There, on the left, is the Tarbaro tree, do you recognize it?' Bhanmati asked me.

I had indeed not recognized in the dark the tree of Tarbaro, protector of wild buffaloes. The new moon had not yet risen.

We had come down a fair bit. Once more, the forest of chhatim, its sweet and intoxicating fragrance!

'Let's sit here awhile,' I said to Bhanmati.

Later, as we went down the forest path in the dark, I thought, Lobtulia was gone; gone too was Narha and Phulkia-baihar, but the hills of Mahalikharoop remained, as did the forestland of Bhanmati's family on the Dhannjhari range.

Perhaps a time would come when men would no more be able to see forests: all they would see would be fields of crops, or the chimneys of jute and cotton mills. They would come then to this secluded forestland, as though on a pilgrimage. For those people, yet to come, let the forest stay pristine, undisturbed.

2

At night, sitting up with Jagru Panna and his elder brother, I listened to them talking about their lives. The debts owing to the mahajan remained unpaid, and now they had to borrow money to buy two buffaloes, it had to be done. Earlier, a Marwari trader from Gaya used to come to buy ghee from them; it was more than three months since he last came. They had almost half a maund of ghee stored at home, but no buyers.

Bhanmati came to sit in a corner of the verandah. Jugalprasad was a heavy tea-drinker; I knew he had brought along his store of tea and sugar. I also knew that he was too shy to bring up the question of hot water. I asked Bhanmati, 'Will it be possible to heat up some water for tea?'

Princess Bhanmati had never made tea. Tea drinking was not part of the local custom. After we had told her how much water would be needed, she came back with boiling water in an earthern pot. Her younger sister brought a few stone bowls. I entreated Bhanmati to have some tea but she did not wish to. Meanwhile, Jagru Panna had finished a small bowl of tea and now asked for some more.

Everybody else got up after they had drunk their tea. Bhanmati did not leave. 'How many days will you stay here, Babuji?' she asked me. 'This time you've come after a very long gap. I certainly won't let you go tomorrow. Let me take you to the Jhati Springs tomorrow: there, the forest is even more fearful and wild elephants roam the place. And you will see lots of wild peafowl. It's wonderful, there's no place like it in the world.'

I wanted very much to know how little was Bhanmati's world.

'Bhanmati, have you ever been to a city?'

'No, Babuji.'

'Tell me the names of a few cities?'

'Gaya, Mungher, Patna.'

'You've not heard of Calcutta?'

'I have, Babuji.'

'Do you know in which direction it lies?'

'Who knows, Babuji!'

'Do you know the name of the country that we live in?'

'We live in Gaya district.'

'Have you heard the name, Bharatvarsha?'

Bhanmati indicated by shaking her head that she had not heard of it. She had never travelled anywhere beyond Chakmaki-tola. In which direction was Bharatvarsha?

A little later, she said, 'Uncle had bought a buffalo that gave a lot of milk—three seers in the morning and three in the evening. Babuji, we were better off those days. If you'd come then, Babuji, I'd have treated you to such good *khoya*. Uncle used to make it himself. What delicious *khoya* it was! There's no use talking of *khoya* now when there's hardly any milk to be had. Those days we were greatly respected.'

Then, with a sweeping gesture that embraced the expanse surrounding us, she said with pride: 'Do you know Babuji, all this land was part of our kingdom? The whole world! The Gonds whom you see in the forest, and the Santals, they are not of our tribe. We are royal Gonds. They are our subjects, and they regard us as kings.'

I was both amused and saddened by her words. Even those who are burdened by debt and forfeit their buffaloes every other day to the mahajan, do not desist from boasting of their royal genealogy.

'I know Bhanmati, of the greatness of your lineage . . .'

'Listen, Babuji,' she went on, 'a tiger got the buffalo, the one that Uncle had bought.'

'How did that happen?'

'Uncle was grazing it at the foot of that hill and he was sitting under a tree when the tiger got it.'

'Have you ever seen a tiger?' I asked her.

Bhanmati raised her dark arched eyebrows in an expression of great surprise: 'Me not seen a tiger, Babuji! Come to Chakmaki-tola in the winter, tigers come and lift cattle from our very doorstep—'

And she called out, 'Nichhni, Nichhni! Come here . . .'

When the younger sister had come, she said, 'Nichhni, do tell Babuji what used to happen every night last winter when the tiger would come into our yard. Jagru set a trap. But it didn't get caught.'

After some time, she suddenly said, 'Oh! Babuji, will you read out a letter? A letter had once come from somewhere, but there was no one to read it, it's just been put away. Nichhni, go and fetch the letter, and bring Uncle Jagru with you—'

Nichhni could not find the letter. Then Bhanmati went herself and after a lot of searching she found it and put it in my hand.

'When did this come?' I asked.

'About six or seven months ago,' said Bhanmati. 'I put it away so that you could read it out when you came. None of us can read, you know. Nichhni, do go and fetch Uncle Jagru. The letter is to be read. Call everyone here.'

By the light of Jugalprasad's fire, I sat down to my task of reading aloud an unread letter, now some seven months old. The entire household, wanting to hear what the letter said, sat in a ring around me. The letter, written in kayethi Hindi, was addressed to Raja Dobru Panna. A certain moneylender from Patna was enquiring of Raja Dobru if he had any forest of tendu leaves, and if so, was he willing to lease it out?

The letter had nothing to do with these people around me, for they had no forest of tendu leaves in their land. There had been a king called Raja Dobru, but that he had not an inch of land excepting for their ancestral home in Chakmaki-tola was surely not known to the same mahajan writing from Patna; he would not have otherwise spent money on postage to write such a useless letter.

Jugalprasad was cooking a little further from where we sat. The light from his wood fire lit up the verandah. Moonlight fell on the other half of the verandah, although it was only the third day of the second lunar cycle. It was only sometime ago that the moon had come up from behind the Dhannjhari range. Before us was the half circle of the range—you could hear the little boys shouting and playing in the village in Chakmaki-tola. The night spent in this rustic place was so very beautiful. How happy I was listening even to the most ordinary tales that Bhanmati had to tell me. I remembered what Balbhadra had said about progress the other day.

What do human beings really want: progress or happiness? Was it of any use making progress if no happiness came with it? I knew so many people who had certainly progressed in life but had lost happiness. Excessive indulgence had blunted the edges of their desires, now there was nothing that brought them joy. Life had become monotonous to them, of a uniform colour and without any significance. No stones shored their inner being; no sap flowed within.

If I could have lived here ... married Bhanmati ... in the moonlit verandah of this very mud house, the innocent forest maid would tell me her childish tales as she cooked, and I would sit and listen to her. And when the night grew dark, I would hear the hural cry in the forest, the hyena laugh, and wild elephants go stomping by. Bhanmati was dark, but in all of Bengal, you would not find such a healthy lissome slip of a girl or such a vibrant innocent being. She was compassionate, kind and affectionate—how many times had I proof of it ... Even thinking about it gave me pleasure. A beautiful vision! What was the point in progress? Let Balbhadra make his way to Sengat and improve his situation. Let Rashbehari Singh improve his.

Jugalprasad announced that the meal was cooked; should he lay the seats? There was no dearth of hospitality in Bhanmati's home. Vegetables were not easy to come by in these parts, but Jagru had managed to get a brin-jal and some potatoes for me. Then, there was dal made of kalhai, a cooked bird and delicious butter freshly churned from their buffalo milk. Jugalprasad was an excellent cook besides.

Tonight, Bhanmati, Jagru, Jagru's brother and Nichhni—all of them—would eat with us. I had invited them, for they never had such food. 'Let them all sit too, near us,' I said. 'It would be easy for Jugalprasad to serve us: let's eat together.'

They did not agree to this. They wouldn't eat until we had finished our meal.

The following day as we were about to set off, Bhanmati did something unexpected.

Suddenly, she held my hands fast in hers and said, 'Babuji, I will not let you go today . . .'

I stared in amazement at her face. It was painful.

We could not set off in the morning because of her pleas. We took leave after our midday meal.

Once more, we took the path through the dark forest. By the side of the road Princess Bhanmati seemed to be standing—not a girl, but a youthful Bhanmati—one I had never seen before. Her eager eyes were fixed on the path awaiting her lover; perhaps he had gone hunting on the other side of the hill: any moment now, and he would be here. In my heart, I silently blessed the young woman. In the still and ancient forest of chhatim flowers, in the cover of an enchanting evening light, in the Dhannjhari hills glowing with fireflies, may the secret tryst of a forest maid be fulfilled.

On my return to the estate, I took leave of everyone and, within a week, had left Lobtulia.

Raju Parey, Ganauri, Jugalprasad, Ashrafi Tindale and several others walked beside my palanquin and accompanied me as far as the limits of Lobtulia where the settlement of Maharaj-tola had newly come up. Motuk-nath recited Sanskrit verses of benediction.

'Huzoor, when you are gone, Lobtulia will be made *udaas*,' said Raju.

I might say here, that in these parts *udaas* was used to encompass a vast range of meanings. If, for instance, the maize was not fried properly they said, 'the frying is *udaas*': I cannot say exactly in what manner the word was used of me.

While I was bidding goodbye, a young woman had cried. She had come to the katcheri early this morning. When the bearers lifted up my palanquin, I found her sobbing. She was Kunta.

Of the few worthy things I had done in the course of my work as a manager, one was to settle a plot of land on the hapless Kunta. For Manchi, the carefree girl of the forest, I could not do anything. We never came to know who had taken away the unfortunate girl and where they had taken her. If she had been here today, I would have given her land in her own name, without any salaami.

I remembered her even more intensely when I spotted Nakchhedi's home on the boundaries of Narha-baihar. Suratiya was busy with some work outside the house. 'Babuji, Babuji,' she called out as soon as she saw my palanquin, 'Stop a bit—'

She came running to the palanquin. Behind her came Chhania.

'Where are you going Babuji?'

'To Bhagalpur. Where is your father?'

'He's gone to Kallu-tola to fetch seeds for the wheat crop. When will you come back?'

'I shan't be coming back.'

'A likely story! It's a lie . . .'

When we crossed the limits of Narha-baihar I put my head out and looked back, once.

So many villages, roofs everywhere, people chatting, the laughter and cries of children at play, cattle feeding, and stacks of harvested crops. It was I, who in the last seven years or so, had the forests cleared and set up in their stead this joyous settlement, bustling with activity and filled with crops. Yesterday, they had all been saying, Babuji, even we are amazed looking on what you have done. How greatly has Narha-baihar and Lobtulia changed!

Now, as I moved on, I too, thought: How greatly have Narha-baihar and Lobtulia changed!

I bowed from afar to Mahalikharoop and to Mohanpura Forest lying in the distance. You primeval gods of the forest, forgive me. Farewell.

3

Many years have gone by, more than fifteen years.

I thought of these things sitting beneath the nut tree.

There was hardly any daylight left.

The almost forgotten forestlands of Narha-baihar and Lobtulia that had been destroyed by me, the wondrous plant life around Saraswati kundi— they come back to haunt me with sadness, like memories of dreams. And in the same breath I wonder, how is Kunta? Has Suratiya become a young woman now? Is Motuknath's little school still to be found? What is Bhanmati doing in their hill-ringed forest? Rakhal-babu's wife, Dhruba, Girdharilal, who knows how each of them is keeping after all these years . . . !

And Manchi, I remember her sometimes: Has a repentant Manchi gone back to her husband, or does she pick leaves in a tea garden in Assam even now?

It has been so long that I have lost touch with them.

NOTES

1 Bhairavi: One of the ten Mahavidyas or forms of Mahadevi (the all-encompassing female deity in Hinduism), while Bhairav is the corresponding form of Shiva. 'Bhairavi has a fierce appearance, her primary role in the cosmic process is destruction. Her complexion is said to be as bright as thousands of rising suns. She wears a garland of skulls and clothes made from the skins of demons she has killed; her feet and breasts are covered with blood. Her four hands hold a rosary and a book and make the signs of fearlessness and granting wishes. The *Kalika-purana* says that her eyes roll from intoxication and that she stands on a corpse' (David Kinsley, *Tantric Visions of the Divine Feminine* [New Delhi: Motilal Banarasidas, 1998], p. 11).

2 paan-money: Euphemism for bribe, suggesting that the amount is trifling.

3 Sven Hedin (1865–1952): Swedish explorer and author and orientalist, most famous for his numerous dramatic expeditions throughout Central Asia from the 1890s to the 1930s. In 1893–97, he travelled through Russian Central Asia, crossing the Pamirs and exploring in the Tarim Basin. In crossing part of the Takla-Makan Desert in Inner Mongolia to the Khotan River only Hedin and two others of his expedition survived. Hedin was trained in physical geography and was a skilled draughtsman and artist: his books, accompanied with photographs, paintings and maps were excerpted, translated and republished in dozens of languages.

4 The Gila River Basin described in Hudson's books: The Gila River flows through New Mexico and Arizona in desert south-western USA. It is not clear whether the Hudson here refers to the explorer after whom Hudson River in New York State and Hudson's Bay in Canada is named. It may be a reference to William Henry Hudson (1841–1922), the author of *Green Mansions* (1904), a book celebrating Edenic wilderness, set in the South American Amazon.

5 Hindi *Gul-e-bakawali, Laila-Majnu, Betal Panchisi, Premsagar*: Examples of popular literature derived from a range of sources.

Kissa-e-Gul-e-bakawali (the full title) is derived from a Persian *masnavi* or romance. It was first rendered in Bengali prose by Izatullah Bangali in 1722 and translated into Urdu by Pandit Nihal Chand Lahori in 1803.

Laila-Majnu, the legend of madness in love, in which Majnu is considered as a model of mystic love from the eighth century onwards, was celebrated by the twelfth-century Persian poet Nizami. Written as a *masnavi* first by Amir Khusrau (1254–1325), then in Kashmiri by Mahmud Gami (1765–1855), popularized in Hindi in the nineteenth century.

Betal Panchisi, also known as *Betal Panchavinsati* (Twenty-Five Tales of the Ghost), a collection of stories about the legendary king Vikramaditya. One of the major Hindi texts written by Lalluji Lal (1763–1825/35), a Sanskrit scholar and teacher at the Fort William College, Calcutta.

Lalluji is best known for his *Premsagar* (1810) based on the tenth canto of the *Bhagavata- puran*, the story of Krishna's early life. Written in Khariboli language with a mix of Brajbhasha, *Premsagar* proved immensely popular and became a great model for Hindi prose.

6 Greek king Heliodorus: Heliodorus was the Graeco-Bactrian king, Antialkidas' ambassador at the ancient central Indian city of Vidisha. The Heliodorus pillar in Besnagar, Madhya Pradesh, was 'discovered' by Alexander Cunningham in 1877 and the lithic recordings identified only around 1915. One of the inscriptions on the pillar (*c.*120–100 BCE) identifies it as a Garudadhvaja set up in honour of Vasudeva whose emblem is Garuda, thus suggesting that Heliodorus was a devotee of Vishnu. Evidently the theme was of great interest to Bibhutibhushan: On 1 September 1943, he started writing about Heliodorus, a love story between a Greek soldier and an Indian woman, and laboured long over the historical background. It was variously entitled 'Heliodoruser Galpa', 'Hindu O Greek' and, finally, 'Swapna Basudev'.

7 *sankirtan*: Collective singing of *kirtans*, devotional songs, typically about the life of Krishna, in which a group repeats lines sung by a leader, popularized by the Vaishnavite preacher-saint Chaitanya (1486–1533) in Bengal.

8 Bharatchandra's rendering of Ma Annapurna: Bharatchandra Rai Gunakar (1119–67) Bengali poet best known for his *Annadamangal* (celebrating Goddess Annapurna) and *Vidya-Sundar* (a romance). In the former, Sati manifests herself to her consort Lord Shiva as the ten 'Dasamahavidyas', or the ten manifestations of Mahadevi. The reference here is to her manifestation as the withered and emaciated Dhumavati.

9 Harry Johnston, Marco Polo, Hudson and Shackleton:

Sir Harry Hamilton Johnston (1858–1927): British explorer and colonial administrator, served in various parts of British Africa from 1885. Combined his interest in the natural sciences with political negotiations for Britain. In 1884, made an expedition to Mt Kilimanjaro that uncovered valuable scientific data and strengthened Britain's political hold in East Africa. A talented painter, linguist, naturalist, photographer, cartographer and writer, Johnston travelled extensively by foot and boat through huge sections of the continent, 'discovering' and documenting.

Marco Polo (c. 1254–1324): The first traveller to trace a route across the whole breadth of Asia, Marco Polo had set off with his father and uncle on their second trading speculation from native Venice to China in 1271 where they lived for about 20 years. They came back to Venice after sailing for Persia. In 1298, Marco was made prisoner in a sea battle and, while in captivity in Genoa, he dictated his adventures to a scribe. Described in his *Livres des Merveilles* or *Book of Marvels*.

Henry Hudson (c.1570–1611): English explorer who made four voyages to the Far North financed by merchants who hoped he would find a short route to the coast of China. In the service of the Dutch East India Company, ascended what was later named the Hudson River in 1609. In 1610, Hudson sailed from London in the *Discovery*, was overtaken by winter and amidst terrible hardships, set adrift with one of his sons by mutineers. Only a starving remnant of the original crew returned to England with his records. Historians have since uncovered records of his enterprising wife Katherine's correspondence with the East India Company after his death. After a series of lawsuits, she travelled to Ahmedabad to trade in indigo and other products, returning to England as a wealthy woman in 1622. Another surviving son also became a factor with the East India Company, did well for himself and settled down finally in Balasore, Orissa, where he died in 1644. One wonders what Bibhutibhushan might have made of these connections.

Sir Ernest Henry Shackleton (1874–1922): After an abortive expedition to the Antarctic region in 1903, Shackleton led another in 1907 and, in 1909, planted the Union Jack on Mt Gauss, 97 miles from the South Pole, the nearest point to it then reached. Commanded the imperial trans-Antarctic expedition of 1914–17 with his ship *Endurance*. He wrote two books about his adventures: *The Heart of the Antarctic* (1909) and *South* (1919).

10 Kayethi Hindi: Version of Devanagari script used for legal and administrative work since Mughal times in parts of North India.

11 *Raghuvamsa* and the subtleties of Bhatti's grammar: *Raghuvamsa* is an epic poem in Sanskrit by Kalidasa (fourth to sixth century CE) on King Raghu, the celebrated king of the solar dynasty, and his descendants.

Bhatti, aka Bhattaswamin, a grammarian of the sixth century CE. His *Bhattikavya* is a long poem of 1650 verses composed to illustrate classical Sanskrit grammatical rules and metaphors.

12 Santal Revolt of 1862: Most likely a reference to the Santal Uprising of 1855 in Bihar. According to historian Anil Seal, the uprising was 'messianic in inspiration' and the Santals were 'hostile to the British not as foreigners but as rulers'. Like many other contemporary movements, it was 'grounded on local grievances and local aspirations, and dependent on local leadership' (*The Emergence of Indian Nationalism: Competition and Collaboration in the Later Nineteenth Century* [Cambridge: Cambridge University Press, 1968], pp. 12–13).

13 Company: The East India Company, founded in 1599 by London merchants with a royal charter granting it monopoly of trade with India. It began trading in India from the early seventeenth century, growing in size and prestige and virtually running a government in the subcontinent, until the takeover by the Crown after the 1857 Uprising.

14 *nayamatma* . . . : 'The spirit is not to be achieved or realized by the fainthearted.'

15 *vidvastu* . . . : 'The words of the poet-philosopher are to be revealed only to the truly learned; they are like half-opened flowers to the student desirous of learning, and to the dull are of no value.'

16 *pura yatra* . . . : 'Now there are riverbanks where once the waters flowed . . .'

17 Kapalkundala: The eponymous heroine of Bankimchandra Chattopadhyay's (1838–94) second novel, *Kapalkundala* (1866). Bankimchandra's heroine is a foundling who is brought up in the forest; her subsequent marriage and attempts to fit into the norms of conjugality end in tragedy.

18 He had a name like Dron precisely because he was an ancient man: Probably referring to the Drona (known as Dronacharya), who taught the Kaurava and Pandava princes the science of arms and archery in the epic Mahabharata.

19 Adarsho Hindu Hotel: Literally, 'The Model Hindu Hotel', a type of generic eatery catering to budget customers in crowded places like railway junctions, with a brahman cook or *thakur* ensuring caste purity. Also the title of a novel by Bibhutibhushan (1940) celebrating the fortunes of its protagonist, the honest and enterprising cook, Hazariprasad Thakur, whose hotel by that name becomes a byword for excellent food and service. The gap between the commercial eatery run only for profit and Hazari's personalized service, of course, makes for the

irony in the line 'The original and absolutely authentic Adarsho Hindu Hotel' in *Aranyak* where the narrator imagines the degraded environment of an industrialized belt.

abwab: miscellaneous cesses, imposts and charges levied by zamindars and public officials

adha-bakhra: half the value of a crop fixed by the appraiser; share of a half (the other half is given as revenue)

ahir: caste of cultivators

akash [neem]: Indian cork tree, Hindi–neem chameli; a tall tree cultivated throughout India.

amil, amildar: revenue collector or contractor.

amla: a clerk.

amlaki: Indian gooseberry, Hindi–avla, amla; a moderate-sized deciduous tree; the fruits ripen from November to February and are fleshy and nutritious.

anna: one-sixteenth of a rupee

aristolochiaceae: snakeroot, Indian birthwort. Hindi–Ishvari; twining perennial and a native of India, also called hansalata.

arjun: a large evergreen tree flowering from March to June. Occurring throughout the greater part of India.

ashan: laurel, also called piyasal; about 80 to 100 feet tall, found mainly in the Chhotanagpur region.

asami: cultivator, tenant

ashraf/i: title of rank

babla: babul acacia; Hindi–babul, kikar; a medium-sized tree distributed throughout the drier regions of north, central and south India.

babul: usually title of respect in Bengal, but often used by the British in India (and subsequently by Bengalis) disparagingly to denote Indians educated in English or fops.

badam: Indian almond tree; Hindi–jangli badam; native of the Mediterranean region, cultivated chiefly in Himachal Pradesh and Kashmir.

bahera: *Belleric myrobalan*; Hindi–bahera.

baiji: a prostitute, especially one skilled in song, dance and entertainment.

bajra/i: pearl millet; cultivated in many parts of India for its edible grains.

bakain: Persian lilac, china tree; Hindi–bakain; a small tree grown as a hedge plant and also used medicinally.

bangar: arable upland plain

bargadar: sharecropper

bathua: pigweed; a common herb whose leaves and stalks are used as vegetable and fodder.

bhandi: Nepal geranium; Hindi–bhanda; a perennial herb found in the temperate Himalayas, Kashmir, Khasi Hills and the Nilgiris.

bhang: hemp; Hindi–ganja, bhang; yields narcotics besides other products. Commonly found in waste grounds.

bhura: Type of coarse cereal.

bigha: measure of land corresponding to about one-third of an acre

benth: cane; Hindi–bet; a common and extensive climber; the stems are used for making baskets, furniture, etc.

bhuinhar/bhumihar: high status land-owning caste unique to Bihar.

chakladar: a title (medium level).

char: an island formed by a deposition of silt on the riverbed.

chihor: thick and woody creeper bearing fruits.

chhatim: Dita Bark tree; Hindi–chatiun.

cheena: common or Proso millet; Hindi–chin, morha; grown mainly in Bihar and Uttar Pradesh—a nutritious grain, but used as forage grain in other parts of the world.

chhetri/chhatri : local variant of kshatriya or warrior caste.

chihar: camel's foot climber; Hindi–malijan; a large woody climber found in Assam, Bihar, Madhya Pradesh and Punjab.

chinar: oriental plane tree; A tall tree native to Europe and West Asia, commonly found in Kashmir.

daroga: the head of a police station.

desh: native country.

dhatup: fire-flame bush; Hindi–dhatua; A common ornamental shrub producing gum.

diara: same as char land.

dihi/dih: cluster of villages or mauja.

dihi-katcheri: sub-katcheri.

doshad, gangota: low-caste ryot.

dhrupad: a North Indian classical style of singing.

dudhli: Hindi–basingh; a shrub or a small tree occurring in Himalayas from Nepal to Kumaon and Khasi Hills.

farman: a mandate or an order.

gajari: Hindi–ganj; a woody climbing shrub found in Punjab, Bihar, Uttar Pradesh and Madhya Pradesh.

gola: warehouse/storehouse.

goldar: wholesale merchant owning a warehouse.

golgoli: yellow silk cotton; Hindi–galgal, gooloc; a small deciduous tree with numerous branches and golden-yellow flowers, appearing from February to March; found all over India, particularly in hot, dry regions.

gomasta: agent, clerk or confidential representative.

gotra: clan, all members of which are supposedly descendants of a rishi or sage.

gurguri: a hookah.

gurmi: wild fruit-bearing creeper.

guru-bhai: disciples of the same guru, with whom one shares 'brotherly' bonds.

haat: periodic village fair or mart.

hansalata: See aristolochiaceae.

haritaki: *Chebulic myrobalan*; Hindi–harir.

hemanta: the season between autumn and winter.

hinglaj: Hindi–hingan; a small spiny evergreen tree growing in drier parts of India; the fruits are often made into garlands.

hustabood: assessment of the resources/assets of a revenue-yielding land.

ijara: form of revenue.

ijaradar: farmer of any item of public revenue.

irshal: despatches of remittances to the zamindari or the state treasury.

izzat: honour, credit, reputation, prestige.

jab: barley; Hindi– jau.

janab: respectful form of address (from Arabic), literally meaning 'sir'.

janar: species of maize.

jati: caste.

jhau: Bushy shrub especially near riverbeds and sea coasts.

jhum: cultivation involving burning of vegetation and keeping the soil fallow for a certain period before the next round of planting.

jowar: sorghum; Hindi–joar, jowar; cultivated widely; the grains are used as food and the stems and leaves as fodder.

kadamba: kadam; Hindi–kadamba; a moderate graceful deciduous tree with a straight stem of about 30 feet and creamy yellow ball-like flowers.

kaibartta: large cultivating and fishing caste of Bengal.

kaloar/kolu: ironsmiths and hardware merchants (in Bengal, kolus are the same as telis).

kalhai: kind of dal.

karari estate: conditional, covenanted land.

kash: thatch-grass; Hindi–kans; a perennial grass found throughout India.

kata-bansh: thorny species of bamboo.

katcheri: estate office.

kelikadamba: species of kadamba.

kend: Nepal ebony persimmon or black ebony of North India; leaves used for bidis.

khalsa land: land held and managed directly by the state.

khamar: place were grain is stored and winnowed.

kheri: shama millet; annual tufted grass growing in Bihar, Maharashtra and other parts of India; the grains are eaten in times of scarcity, otherwise used as fodder.

kulinism: system of hypergamy best known among the kulin brahmans of Bengal.

kund: species of berry.

kundi: a tank, lake, or a basin.

lathiyal: man proficient with his stick hired or retained by the zamindar as a mercenary or a private muscleman.

mahajan: merchant, banker; loosely used to mean moneylender.

Marwari: native of Marwar in Rajputana, but found throughout India as traders, bankers and brokers.

matar: field peas, used as a dal.

maund: measure of weight corresponding to 40 seers.

mofussil/mufassal: countryside districts, as opposed to the principal town.

mohuree: an accountant.

moinakanta: thorny shrub growing wild in the country.

munsif: lower-category judicial official.

naib: deputy.

namasudra: members of a caste mainly engaged in boating and cultivation.

natua: a practitioner of nat.

nazrana/nazar: gift, usually from inferior to superior; often forced contribution.

paisa/pice: small copper coin, one quarter of an anna.

pakur: large evergreen tree with spreading crown and drooping branches.

palash: 'flame of the forest'; Hindi—palas, dhak; a small deciduous tree with flaming scarlet-orange flowers, occurring throughout India.

pargana: district, province, tract of country comprising many villages.

patowari: village accountant.

peada: peon (assigned for postal duties).

phanimansa: thorny shrub growing wild in the country.

piyal: tall tree (almost as tall as the sal), flowering in the monsoons; its seeds are used as manure and crushed to make oil; mainly found in the Santal parganas.

praja: subject, tenant.

raiyat, ryot: literally, a subject; landholder paying revenue to zamindars or directly to government; cultivator, peasant.

raiyatwari: system of land revenue settlement made by government with each individual cultivator without the intervention of a third party.

raj: principality, kingdom.

rajput: of the kshatriya caste.

reri: castor; Hindi—arandi; a small tree usually found in Andhra Pradesh, Maharashtra and Orissa.

rupee: standard coin of the British Indian monetary system

sabai: Baib or sabai grass; Hindi—babni; A perennial tufted grass growing in many parts of north India.

sadgop: cultivating caste of Bengal.

sal: tall tree; Hindi—sal; largely found in the north-east and central India; in addition to many products, the wood ranks second to teak.

salaami: a sum of money or a gift given to a person in authority as a mark of obeisance.

sandhyamani: flowering creeper.

saptaparna: laticiferous tree of medium height, native to South Asia and Africa (same as chhatim).

satvik: not actuated by any desire.

seer: measure of weight corresponding to about two pounds.

segun: teak; Hindi—segnan; grows primarily in Bihar, the Terai region, central India and the western peninsula.

shefali: tree of sorrow, night flowering jasmine; Hindi—sephalika; a large shrub or small tree; flowers strung and worn as ornaments.

shikasti: land damaged by flood or inundation; deficiency in rent collection as a result of flood or inundation.

shisham/seesam: East Indian rosewood, Bombay blackwood; a large tree common in Bengal, Bihar, Madhya Pradesh and the western peninsula.

shishu: sissoo; an excellent timber-bearing tree.

shiuli: fragrant small white flower with bright orange stalk usually flowering in autumn.

sipahi: a person who stands guard.

simul: red silk cotton; Hindi—simul; a tall tree with a spreading crown and bright red flowers, found throughout India.

sthalpadma: kind of lotus.

supari: areca nut.

taluk: subdivision of a zila or a district.

tehsil: revenue subdivision of a district.

tehsildar: revenue official in charge of a tehsil, subdivision of a district or estate.

tendu: Coromandel ebony persimmon; Hindi—tendu; distributed all over north India; leaves used for wrapping bidis.

terai: moist land in general, especially applied to the strip of jungleland along the foothills of the Himalayas.

teuri: wild creeper with faintly blue flowers.

thakur: lord; man of rank, usually used to address rajputs.

thumri: a North Indian romantic song in classical music.

tindale: supervisor of gang of workers.

yakshi: originally Pali for tree spirits (female); later, demi-gods and attendants of the Buddha; also a female water sprite, relatively low among the hierarchy of heavenly beings.

zamindar: landholder; a collector of revenue on behalf of the government, paying revenue to the government directly.

Sources

S. P. Ambasta (ed.). *The Useful Plants of India*. New Delhi: Publications and Information Directorate, Council of Scientific & Industrial Research, 1986.

Sushil Kumar Chattopadhyay. *Bibhutibhushan: Jiban o Sahityo*. Calcutta: Jignasa, 1970, pp. 399–417.

The Cambridge Economic History of India, Volume 2: c.1757–c.1970 (Dharma Kumar ed.). New Delhi: Orient Longman, in association with Cambridge University Press, 1991.

Umrao Singh, A. M. Wadhwani and B. M. Johri. *Dictionary of Economic Plants in India*. New Delhi: Indian Council of Agricultural Research, 1990.

TRANSLATOR'S ACKNOWLEDGEMENTS

My warm thanks to Taradas Banerjee, Sarmistha Dutta Gupta, Anuradha Roy and Rusati Sen (and my anonymous reviewer) in making possible the publication of this translation. I am indebted to Prasanta Bhattacharya, Lily Ghosh and Rekha Sen for help with proofing; Arun Arya, Jaya Menon and Supriya Varma for references; Shanti Dighe for translations of Sanskrit verses, and Prasanta Bhattacharya and Kumar Shahani for many related and unrelated interchanges.

The translated *Aranyak* branched into notes and glosses during my stay in Oahu, one of the seven Hawaiian Islands, in 2000. To Vrindya Dalmiya and Arindam Chakraborty and the Rama Watumull Foundation, I am grateful for affording me the rare conjunction of living in one of the most beautiful and most despoiled places on earth. The Pacific was one of the many distant regions loved in the imagination by Bibhutibhushan Bandyopadhyay. The islands are inscribed with continuing histories of migration, settlement and colonization and decolonization of plantation economy, nuclear and tourist colonization and the more recent indigenous sovereignty and landclaim movements; to experience these histories in everyday life was to recognize *Aranyak* as a planetary metaphor.